The
Department
of Curiosities

The Department of Curiosities

Karen J Carlisle

Kraken
Publishing

The Department of Curiosities: For the Good of the Empire

 A catalogue record for this book is available from the National Library of Australia

NATIONAL LIBRARY OF AUSTRALIA

ISBN: 978-0-9944850-4-5
Series: Carlisle, Karen J.

Also available separately as eBook

This book is written in British English.
Typeset in Times Roman 10pt.

Published by Kraken Publishing.
Adelaide, Australia.
www.krakenpublishing.com

For my sanity,
and all those keeping
the Black Dog at bay.
We can do it.
One day at a time.

Contents

The Department of Curiosities

Of Rivals, Surprises, and Escapes

I should have left you where I found you," Tillie whispered. She shoved her gloved hand into her coat pocket and pulled out the brass-covered sphere, the size of a large marble. She held it out before her; even in the dimness of the unlit hall, the finely-threaded steel and brass pins inserted part-way into the sphere glistened. Its chain slithered over her wrist as she turned it over. The inner content of the brass sphere was just visible; an amber glass orb fitted snugly into its metal shell. It spun to face Tillie. Its thin wedge-like pupil locked onto her, widening to fill two-thirds of the aperture, as if trying to consume every morsel of available light. She avoided its stare.

"Oh, don't look at me like that," she whispered. "I'm not going to fall for that one again."

A clatter echoed down the dark corridor. She froze mid-step. Something thudded on the floor. The sphere's pupil snapped down to a narrow slit. She spun in the direction of the noise. The Chinese urn at the other end of the hall had toppled onto the carpet runner. She squinted into the darkness, searching for the culprit. The hall was empty.

A picture formed in her mind: green eyes, dark fur. She shook her head.

"No, I don't think Professor Waldran has a cat." Tillie looped the ocular ball's chain over her head, allowing it to fall onto her bodice. She hitched up her skirts and anchored them in place with a small leather cord that snaked from the underskirt and latched onto a grommet on her belt. If the unwelcome ruckus continued in the hallway they might need to execute a quick escape; they weren't exactly invited to this party.

Downstairs, the noise of the invited guests crescendoed. Piano music wafted up the stairs; party-goers warbled an unrecognisable tune, conveniently masking the unwelcome noises in the hallway. Everything was ordered and civilised - as it should be. Everyone remained in either the Dining Room or the Drawing room - as was to be expected during a dinner party. Everyone, that is, except the other intruder who had announced his presence by knocking over the Chinese urn at the opposite end of the hall.

Tillie edged backwards. Her fingers searched for the niche under the stairway where she could slip out of sight.

At the end of the hallway a lantern flickered, bobbing slowly as it moved closer. Her breaths quickened. She shrank into the niche and held her breath as her rival's shadowy outline crept past the urn and climbed the staircase up towards the private family rooms. Was he searching for the Professor's secret also? How did he know? She needed to find the workshop before him. She crept out of her sanctuary.

Downstairs, the piano music fell silent. She heard the faint creak of a badly oiled door hinge and the click of a latch as a door closed.

She waited. Had the guests heard the noise? She tilted her head to listen. There were no footfalls on the stairs. The music started again. She let out a slow, measured breath, emerged from her hiding place and sneaked up the stairs, following her rival.

The staircase continued upwards, past the family's private floor and beyond the closed door on the right that lead to the servants' quarters and the attic. To the left of the stairs, a short corridor extended forward. Four doors lay beyond, concealing all from prying eyes.

Tillie smiled. She was confident Waldran's workshop was behind one of these doors. He'd want to keep his work close, away from the curious eyes of spying servants. This was their Master's domain; they would not dare intrude without permission.

She peeked along the hallway. There was no sign of her rival. She tested the doorknob to the servants' stair. Locked. He must still be on this floor. Her heart skipped. Had he found the workshop first?

She scanned the area around the doors. The first three door alcoves were immaculately clean; the alcove on the far right boasted a thicker layer of dust on the surrounding floor. Waldran would forbid the maid entry to his private workshop. There'd be no dusting, no cleaning... She flexed her fingers as she crept towards the next door. That was the one.

Her shoulders relaxed. Her footfalls fell silently on the soft carpet runner as her pace quickened.

The chain shook around her neck. The amber eye spun in its metal casing, searching in the direction of the door. Its pupil dilated.

<<*Yes!*>> The Orb's unspoken statement echoed in her head.

She clasped the bauble in her hand and turned it to face her.

"What do you mean 'Yes'?" she whispered.

The Orb stared back blankly in reply.

Tillie scowled. "I hate it when you are so cryptic."

She retrieved a small brass ear trumpet from a pocket under her bustle and placed it against the door. She strained to listen: a faint scuffle. A short scrape, and all was quiet again. Had the stranger absconded with her prize?

She pocketed the listening device, slowly turned the doorknob and eased open the door.

The Orb's pupil snapped shut. *<<Danger!>>*

Its voice invaded her thoughts. She grasped her head in her hand.

"Shh!" It was an automatic response. Tillie clutched the Orb in her free hand and froze, hoping she'd not betrayed her presence. She held her breath and tried to listen beyond the door. Silence. Then a faint scrape, a flutter, and nothing.

She released the Orb; it fell onto her chest.

A breeze chilled her hand on the door jamb. She peered through the thin crack of the partially-open door. A puddle of pale light rippled in the shadows near the window. The room appeared empty.

Where had he gone?

"Anything?" she whispered. The Orb usually had an insight on things unseen. But now it lay quiet, its only reply a widening of its aperture.

Tillie glanced along the hall toward the stairs. They were in full view of any latecomer.

"We can't wait here all night." Tillie pushed open the door.

Another rush of cold air greeted her. The far window was open. Parted curtains fluttered in the brisk breeze. Light, from a discarded lamp on the desk, danced fitfully. She entered, closed the door behind her and leaned against it.

A key nudged her in the back. She grinned. How fortuitous. She locked the door and slipped the key into her pocket.

The Orb twitched. Its thoughts formed in her mind.

"No, I don't think the Professor would leave the window open at this time of year," replied Tillie.

The Orb whispered again.

"No, he wouldn't leave the curtains open for all of London to see his work in progress." Questions, questions. She rolled her eyes. Now the Orb chose incessant chatter. She was grateful that the rest of the world could not hear it. That would only lead to more questions - questions she could not yet answer.

"Quiet!" she whispered through gritted teeth.

Tillie crossed the room, collecting a poker from the fireplace on the way, and navigated her way through a narrow path between stacks of crates near the desk until she reached the window.

She poked at the curtains. Nothing. Her grip on the poker relaxed. She peered out the window. A sea of slate-tiled roofs stretched in every direction.

There was a tink of breaking tile. A grating sound, near one of the chimneys, caught her attention. Something scrambled in the dark. Tillie grasped the sill and leaned out the window. A lone fleeing figure, barely visible against the night sky, fled over the roof edge.

<<*Gone.*>>

Tillie turned back to face Waldran's workshop. "Yes, but hopefully not with our prize."

A large oak writing desk with a full set of writing accoutrements stood before her. Note papers lay scattered across its surface. Black ink dribbled from an overturned ink bottle, partially obscuring the handwriting. The liquid glistened in the lamplight as it dripped off the table edge. Tillie tapped her finger on the liquid. It was still fresh.

Tillie wiped her finger on the desk blotter and surveyed the rest of the workshop.

Bookshelves lined the wall on the left, their contents encased in floor-to-ceiling glass doors. An octagonal display case sat in the far corner, packed with a collection of curiosities. To the right was a long work bench. A large muslin-covered object perched on the near end.

Her fingers twitched. What was Professor Waldran working on? She edged past the crates toward the mysterious object; her foot nudged something under the desk chair.

What—? She bent down and searched the floor under the desk. Her fingers wrapped around a small book. Tillie examined the object under the desk lamp; a notebook bound in red leather. Pages crackled as she opened it. Inside were diagrams of pulleys and levers drawn in faded brown ink; it seemed curiously familiar.

The Orb scanned the pages. Images of a hand and quill filled her mind. <<*Backwards.*>>

Tillie held the book up near the window and studied the reflection, but was still unable to decipher the accompanying text. Perhaps it was in code? She leaned closer to the lamp to see he markings clearer. Her finger nudged its hot glass globe. She flinched. The book fell onto the desk with a thud.

She held her breath. Had she been heard? She cocked her head to listen. Muffled noises below attested the party was still in full swing, but there was no telling when Waldran would grow bored and retire for the evening. There was no time to dally with this distraction now. She picked up the book, tucked it into the hidden pocket under her bustle and flattened her over-skirt neatly back in place.

She returned her attention to the shrouded object sitting on the workbench. Why would he bother to cover up one of his creations, in his own workshop? She moved closer the intriguing object and licked her lips. Her fingers reached out and brushed the cotton. Tillie's fingers recoiled from the cloth.

The Orb jiggled on the end of its chain.

"All right, I'll look!" She reached out and grabbed a patch of heavy muslin and slowly slid it off the object underneath.

Metal glistened in the lamp light. It was man-sized skeleton made of brass and steel. Tillie's heart jumped. An automaton! The workmanship was exquisite. Her eyes widened. Such a treasure. The cage-like body contained a complicated mass of pulleys and levers. In the place of a heart was a box filled with an intricate arrangement of clockworkings. Delicate wires led down the arms to the metal fingers with each joint a perfectly rounded pulley.

Its skull was the size of a man's. She leaned over the bench and craned her head to examine the automaton more closely. The back of the cranium was open, exposing more clockwork mechanicals; the front was of solid metal with empty sockets that stared back into her eyes. She moved the lamp closer. Several fine wires emerged from the socket walls, each one ended with a small movable bolt ready to screw something in place; something approximating the size of a large marble.

<<Home.>>

"Home?" Tillie's voice wavered in reply to the bauble around her neck.

There was a faint click as the Orb's pupil snapped shut with a click. *<<Danger!>>*

Clicking continued intermittently, evolving into a constant ratcheting.

"No need to repeat yourself," she said.

The Orb twisted on her chest.

If it wasn't the Orb, then...? She stepped away from the bench, tilting her head to determine the origin of the noise. It was...

Tillie froze. The noise was coming from the automaton itself. She screamed and jumped backwards, hit her hip on the edge of the solid desk and overbalanced onto the crates behind it.

Long, metallic digits grasped at the air where she had stood just seconds before. The eyeless skull turned in her direction.

Loud footfalls echoed from the stairs. Her pulse raced. The music had ceased. The entire household would be upon her in moments.

<<Run!>>

Footsteps hurried along the corridor. Tillie spun to face the door. Doors rattled. She stepped back toward the window. The automaton's arms flailed in her direction. Closer. It would be upon her before Waldran reached the door.

"Look what you got us into!" she hissed at the Orb. She eyed the metal man as her fingers fumbled at the curtain behind her, and groped for the window sill.

A hand grabbed her shoulder from behind; her scream was cut short by a gloved hand over her mouth. Her bustle scraped the sill as she was dragged through the window. Glass rattled as its sash slammed shut behind her. The automaton's metal fingertips screeched against the glass, its grinning skull staring blankly at her.

Muffled thumps pounded on the workshop door.

"I think it would be wise to remove ourselves." The stranger released his grip. "It appears you have alerted the household." He retrieved a metal spike from his shoulder satchel and wedged it into the window frame.

The pounding on the door grew louder.

"It will take them longer without the key." she smiled.

The stranger nodded, assisted Tillie to her feet and led her across the roof. Her rival had now become her protector.

Tillie's footing was unsteady on the uneven tiles. "I must congratulate you on your nimbleness," she said.

The man stopped near the chimney, placed a metal box on the outside edge of the roof and pressed it firmly. A spike rammed into the brick. Two hooks sprang from the box, inserted themselves between the tiles and clamped onto the roof. He bent down, pressed another button. A metal ladder unfurled from the bottom of the box. Chain clinked as the end hit the cobblestones below.

He reached out to Tillie. "After you," he said.

She peered over the edge. The ladder was a foot wide and looked flimsy - barely strong enough to carry the weight of a young chimney sweep. "After you," she said.

The man swung off the roof and scuttled down the ladder. Tillie tested the first rung. It seemed solid enough. The ladder rattled.

"Come on," he said.

Tillie followed him down the ladder, her foot searching for each rung. The stranger eyed her as she descended. Her cheeks burned; she pulled her skirts close, ignoring his offer of assistance when she reached the ground.

"Sir, we have only just met and have not been properly introduced," she snipped.

The man tugged on the chains. The ladder retracted upward. The hooks scraped free of the roof as the contraption fell away from the wall. The man nudged her to one side and caught the contraption.

"I suppose I must introduce myself," he said. He unwound the charcoal coloured scarf from his face to reveal a man in his early thirties with a most impressively waxed moustache. "Professor Avery Allington of the Department of Curiosities, on loan from the Royal Society. I am at your service, Miss Matilda Meriwether." He bowed.

"How did you know—?"

"Your name?" The stranger's green eyes glinted. "The Department has its ways." He scrutinised Tillie's bustle. "I think you have something of mine that I accidentally dropped?"

Her eyes widened. Such familiarity!

"A red leather notebook?" He held out his hand. "Mine, I believe," His flawless waxed moustache raised with his smile.

The book? The one with the diagrams?

"It belongs to you?" she asked.

"It belongs to the Crown," he replied.

<<*No!*>> The Orb wiggled.

Tillie's eyes narrowed. She wasn't about to let the prize out of her sight.

"We may be able to come to an arrangement," she said.

"Miss Meriwether, I was told you were worth watching."

9

Of Silks, Kippers, and Secrets

T illie lay in an over-sized feather bed, revelling in the comfort engulfing her. She dared not open her eyes for fear that she would be thrust back into reality.

A clock chimed in the hallway. *Five, six, seven.* The final echo of the gong rolled past the bedroom door and down the stairs.

Professor Allington's Bots would be patrolling the halls: small brass half-spheres on wheels, with tiny hair triggers set to react to any sound of an intruder. Each carried a small canister of gas to incapacitate, and an alarm to alert the household. The clever little devices reminded Tillie of a 'pet' tortoise she had as a child, though she thought it prudent to avoid the Professor's pets.

Tillie snuggled deeper into the warm bed covers. Rarely did she have the opportunity to safely remove the Orb from around her neck. At last she'd had a full night of silence, free of the disturbing dreams that accompanied its presence. Free to let her mind wander in peace, and free of its constant chatter, which invaded her private thoughts.

Just a few more minutes.

Tillie's Aunt Prudence did not approve of sleeping in late. Nor did she have such modern security measures. Tillie longed to take full advantage of both luxuries.

Dear Aunt Prudence. Though always aware of her duties as a chaperone, Tillie's Aunt had encouraged her independence, and funded her adventures. Aunt Prudence never questioned Tillie's late-night jaunts - as long as all social appearances were upheld.

But, permissive as Aunt Prudence was, she would not approve of Tillie staying overnight, unchaperoned, in the Professor's house - even if he was to be her new employer. She clutched the bedsheets. It couldn't be helped; she dare not let the discovered notebook out of her sight without an assurance she could study it further.

Her grip relaxed. What Aunt Prudence didn't know...

Still, there would be hell to pay if Tillie didn't send an explanatory note. She'd remedy that before breakfast; for now...

Peaceful sleep.

The rhythmic click of heeled shoes marched up the stairs and along the hallway and halted outside her door. A faint knock tugged at the edges of her consciousness. Tillie reluctantly opened one eye a crack, fighting the urge to remain oblivious to the world beyond the door. To dwell in the contentment of the endless layers of bedding was preferable.

The room was dark. A single sliver of light seeped through the crack between the closed window drapes. The Orb glinted on the bedside table, just out of arm's reach. Its whisper danced around the edge of her consciousness, barely audible.

She'd found it amongst belongings inherited from her father. It had called to her. Its reassuring tone reminded Tillie of her father's voice - quiet, comforting and ready with advice, at *its* leisure. It was one of the few tangible links to her past; a reminder of a loving father, of what he'd been and of an enigma yet to solve.

Tillie pulled the covers over her ears in an attempt to restore silence for a little longer; just a few more minutes to steel her thoughts against the beckoning murmur...

Another knock.

"Miss Meriwether?" It was a woman's voice. The key rattled in the door lock.

She sat bolt upright in bed and glanced at the key jiggling in the lock; she'd let her guard down and left the key in the door. She'd allowed herself to be distracted by a pretty face and perfect moustache. She smiled as she remembered the Professor's smile, the reassuring touch of his hand; the hand that intended to relieve her of the hard-earned notebook! The memory snapped her mind awake. She scowled and whipped off the bed covers.

Adrenaline-fuelled reflexes urged Tillie to her feet. In one swift move her robe swirled about her, landed on her shoulders, and she was at the door grasping the key in the lock.

"Please, Miss Meriwether. You have an appointment with Professor Allington for breakfast. I've brought you some clothes."

Tillie sighed. She was the Professor's guest. Courtesy demanded she did not keep him waiting. The key clicked as she turned it in the lock.

The petite maid entered with an enormous box, almost as tall as she, under each arm. With economy of movement, she deposited the boxes on the bed, crossed to the window and pulled back the heavy drapes, allowing sunlight to bathe the bedroom.

The Orb still lay on the bedside table, momentarily forgotten. It glowed in the morning light, as if to remind Tillie of its presence. Tillie glided across the room and scooped up the Orb. Its whisper, now audible, was frantic.

<<Secret,>> it hissed.

Tillie watched the maid's reflection as the girl opened the window and glanced in the direction of the nightstand. The maid smiled. Tillie sucked in a quiet breath. Blast! Her reflexes had not been swift enough.

The Orb growled at her.

<<*I'm sorry,*>> she replied.

<<*Information.*>> The Orb's voice was clear in her mind.

She nodded. Servants know everything, *see* everything. If she were to glean more information about her host, she would have to befriend the girl.

"The fresh air will put the colour back in your cheeks, Miss," said the maid.

"Call me Tillie." She smiled. "And what shall I call you?"

"My name is Grace, Miss." Purple and green ribbons fluttered in her hair as she curtsied in Tillie's direction.

"I like your ribbons, Grace," said Tillie.

The Orb fidgeted on the end of its chain dangling from between her fingers behind her back.

"They are Her Majesty's favourite colours, aren't they?" she asked.

Grace nodded in reply and returned to the unopened boxes.

Tillie's shoulders slumped. Starting a conversation, let alone getting the girl to talk, wasn't going to be easy.

She slipped the Orb's chain around her neck while Grace unpacked the boxes. She tucked it under her night gown. It was the greatest of her father's mysteries, left for her to unravel. And it would remain hidden - until that secret was unlocked - especially from curious Professors who insist on acquiring her finds.

"Which would you prefer, Miss?" Grace's voice pulled Tillie back to the task at hand.

An assortment of silk, cotton and linen dresses, all in the latest fashions, had been laid out on the coverlet. Assorted linens and unmentionables were unpacked from amongst the layers of soft tissue paper in the second box. There was a pair of collapsible bustles, ideal for transport, with ample room for her concealed pockets and holster. Two new pairs of leather boots stood at the foot of the bed.

Tillie sighed and ran her fingers along the intricately pleated trim of a dress, in a most pleasing burgundy-coloured silk. The material slipped smoothly under her fingers, caressing their tips as they caught in the soft folds. She yearned for its gentle kiss on her skin. Tillie sighed. It had been too long since she'd indulged. A door opened to memories of her childhood. Bows and ribbons and...

She snapped her fingers away from temptation. Her old clothes were practical and carried no obligations.

"They are not mine," she sighed. *Pity.*

"Compliments of the Professor." Grace slipped the old clothes away from Tillie's reach, folding them and stuffing them into the empty boxes.

Tillie raised an eyebrow. Aunt Prudence would not approve of her accepting such intimate gifts from a complete stranger. She was surprised at her discomfort; she wasn't usually concerned with conforming to the expectations of Society. She'd avoided the trappings of 'coming out' at Court and its social entanglements for almost four years and was disinclined to be indebted to anyone.

Should she accept such a personal gift from a stranger, even one who had most likely saved her life? She had no desire to be trapped into commitment. She eyed the shimmering silks and pressed linens. She took a deep breath. Perhaps...? If it was required as part of her new employment, she would owe the Professor nothing.

The Orb chuckled.

Her eyes widened; she'd never *heard* the Orb chuckle before.

"Perhaps they are from The Department of Curiosities?" She did not intend to speak out loud. She bit her lip. Too late.

Grace looked up from her tidying, holding one of Tillie's worn boots in her hand.

"Of course." Grace smiled.

"Yes." Tillie's conscience settled; little more encouragement was required to dress for breakfast. "Which would you suggest?" she asked.

Grace held up a silk day dress of blue and purple stripes. The silk shimmered in the morning light.

"Perfect."

Tillie donned the new bustle and petticoats. Soft, silken hose slid effortlessly over her leg and clung to her skin like soft spiderwebs. Her heart fluttered. How she loved silk!

She straightened her skirts, ensuring the recent leather-bound acquisition was securely tucked away in the pockets hidden beneath the voluminous overskirt that draped the bustle. A small purple bonnet, with fluffy white and green feathers, finished off the ensemble.

"Professor Allington is expecting you in the dining room, Miss Tillie."

"Thank you, Grace." Tillie pinned a brooch to the collar of her bodice and nodded. There was just enough time to write Aunt Prudence a quick note.

Breakfast beckoned.

The smell of smoked kippers greeted Tillie as she entered the dining room. The buffet boasted a full range of delights, including her favourites: ham, fried mushrooms, eggs, toast and jam. Kippers were not high on her list.

A large newspaper hung, as if suspended, just above a chair at the end of the well-appointed breakfast table. Only curled fingers supporting it on either side, confirmed that its reader occupied the chair at the head of the table. As this was the Professor's residence, Tillie surmised the fingers were his.

Tillie tugged self-consciously at the cuffs of her newly acquired dress. It was too late to regret her wardrobe decisions now. A gentleman would say nothing. Hidden beneath her bodice the Orb twitched, as if laughing. She took a deep breath and sat at the opposite end of the table.

One corner of the newspaper crinkled forward. Professor Allington reached for a piece of marmalade-laden toast. He peeked over the broadsheet, as his gaze flicked towards her plate of fried mushrooms.

"Good morning, Miss Meriwether." The corners of his eyelids wrinkled slightly. The newspaper rolled further forward to reveal the smiling face of the previous night's rival, rescuer and, now, work colleague. "I highly recommend the eggs," he said.

With her host's duty of providing nourishment and the discussion of the breakfast menu completed, Professor Allington was all business, not bothering with small talk of the weather or the state of the roads: "May I ask what you were doing at the Waldran residence last night?"

Sunlight, from the window behind him, danced across the surface of his tea as he smiled sweetly and lifted the cup to his lips. Tillie blinked; was that a glint in his eye or merely the reflected morning sun?

She considered her position. His countenance was certainly agreeable, but experience had taught her caution. It was one thing for him to have saved her from the grip of the automaton, but could he be entrusted with her secret? Minimal information and prudence were always recommended when her emotions could not be trusted. Avoidance worked equally well. Tillie sipped her tea. It was expensive, a blend of Assam and Darjeeling.

"A gentleman would not ask about a lady's private business," Tillie replied, scrutinising the Professor carefully for his reaction.

His gaze faltered and flicked towards the butler who diligently ignored them both. The Professor's cheeks reddened, for just a moment. He straightened his shoulders and turned his eyes back towards Tillie, this time avoiding her direct gaze.

"My apologies, Miss Meriwether."

Tillie felt a twinge of regret. A lady would not have pointed out his slip in etiquette. It seemed that the Professor may prove to be many things, but at least he *considered* himself a gentleman.

"Do forgive my choice of words, Professor Allington. What I meant was that it's a family matter."

The Professor fidgeted with his toast before correcting its insufficiency of marmalade, then sipped his tea slowly. Finally, he cleared his throat and spoke, returning to a more business-like manner: "There is the matter of a red-leather bound notebook to finalise."

"Ah, yes, but why should I hand over my prize?" replied Tillie.

"That *prize* was stolen from Her Majesty's Private Collection." The glow that bathed his face receded as he lowered the tea cup. The glint in his eye remained.

"What proof do you offer to back your claim?" She spread a thick layer of quince jam on her toast. If she must relinquish the notebook, she would make him work for it. It was not the prize she had been searching for, but it seemed the fortuitous find might prove lucrative.

The Professor snapped his fingers in the direction of the butler.

She was pleased that he was not easily shaken. She could not abide a weak man. This was a man who was used to getting what he wants.

<<*Arrogant.*>> The Orb was free to express its silent opinion, without fear of recrimination.

Tillie smiled in agreement and brushed her hand against the pleated edge of the lapel covering the Orb. The smooth silk seduced her fingers, reminding her of the finery still in the bedroom above. She lowered her hand and dug her nails into her palm. He would not buy her.

The Orb remained silent.

The butler stepped forward and handed a letter to Tillie. It was addressed to Professor Allington. The seal was broken. She unfolded it and read:

"*Dear Sir,*

I wish to engage you in a forthcoming task. Her Majesty Queen Victoria, in her generous patronage of the Department of Curiosities, has instructed we retrieve an item which once resided in her personal

vault. The item being one red-leather bound notebook, authored by Leonardo da Vinci.

This volume must not fall into the enemy's hands.

Our Intelligence informs us it is currently in the possession of The Inventor.

I request your immediate attention on this matter.

Yours most sincerely,
General Sir Edward Sabine,
Director, Department of Curiosities."

Da Vinci? Property of the Queen? Tillie's heart jumped. No wonder the Professor was unwilling to relinquish ownership. Her fingers twitched as she tried not to betray her excitement.

She glanced at the bottom of the letter. A small drawing of a cog superimposed by a lightning bolt followed the signature. At the very bottom was another signature and a seal: a Queen riding in state, carrying a sceptre in one hand and attended by a page.

"Is that...?" Tillie looked up from the letter.

The Professor nodded. "By Royal Appointment, as it were." With a nod, the butler retrieved the letter, refolded it and slipped it into his jacket pocket.

Tillie was many things, but most of all, she was loyal to the Crown. She would obey her Queen, without question. It may be inopportune to have lost the notebook to the Empire, but it would not stop her seeking her original prize. Clearly the Department of Curiosities had access to privileged information. Perhaps such information would prove useful in her personal quest.

She retrieved da Vinci's notebook from her bustle pocket, under the amused and ever-watchful eye of Professor Allington.

She held the notebook in the air, her hand firmly clutching its leather-bound cover.

"I do not surrender this to you, but to Her Majesty," she said. "I expect your payment for services rendered."

"The Department of Curiosities pays very well to those who are loyal. Consider your new wardrobe as your first payment." A twitch of the Professor's moustache was the only hint of his smile.

<<*Touché!*>> The Orb rejoined her side of the conversation.

Her fingers tensed, as she remembered the outfit's provenance. She willed herself not to blush. Only silly girls blushed. After her challenge of the Professor's gentlemanly credentials, she owed him that one rebuff. But just the one.

"And I must congratulate the tailor on the fit," he continued.

Tillie's heart froze. A chill dread crept over her and prickled her skin. Tailor-made clothing took time to make.

"How did you know what...?"

"Oh, I have been following you for some time," he replied.

She swallowed. Aunt Prudence had warned her she would find herself in trouble one day. Her gaze darted around the room, noting the position of the doors and windows, any means of escape. She cleared her throat and looked him directly in the eye.

"I *have* advised my aunt of my whereabouts." Making one's abductor aware that one will be missed is also a good stratagem for continued safety.

The Professor's eyes widened. His cup clattered on its saucer.

"My apologies, Miss Meriwether. What I meant to say was: The Department of Curiosities has been investigating your recruitment potential for some time." He leaned forward and spoke softly: "I assure you, there was no impropriety meant. You have Grace to thank for the tailor's work. The Department requires all its operatives to be appropriately attired. The garments are part of your employment agreement. We are honoured you have accepted our offer."

Tillie nodded, but she still didn't know exactly what she was agreeing to. Her gaze met the sharp stare of his clear green eyes. They definitely glinted. She stared into them, trying to decipher the truthfulness of his words.

"What does the Department of Curiosities do, exactly?" she asked.

"We collect and study curiosities, scientific or otherwise, many of which can be put to good use for the Empire."

"I will want a written letter of employment."

The Professor nodded.

"And the freedom to pursue my own investigations. No questions asked," she said.

"Of course." The Professor smiled. "As long as it does not interfere with Department business."

She reluctantly relinquished the notebook and slid it across the table. The Professor snatched it up, unwound the strap and opened the notebook to examine its contents. The moustache dipped in a frown.

"It's written backwards, and in code. You'll be needing a cryptographer." She chuckled. The Orb expressed its satisfaction. "Fortunately, I'm a cryptographer," she said. "But, unfortunately, I do not speak Italian."

"You are full of pleasant surprises, Miss Meriwether. I'm sure you'll prove a great asset to The Department." He closed the notebook and returned it to her. "Perhaps it's best you keep it for now. I'll see we find a translator to help with your decryption."

Tillie leaned back in her chair and smiled, satisfied with the agreement. She savoured the aroma as the butler filled her teacup. She sipped the brew. Tea had a refreshing way of invigorating the memory; something else had caught her attention as she had read the letter.

"Who is 'The Inventor'?" she asked.

"One of our... rivals" replied the Professor, "working against the Empire. He was rumoured to be attending Professor Waldran's soiree last night."

<<*Foe.*>> The Orb's silent hiss echoed in Tillie's mind.

She nodded.

"Then we have something in common," she said. "We both want to see him hang."

The Professor executed a perfect eyebrow arch.

Tillie regretted her outburst as soon as she had spoken. Such things are best left unsaid in polite company.

"It is a personal matter," she said, as she sipped her hot tea.

Professor Avery Allington sat at the head of the breakfast table, crunching on the last of his marmalade toast. He wondered if there were any kippers left. Miss Meriwether hadn't touched the kippers. She preferred the honey-cured ham and toast with quince jam. He watched as she slowly sipped her tea. The aesthetically-pleasing curve of her hand echoed that of the handle of her tea cup.

She wore a dress of silk, trimmed with velvet. The colour complimented her very well indeed. The Professor congratulated himself on such an excellent choice of attire, as his gaze drifted to an unfamiliar brooch adorning the collar.

"More ham, Miss Meriwether?"

Professor Allington's voice broke the awkward silence, causing her tea cup to tilt at a most precarious angle. A drop of tea fell into her lap. He frowned. Would it stain? He had no knowledge of such things.

"No, thank you, Professor Allington." She wiped her mouth gently with a napkin as she shook her head slowly.

The Professor motioned to the butler. "Kippers please, Wallace."

Wallace leaned forward and deftly slid them onto his plate.

"And order some more quince jam and honey cured bacon, will you?" he whispered, making sure that his guest did not overhear. Wallace nodded and left the Professor to his self-congratulatory reflections.

Tillie's heart raced. The Professor had been examining her brooch, a gift from her father. She brushed the spilt tea from her napkin, hoping he would lose interest in the bauble. Tillie stole a glance at the other end of the table. Professor Allington's eyes had lingered too long.

<<*Fool.*>>

Even the Orb had realised wearing it could prove her undoing. Such a personal keepsake could be traced back to reveal her true identity. Her hand twitched. She resisted the urge to remove the brooch.

Warmth spread slowly up her neck. She could feel her cheeks reddening. Tillie took a renewed interest in the tea-stained napkin; she twisted it in her fingers and hoped that the Professor would not notice her reaction.

There was a knock on the door.

Thank goodness. Her fingers relaxed.

The maid, Grace, entered the room. She handed the Professor a letter, leaned close and whispered something to him. Again the raised eyebrow. Once may have been endearing, but using facial hair to communicate emotions was not exactly a scientific method. The affectation was starting to get on Tillie's nerves.

The Professor nodded, smiled and read the missive. His eyes flicked in her direction, betraying the subject of the contents, then returned his attention to the letter.

Tillie glimpsed the outer seal of the dispatch. The mark was similar to that on the General's letter.

"Well, we shall see what the Queen makes of you," he said. "Her Majesty has called a meeting with the Department, and you have been instructed to attend."

Tillie took a hesitant step into the spacious Drawing Room. Her gaze skimmed over the crimson damask that festooned the walls and gilt furniture, and barely registered their presence. Nor was she fully capable of appreciating the soft thud of their footfalls on the floral carpet. Her attention was focused on the woman before her - Her Imperial Majesty, the Queen-Empress Victoria.

Tillie adjusted her bonnet and fidgeted with her white gloves. What was the dress code for meeting the Queen?

Professor Allington strode forward and halted next to a tall, grey-haired man standing several feet away from a raised dais. Tillie followed and fell in behind the two men. She glanced up at the figure seated on the dais: a straight-backed, serious-faced woman, shrouded in black and corsetry. She had worn the colour of mourning since her beloved Albert had died, twenty-one years earlier. She regarded the trio with her sharp blue eyes, her gaze lingering on Tillie. The loss had obviously not dulled her intelligence nor crushed her will to make the British Empire all-encompassing.

She looked every inch the Queen. Though short in stature, Her Majesty was not lacking in authority. And she knew it.

The Queen proffered her hand. The two men stepped forward and kissed her hand, bowed and stepped back to a less intimate distance. Tillie remained behind them trying not to betray her stupefaction.

"Lord Allington, General Sabine. Welcome." Her voice was clear and confident.

<<Lord?>> the Orb echoed.

The word took a moment to filter through Tillie's awe. Her eyes widened. *Lord?*

A faint click distracted her as the General twisted his palm over the top of his walking cane. Her head swam as her world shimmered and danced. Her ears buzzed. A whooshing sound in her head drowned out the conversation. The Orb twitched against her neck, its protestations lost in the confusion, and quite beyond her understanding. She felt it reach out, unable to break through the static. Its voice slipped away.

Tillie fought the urge to straighten her bustle and tidy her skirts. Was she supposed to remove her bonnet? Her heart raced. Her cheeks flushed. Was the room getting hotter? She rarely experienced such light-headedness. Was this the *vapours*? How disappointingly pedestrian. She dug her fingers into her palms, hoping the pain would clear her head.

"General Sabine has informed me that *my* Department of Curiosities has a new recruit," said the Queen.

Lord Allington nodded. "May I present Miss Matilda Meriwether, Your Majesty." His voice seemed muffled.

Queen Victoria eyed Tillie as the two men stepped aside. Tillie stood alone before the inquisitive stare of her monarch. She swallowed; her head was still spinning and her balance tenuous at best. She bent her knees as much as she dared and managed a flustered curtsy, more like a bob than a formal bow.

Queen Victoria studied her subject, nodded to Lord Allington and reached down the side of her throne and flicked a switch.

To Tillie's relief, the Orb now ceased trying to communicate. Her head cleared and the voices became more lucid.

Victoria Regina, Her Majesty, Queen of the United Kingdom of Great Britain and Ireland, Empress of India, rose from her throne, inspected Tillie's bonnet and smiled.

"We are glad that one of our own fair sex is finally accompanying these men," she said. Tillie's heart slowed, the unexpected greeting quelling her nerves. She bowed her head slightly, still avoiding the Queen's direct gaze, and studied the tiled flooring; a fine crack cut across the corner of the tile on which she stood.

The Queen stepped down from her dais. The rustle of her expensive silk skirts warned Tillie of her approach.

Again, a hot flush ravaged her body. The Orb shifted under her bodice, cooling her breast. Though Tillie was still unsure if she entirely trusted the Orb, she had learned it was uncanny in its assessment of any given situation. And, so far it seemed to have her best interests at heart. Yet now, when she would have gladly welcomed advice, it remained silent.

She breathed slowly, willing the redness from her cheeks and attempting to calm the flutterings in her stomach. It appeared she was on her own.

A pair of exquisitely embroidered black silk shoes invaded her field of view. A small lace-gloved hand touched her cheek and lifted her chin to direct her gaze forward.

Tillie's heart froze as the Royal lips gently kissed her forehead. A heady aroma gently enveloped her with the scent of roses, musk, ambergris and bergamot. Her head swam. Before her was the face of a monarch. Confident blue eyes searched her own. The eyes smiled.

Tillie held her breath, willing herself not to succumb to a fainting spell.

Queen Victoria waved the two men away from Her presence. Lord Allington and General Sabine stepped back, out of view.

The Queen leaned in closer, her perfume now surrounding them both as if in a protective cocoon.

"They may have position and learning," she said, "but remember there are some things that only women can understand, some places only women can go, some things we can discover that they cannot. That is our strength, my dear. We are often ignored. No one suspects us."

Queen Victoria's gaze shifted towards the two men who awaited her permission to return. Her smile was mischievous. The men shifted uneasily. Tillie felt heat creep up her neck and settle in her cheeks. This time there were no flutterings.

"They think they own our world. They do not." Queen Victoria's fingers tweaked Tillie's cheek. "The Crown does." The Queen chuckled. "I do. And I intend to own more."

Tillie's hands trembled.

"That is the promise of Our *little experiment*," the Queen whispered. "A new frontier for us, Miss Meriwether." She leaned even closer. "We have been following your progress for some time now."

Queen Victoria pressed something into Tillie's palm, clasped her own hand around Tillie's and gently squeezed it shut.

Tillie caught her breath. Her eyes flicked up to catch the Queen's steady gaze. Then Her Imperial Majesty, the Queen-Empress Victoria winked.

"We shall speak again." Queen Victoria stepped away from the intimacy. "We are pleased," she announced to the room. "We will have our orders dispatched immediately. Good day, Gentlemen. Good day, Miss Meriwether."

The audience now concluded, the Queen pivoted on the heel of her silken shoe and returned to her throne. Tillie curtsied, rejoined Lord Allington and the General, and was ushered from Her Majesty's presence.

✦

Tillie stared out the carriage window. Purple tassels bounced along the inside edge of the roof. Wheels clattered on the cobblestones, almost hypnotically, drowning out the murmur of Lord Allington's polite conversation. Random words rose above the noise of the carriage.

She stared at her closed fist and ignored him. The Queen - his employer - had given her something, something secret. Something that currently burned a hole in her right hand. Her fingers twitched. Curiosity demanded she take a peek.

<<*Wait,*>> the Orb whispered in her mind. She clenched her fist tighter and kept the contents safely hidden.

The carriage rumbled and jolted.

"I say, I have never seen you lost for words before," Lord Allington chuckled.

Tillie's attention snapped back to the conversation. "I beg your pardon."

"Her Majesty had a lot to discuss with you."

She nodded. He eyed her expectantly.

<<*Secret,*>> the Orb urged silently.

She agreed. If Queen Victoria had wanted the missive seen, she would not have been so clandestine in the giving.

Tillie turned back to face the carriage window and focused on the Terrace houses along the street.

"Her Majesty liked my bonnet," she said.

It seemed an age until Tillie managed to find time alone. Lord Allington had insisted she remain as his guest until after she had visited The Department's main office. Guard Bots lurked in every corner. His staff were overly-helpful, and possibly ever-watchful.

Tillie waited until Grace was called on an errand, then slipped back into the guest bedroom and locked the door.

She closed the drapes, lit the gas wall sconce near the dressing table and examined her closed fist. She held her breath. What could Queen Victoria want to give *her*? And why keep it secret from Her own men?

<<*Open,*>> the Orb cooed.

The internal voice was calm and reassuring. She let her breath escape slowly and relaxed her grip, extending the fingers of her right hand one at a time. A piece of meticulously folded silk lay in her palm. The wax seal of Victoria Regina stared back at her.

Tillie removed her linen gloves and slipped a letter knife under the seal, diligently avoiding any breakage of wax. She unfolded the note and scanned the lines. Minuscule numbers and letters filled the page. Her eyes widened. It was the same cipher that her father had used and taught her as a child.

A chill crept up her arm. How could the Queen possibly know her father's cipher? Only three people knew her father's secret code - or so she thought. If the Queen knew the code, then she *must* have known Tillie's father. And, if she knew her father then...

Tillie's heart froze. The Orb chilled against her skin.

After her father died, she had been ostracised - a child abandoned by polite society. Her Aunt and Uncle Meriwether took her in. A change of name had distanced her from her father's sins. She had presumed that only they had known her true identity. But, if the Queen knew her father's identity, then she also knew Tillie's secret.

She leaned on the dressing table. Her heart felt as if it was being crushed in her chest. Her hand trembled as she read the rest of the message. There was a single word below the message:

Homunculus.

It was a pet name given to her by her father. It was unmistakably a key to the cipher.

"She knows who I am!" She struggled to breathe.

If the Queen knew the truth, why was she giving Tillie secret messages? Why would the Queen even talk to her? Tillie slumped onto the chair by the dressing table. Why had She not denounced Tillie as a traitor's daughter?

Tillie breathed slowly, fighting the wave of panic threatening to engulf her. What else would the message reveal? She pulled a pencil and scrap of paper from her bustle pocket and scribbled down the deciphered message.

There were instructions. Queen Victoria intended to contact her directly, by code and at specific times. The note was signed *V.R., Liberator.* The Royal stamp was unmistakable.

<<*Liberator.*>> The Orb's voice filled her thoughts.

Her grip loosened on the silken note. It fluttered onto the table.

Liberator; the name was almost as familiar as her own. It was the name of her father's employer. The name of the person whose identity he died to protect. If Queen Victoria was this *Liberator*, then *why* had Tillie's father died a traitor?

The Orb remained uncharacteristically silent. Tillie was grateful. She sat in silence and sifted through her memories. What was it Queen Victoria had said? *Our little experiment.* Tillie could hear her father's voice repeating the same words.

The sound of the hall clock seeped into the room. Her heartbeat synchronised with click of the clockwork. Each tick matched the beat of her heart. With each tock, pieces of her life fell into place. Each swing of the pendulum reforged a memory.

Tillie glanced over her instructions. She could not refuse the Queen, even if she had betrayed Tillie's father. She was Victoria's creature, her *Homunculus* - as was her father before her.

Of Traitors, The Department,
and Curiosities

usset leaves swirled up the side of the carriage as the horses trotted along Cromwell Road towards Hyde Park. The colour reminded Tillie of the toffees her father gave her as special treats, as a child. Her chin crumpled. It had been years since she'd savoured sweet toffee...

An errant leaf darted through the open window. It flicked at her nose, danced across the compartment and taunted Lord Allington as his journal pages flicked in the wind. He scribbled another note in his journal and batted the leaf away.

"Can't you close the window?" he mumbled. "I can't finish my notes in this wind."

Tillie shook her head and turned her face toward the window. A flurry of air streamed across her face and tugged at her curls. She grinned, and fought the urge to lean out the window, to taste the freedom it promised.

A crisp breeze swirled in and plunged down her neck. She shivered and tugged her fur-lined collar tight, to shield her neck from the chilled wind. She pulled the window shut; she couldn't afford to catch a chill.

Lord Allington glanced up from his notebook. A smile played over his lips.

"Spring will be late this year," he said.

"Then I shall just have to find ways to stay warm."

He muttered a reply and returned to his scribbling.

Her brow winkled with disappointment. When they had first met, he promised to be entertaining. Now he seemed as self-absorbed as every other man she had met. Ordinarily, she'd abandon such a tiresome acquaintance and search out a more promising companion. But she needed time to examine the da Vinci notebook, and to access The Department of Curiosities' files.

A cheeky smile flickered across her lips. She wondered what he would do if she grabbed his notebook and sacrificed it to the wintry world beyond the carriage window.

<<*Boring.*>> The Orb reminded Tillie of its presence.

"Yes, such a pity." She sighed and returned her attention to the intoxicating chaos beyond the window glass.

"Hmm, pardon?" Lord Allington ceased writing.

Tillie reproached herself for expressing her emotions publicly. She didn't need to reply to the Orb vocally; it could read her every thought.

"It's a pity the weather is not warmer. We could have taken an open cab," she replied.

Lord Allington shook his head and returned to his work.

She continued to watch the dance outside the window; it provided a welcome distraction to his interminable scribbling.

"Sir?" A disembodied voice filled the air. Lord Allington retrieved a small brass funnel from its harness near the roof.

"Yes, Smythe." He spoke into the curved communication funnel.

"We're arriving at Prince's Gate," came the tinny reply.

"Thank you, Smythe." He replaced the communicator device and slipped his notebook and pen into his coat pocket.

Tillie caught sight of the Natural History Museum as the carriage turned to head north and stopped outside a large red brick building.

"We're not going to Hyde Park?" she asked.

Lord Allington shook his head, exited the carriage and started towards the building. He hesitated mid-step, returned and offered his hand to Tillie, as she gathered her skirts to alight from the carriage. She took his hand and stepped out of the warmth of the compartment.

The morning sun highlighted the ornately-patterned brick of the Department of Curiosities' headquarters. Carved-stone balconies topped each of the full-length bay windows of each floor. Three in all. She raised an eyebrow. The Department must be well-funded; the glass would have cost a fortune.

<<*Behave yourself,*>> Tillie instructed the Orb. <<*Not a peep out of you. I need to keep my wits about me and I don't need your distractions.*>>

"Welcome to the Department of Curiosities, Miss Meriwether," said Lord Allington, with a grin.

❂

Tillie and Lord Allington were greeted at the door by a stout man with grey eyes hidden behind metal-rimmed spectacles, and a lack-lustre moustache. A faint smell of sulphur lingered about him.

"Good morning, Harrow," said Lord Allington.

"Good morning, Sir." He tipped his bowler in Tillie's direction. "If you would follow me. The General is expecting you."

The entry hall was well-appointed, witness to an excess of money tastefully spent. Tillie's hand trembled as she traced her fingers along the wall-papered panels. Her fingertips caressed the softness of the golden silk and velvet damask. Her heart fluttered.

A series of faint clicks caught her attention as Harrow led the pair further along the corridor. She tilted her ear toward the sound, trying to decipher the direction of its source.

The clicking grew more insistent with each step, until a high pitched whir filled the hall behind her, and circled to the right as it closed in.

"Stop!" Harrow held his hand up in warning.

Tillie froze mid-step, just in time to avoid tripping over a small half-spherical mechanical.

"How cute," she cooed. "It's one of your little Bots, Lord Allington."

"I cannot claim them as mine," he replied. "They were created by a past member."

Tillie eyed the twitching mechanical. It resembled the mechanical tortoise her father had made for her twelfth birthday - one of her favourite toys, as a child. A seam opened down the centre of the Bot's shell. The cover slowly separated and opened, like flower petals, to reveal two segmented metal arms, which gesticulated furiously in Tillie's direction.

The Bot hissed as it rumbled closer to her. A third, smaller appendage, resembling a pipe cannon, telescoped out from the Bot's innards.

She gasped. Her tortoise had never done that!

The Orb buried itself into her chest.

Harrow rummaged through his coat pockets and pulled out a small bronze brooch. With a nervous-looking smile, he tossed it towards Tillie. It sailed past her ear. Harrow grimaced.

Lord Allington snatched it out of the air and glared at Harrow. Again, Lord Allington's dexterity impressed her. Harrow, on the other hand, was proving not only negligent, but a poor shot as well.

The Orb sat in smug silence.

"Put this on," Lord Allington instructed.

"A brooch?" she asked.

"Protection," he replied.

The Bot's hissing slowed; it jerked from side to side, as if searching for its lost target. The pipe cannon retracted, followed by the two antennae. The metallic petals folded back on themselves and closed with an emphatic clack. It hesitated for a moment, then spun around and whizzed off to wait under a mahogany side table.

"I don't think much of your welcoming committee." She shot a glance at Harrow who now stood ahead of them, at the bottom of the stairs.

Harrow's frown faded.

"As a security device, your Bot's don't look all that intimidating," she continued.

She tugged at the cog-shaped brooch, trying to dislodge the sharp point of its lightning bolt motif that had entangled itself in the pleated trim of her bodice.

"I think it was confused," Lord Allington replied, as he indicated his badge. "The badge produces a signal, which the Bot recognises as an ally. It then allows the wearer access. Harrow and I both have one, so it detected you as an intruder."

Tillie eyed the badge. It was a rather ordinary looking thing, styled with the emblem of the Department of Curiosities. Unfortunately, it did not match her outfit at all. Had she known she was to be given such a garish token, she would have chosen to wear her red gown, in place of the pale blue silk and white lace.

"I am sorry, Sir. I wasn't informed that our visitor would not be pinned."

Lord Allington's moustache dipped in disapproval as he glared at Harrow.

Harrow turned, led them up the stairs to the first floor and into a large drawing room at the front of the building.

The afternoon sun shone through three full-length windows. A tall figure stood silhouetted; his long shadow interrupted the wall of light bathing the parquetry floor.

"Good afternoon, Allington. I trust your journey was uneventful."

The voice seemed familiar. The man turned to face them. His face was framed by grey hair, sedate mutton-chop sideburns and a most spectacularly folded cravat.

"Yes, General, thank you," replied Lord Allington.

The General approached them. Tillie stood at attention as if waiting his inspection.

Sunlight glinted off the head of General Sabine's walking cane. Tillie glimpsed a hint of the now-familiar shape of a cog pierced by lightning through his gnarled fingers. He transferred his weight off one leg and leaned on the cane as he approached them.

Tillie relaxed. His limp stirred vague memories of her own grandfather, his prosthetic leg clicking as he bounced her on his knee. Her father had made the mechanical, the first of many designed and constructed for veterans of the Dirigible War. Before the ban.

<<*The poor man.*>> She clenched her hand, resisting the urge to help the General. <<*Do you suppose it's a war injury?*>> she asked the Orb.

<<*Age*>>, the Orb replied curtly.

<<*Hush!*>>

The wrinkles around the General's eyes deepened as he greeted her with a smile. He seemed older than she remembered.

"Ah, Harrow." The General nodded at the doorman hovering beside them. "It must be time for morning tea. There's a good chap."

Harrow's lips hardened. He scurried from the Drawing room. A small Bot whizzed into the room, past Tillie's feet and nestled amongst the curtains near the window. Her hand moved up to her new Department badge to ensure it was still in place.

"It's a pleasure to officially meet you, Miss Meriwether. I must apologise for not introducing myself earlier. My time was not my own; I had an urgent errand to attend to, for Her Majesty."

The wrinkles at the corner of his eyes deepened. Was that fear in his eyes? A hardened military man scared of a woman half his height...?

"I understand." Tillie nodded. Her life had been shaped by Her Majesty's wrath. Now Queen Victoria had claimed her as Her own. Her shoulders tensed. And *no one* defied Her wrath, not even Her very own Homunculus.

"Is there a problem, General?" she asked.

"Forgive me." The General shook his head. "I knew your uncle, Miss Meriwether." His wrinkles softened. "We fought in the Dirigible War together. I was aware Meriwether's niece was Australian; I expected a Colonial accent. How long have you resided in England, my dear?"

"Fifteen years; since I was a young child."

"Ah, that explains it."

Tillie bit her lip. No one usually bothered to check on family in the Colonies. She wasn't sure how curious the Department was, and how exhaustively they would search. She swallowed; an urgent change of subject was required.

"And what exactly is the Department of Curiosities?" she asked.

"Has Sir Avery not been forthcoming, as usual?" The General seemed to lean more heavily on his cane.

Lord Allington remained silent.

Tillie shook her head. "He does seem to prefer to keep an air of mystery."

He didn't flinch.

The General thrummed his fingers against the head of the cane. "I understand you have found an item for us, Miss Meriwether."

"Ah, yes, the notebook your man negligently left behind." She clasped her hands behind her back. She could feel the book's spine in her bustle pocket. The da Vinci notebook. Her heart pounded; she needed to examine it before she relinquished it to Queen and Country.

Lord Allington cleared his throat but said nothing.

Queen Victoria's words echoed in Tillie's memory: *Not by their rules.* A smile flitted across her lips. She would not let him off lightly, nor play the part of the submissive female.

"I shall require compensation before I hand it over, General," she said.

The General eyed her, but remained silent.

She straightened her shoulders. "I wish to study the notebook."

"I was told you're a cryptographer." The General straightened his back and shifted his weight off his walking cane. "You'll be an asset to The Department, my dear. And, as one of our operatives, you will be granted access to the archives. However, I must insist the notebook remains within The Department at all times."

Tillie's heart sank. She would've preferred to do her work in private. She looked the General directly in the eye.

"I must have your word I can study it before it is whisked off into your archives," she said.

"I like you, my dear," the General replied, with a grandfatherly smile. "I can give you one week. After that it must be archived and returned to its rightful owner. I will arrange for a room to be at your disposal."

She let her muscles relax.

General Sabine moved toward the north wall and motioned for her to follow. A collection of framed certificates decorated the panels behind his large, ornate desk. She peered at the calligraphed documents and strained to decipher the impressive credentials: Oxford, Cambridge, Royal Society of London... something in a foreign language.

Aunt Prudence would be suitably impressed. If the General had been younger, she would be writing up invitations already.

The Orb remained silent.

Tillie chuckled. It was probably sulking.

A Bot trundled across the room, hesitated, then skittered after them, bouncing off her boot, leaving a scuff on the new leather.

The General flicked a switch on his cane, instigating a series of clicks followed by a high-pitched whir. A crack opened in the wall behind the desk. The halves slid apart to reveal a map of the world.

"I have been remiss, Miss Meriwether," said the General. "With regards to your earlier question: The Department of Curiosities deals in discoveries of things of a curious nature, which may have potential to benefit the Empire. Some curiosities have tactical or economic value. Some discoveries are best kept secret as there are those who may exploit them in a... non-beneficial manner."

"We are the keepers of those secrets," added Lord Allington as he joined them.

"Most are best not revealed as they would incite panic," continued the General. "That would definitely not be in the best interest of the Empire."

Lord Allington approached the map and indicated different coloured areas on it. "Each colour indicates the influence of various curiosities."

Tillie's fingers twitched. All this talk of curiosities! She wanted to examine a certain *curiosity*: the da Vinci notebook. She flexed her fingers. She must be patient; it seemed her new employment may prove valuable in discovering information about the automaton and its creator. Lord Allington had introduced himself as 'Professor' when they'd first met; perhaps she could appeal to his scientific vanity?

<<*Careful,*>> the Orb instructed.

Her jaw clenched. <<*I know what I'm doing.*>>

The General's cane chirped quietly, distracting him from their conversation.

"What Curiosity were you hoping Lord Allington would find at Professor Waldran's residence, General?"

Lord Allington glanced at the General before answering. "The notebook, of course."

She took a measured breath. She should have guessed a member of a clandestine organisation would not give up his secrets easily. This time she would be more direct.

"What about the automaton?" she asked.

The General's eyes widened. His hand slipped from the head of his cane, causing him to almost lose his balance.

"What automaton?" he asked.

<<*No!*>> The Orb expressed its displeasure at the current turn of the conversation.

Tillie's head throbbed as its words echoed in her mind. She realised her mistake. But it was too late.

Lord Allington spun on his heel, turning away from the wall map. His moustache twitched most annoyingly.

The rogue Bot bumped her foot and ricocheted off towards the windows. It spun back around and shadowed her as she approached the General, who had now recovered his balance with remarkable dexterity for a man of his age. She was now the centre of attention.

With one step, Lord Allington closed the gap between them and returned to the conversation.

"Ah, General, I was going to mention that in my report," he replied.

"Perhaps now would be an opportune time." General Sabine peered over his spectacles and glared at Lord Allington. The impatient tap of his cane on the wooden floor echoed in the large room.

Tillie's pulse raced. The Department of Curiosities seemed to have had no prior knowledge of her discovery.

The men continued their conversation; Lord Allington apprised the General of the previous night's events.

The Bot trundled back and nudged against her foot. The mechanical was just as annoying as the clockwork turtle that kept young Tillie company while her father worked long days - and nights - in his laboratory. It had followed her around like a puppy, just as the Bot was doing now.

"I have a badge, leave me alone!" She flicked it away with her boot and edged closer to the men, trying to hear their hushed conversation.

The Bot spun around and careered into the toe of her boot, skimmed along her foot and spun away towards the doorway. It performed a strange little dance, circled around her feet as it buzzed, like a furious bee.

"I am trying to listen," she whispered through gritted teeth.

She leaned down and snatched up the Bot as it returned to annoy her. She curled her fingers around its body. The metal vibrated. Its wheels spun as it twisted in her hand. She flipped the Bot over and, without thinking, flicked a small switch hidden beneath. Its wheels whirred, slowed and halted. The Bot lay motionless in her hand.

She sighed. Now she could concentrate. She turned back to listen to the conversation.

Both men stared at her in silence.

Lord Allington's over-expressive moustache remained suspended mid-air. The silent tableau remained frozen for several moments.

The General tapped his cane.

"You are full of surprises, Miss Meriwether." His voice was flat. His accusatory stare burned. Even the Orb stirred uncomfortably, under his scrutiny. Her heart twisted in her chest. What had she done wrong?

<<*Caution.*>> The Orb's warning wormed through her mind. Her fingers gripped the Bot's carcass.

A series of pips emanated from the General's cane.

<<*Exposed!*>> The Orb shrieked.

The General examined his cane and turned to face her. The pips increased in frequency. He raised an eyebrow, lifted his cane and walked towards her. An ominous hum emanated from its brass head. He advanced, as if led by an auditory beacon. The cane produced a sequence of short, quick noises. He frowned.

Tillie stood her ground; nothing would prevent her from studying the notebook. She willed the Orb to remain still.

The General halted and lifted his cane in her direction. He pointed it towards her chest. A series of frantic clicks crescendoed. His eyes widened. They were old, framed with deep lines of experience. What secrets were hidden behind them?

Her skin prickled. The Orb? Had his confounded cane detected it?

"What do we have here?" The General reached out and seized the inanimate Bot. He turned it over, examined it briefly and handed it to Lord Allington. His wary gaze never left Tillie.

She rubbed her hand. The Orb was safe. She mentally pleaded with the Orb to remain silent to avoid detection.

It acquiesced.

Lord Allington laid the mechanical on the General's desk and began to disassemble it. He glanced at the overabundant array of desk drawers.

"Where do you keep your Mag-specs, General?" he asked.

"Third down, half drawer on the left," the General replied, his eyes still fixed on Tillie. "The very left."

Tillie's mind raced. What was so important about the Bot? What *had* she done?

Lord Allington flipped through several lenses stacked on either side of the Mag-spec's frame then sifted through the mechanical's brass components, scrutinising each in turn.

Visions of her father crowded Tillie's memory; she was a child again, watching her father build her first mechanical turtle.

Lord Allington scraped the inside of the casing and flicked flecks of rust from his silver tweezers.

"It's one of the older models, General." He flipped down another lens. "*That* doesn't belong there." He burrowed into the Bot's shell and retrieved a small section of clockwork and cogs with copper wire coiled around a metal pin.

He looked up, his green eyes filling the entirety of both lenses. There was something about the look in his eyes... a look of determination and concentration. Just like her father.

Tillie's fingers slipped away from her palm.

The Orb twitched under her bodice. A prick of heat scalded her skin.

Lord Allington mumbled and returned to his investigations of the Bot. After a few minutes, he leaned back in his chair and removed the Mag-specs.

"Clever," He shook his head. "Very clever. It's a listening device," he announced.

The General scowled. "How did it get past, undetected?"

He lifted the cane to his ear and shook it gently, then flipped the top of the decorative head and examined its internal workings. He nodded and flicked his wrist. The top flipped back and closed with a metallic ting.

"A what?" asked Tillie.

"A device that listens to our conversations," he replied.

"I don't follow." She frowned; Mechanics was not her field.

"The cane detects minute magnetic fields produced by moving mechanicals or electrical currents, hence it detected the Bot." He grinned. "General Sabine's area of research is magnetic fields."

"Handy toy." She moved closer to examine the disassembled Bot. Why hadn't it detected the Orb? "How did it detect the Bot when it was turned off?"

"It wasn't turned off," replied Lord Allington. "Well, not entirely." He indicated the switch under the Bot's casing. "This switch only controls its dampening magnetic field."

She shook her head.

"I still don't follow." She'd never grasped mechanics, no matter how much her father had schooled her.

"This Bot has been modified with a nullifying magnetic field. It masked its signal and prevented it being detected. When you..." He glanced at the General. "When it was turned off, the cane could detect the listening device."

Tillie nodded.

The General had remained quiet during Lord Allington's explanation. Only now did he speak.

"We were fortunate you knew how to switch the Bot off, Miss Meriwether." The General frowned.

Tillie's stomach knotted. She preferred '*my dear*'. His voice no longer reminded her of her grandfather. Now it sounded more like one of her scolding tutors.

Lord Allington pulled a small lead box from one of the desk drawers, and packed away the parts of the corrupted mechanical.

"They know about your cane, General." He snapped the lid shut. "And that means..." His face paled.

"We have a traitor." The General stomped the end of his cane on the floor. The sound echoed through the room. He turned and bellowed in the direction of the hallway. "Harrow."

There was no answer.

"Harrow!" roared the General.

Tillie flinched. Before her was a man of authority, hardened by service in the military. Any hint of a sweet grandfather-figure was now lost to her, likely nothing more than just a childish fancy.

Her shoulders slumped. Perhaps the security she had sought with The Department of Curiosities was a hopeful fantasy? As in all things, reality was much more fragile.

The General shot her an accusatory glance, and tapped his cane again. Only now did she realise why the General had turned on her. She swallowed, her throat dry.

<<*He thinks I'm the traitor?*>> she said.

The Orb remained silent.

She turned to Lord Allington, the man whom she had followed into this precarious venture. His calm green eyes seemed to hold no recriminations. They were as inviting as ever. A small crease grew at their edge, revealing a small smile.

"What traitor would be so foolish as to incriminate themselves so obviously?" he said.

"If this is how you treat all your recruits, then--"

"We are indeed fortunate that Miss Meriwether had the intelligence to deduce the Bot's deactivation mechanism," he said.

The General frowned.

Tillie pursed her lips and crossed her arms.

"How can *I* be your traitor?" she scoffed. "I had no idea of the Department's existence before *your* man practically assaulted me. I'm beginning to wish I had left him on that rooftop."

"General, it's obvious Miss Meriwether is just as surprised as we are. And, surely, it would take someone with knowledge of The Department, to circumvent our security?"

The General did not reply.

"We need to be on our guard," he said. "*All* of us. I recommend we review the entire Department immediately."

"As always, I respect your advice, Allington." The General relaxed the grip on his walking cane and eyed his colleague. "You will now be responsible for Miss Meriwether. I will get Harrow to begin investigations into this."

"Excellent notion, sir," said Lord Allington.

"Harrow!" The General stomped towards the double-door entrance. "Where is that man?"

Harrow poked his head through the doorway.

"Where have you been?"

Harrow mumbled in reply.

"I need to see a listing of all security measures, at once." The General's face reddened as he twisted this cane into the parquetry floor.

"My apologies, Miss Meriwether. We will meet back here in two days. We should have your translator by then, and you can examine your precious notebook." He paused and looked her directly in the eye. "Though it must remain within the Department of Curiosities. Understood?"

Tillie nodded.

"You see to it, Allington." The General spoke in clipped tones. "In the meantime, I have a traitor to deal with."

Of Diaries, Ghostmen, and Unpleasant Surprises

The pale yellow glow of the low-lying sun flashed through the carriage window and darted across Tillie's lap. It gleamed off Lord Allington's intriguing self-inking nib pen as he scribbled in, yet another, notebook and mumbled to himself about traitors and listening devices. The litany continued for the entire journey, ignoring the enticing world beyond the comfort of leather-padded seats and purple tasselling.

Tillie was relieved by his preoccupation. At least she didn't have to answer questions about her unexpected knowledge of the Department's security Bot. She bit her lip. How could she explain what she didn't know? Perhaps her father's mechanical turtle had inspired the Department's invention - or them, his?

She shifted in her seat. She hadn't known her father worked for Queen Victoria. Perhaps he'd worked for the Department of Curiosities as well? And if so, would the Department have archival evidence to prove he wasn't a traitor?

She straightened her shoulders. She *had* to access their records. She had to know, before Lord Allington got too curious. She swallowed.

That day would come; the longer she could delay it, the more time she had to search. If they had evidence, she would find it.

She snuggled into the carriage seat opposite Lord Allington. She was on her way home, for the first time in almost twenty-four hours. Her eyelids drooped.

Home was a fashionable cut-brick house of brightest red, with white quoins around the windows and doors, twisted brick chimneys and slate roof tiles. For six years she had resided in Pont Street, under the guardianship of her Aunt Prudence Meriwether. Aunt and Uncle Meriwether had taken her in after her father's accident, amid rumours of his treachery. The caveat had been that she relinquish her father's name, and never mention her past. She stayed on after her uncle's death - for Aunt Prudence's sake, of course.

Tillie smiled, closed her eyes and fingered the ring her aunt had given to her on her eighteenth birthday. Nothing could match the security - and freedom - Aunt Prudence allowed her, not even the Department of Curiosities. There were certain things the Department could not provide: unconditional freedom, Mary's delicious cooking and the book of her father's cyphers.

"Arriving at Pont Street, Sir," Mr Smythe's tinny voice emanated from the carriage's brass communication funnel.

The carriage rocked as it halted outside her home. Tillie's eyes snapped open. Lord Allington smiled and opened the door.

"Will you need assistance, Miss Meriwether?" he asked.

"No. Thank you for the offer, Lord Allington, but my aunt will be home." Tillie's heels clacked on the cobblestones as she stepped down from the carriage, glad to feel familiar ground under her feet.

<<*Unescorted,*>> the Orb observed.

She grimaced at the reminder. Yes, appearances were everything.

"It's better I arrive unchaperoned, than in the company of a strange man." She smiled sweetly at Lord Allington.

His eyebrow lifted, only briefly. She cleared her throat and looked him directly in the eye, ignoring his obvious affectation. It had become quite irritating. There was a faint flicker of... something, as he returned her gaze. Then it was gone.

"As you wish, Miss Meriwether." He closed the carriage door with a click. "I will send Smythe to collect you in two days."

Her stomach knotted; it was a risk allowing him to leave. What if Smythe didn't return? Would she be able to find her way back to the Department of Curiosities, and its potential-filled vaults? She tried to retrace the carriage's journey in her mind. The building had been somewhere near the Royal Albert Hall. She straightened her skirts. She had to trust him - and the General - and take them at their word.

She nodded, ascended the front steps and tapped on the door.

Aunt Prudence would not be pleased, even though she'd sent word about her change in plans. Tillie winced. She could already hear Aunt Prue's wrath. She would stand on the hall stairs, lecturing Tillie on the almost impossible task of ensuring at least the pretence of propriety was upheld.

No matter, Aunt Prudence enjoyed the dance: there would be a scolding to endure, but then her aunt would be all smiles. She would be supportive, as always.

Tillie smiled and tapped on the door again.

Dear Aunt Prudence; she was such a delicious contradiction.

Tillie straightened her new kid-gloves then rang the doorbell. Still no answer.

She glanced over her shoulder. The carriage remained at the kerb. The horse's tail twitched, its hooves fidgeted on the cobblestones. Smythe sat, his face expressionless and his eyes forward.

She slipped her hand into her purse and retrieved her key.

Tillie's heels clicked on the tiled floor as she made her way to the Parlour where Aunt Prudence would often nap in the afternoon. She tapped on the Parlour door, and eased it open.

The room was dark, the drapes still drawn and the fire unlit.

"Aunt Prudence?" She waited for her eyes to adjust to the dim light, tiptoed up to her aunt's favourite arm chair and sank her fingers into its deep blue velvet upholstery. "Are you still sleeping?" She smiled and peeked over the back of the chair.

It was vacant.

<<*Empty,*>> whispered the Orb.

"I can see that. I'm not blind." She shook her head and examined the fireplace.

The Parlour was her aunt's refuge, always warm and inviting. Tillie wrapped her fingers around the fire poker and jabbed the remnants of charred wood and coals in the hearth. They were cold and black.

She frowned and scanned the room, with its blue velvet wallpaper, padded velvet-upholstered furniture and plush carpeted floor. A pile of books had toppled from the bookshelf and lay strewn across the floor behind the settee.

A chill ran down Tillie's spine. Her footsteps padded on the carpet as she edged back to the hallway.

<<*Silence,*>> hissed the Orb.

She paused to listen. Nothing. She crept along the passageway and past the hall table. The midday post still sat on its silver platter. On top was a familiar note addressed to Aunt Prudence, in Tillie's own handwriting.

Her heart raced as she made her way past the stairs and further along the hall towards the study. The house was too quiet. No noise from the kitchen; Mary should be preparing for dinner by now.

There was no noise from...

There was a thump on the stairs above her. Her heart lurched. She hitched up her silk skirts, secured them in place, then snatched up one of her aunt's favourite ceramic Chinese vases, and crept up the main stairs.

A single shaft of light shone on the carpeted stairs, casting them half in shadows, half in light. She squinted, attempting to adjust to the varying light levels.

<<*Intruder!*>> The Orb's psychic scream pierced her mind.

The vase slipped from her fingers and thunked down the carpeted steps. She clutched her head. Her hem tumbled around her ankles. She caught the banister with her free hand.

A pale grey limb snaked out of the shadows and grasped at her sleeve. Its sinewy fingers fumbled at the blue silk.

"Not my new silk dress!" Tillie jerked her arm away in time to avoid any damage. She tugged up her skirts and dashed back down the stairway and into the darkened hall.

Footsteps scampered on the floor above. More thumps came from the direction of the stairs.

<<*Three,*>> the Orb advised in military fashion.

Tillie scooped up the vase and thrust it before her at arm's length, ready to strike at anyone - or anything - that dared to approach. She reached out with the other hand and felt her way along the hallway, back to safety beyond the front door. Her silk sleeves swished against her bodice as she swept the vase left, then right, in an attempt to ward off any unseen invader.

A strong hand grabbed her wrist and yanked her aside. A pale grey face greeted her with a sneer.

"Where?" Its slurred word was barely discernible.

Tillie screamed and brought Aunt Prudence's Chinese vase crashing down onto the man's ghost-like head. She wrenched her hand free. The Ghostman's grip loosened and he fell to the floor, with a satisfying thud.

The faint outline of his companion lingered further along the hall. He was not alone.

<<Run!>> The Orb's shriek flooded every corner of her mind.

She retreated toward the front door, groping for the doorknob in the darkness behind her.

A sliver of light pierced the gloom, reflected off the hall mirror and lit her escape route. There was another flash of pale grey skin.

Damnation! She'd forgotten there were three of them.

Now weaponless, she pressed against the wall, trying to meld into the shadows.

<<Trapped!>> hissed the Orb.

<<I told you before; I'm not blind.>>

A metal knob dug into her shoulder as she was besieged by her aunt's red wool cloak. Where there was a cloak, there was a... She smiled and stretched out her fingers.

Her fingertips brushed against Aunt Prudence's parasol; its smooth, ornately-carved, and unexpectedly heavy, ivory handle was icy cold to the touch. She wrapped her fingers around the parasol's shaft, drew it silently from its stand in one smooth movement and swung the ostentatious handle directly into the face of the oncoming Ghostman. There was a gratifying crack, followed by warm splashes on her face.

And then there was one.

Tillie turned towards the remaining intruder who blocked her way. She hefted the parasol's handle in her hand, comforted by its extra weight. They may not have expected such resistance from a household of women; she would show them otherwise. She was ready to defend herself, her home and her family.

She gritted her teeth and braced herself for the oncoming fray.

The Ghostman lurched forward, then hesitated. In the mirror's reflected light, Tillie caught sight of his grey, otherworldly-eyes; he glanced over his fallen accomplices then focused his attention on her. He grinned, and reached inside his coat.

She stared down the barrel of the large pistol. Too close. Even in this poor light, he would have to be inept to miss his target. Her fingers trembled.

She made mental note of the distance between them; she could not outrun the bullet. She raised the parasol in a futile attempt to protect herself, and wondered if the Department of Curiosities had a bullet-shielding parasol in their archived vaults?

A brilliant light engulfed her. There was a loud crack.

She flinched and prepared herself for the inevitable agony.

But there was nothing.

No pain. No sound.

The world slowed as Tillie's eyes adjusted to the midday sun. Shadowy outlines formed. A tall figure stood silhouetted in the open doorway. Her heart raced. Her hands trembled. Her vision shimmered.

Not another one! The Orb must have miscounted. Every muscle in her body tensed, preparing for another attack.

The figure spoke, his voice almost drowned out by the pounding of blood in her ears.

Sir Avery Allington dropped his arm. Smoke drizzled from the muzzle of his pistol. He surveyed the hall. Before him lay a crumpled body. Blood oozed from the bullet wound in its side. A crimson pool seeped into the oriental carpet and formed a gory halo around its head. Another body lay at Miss Meriwether's feet. A third lay motionless, surrounded by a multitude of fine porcelain shards, too far away to assess its injuries.

Miss Meriwether stood defiantly among the fallen, looking charmingly dishevelled. Her bonnet hung precariously, held by a remaining hat pin, to reveal a less than pristine coiffure. She brandished a red parasol, swinging it like a golf club around her legs. Her skirts were hitched up, revealing the ankles of her new leather boots.

"Lord Allington?" Her voice was faint.

"Are you unharmed?" he asked.

"I believe so." She tucked a lock of blonde hair back into her bun.

The hat pin fell silently onto the carpet. The bonnet followed, and landed in the pool of blood with a plop. She lifted her face towards him. It was spattered with blood.

Tillie's head spun. The buzzing in her ears would not stop. She leaned on the edge of the hatstand and shook her head, attempting to regain a measure of control. It would not do to faint in front of a work colleague; they'd barely been introduced.

Lord Allington's face loomed before her, blocking out the view of the hallway. She blinked to refocus. A wrinkle flitted over his forehead. He avoided direct eye contact and seemed to develop an odd fascination for the flooring.

The front door rattled and tapped against the wall. A wintry breeze chilled her ankles.

Her cheeks burned. He wasn't staring at the carpet, he was staring at--

With a quick flick of the wrist, she unhooked the leather cord from her belt and allowed the layers to fall to the ground to obscure her stockings from view.

"Sir Avery, are you in need of assistance?" Smythe's voice sounded strange without the augmentation of the carriage's Communication Device.

"No, thank you, Smythe." Lord Allington cleared his throat and stepped away to a less intimate distance.

Tillie did likewise. For the first time, she observed the chaos that surrounded her.

"Aunt Prudence will not be pleased," she whispered.

<<*Attacked?*>> the Orb replied.

She sucked in a sharp breath as a cold wave of terror consumed her. Her stomach knotted.

"Aunt Prudence! We must find her."

Smythe stepped forward. Lord Allington raised a hand to halt him, and pointed up the stairs.

"Was she at home?" he asked.

"She usually naps in the Parlour in the afternoon." Tillie frowned. "But she's not there." She remembered the disorderly state of the Parlour. "And I don't know where the maid is."

"Keep watch at the front door, Smythe," said Lord Allington. "Make sure we aren't interrupted by more intruders."

Smythe nodded and stepped back into the doorway.

"It's gone six," said Lord Allington as he edged towards the Dining Room. "I would expect she would be preparing supper by now."

Tillie shadowed him along the hallway. Each step grew heavier. She clutched the parasol until her knuckles whitened, ignored the growing ache in her fingers and focused on his reassuring steps. Left. Right. Left. Right. At least she wouldn't have to face the Dining Room alone.

Lord Allington opened the Dining Room door and scanned the room. He drew a deep breath and placed his hands on each side of the door frame, blocking Tillie's view.

The faint smell of burnt bread wafted into the hall. Tillie raised herself up on her toes, trying to peer into the room. The servant's door leading to the kitchen was open. She hesitated.

The Orb twisted under her bodice. It scavenged her thoughts, leaving trepidation in its wake. She winced.

<<*Leave,*>> it demanded.

Tillie took a deep breath. She would not let it break her resolve now. She had to know the truth. She demanded its silence. It acquiesced.

"Is it..?" Her voice trailed off.

"No," Lord Allington replied.

She placed her hand on his shoulder to raise herself higher.

"I assume it's the maid," he said.

Tillie's heels fell to the tiled floor with a crack. "Is Mary--?" She dared not complete the sentence.

"She's dead." His voice was soft. He dropped his arm and stood aside.

Tillie straightened her shoulders and stepped into the room.

A crisp linen table cloth had been laid in preparation for supper. Its bleached whiteness accentuated a ragged streak of blood that arched across from the opposite side of the dining table and splattered the fine white china dinner service set at Aunt Prudence's customary place. The silverware lay neatly on either side: fork, spoon... The knife was absent.

She edged closer to the table. Mary's sensible black shoes peeked out from behind the table drapery. Her stockings were visible.

Tillie reached down, tugged at Mary's skirt and covered her ankles. Aunt Prudence always insisted on propriety at all times.

The table knife glinted in a pool of blood next to Mary's head. Tillie closed her eyes and turned away. Too late. The image was now carved into her memory; it could not be unseen. Mary's throat had been slit, the gash still oozed blood.

Tillie's free hand began to tremble. "Aunt Prudence?"

"We won't find her here." Lord Allington's voice was calm, consoling. "Supper's not yet served."

"Her dressing room." Her voice cracked. "Aunt Prudence always dresses for meals."

She tucked up her skirts and dashed from the Dining Room, parasol still in hand.

Lord Allington's feet thudded on the carpet behind her as they ascended the stairs to the first floor. Tillie led the way along the unlit corridor. There was no time to light the gas now.

The door to her Aunt's dressing room was closed. Tillie leaned against its solid oak. Her aunt's red parasol dangled in her free hand. She buried her head in her arm, trying to gather the courage to enter.

"Shall I go first?" said Lord Allington.

"No." Her reply was muffled. "I must make sure that everything is in order."

"Are you sure?" he asked quietly.

"Yes, I am sure."

Aunt Prudence would be horrified if she was not ready to receive guests. Tillie pushed herself away from the door, and straightened her shoulders. She clutched the parasol's handle to steady her trembling hands. A deep breath filled her lungs as she fumbled with the doorknob. The latch clicked loudly. She nudged the door open, slipped inside and pushed it partly closed behind her.

The setting sun spilled into the room and pierced the gloom. A faint winter breeze caught the edges of the open curtains and tugged them open to reveal the neighbouring roof line. Neglected flames flickered low in the fireplace, their light trapped within the hearth.

Prudence Meriwether sat hunched at her dressing table. Her hair fell over her neck and shoulders. Her head lay on the Burwood surface, as if she had fallen asleep. Her pale hand dangled above the hair brush discarded on the floor.

<<*Hope,*>> the Orb tentatively offered.

Tillie shook her head and edged closer.

A drop of blood marred the collar of her aunt's pale green dress. The bejewelled head of a hat pin was wedged deep into her ear canal.

She had an urge to touch it, to pull it free. She swallowed. If she could just remove it... Perhaps she would wake from this terrifying nightmare. She stretched out her fingers. They trembled. She let them settle on Aunt Prudence's shoulder. Her skin was cold.

Tillie's hand hugged her aunt. There was something metal under her blouse. She felt along her aunt's neck. A chain? The only jewellery Aunt Prudence wore was her wedding ring. Tillie's eyes widened. What secrets had her aunt been keeping?

She glanced at the locked drawers of her aunt's dressing table. She'd always wondered what secrets were hidden in them. Her fingers twitched. She'd never looted the dead before. Curiosity got the better of her; her fingers crept under the collar of Aunt Prudence's blouse.

A log cracked and dislodged in the fire.

Her fingers recoiled from the lifeless body. She sucked in a breath. Aunt Prudence was gone. Her father was gone. She was alone. Again.

A cold wave of nausea engulfed her. She shivered. Her death grip on the parasol failed. It fell to the floor. Her legs faltered.

Tillie crumpled to the floor. Her arms flailed at a nearby chair, as she struggled to steady her fall. Her hand trailed across the dressing table and knocked a ceramic vanity bowl, sending it clattering into the mirror.

"Miss Meriwether!" Lord Allington burst through the door.

Tillie's throat was dry. She remained silent.

"Miss Meriwether?" His voice grew louder. There was movement at the dressing table as he examined the body. She held her breath. Would he find the chain around Aunt Prudence's neck? He turned and concentrated his attention on Tillie.

"I am sorry," he said finally. "She's been dead for some time."

She let out a quiet breath. Aunt Prudence's secrets were still hers to discover. She opened her mouth to speak. Her voice would not obey. The taste of salt touched her mouth. Lord Allington leaned closer, wiped a tear from her cheek and offered her a handkerchief.

She could see his face in the mirror. His gaze traced the outline of her face. A frown flickered over his lips; his attention now directed at the floor. The moment was gone.

"You seem to have dropped your parasol," he said.

"It belongs to..." The words caught in her throat as she corrected herself. "It *belonged* to Aunt Prudence," she said.

"Then it has done a great service in exacting its revenge."

"Yes." Tillie accepted the parasol and cradled it in her hand. It had served her well. Would that it could have served her after her father's death. Would that it could track down his murderer and deliver him to her. Aunt Prudence's parasol still had work to do.

<<*Revenge,*>> whispered the Orb.

Revenge: The word lingered in her mind, searching for a kindred thought. There was also *justice* - for the false accusations against her father, and *retribution* - for his murder. Yes, *revenge* had a nice ring to it.

Lord Allington returned from his inspection of the open window. He cleared his throat. She followed his gaze downward. Her hand was polishing the parasol's handle.

"It appears the blaggards entered via the window." A faint hint of concern coloured his voice. "There are footprints on the sill and the roof."

"Purification is the key." She continued to polish the ivory.

"I beg your pardon?"

Her hand froze; she had spoken out loud, her thoughts no longer private. She glanced up from her work. There was a hint of concern in the set of his mouth.

"It will need more than just spit and polish to clean this." She pocketed the sanguine-smudged handkerchief and feigned a sweet smile. "You were saying?"

"We may be able to track them over the slate," he continued.

"You seem to have a strange fascination for rooftops, Lord Allington," she replied,

His moustache twitched. "Lord Allington was my father." He proffered his hand.

"Then what shall I call you?" she asked.

"My name is Avery." He helped Tillie to her feet.

"Thank you, Sir Avery."

"We will need help with investigations and clean up," he said. "I will get Smythe to inform the Department."

Tillie fiddled with the lace edging on the parasol.

He fetched Aunt Prudence's lace dressing gown from the end of the bed, and covered the body. He paused.

"Are you recovered?" he asked.

"I am recovered," she whispered.

"In the circumstances, I think it unwise to remain here," he replied. "I'll fetch Smythe to carry your luggage."

Tillie dropped the parasol and fumbled for the chain under her aunt's blouse.

<<*Hurry,*>> the Orb urged.

She unhooked it and pulled it from its hiding place. A small, tarnished silver key dangled from her fingers. She examined the locks on the dressing table drawers. Her heart skipped. It looked to be a perfect fit.

<<*Secrets,*>> hissed the Orb.

She slipped the key into the lock, and hesitated, remembering the first time she'd asked her aunt why the drawers were locked. Aunt Prudence had just smiled and replied: You have your secrets, and I have mine. Tillie had learned to respect privacy and secrets. Her father had taught her that. She frowned; Father had many secrets.

<<*Share?*>> whispered the Orb.

She glanced at the bedroom door. She understood its meaning. Sir Avery would soon return. There could be documents about her father, her true heritage, locked in these drawers. She needed to discover any secrets before the Department could steal them away.

She twisted the key in the lock. Tumblers clicked. Cogs ratcheted. The drawers slid open. There was nothing of note in the first drawer, and nothing at all in the second.

Nothing. Tillie huffed.

The Orb jiggled, as if snickering.

"Oh, do be quiet. I didn't ask for your opinion." She frowned. Had Aunt Prudence been teasing her all these years? Surely face powders, creams and kohl weren't a secret worth locking away in one's private rooms?

Tillie bit her thumb nail. There had to be something. What if...?

Her heart sank. The Ghostmen couldn't have discovered it. The drawer was still locked and she had the key. She shook her head. No, there had to be something.

She curled her fingers around the drawer handle, pulled out the empty drawer and flipped it over. Nothing.

She snaked her hand into the empty cavity where the drawer had been, and scrabbled her fingers across the inside of the dressing table. Top. Sides. Bottom. Her fingernails caught on an edge on the bottom of the cavity. Her eyes widened. She traced her fingertips along a flat, rectangular compartment large enough to hold a large journal.

She crouched down next to her aunt's body and peered into the cavity. On the top of the box was a set of three numbers on a brass tumbling dial. A combination lock. Numbers ran through her mind: dates, addresses, anything significant. She fell back onto her haunches.

<<*Birthday,*>> announced the Orb.

She frowned. No, it wouldn't be that obvious. She rubbed her fingertips over her temples. This could take all night.

<<*Father,*>> insisted the Orb.

She shook her head.

A pinprick of intense heat burned into skin as the Orb buried itself into her chest. Tillie winced.

"All right, all right."

She dialled in her father's birthday. Nothing.

<<*Matilda.*>>

<<*My birthday? But, why--?*>>

The Orb pushed against her sternum.

"All right." She dug her nail between the numbers on the first dial and turned the numbers.

Two.

Click.

She sucked in a breath. The Orb shifted under her blouse.

"Beginners luck," she replied.

She turned the next dial.

Two.

Click.

She bit her lip. It couldn't be?

Five.

There was a faint tink, like an unwinding spring, in the bottom of the dressing table. Gears whirred and clacked as the compartment clicked open.

The Orb jiggled. She clasped her hand on her chest to settle it. She stared at the open compartment.

"How could you possibly know that?" she whispered.

Inside was a leather folder. Under it were bundles of envelopes tied with black ribbon. Tillie examined the letters. She'd seen that handwriting before. But where? Was it her father's? Her heart raced. Were they letters from him, hidden to protect her real identity?

She flipped over the letters. Her heart sank. There was no return address.

Her hands trembled as she untied one of the black ribbons, unfolded the paper and skimmed the contents.

'...details of this month's expenditures, on behalf of Miss Matilda Meriwether, to be forwarded to allow for prompt reimbursement.'

She peered at the signature; it looked like: *Victoria R.* She fell onto the floor with a thud.

"No, it can't be."

She squirmed closer to the dying fire. The signature was unmistakable. She'd seen it before, on the silk note the Queen, herself, had slipped into her own hand. *Victoria Regina. Liberator.*

She snatched up the remaining letters. Each was in the same handwriting, going back at least six years. She opened another letter, and another. Each was a signed receipt for various expenditures. The Queen had paid for her schooling, holidays, clothes, costs for her adventures, even piano lessons, though she would have dearly loved to have learned the violin.

Tillie dragged herself onto the chair near the fire and opened an early-dated missive from the bottom of the pile.

"I commend the child into your care. Arrangements have been made for her new name. Expenditures will be covered. I shall require monthly reports of the child's progress. Other than these communications, this matter will be spoken of no further.

-Victoria R"

Queen Victoria was her guardian, not Aunt and Uncle Meriwether. The Queen knew. She knew *everything.*

Tillie unbuttoned the top of her blouse and wiggled her fingers under her corset to retrieve the silk note from the Queen. She stared at its signature in the firelight: *V.R., Benefactor.*

<<Benefactor?>> The Orb stopped moving. A chill gouged her chest where it lay.

She nodded. The Queen had chosen the name carefully, and with irony.

Aunt Prudence had always known the details of her secret adventures. It was as if she had her own spies. Tillie swallowed; or the Queen's spies. Had Aunt Prudence been updating Tillie's true guardian, the Benefactor, of her every venture?

The Orb twitched.

Tillie crumpled the receipt. She peered at her aunt's body through tear-rimmed eyes. Was this woman any relation at all, or just a highly-paid nanny, an employee of the Crown? As was she.

She threw the paper into the fireplace. There was always a price to be paid.

The Orb remained silent, as if listening for something.

A soft, rhythmic thud of footsteps heralded Sir Avery's return as he bounded up the stairs. She was out of time.

<<Hurry,>> urged the Orb.

Her muscles tensed. Was the Department full of the Queen's spies as well? She didn't want Sir Avery discovering her secret. He'd investigate and document it all down in his notebook.

Tillie scooped up the letters; she couldn't have the Department discovering her true identity. They wouldn't want the daughter of a traitor rummaging through their files or accessing their precious curiosities. She scrunched up the letters. Her secret must be kept safe.

Footsteps padded along the carpeted hall and paused half way. There was a knock on Tillie's bedroom door, two doors down.

She stared at her aunt's bedroom door and contemplated her next move. There was no time to relocate the records. There was no need to keep them. The Queen already knew the truth. When she found proof of her father's innocence, Her Majesty would ensure all was put to rights.

The door clicked shut along the hallway.

She bundled the missives into the fire. The poker made sure each one caught alight. The smell of burning papers wafted through the room.

The footsteps halted outside. There was a tap on the door.

Tillie retrieved the drawer and slipped it back into the empty cavity. She locked the drawer as Sir Avery knocked on the dressing room door a second time.

"Miss Meriwether? Are you still in there?"

She turned her back on her aunt's lifeless body, slid the key inside one of her now-bloodstained kid gloves as the door opened.

Sir Avery glanced over the room. His gaze lingered on the flames now licking the edge of the hearth. His moustache twitched.

"I thought you'd be packing," he said.

She fluttered her eyelids; Aunt Prudence always said it made an excellent diversion while one constructed a polite answer to a difficult question.

"I didn't want her to be cold."

"Ah." His gaze dropped to the floor. "Your aunt will be looked after. Smythe has alerted the appropriate authorities."

"Thank you, Sir Avery."

"We have one hour before they arrive. I suggest we leave before then."

She nodded. "That should give me time to get my things."

He motioned towards her spattered clothing. "And change your attire?"

Tillie turned to the mirror. Her bodice, face and gloves were smeared with blood of the Ghostmen.

"I did not know that ghosts could bleed," she whispered.

"There are no such things as ghosts, Miss Meriwether," Sir Avery replied.

Of Gentlemen, Traitors, and Despicable Acts

General Edward Sabine sat at his desk, his head buried in the box of brass and iron workings. There was something familiar about one of the mechanical's gears.

He grumbled, shook his head and tweaked several knobs on his Mag-specs. A larger magnification was needed.

"Harrow!" He glanced up from his investigations and reached for his polished wooden pipe.

Footsteps tapped on the hallway floor.

"Harrow, could you find me a stronger set of Mag-specs?"

Harrow nodded as he hurried into the room.

"Yes, General." He slid to a halt on the polished parquetry floor, turned on his heel and retreated back along the hallway.

The General drew a deep breath and savoured the warm, spicy flavour of the tobacco smoke. He leaned back into his mahogany chair and stretched out his arms, allowing his chest to expand and maximising the nicotine intake. His thoughts clarified.

He pushed the box, with the dissected Bot, to one side and scrutinised the remaining pieces on the desk.

The demise of such a small device had revealed enormous consequences. The Department of Curiosities had a traitor. Someone with mechanical skills. The General's pulse raced. He sucked on his pipe, held his breath and waited for the nicotine to calm his nerves.

Many secrets had been discussed in the Upper Levels. His heart faltered. He bit into his pipe and drew another quick breath. How long had the listening device been active? How much had been overheard? How many secrets had been compromised? And who had they been passed onto? He swallowed; more importantly, had the security breach gone beyond the Upper Levels?

There was a tap on the door. Harrow cleared his throat, crossed to the desk and handed the General another pair of Mag-specs, as requested.

The General settled his pipe on its silver tray. He perched the Mag-specs on his nose, clipped the arms behind his head and shoved the inferior pair across the desk in Harrow's direction.

"What are you searching for?" Harrow asked.

"There is something here," replied the General. "Looks like small scratches, could be a maker's mark."

"Like in watches?" asked Harrow.

"Yes," he replied. "For some time now the Empire has required all gear and mechanical makers to mark their wares."

"I didn't know that," said Harrow.

"No. It's not widely known." The General glanced up and smiled, the corners of his eyes like craters under the extended magnification of the Mag-specs. "It's been very useful to us."

Harrow picked up one of the separated gears and peered at it. "I can't see any markings."

"You won't. Not without a pair of these." The General turned the gear over. "Ah, found one!" He sat bolt upright in his chair. A smile played on his lips.

Harrow dropped the gear he had been examining.

"Now we can track down our traitor, Harrow!"

"Well done, General." Harrow smiled faintly.

Cogs turned in the wall clock. Chimes echoed through the room.

"Nine o'clock?" The General slipped off the Mag-specs and snatched up his pipe. "Any reply from Her Majesty?"

"No, General. We only sent the communication two hours ago."

He frowned. "Check again, Harrow."

A Bot scuttled out from under the General's chair and skittered toward the hallway after Harrow.

He puffed furiously on his pipe. A cloud of smoke encircled his head. The sweet aroma drifted towards Harrow and ushered him out of the room.

Harrow scurried down the main hallway towards the Communication Room. A Bot trundled after him. He growled and kicked it away, as he unlocked a heavily re-enforced metal door. He slipped inside and locked the door behind him.

The room was compact and efficiently-packed with an array of devices, each securely bolted to a curved desk which filled the room. A brass telegraph machine dominated the left side of the desk.

On the other side was another contraption, with a web of wires attached to a curious-looking button in place of a lever. A cluster of small, round keys were suspended on rods emerging from the side of the box. Each was positioned to allow easy access from the desk's central hub.

More wires erupted from coils on the opposite side of the modified telegraph machine, and led to a third, vertical contrivance. More round keys emerged from a domed section at its crown. At the centre of the machine sat a brass half-cylinder, wrapped with a sheet of paper.

Harrow sat in the operator's chair, like a spider testing its wired web, and glanced at the paper on the cylinder. His eyes widened. He reached out across the elaborate machine and snatched the communiqué from its housing.

The message read:

My dear General Sabine,
In reply to your query. Information too sensitive for wired communication. Your ears only. Require your attendance immediately.
Victoria RI.

Harrow removed his spectacles and pinched the bridge of his nose. He inhaled a measured breath, replaced his spectacles and re-read the missive. His breath escaped slowly, through clenched teeth. He reached across to the telegraph machine on his left, flicked a small switch under the lever and methodically tapped out a message.

The corner of his mouth twitched. He had no option but to inform the General of the note's contents. His employer would not be happy.

General Sabine glanced across the Queen's Drawing Room. It was after supper, but he knew She would not forgive him if he did not attend Her, even at this late hour.

Her Majesty remained seated, Her back straight, surrounded by acres of ebony silk and velvet. No frills. No nonsense. She was the Empire's ultimate authority. Never to be swayed. Never to be moved. Never to be questioned.

The ritual was always the same. He would go to Her, state his case and await Her pre-prepared reply. If anyone could make him feel insignificant - while at the same time feel the most important man in the world - it was Her Majesty Queen Victoria. She excelled at it.

She scrutinised him as he approached, following his every move. He paused several feet away from Her presence and focused his attention on her gloved hand, the first obstacle in the courtly dance. He'd learned over the decades that, like a cat's tail, any twitch or slight gesture of that hand could reveal Her present mood. It remained motionless. Perhaps She'd discovered his stratagem?

He lowered his gaze to avoid direct eye contact and noted the patch of carpet on which he stood. Here, the pile was more worn, its rich colours dulled by decades of hesitant feet scuffing at the Royal rug.

He waited. The Queen must always speak first.

"Ah, General Sabine."

"Good evening, Your Majesty." He bowed reverently.

"Nice of you to finally accept Our invitation," She said.

"Forgive me, Your Majesty."

"Don't We always?" She replied with a smile.

He could plead his case for his late arrival: the message had not been delivered in a timely fashion, the roads were icy making travel problematic, there had been an attack on one of his operatives. All unforeseeable events. Yet, he would offer no excuses. Queen Victoria did not like pleas or justifications. He knew Her well enough to know that She viewed them as possible subterfuge or an effort to disguise incompetence. She preferred action.

He held his tongue, offering no defence. He simply bowed to his sovereign ruler and waited for Her permission to proceed.

Queen Victoria rose from Her gilded chair and extended Her now-ungloved hand. He kneeled before Her and kissed Her hand. The scent of *Fleurs de Bulgarie* floated in the air around them. Its exhilarating aroma heralded an equally compelling woman.

Ah, Bulgarian roses. For those who had the privilege to draw near to Her royal person, the sweetness belied the strength of the woman wearing the Crown.

He lingered a few more moments, breathing Her scent in one last time, then slowly removed himself from the scented veil. He returned to his place on the trampled carpet and awaited Her Majesty's pleasure.

Queen Victoria re-established herself on the crimson-upholstered settee and patted the arm of Her chair.

The General raised his head and glanced fleetingly in Her direction. They were alone. Her Lady-in-Waiting had withdrawn. Queen Victoria's skirts filled the entire seat and spilled over the armrests.

She seemed taller when She was seated. He wondered if She had a secret cushion, hidden in Her skirt folds, to add to Her height. He swallowed; it was not a fitting question to ask of a monarch. His curiosity would remain unsatisfied.

She motioned towards the parlour chair beside Her. A mischievous grin played on Her lips.

"Do sit down, General. You look flustered."

"I do apologise, Your Majesty," he replied.

"Explain yourself, General."

"Ma'am?" he asked. What had he done to meet with Her disapproval?

"Your message said we have a traitor in the Department of Curiosities."

"Yes, we had a problem with one of the Bots,' he said.

As if on cue, a small hemispherical Bot trundled across the carpet towards their feet.

The General's shoulders tensed. He put a finger to his lips, reached down and scooped up the mechanical. He flipped it upside down and flicked a switch. With a twist, he removed the brass covering and examined its inner workings. All seemed in order.

His muscles relaxed. "This one does not appear to have been tampered with."

"We should hope not!" said Queen Victoria. "The Department supplied them to the Palace."

"Yes, Ma'am. However, it seems one of our Bots has been re-engineered to fashion as a listening device. The culprit was able to neutralise my cane's magnetic detection field." He tapped his cane and frowned. "One of our own has turned traitor."

She regarded the Bot briefly then returned Her attention to General Sabine. "And what is the name of our possible traitor?"

"Our new operative, Miss Matilda Meriwether," he replied.

Queen Victoria took a sharp breath.

After a long silence, he spoke: "She was present when the device was discovered."

Queen Victoria did not reply.

He cleared this throat. "Could her credentials have been... misjudged?"

"What makes you think she is the traitor?" Queen Victoria finally asked.

"She incriminated herself, Ma'am." He held out the Bot, indicating its activation switch. "She knew how to deactivate the Bot." He replaced the cover and set the Bot back onto the carpet.

"Ah..." The Queen glared at the Bot as it trundled around the room, beeped cheerily and squatted under an armchair.

She leaned towards the General and placed Her hand on his.

"Edward," She continued. "We know we can trust you, above all others. That is why we chose you to run the Department of Curiosities."

"Yes, Ma'am. I am, as always, yours," he whispered.

"There are many who work against the Empire. Against Us." She looked him directly in the eye. "Against me."

"Anarchists?" His fingers clenched his cane. "The Men in Grey have been inactive of late. Too much for my liking."

"We have information they are stirring up trouble again. They've manipulated themselves into strategic positions within The Gadgeteers."

"That group petitioning for free trade of mechanicals?"

She nodded.

"Do you think the Men in Grey are behind the traitor?" The General shifted in his seat. He could not shake the feeling Miss Meriwether knew more than she admitted. She'd slipped with the Bot; not even the Queen's household had access to information on their mechanicals.

He sucked in a sharp breath. But the Queen had recommended her. Could Queen Victoria have been deceived? Was Miss Meriwether a spy for the Men in Grey, a cuckoo in the nest? Even Meriwether - her uncle - had admitted he'd never met her before she arrived from Australia.

He clenched the cane tighter. He was responsible for the Queen's safety. It was his job to investigate every possibility. He let out a slow breath. He had to ask...

"We have only one new recruit, Ma'am."

Queen Victoria smiled and patted his hand.

"I need..." She paused and corrected herself. "*We* need to have those we trust in such crucial roles." Her piercing blue eyes held his gaze. "Miss Meriwether is one such person. I suggest you look elsewhere for your traitor."

"But, Ma'am?"

Queen Victoria glared at him. She shook her head. The glare faded. She smiled.

"No. She is mine, Edward."

The General opened his mouth to speak. There were no words. He knew Queen Victoria had interests everywhere but... a secret confidante planted in the Department?

"We have known her family for many years and have been guiding her since she was a child, under the care of a trusted friend and subject. Miss Meriwether is *my* creature. She is not your traitor."

The General remained silent. He wanted to ask why She'd recommended the girl as an operative for the Department of Curiosities. His heart sank. Was She testing him?

The General took a deep breath, a hint of *Fleurs de Bulgarie* flirted with his nostrils.

No. He was a loyal supporter and long-term friend. He shouldn't require Her to explain her decisions. He should *not* ask such things of his Queen.

"My dear Edward, it was serendipity that found the Department of Curiosities and Miss Meriwether on the same path. We intend to use this to *Our* advantage. She is unknown to your operatives. We will engage her to find our traitor." Her voice was quiet and soothing.

The General nodded. His smiled returned. How could he have doubted his Queen?

"You must give her full assistance and complete access on all levels." Her royal blue eyes twinkled.

"Appoint her to Communications. It is the perfect position to gather information and won't raise suspicions when she reports back to Us."

"Of course, Your Majesty," the General replied. It was a sensible plan.

"Thank you, Edward." She slowly removed Her hand and smiled sweetly at the General. She straightened Her shoulders and slipped Her gloves back onto Her petite hands. The smile was gone, replaced by the studied neutrality of a sovereign.

"Next time, General, try to make it in time for tea," She said.

This was the General's cue to depart. He rose to his feet and bowed. He was privileged to have such rapport with the Queen.

"One thing, if I may Your Majesty?"

"Yes, General," the Queen replied.

"May I suggest you have all the Bots recalled, as a precaution. I will have Harrow send replacements, this evening."

Things do not always happen as planned. This had become

abundantly clear to Tillie over the past twenty-four hours. Gone were her carefully researched plans in her quest to clear her father's erroneously-dishonoured name. Gone were the remnants of her adopted family who had supported her. And, now it seemed, her independence was also gone; an unexpected duty had been thrust upon her. One she could not refuse.

True, her new employment was fortuitous; it could allow her access to new information in her search for the truth needed. But she was now trapped in uncharted territory, with duties to both Queen and Crown, and no longer able to choose her own path at will.

She glanced at her bedroom door. Her fingers twitched. Sir Avery stood guard outside in case more Ghostmen should be skulking in the shadows. She turned the key in the lock, removed the Orb's chain from around her neck and placed it on the table next to her bed. She was not in the mood for its chatter.

Tillie glanced over the mantelets, redingotes, flounced and pleated skirts and passementerie and sighed. Without Mary's help, dressing would be a more arduous task.

She retrieved her favourite bodice from the wardrobe, folded it and tucked the cuffs inside the neat package. She wrangled the acres of skirts into her portmanteau, then collapsed onto the bed and groaned. She'd never had occasion to discover the intricacies of the art of packing. How did Mary ever manage to fit it all in? It was a puzzle worthy of scholars.

There was a faint tap on the door.

"I must speak with Smythe. I shall return shortly." Sir Avery's voice was calm and soothing.

She nodded and waited until he was on the stair before she turned the key in the lock. The Orb glowed faintly on the bedside table. She sighed. Finally, she was alone.

She darted across the room, leaned into the unlit fireplace and groped along a brick sill inside the lip of the hearth's mouth for her secret belongings. Soot trickled onto her fingers. She flicked away the grit. A small metal box dislodged and clattered into the coals below.

Another pair of gloves ruined. She scowled. Unplanned relocations were damned inconvenient. She tugged off her soot-stained gloves, retrieved the box and dusted it off, wrapped it in a linen handkerchief and secreted it in one of the pockets under her bustle.

She leaned further into the hearth, grabbed the edges of one of the bricks and wiggled it free from the back of the alcove. She reclaimed a leather wrapped parcel from the small cavity and gently placed it in her valise.

Even in her own household, she had learned to be cautious. This had now proved to be a wise choice; the Ghostmen had not discovered her father's precious journal. She patted the valise. It was safe in her possession.

Footsteps bounded up the stairs and made their way along the hall to her door.

Tillie brushed the soot from her magenta bustle dress and fetched the Orb from the bedside table. Ignoring its indignant protests, she replaced it around her neck and concealed it beneath her bodice.

She crossed the room, reached for the door key, and hesitated. The Queen had promised her life would not become one of dependence on men. Yet she'd bound herself in service to a covert government department of men, in the quest to save another's reputation.

She took a deep breath. Onward and upward.

The key turned in the lock and clicked. She smiled sweetly as she opened the door.

"Ah, splendid timing, Miss Meriwether," said Sir Avery as she emerged from the room. "Mr Smythe has just returned. Once he has attended to the business below, he will fetch your luggage."

Tillie was relieved when they finally arrived at the Department of

Curiosities; after the evening's tragic turn of events, she wasn't in the mood for even polite conversation.

Fortunately, the Orb had remained quiet on the return carriage ride. Even Sir Avery had refrained from scribbling in his notebook, though he spoke little during the journey.

Harrow entered the Drawing Room, announced their return to General Sabine and withdrew to the doorway, beyond her attention.

Shadows stretched across the Drawing Room and danced in the flickering gas light. The room was still impressive, even with its grand bay windows shuttered and patterned floor shrouded in darkness.

"Ah! Welcome back, Allington, and my dear Miss Meriwether." The General stepped out of the shadows. "Do excuse us for a moment, Miss Meriwether. I have urgent business to discuss with Allington." He turned and engaged in a short, but furtive, discussion with Sir Avery.

My dear Miss Meriwether? Tillie raised an eyebrow. The General seemed to disdain her on one visit, and delight in her presence at the next. Perhaps age was catching up with him? Dear old Uncle Meriwether had often been confused before he faded away, and he had been at least a decade younger than the General.

She waited for an acerbic remark from the Orb. It remained silent. Their last encounter with the General, and his cane, must have been an adequate incentive for the Orb to refrain from comment to avoid detection. She was thankful; she was unsure if she could have dealt with both the Orb *and* the General, at the same time.

The men concluded their discussion and turned to face Tillie.

"I hear you have had an ordeal with some..." The General glanced at Sir Avery. "Ghostmen?" he asked.

Sir Avery nodded.

"Are you recovered, my dear?" the General asked gently.

"Yes, thank you General but..." her voice trembled.

"I *am* sorry to hear about your Aunt. Colonel Meriwether was a good friend. They shall both be missed." said the General. "I understand she was a good friend of the Queen."

Sir Avery's moustache twitched. "I hadn't realised," he said.

Tillie nodded.

"Rest assured the Department will investigate your aunt's death fully, Miss Meriwether," he said.

The General turned to his aide who hovered impatiently near the doorway.

"Harrow!"

Harrow clicked to attention. "General, Sir?" he replied cautiously.

"See to it personally, Harrow," the General instructed.

Harrow nodded and turned to leave.

"And Harrow..." The General's smile faded. "Her Majesty has requested the replacement of all the Palace Bots. I told her you would take care of it at once."

Harrow nodded. He smiled and strode into the corridor.

"Her Majesty seems to have taken a fancy to you, Miss Meriwether." The General turned to his charges and tapped his cane on the floor.

"Miss Meriwether?" A frown flickered over Sir Avery's forehead.

"Yes, Allington," replied the General. "She has Miss Meriwether assigned as our new Communications expert."

Tillie's heart skipped. "Communications?"

The General nodded. "You are a Cryptologist. It was a logical decision."

Sir Avery grinned. "Harrow will not be pleased. He enjoys knowing everything before we do."

"It is by the Queen's command," replied the General. "He will adjust." He pointed along the hallway in the direction of the secured room. "We have a telegraph room for Upper Levels." He leaned closer to Tillie, and lowered his voice. "You get access to something a little more impressive, my dear."

Both Tillie and Sir Avery eyed the General curiously.

"Are you sure, General?" asked Sir Avery.

"Do you want to defy the Queen's orders, Allington?" The General twisted a small silver ring below the head of his walking cane.

There was a clack in the ceiling above the Drawing Room doorway. The double doors clicked shut. Several thuds followed as locking mechanisms fell into place.

The bay window curtains fluttered as unseen wires and pulleys drew them closed.

"I have something to show you, my dear." The General ushered Tillie towards his desk, opened a small panel in its side and pushed a button. The panel slid back into place. He turned his attention to the wall behind them.

A door-sized section of wall slid open to reveal a windowless niche, barely a few yards square, lit by a cylindrical tube of light in its ceiling.

"After you, Miss Meriwether."

"All three of us?" she asked.

"It was designed with that number in mind," he replied.

Tillie entered the closet-sized room. An illuminated tube, encased above a glass panel, crackled above her with an eerie white light. It radiated no heat. She frowned.

"Not gaslight?" she whispered.

"Something new." Sir Avery smiled as he stepped into the compartment.

"A little gift from Mr de la Rue and Mr Tesla." The General followed her into the compartment. "Safer for confined spaces."

Tillie pulled her skirts close and stepped back into one corner until her bustle pressed against the wall. Her secret metal box prodded her in the thigh. She frowned.

"Either you have few female operatives, or your architect is unmarried, General."

The two men eyed her.

"Perhaps he should consider a lady's fashions next time you require secret rooms."

"Just so, Miss Meriwether." The General chuckled and pulled a lever on the wall beside him. The door closed.

The room shuddered. She pressed her hands against the wall on each side to steady herself.

"It's perfectly safe," whispered Sir Avery.

Tillie's stomach seemed to float for a second, then plummet. A wave of nausea rolled upwards. She swallowed, trying to keep the contents of her stomach contained.

"What is this place?" she hissed through clenched teeth. She grasped her bodice with one hand to stop her stomach from turning somersaults.

"This is the *Ascending Room*," replied Sir Avery. "It will take time to adjust to the movement. It *is* perfectly safe, I assure you."

A low rumble convulsed the Ascending Room walls.

"Is that usual?" she whispered.

He frowned. The General clutched his cane.

The Ascending Room shuddered to a halt. A boom reverberated through the walls. The Ascending Room jerked fiercely to one side. Tillie lurched forward. Sir Avery caught hold of her as she slammed against the wall. Her heart froze. She gripped the walls. Acid crept up her throat. She felt as if she was descending into hell.

"Perfectly safe, is it?" Her voice was shaky.

A low thundering noise rolled towards them, culminating in a loud cracking boom.

Tillie never heard Sir Avery's reply. The world went black.

✿

Of Resurrections, Discoveries, and Eliminations

P edestrians stepped in and out of pools of light, following the string of street lamps. They strolled on their way to the theatre or shuffled home from work, oblivious to the oncoming consequences. Somewhere in the bowels of the building, there was a low rumble. Then silence.

A second explosion shuddered the building. The resounding crack garnered sufficient witnesses to its demise. Men shouted. Women screamed. Everyone stared, pointed or ran for cover.

Glass warped and shimmered. The red brick walls bowed outwards. Cracks appeared around the magnificent bay windows and raced along the mortar joints. The cracks widened until the walls shattered across the footpath.

Lingering bystanders scattered in panic, as red dust and debris showered them.

The top floor lay suspended in the air - just long enough for the stragglers and curious observers to draw a quick breath - then succumbed to gravity, crushing the ground floor, as the entire structure collapsed.

A curtain of thick, white smoke filled the air. The plume leaned over and fell to the ground as prevailing winds rolled it across Prince's Gate.

Harrow emerged from the dense smoke, his bowler buffeted with the force of the explosion. He secured it in place with his gloved hand, and re-positioned his goggles to protect his eyes from the swirling dust and grit. He stared across the street, determined not to glance back at the ongoing destruction.

A figure stood across the street, calm amongst the chaos of fleeing citizens and flying debris. His long coat flapped in the heated gusts, revealing glimpses of his dark, double breasted suit. Wisps of red hair peeked from under his matching square-topped bowler; the lower part of his face was obscured by a leather mask with a circular filter attached to either side - a popular accessory during the measles epidemic, a few years before.

Harrow halted next to the masked man and nodded. Only then did he turn towards the building. Rain drizzled down the back of Harrow's neck. He turned up his collar. White smoke unfurled around them and gradually thinned, caught in the afternoon wind.

Flames licked along the debris and climbed the walls. They leaped high into the night sky and illuminated the footpath and cobblestones.

"Well done, Harrow." The man's flat accent rose above the roar of the blast.

"Thank you, sir."

"That should put an end to this nonsense." The man adjusted the filter on his mask. "Are the Bots ready for deployment?" His words were muffled.

"Not quite, but the Queen is expecting them tonight."

"Good. Good," came the reply.

"Should I return with you, sir?" asked Harrow.

There was a short silence as the last wisps of smoke disappeared down the alley behind them. Bricks scraped and thuds rang across the street and echoed off the surrounding buildings.

A crowd was gathering in the flickering light, shovelling debris from the collapsed doorway. Men shouted directions and held back gawping spectators.

"Not yet," he replied. "Make sure they are ensconced at the Palace before you contact me. I think we should keep you hidden for a while longer. There is still the ever-suspicious Mr Brown to be wary of. Best not raise the hackles of her Scottish Terrier until then."

"Indeed, sir," said Harrow. "I shall have to find alternative means of communications, sir. I fear my encrypting machine will not have survived the fulmination."

The man removed his leather mask and sniffed the air. He would have been a particularly handsome man, if not for his weathered skin, permanent scowl and the greyish tinge to his sclera.

A gust of wind disturbed the fine debris. Harrow sneezed as the dust tickled his nose. The man let out a quiet shriek and whipped his filter mask back over his face.

Bells clanged in the distance, signalling the arrival of emergency assistance. Too little. Too late.

A large metal engine came into view at the end of the street. Its pistons hissed and wheels rumbled above the groans of the dying building. Steam belched from its engines and blended into the vestiges of the explosion's fumes and debris.

"Contact me as soon as everything is in place." The man grumbled and pulled on his mask.

"Yes, Sir."

The masked man turned on his heel. Debris crunched underfoot as he strode off in search of the nearest pharmacist.

Mr Brown sat in his chair and sipped his drink from a very expensive crystal glass. A half-empty bottle of Begg's Best stood on the table beside him. His pale blue eyes glared at Harrow. The ribbon on the back of his Glengarry cap danced as he shook his head vigorously.

"You can nae see her now," Brown growled. "I am to take charge of your wee Bots."

"I have my orders," Harrow replied.

"So do I." Brown downed the last of the whiskey and slammed the glass on the side table. "Hand them over."

"This is Her Majesty's personal Bot." Harrow presented the Scot with an ornate wooden box.

Brown snatched the box from Harrow's hand, held it to his ear and shook it tentatively.

"How do I know this one is safe?" he queried.

"You have General Sabine's personal guarantee," Harrow smiled.

"Well, I suppose that will have to do," replied Brown. "The woman trusts him."

"As she trusts you."

With a quick nod of his head, Harrow deliberately lifted his nose and studied the Scot. Brown's jaw could have been chiselled from Scotland granite itself. By Her Majesty's command, he'd forsworn his clan colours for a kilt and jacket in the grey of half-mourning - for Her beloved Albert.

Though the Widow of Windsor had tamed him, Brown still had a strong fist and enjoyed Her adoration. Two very dangerous attributes. Any disrespect would be reported. And Harrow didn't relish being the object of Her wrath.

He, like much of London Society, found Brown to be a gruff man, accustomed to ill-manners and of unaccommodating speech. He spoke his mind freely in Court and, it was said, even more freely in Her Majesty's presence. Such a flagrant disregard for etiquette was unbecoming of a gentleman, betraying the man's roots.

He resisted the urge to sneer. Brown would always be a *ghillie*.

Harrow rose from his chair.

"I trust you will have these deployed before retiring for the evening," he said. "We both want Her Majesty to remain safe," said Harrow.

"Her safety comes before all else." Brown growled, like the loyal Scottish terrier he was.

"Then good day to you." Harrow clicked his heels and removed himself from Brown's company as speedily as courtesy would allow.

Tillie's head throbbed in the dark. It felt as if it would explode. Her left arm screamed in agony and complained about being pinned under her torso in an awkward position against a *chaise longue*. Velvet tickled her nose.

She rolled off the offending limb; her hand brushed soft tassels along the edge of the upholstery. A crushing ache gripped her torso. She sucked in a deep breath, and regretted it instantly.

Pain stabbed the side of her chest. She clenched her teeth and--

The Orb screamed.

She cradled her aching skull in her hands, as it joined in chorus, and breathed rapidly to compensate for her enforced shallow gasps.

There was a thunk on a metal door. She jerked. Her muscles spasmed, renewing the pain.

"Miss Meriwether!" The voice was muffled.

She ventured a slow, shallow breath and tried to relax to fight the pain, as she flailed for a source of light. The knocking continued in earnest.

"Are you in distress, Miss Meriwether?"

There was a pause. Metal scraped. The door flew open; light flooded into the room. Her pupils ached. Sir Avery rushed through the door and scanned the room. The corridor light glinted off a large gilded frame on the opposite wall, behind him. His shoulders relaxed and any hint of concern vanished. Once again he resorted to his irritating trademark eyebrow calisthenics.

She flexed her fingers, resisting the temptation to manually beat his brow back into position; he was fortunate she was in too much pain to move.

"Do you need assistance?" he asked.

"I am not entirely sure." She gripped her ribs as she spoke. Talking hurt too.

"But, you screamed," said Sir Avery.

"Did I?" She frowned. Maybe the pain has befuddled her brain?

"Most definitely. I thought you may have been attacked or hurt."

"I *have* been hurt." She grimaced.

"... again?" he asked.

She shook her head, grasped the edge of the *chaise longue* and winced. He stepped forward and offered his hand. She glared at him.

"I can stand on my own."

He bowed his head, turned to face the open hatchway and activated a switch on the wall. A cylindrical light tube crackled to life beside him. Pale white light crept through the room.

Tillie pushed on the arm of the *chaise lounge*. Tears lapped the edge of her eyelids. She bit the inside of her lip, trying to not to cry out as she struggled, unassisted, to her feet.

She took a tentative breath and assessed her situation. Only her ribs, left arm and head experienced any significant pain.

<<*Are you intact?*>> she asked the Orb.

It remained quiet.

Had the Orb been damaged? She grabbed at her chest. Pain spread through her chest and shot down her arm. She moaned. Her hand gripped at the rich folds of loose silk that now wrapped her body. She glanced down. She wore a man's Chinese dressing gown of brown and turquoise with a quilted collar.

She smirked. It was something she'd expect Sir Avery would wear in his study. She reached to touch her head. But no Turkish cap. She grimaced and held her breath, trying to quell the spasms of pain.

<<*Mistake!*>> The Orb chided silently, announcing its survival.

<<*You're correct. I think it is more the General's style,*>> she confessed to her silent companion.

"Are you sure you are well?" Sir Avery's gaze flicked downward, then settled on the wall behind her. He cleared his throat.

The collar had shifted, revealing a large expanse of skin on her shoulder. The Orb glinted in her décolletage. Heat spread up her neck and onto her cheeks. She tugged the gown closed and glanced at Sir Avery. His back was now turned to her. Had the Orb been exposed?

"My clothes?" She gripped the dressing gown at the collar and frowned.

"I fear your garments did not fare well."

He indicated her beautiful magenta dress, draped over the back of a chair at the end of the *chaise longue*. The silk was filthy, its magnificent magenta velvet detailing and pleated hem were in tatters. She slumped back on the *chaise*, unsuccessfully ignoring the pain as she did so.

"I am beginning to think you have got the better half of our arrangement," said Sir Avery. "This is the second outfit ruined in one day."

"I do apologise," she replied. "However, I dare say you may be enjoying the arrangement more than you admit." She adjusted the silk robe, leaving just a hint of her naked shoulder, hoping to distract attention away from the Orb that lay hidden beneath her stays.

Sir Avery cleared his throat and seemed to take a sudden, and rather ardent, interest in her hat that lay on top of her gown.

"One of the feathers is broken," he said.

"I don't think that is the only thing that is broken," Tillie replied. She moved her torso carefully and tugged at her stays; they felt odd.

"You have a broken rib," he said as he examined the trim of the spoiled dress.

She grabbed at her chest. She could feel the constricting bandages beneath the silk gown.

Not stays? Her heart skipped. Who had dressed her? Had they seen the Orb? She managed a shallow breath and tried to calm her nerves. Instead, she only succeeded in flooding her entire torso with excruciating pain.

"What happened?" She gritted her teeth, trying to suppress any admission of pain.

"Sabotage," he replied. "Our traitor detonated a considerably large incendiary device. The entire Upper Levels have collapsed on us. I am afraid we will be grounded here for several days as our men dig us out."

"Several days?"

"Yes," he said, still averting his gaze. "Unfortunately, the Lower Levels' exit tunnel also succumbed to the blast."

"Lower Levels?" she replied.

"The Department has offices under the main building. The Upper Level staff are unaware of their existence. Thanks to our engineers, this level withstood the explosion. It's fortuitous we were in the Ascending Room at the time. Fate, and Her Majesty, work in mysterious ways."

"Her Majesty?"

"She insisted we build the Ascending Room, so she didn't have to climb down the iron ladder." He draped the bedraggled dress over his arm. "The General requires your attendance, though first we shall have to find you more appropriate attire."

He closed his eyes as he turned to face her. She smiled and pulled the dressing gown back over her shoulder. He nodded his head, left the room and closed the door behind him.

Tillie turned her attention to the remaining undergarments on the chair. Thankfully her stays had been spared from the incident. She felt vulnerable without their protective sheath. It did not do to entertain male company in such a state of undress. The corners of her eyes crinkled. Dear Aunt Prudence would have chided her on lack of propriety of the situation. She wiped a tear from her eye.

She loosened the cords in the back eyelets, slipped the stays around her back and secured the metal busk. As she reached tentatively for the lacing, a twinge heralded the oncoming torment as her ribs reminded her of their existence. She froze, not daring to move and scanned the room; Matilda Meriwether would *not* be beaten.

The metal hatch door, with its circular locking wheel, looked like it belonged in the bowels of a steam ship. The light from the illumination tube reflected in the glass doors of the corner bookshelf on the other side of the door, and danced over the room. A modest oak desk stood near the back wall.

She studied the bookshelf doors. The handles were too small. There was no anchor point on the light fixture and she didn't fancy getting too close to the crackling tube. She hooked the lacing loop around the wheel handle of the room's door. The large portrait of Her Majesty, Queen Victoria on the wall opposite the *chaise lounge*, judged her every move.

<<Careful,>> reminded the Orb.

<<I know what I'm doing.>> She swallowed and stepped forward, allowing the loop to slowly tighten, and stopped only when the pain threatened to return. She used the handle to cinch each lace crossing until the stays were firm. She let out a slow breath. Success!

She examined herself in the glass doors of the corner bookcase. The stays were still loose, but she dare not lace them any tighter with a broken rib. She would not yet fit into her dress. How could she present herself to the General dressed only in her undergarments and a borrowed men's dressing gown?

<<One last pull.>>

<<Bad idea,>> whispered the Orb.

<<*What would you know?*>> Tillie held her breath, caught the central loop in the door handle and pulled at the cord lacing. A wave of pain washed over her.

Tillie groaned. Her head *still* ached. A faint buzz crackled in her ears. She opened her eyes and peered across the dimly lit room. Sir Avery sat slouched in the chair behind the desk. His chest fell rhythmically as he slept. A portable illumination tube crackled on the desk in front of him.

She sat up on the *chaise lounge.* Her hand brushed against a voluminous skirt of green trimmed, cream taffeta. The gown's waist was high, leaving the lower half of her torso unrestricted. The silk rustled as she stood in the puffed confection. She viewed her reflection in the glass doors of the bookcase and huffed. It was something her grandmother would have worn.

A cool draft enveloped her ankles. She tugged at the inadequate skirt, trying to cover her exposed stockings; the dress had obviously been made for a shorter woman.

The bodice slipped slightly as she moved. She turned, positioning her head to view the back of the dress, without pulling at her rib. The low-cut bodice was loosely laced, causing the excessive movement and catching on the Orb's now visible chain. Her fingers floundered at the lacings, and jerked away at the first twinge in her torso.

<<*Told you.*>> The Orb chuckled.

"Quiet!" Tillie hissed.

"Pardon?" Sir Avery snuffled and pulled himself up in the chair.

She pulled at the loose bodice.

"Oh, I must apologise," he said. "I'm not adept with women's clothing." He rose from his chair. "We have no female servants in the Lower Levels. I'll organise for Grace to attend you when we resurface."

She blushed and clutched at her chest where the Orb was hidden beneath her stays. Surely he'd noticed the Orb?

"Are you in pain?" A crease appeared in his brow.

"Did you...see anything?" she asked.

He shook his head. "I am a gentleman, Miss Meriwether. My eyes were closed the entire time." It was his turn to blush. "Again, I apologise for such impropriety."

Tillie sighed with relief. Her secret was safe. She grabbed her side as her rib reminded her of its condition.

Tillie entered General Sabine's Lower Level office. It was significantly smaller than the room he had occupied in the Upper Levels. A large map covered the wall behind his desk - a perfect replica of the large oak desk that had been destroyed, somewhere in the rubble overhead.

"Good morning, my dear. I am glad you could join us," chirped the General as he sipped on a cup of tea. "How are the ribs today? That was a particularly nasty bump you took to the head."

"Much improved, General," she replied.

"Tea?" he said.

She nodded.

He pushed a large brass button on the side of the desk. Within minutes, an extremely tall, red-headed man poked his head through the doorway.

"Sir?"

"Miss Meriwether is ready for some breakfast, Saunders." The General's tea cup chinked softly on its saucer. "Another pot of tea, I think."

Saunders nodded and disappeared back into the warren of corridors.

Tillie's stomach grumbled. She tugged at her bodice. She had not eaten since breakfast, yesterday.

"How long have I been here, General?" she asked.

"Two days," the General replied.

"Two days!" She slumped into the chair opposite his desk.

"Relax, my dear. Allington makes an excellent nurse."

Warmth spread up Tillie's neck and across her cheeks. Her fingers tensed as she tugged at the neckline of her borrowed attire. The Orb remained silent. She relaxed, thankful of the temporary respite from its intrusive chatter.

Small crinkles formed at the edge of the General's eyes as he smiled. "He is both a gentleman and trustworthy." He stood, picked up the portable illumination tube from his desk and ushered her to the door. "Come, I have something to show you."

The air grew heavier as the General led her deeper into the polished, white-tiled passages to an octagonal room. The thrum of industry hissed, clattered and clanked behind the door in each wall. A mosaic of the, now familiar, symbol of the Department of Curiosities decorated the floor.

Directly across from the entrance was an imposing iron door. Its circular edge butted the surrounding wall. Bands of metal covered the door's surface, bolted securely to its bulk. Its only hardware was an over-sized brass locking wheel, fashioned in the shape of the cog and lightning bolt, in the centre of the door.

The General flipped open the top of his cane, flicked a switch, and passed it over a section of the iron door. Loud clunks cascaded around its edge and culminated in a heavy thunk from its centre.

Tillie's eyes widened. "How?"

"The miracles of science." He winked at her. "And the power of magnetic fields."

The wheel spun. A faint whirring filled the chamber. Her head reeled in unison as the metal spokes blurred. The walls wavered in the corner of her eye, as a heavy cloak of air enshrouded her.

She ventured a slow breath of stale air. Sharp pain prodded her chest. Her body wavered.

"Easy, Miss Meriwether." An arm slipped around hers, gently supported her and led her into a larger chamber beyond.

A rhythmic click of air whooshed from the side wall. Vertical shafts of light bathed the dim room, revealing sections of continents mapped out on the floor.

The General guided her along the edge of the room, towards a seat, passing across northern Europe and through south-east Asia, to end their journey at an overstuffed leather armchair on the far side of the room.

She sank in the chair and rested her arms on its carved wooden armrests, glad to relieve some of the pressure on her rib cage.

Long rectangular blades clicked behind a mesh-covered vent on the wall beside her. A fresh breeze emanated from it and flitted across her face. She breathed as deep as her injury would allow, drinking in as much oxygen as possible. Her head slowly cleared, as she acclimatised to the restored oxygen levels.

The General pressed a button on the arm of the chair. Small spots of light tracked over the world map painted on the floor. Illumination tubes crackled into life on the walls. Their light brightened until the moving spot lights were barely visible.

Tillie eyed the glass tubes and hesitated. "Are you *sure* they're safe?"

"Safer than gas, here in the Lower Levels."

He smiled and stepped aside, allowing her to view the room's full technological grandeur. An imposing spherical skeleton of brass shells, supported by a quadfurcated pedestal of etched and decorated bronze dominated the room. A detailed globe map sat at its heart.

Each layer swivelled noiselessly, independent of its neighbour. The deepest shell held small bronze model-submersibles. The middle layer boasted silver coloured micro-steamships, barely moving as they skimmed over the oceans of the world sphere. The outermost skeleton held several white-enamelled airships; each moved sporadically over the entire surface of the globe, unrestricted by topography. Not only was the device an ingenious feat of engineering, it was a work of art.

"How beautiful," she whispered.

"I thought you would appreciate it." He beamed proudly. "But I have something else for you."

The General reached down beside the armrest of the chair and pushed a circular button hidden in the centre of a carved flower. With a click, the carved side of the armrest fell open to reveal a secret compartment. He retrieved a key and handed it to her.

"Her Majesty has approved access to the restricted Lower Levels. She trusts you, Miss Meriwether. You do understand the responsibility that comes with that?"

She nodded and accepted the key. "Thank you, General."

"You have been assigned a research room," he said. "Though I must apologise. You won't have access to your Italian translator until we are freed from our tomb. You have also been assigned to Lower Levels communications... once it is repaired. Unfortunately, it was damaged in the explosion."

"You have two communication rooms?" she asked.

"Yes. Very sensitive information is received only at Lower Levels," he replied. "The staff in the Upper Level don't know this level exists. They do not have the required clearance."

"Oh. So what's Mr Harrow's occupation down here, in the Lower Levels?"

"He is Upper Levels staff, my dear. Mr Saunders is my 'Harrow' here in the Lower Levels."

There was a tap on the iron door.

"Perfect timing." The General turned towards the door. "Come in, Saunders."

"Sir." Saunders nodded his head.

"Saunders, Matilda Meriwether is our new Communications expert. See she is informed once the machine is restored."

"Yes, General," he replied.

"Saunders will show you to your room," said the General.

Tillie's stomach grumbled softly. She placed her hand flat on her impertinent midriff.

The General smiled. "After breakfast," he added.

The carriage slowed and pulled off the overgrown muddy lane toward a copse of trees. Two men slipped out of the cab, their pale grey skin and drab long-coats almost invisible in the low light of the half moon. A slender hand thumped the side of the carriage. The driver snapped the reins and trotted his horses onward into the night.

Wet grass squelched under the Ghostmen's feet as they picked their way through the woodland and down to the riverbank. They reached into the low-lying vegetation along the edge of the Thames and recovered their hidden cache: a small boat painted to match the muddy waters of the river.

Water slapped the bow as they climbed into the boat. They eased the craft further into the river and made their way westward to Windsor.

Beyond the outskirts of the town loomed the imposing stone castle, currently home to Her Majesty, Queen Victoria. The Ghostmen skulked through the outlying streets of Windsor town and stole through the castle grounds until they reached the towering wall of the Upper Ward where the trees met the walls, providing significant cover.

Since Queen Victoria had embraced ever increasing technological security measures, manned ground patrols had been significantly reduced. Once over the walls, barring any unpredictable security changes by the Queen's *ghillie*, John Brown, there were only the mechanicals patrolling the doors of the East Terrace to contend with.

The Ghostmen reached inside their cheap woollen longcoats. A muffled ratcheting issued from under the loose folds.

Rectangular-shaped brass poles descended below the hems and settled their ends into the ground. The clicking paused, then, with an excited whir, resumed in earnest. The Ghostmen's feet rose off the ground as the telescopic poles lifted their operators up the stone wall.

A chittering noise met them as they broached the top of the wall. A growing plague of Bots swarmed towards them. The chittering escalated as still more Bots diverted from their patrol to converge on the intruders.

One by one the Bots split open to reveal their antennae.

The brass poles shuddered to a halt; Bots did not require visual cues. They used sound to hone in on their prey. The Ghostmen hovered within footfall of Windsor's walls. Waiting. They glanced behind them. The moon had almost set and there was a hint of pale orange on the horizon. The taller Ghostman grunted, fumbled in his coat pocket to activate the Bot's control box. The Bots froze.

Clicks cascaded through the mechanical army as first one, then another twitched, retracted their antennae, and trundled off on their divergent predetermined patrol routes.

He grinned, his teeth gleaming against his ash-coloured skin. The men leaned forward, pivoted on the brass poles and glided onto the edge of the wall. They reached inside their coats to deactivate the Ascending Gear. The appendages collapsed and retracted back under their mantles.

The men moved, unobserved, along the shadows of Windsor's dark stone walls to the Eastern Terrace.

The Queen's Guard stood at the main entrance to King's Tower. The Ghostmen paused, retrieved small cylindrical pipes from their pockets, then put them to their lips and blew. The darts flew silently to find their new homes in the exposed necks of the two guards.

The taller Ghostman approached the guard and waved his hand in front of his face. The wide-eyed guards snuffled and twitched as the paralysis took hold. Left to the drug's devices, they would soon lose control of their breathing, their hearts would stop beating. The Ghostman bared his teeth in a crooked grin and signalled to his cohort, as he kicked the guards' weapons away and slipped past the sentry post.

Inside, a faint gas flame flickered at the end of the perimeter corridor. The Ghostmen paused, cocked their head in the direction of the light and waited a moment. All was silent. They both extracted a pair of thick-lensed goggles from their pockets. Light glinted on the glass as they slipped them on and peered along the corridor in both directions. They stole along the stairs and corridors until they reached Queen Victoria's private chambers.

One lone Bot now stood between them and their goal. On its golden-coloured back was the Royal seal. It trundled toward them and paused. Its antennae wobbled. It turned, led them off through another room and halted outside the Queen's bedroom door.

The taller Ghostman produced a small metal box and pressed a button on its side. Several key-like projections sprang out of the device. He sifted through them, latching each back into the box until one probe remained, then slid it into the door lock and twisted the device. The faint scratching noises were amplified by the silence of the late hour. There was an audible click; he winced.

They waited. The only noise was the ticking of the Royal Bot as it rolled down the hall and returned to its patrol.

The lead Ghostman pulled a large syringe from its holster. His companion slid a long knife from his belt and nodded to his partner. He adjusted his night goggles and eased the door open.

The fire was nothing but glowing embers, providing little assistance. They scanned the bed chamber. The walls were lined with large framed paintings, the details undetectable by the technology. A large canopy bed dominated the room. A lump moved under the covers; the bed was occupied.

They inched into the chamber. A low, throaty grumble filled the room. They froze, and scanned the room a second time. There was a snarl. A large dark dog stepped from behind the Queen's bed. Its clear eyes shone in the goggles' augmented vision.

The bed covers twitched.

The lead Ghostman lurched forward. The collie had other ideas. Its warning bark pierced the room, summoning help. The moving Ghostman fumbled unsuccessfully for his blow pipe. It dropped and rolled along the floor, past the dog.

The second Ghostman leaped towards the canopy bed. With unexpected reflexes, Queen Victoria sprang from her bed, brandishing an over-sized candlestick in one hand.

"Noble, attack!" she commanded.

The collie sprang onto the knife-wielding Ghostman.

Queen Victoria crouched and launched herself at the remaining intruder. She swung the candlestick and knocked the syringe from the intruder's hand. The metal cylinder skittered under the bedside table.

The Ghostman recoiled from the Queen's return swing and dropped to the floor behind her. His hand flicked under the bedside table and grasped for the syringe. Another swing swished past his ear as he slithered out of range.

Noble attacked the second Ghostman, clamped onto the would-be assassin's arm with his jaws and shook his head violently. The Ghostman screamed in agony and dropped his knife.

Loud shouts and stomps of hurried footsteps echoed up the stairwell outside the door.

The lead Ghostman scowled and lunged at the Queen as she retreated through the open door towards the oncoming reinforcements. The second Ghostman followed, the growling Noble still latched onto his forearm.

"What is all the racket aboot?" John Brown bellowed as he emerged from the adjoining room. He wore a knee-length nightshirt and brandished a large double-barrelled shotgun. Brown, never one for analysing, shot into the fray. Noble yelped and jumped off the Ghostman as he fell.

Confronted by the angry, armed Scotsman and converging militia, the remaining Ghostman concentrated on his prey. He slammed his shoulder into the monarch and shoved her down the nearby staircase. The silver candlestick clattered down the stairs after them.

Brown shot a second time. The slug blasted above the remaining intruder's head and buried itself into the wall on the other side of the stairs. Brown's thunderous footsteps rushed down the steps.

The Ghostman scrambled to his feet at the bottom of the staircase and dashed towards the exit, as more guards emerged from the surrounding doorways and corridors in pursuit.

The motionless body of Her Imperial Majesty, the Queen-Empress Victoria lay crumpled at the base of the stairs.

"Are you all right, woman?" asked Brown.

There was no reply.

Of Symbols, Deceits, and Cyphers

octor Reid closed the Royal bedchamber door behind him, dried his hands on a linen cloth and glared over his spectacles at the assembly of men before him.

"Is she...? Will she...?" Sir Henry Ponsonby tugged on his coat and raised an eyebrow in Brown's direction.

Brown stared past him, seemingly oblivious that he was still in his nightshirt.

"Well?" Brown slammed the butt of his gun on the floor beside him.

"Her Majesty will survive," replied Reid.

There was a collective sigh from the congregation of worriers.

"Her Majesty is concussed. She needs quiet and rest for a few days," he said. "However..." The doctor inspected the linen cloth in his hands.

Mr Brown grunted. "Get to the point, man."

"However, the leg bone is fractured, and the tendons are damaged." The doctor removed his spectacles and placed them in his coat pocket. "It will be some time before it heals properly."

"She won't like that," scoffed Brown.

Sir Henry ran his hand through his hair and sucked air in through his teeth. "What shall we tell the public? We can't let anyone know that security has been compromised."

"I want to know how they got in." Brown's lips hardened, accentuating his frown. "I told you not to trust those wee mechanical bugs. They're no substitute for a man's eyes."

"The mechanicals aren't able to detect dirigible incursions, Brown," said Sir Henry. "We need all available eyes on the skies."

Brown grunted.

"And the Bots have worked until now."

"I dinnae trust that Department lackey." Brown gripped his shotgun. "I will investigate personally."

Footsteps ran up the stairs. A tall, clean-shaven guard approached them, glanced at Brown and tugged down his red coat. He leaned in close to Sir Henry, cupped his hand and whispered in the Private Secretary's ear.

Sir Henry's forehead wrinkled. "Unfortunate." He nodded at the Captain.

"What is unfortunate?" Brown moved closer, shotgun still in hand.

"The intruder you shot at is dead," replied Sir Henry. "And his accomplice has escaped."

"Maybe you will learn to ask questions before you let off both barrels next time, Brown?" The Captain of the Guard sneered at the *ghillie*.

"I do what I must to protect Her Royal Highness," said Brown. "I dinnae see anyone else here at the time." The creases at the corner of his eyes grew deeper as he surveyed the assembled men.

"It wouldn't have mattered, Captain," said the doctor. "The intruder's tongue has been removed. I'd hazard it's the same for his cohort."

Sir Henry cleared his throat. "Gentlemen, the question remains: what do we tell the Prime Minister, and what do we tell the public?"

The doctor stepped forward. "My official statement will say that Her Majesty had an unfortunate accident."

"Omit the assassination attempt?" Sir Henry smiled. "Good idea, Reid. A bit of truth always makes an untruth sound more believable," he said.

The subterranean room provided for Tillie was small, but cosy, complete with a generously-padded armchair and a large velvet fainting couch furnished with feather pillows and a silk coverlet.

Saunders had anticipated her need for a dressing table; he'd scavenged an eclectic selection of mirrors and cobbled them together to create a makeshift vanity on the corner of the desk. A folding privacy screen, fashioned from sheets, stood in the far corner and concealed the bookcase. There was even a gilt-framed painting of Hyde Park.

The illumination tube on the wall dimly lit a portrait of Queen Victoria above the large desk, as if to oversee her work. Tillie shifted in the narrow desk chair.

Mr Saunders had shown her how to operate the newfangled lighting. It made sense not to rely on gas lighting or candles, in the underground rooms; the flames would have consumed the limited oxygen supply following the cave in. He had reassured her it was perfectly safe, but Sir Avery had also given her the same assurance while in the Ascending Room. She eyed the illumination tube on the edge of the desk and shuddered; a twinge crept along her ribs. She did not trust their definition of 'safe'.

Faint footsteps echoed outside her chamber. Her heart skipped a beat. Perhaps Sir Avery would call again? She glanced at the reflection of the hatch-door, in one of the mirrors on the vanity-desk.

He'd been unremitting in his attentions for the first few days of their internment in the Lower Levels. She'd delighted in his gentle words and comforting companionship. But yesterday, he had made excuses after breakfast, only to return for late supper with a new undergarment.

She chuckled. What would Aunt Prudence have said of such a gift? She frowned, placed her hand on her chest and traced the surface of the corset. How had he known her measurements?

She remembered the red-faced Professor apologising awkwardly as he hastened to explain the reason for such an intimate gift, with its construction of articulated metal plates, under the covering of fine silk and lace trim, designed to provide protection. The lines in her forehead faded. She bit her lip, to hold back a giggle.

"*I am responsible for your safety,*" he had muttered. "*And I need to ensure that at least one item of your wardrobe can withstand the rigours of your adventures, Miss Meriwether.*" With that he had bowed and swiftly retreated back into the secret places of the Lower Levels.

She pushed her finger gently against the handle of her fine china tea cup and turned it around on the saucer.

Her attention returned to the mirror's reflection. She had not seen Sir Avery all day. Why didn't he visit? She twisted the ringlets around her fingers, pinned them back in place and tried to ignore how much she missed his annoying eyebrows. What could possibly be monopolising all of his attention? The Department of Curiosities excelled at making secrets. She doubted if she would ever discover his current assignment.

<<*Concentrate,*>> demanded the Orb.

Tillie flicked the handle of the teacup and glared at the Orb on the desk beside her. It had become more vocal now the General's cane was not within range; she'd found a pleasant relief in the infernal thing's silence. She grimaced. Annoying though the Orb was, it had a point; she had a lot of work to do.

She eased the mirrors to the rear of the vanity-desk, propped them against the side wall and arranged her keepsakes on the remaining space.

She took a deep breath, puffed it out quickly as a faint twinge encircled her torso reminding her of her still tender ribs, and wriggled in the narrow office chair. With no convenient bench seat to accommodate the upside-down vase that was imposed by her undergarments, she had forgone a crinoline on day one.

Mr Saunders had found her another gown, this time in yellow with black trim. But the reduced bulk still proved more uncomfortable than the modern bustle when confined within the arms of the captain's chair; such narrow seating was more fit for the practical garments of the male operatives who populated the Department, than for any fashion of women's attire.

She prodded at her skirts, in an attempt to wrangle the even more voluminous amounts of silk of the outdated frock, and crinkled her chin. She'd have to see about some more suitable clothing... And about more women working for the Department.

She sighed and reached back as far as she dared, then tugged at the gown's lacings. The bodice gave way, reducing the pressure on her torso. Another twinge snaked through her ribs.

<<Cypher!>> demanded the Orb.

Tillie huffed and studied the precious keepsakes she had laid out on the mahogany desk: her father's green journal - full of codes, the small metal box from behind the fireplace - now unlocked, and the Cryptocron - a small brass cylinder with an unbreakable seal at each end and encased by ten ivory rings, each etched with a series of pictographs.

She opened the red leather-bound da Vinci notebook. She had only a limited time to discover its secrets; the General's constraints allowed her access only until they broke free of their secret tomb. Then it would be lost to her and returned into the Queen's custody.

The notebook and the Cryptocron were keys to a puzzle. That much she knew from the few coded messages she'd deciphered from her father's journal. She tapped her lip in frustration. But how to use them?

She leafed through the pages. Each page was crammed with scrawled notes, sketches and diagrams. Hidden amongst da Vinci's faded writings were doodles in modern ink. Who had defaced a valuable record of antiquity?

She snapped shut the notebook and slid it to one side of the desk and picked up the Cryptocron. It was hefty for its size. It tinkled as she as she flipped it over in her hand. She'd spent years ruminating on the pictograms carved on the encrypted cylinder.

In order to reveal its contents, a ten letter code word was required, each letter to be dialled separately, aligning the rings in a specific sequence. She clenched the Cryptocron in her hand. But *which* word?

She glanced at the hatch-door and wished the Professor would at least visit for afternoon tea. She could benefit from another logician's opinion on her puzzle.

<<*Secret,*>> the Orb growled. Its iris narrowed as its pupil snapped open and spun in her direction.

"I know," Tillie replied out loud. "But I need to know what is inside."

Muted footsteps passed the hatch door of Tillie's room. Perhaps the Professor would visit *today*? She glanced up at the makeshift vanity mirror on the edge of her desk. The footsteps faded into the distance. She sighed. Not today.

She returned her attention to the Cryptocron and toyed with the dials on the brass cylinder. Each ring had several markings of fine-etched lines and flowing swirls forming pictograms; each pictogram was repeated on several of the rings.

Tillie sank into the chair. She didn't need to be a statistician to realise the possible number of combinations was astounding. She'd already attempted a multitude of combinations: one million, one hundred and twenty-three thousand and fifty-seven combinations, to be exact. And each one had failed.

She sighed, turned the first ring and methodically dialled a new set of pictograms, recording the combination, as she had done many times over the past three years. Something clicked. She grinned and tugged at the end of the cylinder. It refused to budge. The Cryptocron remained sealed.

Tillie huffed, noted down the combination and reset the rings. She tried another combination. The cylinder remained locked. The Cryptocron thunked onto the desk and rattled as it rolled across the surface.

"This is impossible," she grumbled. "There are just too many possible combinations."

<<Notebook?>> suggested the Orb.

"Of course!" She shoved her notes to one side, against the vanity mirrors and opened her father's green journal. "Father would have left a key."

<<No.>> The Orb jiggled against her skin. <<Notebook!>>

"Shh," she hissed. "Can you dial in the combinations for me?"

There was silence.

"I didn't think so." She scanned her father's handwritten pages in search of any notations on how to use the da Vinci notebook to help her crack the code. The Orb had been emphatic about the necessity for its retrieval; it had to contain the key.

<<Cypher.>> The Orb's reply caressed her consciousness, barely a whisper.

"Why are you always so cryptic?"

She dropped her elbow on the desk, plopped her chin in her hand and flipped through the pages. Random doodles filled the margins. She traced the lines with her finger; a palm tree, a crocodile, a depiction of the goddess, Kali, and the Oracle of Delphi. Each one rekindled the memories of wondrous trips to exotic locations, with her father: Egypt, India, the Amazon, full of history and excitement.

Her finger froze on one of the three pillars of the Delphi temple. There was something familiar. Her father's voice echoed in her memory, retelling the tales of their escapades. She shook her head. There was *something* about Delphi, something more recent. She tapped the page. Something important.

She frowned, slid her father's notebook aside and opened the red, leather-bound da Vinci notebook in its place. She turned the pages slowly, studying each before turning to the next.

There! Her heart fluttered. In a corner, hidden amongst the Master's diagrams, was a drawing of a small palm tree. Not usually found in Renaissance Florence.

She tugged on a chain attached to her bodice, pulled a silver lorgnette from inside the silk sash at her waist and examined the ink drawing through the magnifying lens. Familiar swirls lay concealed within the patterns of the palm's trunk. Swirls that resembled some of the pictograms on the Cryptocron.

Tillie held her breath. Could this be the key?

She transcribed the symbols into her notes and returned to her inspection of the sketches, this time with a renewed enthusiasm. A few pages later, she spied a small pyramid buried within a collection of detailed schematic drawings. The lorgnette's magnification revealed more symbols decorating the bricks of the sketch. Next, was a minute cartoon of the temple at Delphi, with six pictograms inked into the base.

She continued, ignoring the passing footsteps, and the fresh cup of tea provided by the ever-diligent Saunders.

Scattered amongst the pages of diagrams, sketches and notes were more inked cartoons in her father's hand. When she was certain she'd found and transcribed all her father's sketches and annotations, she dropped her nib, leaned back in the desk chair and flexed her fingers to relieve the cramped muscles.

She stared at the papers on the vanity-desk. There were over a dozen sketches copied from her father's additions: a pyramid, a temple, Mayan symbols, an Indian god, a sphinx... Each had accompanying symbols hidden in the line work. She studied the Cryptocron and frowned. The symbols were not the same.

The wall clock chimed behind her. Three o'clock; she had been working all night. Hours wasted on a false lead. She rubbed her eyes. The General's caveat on the da Vinci notebook rang in her mind as the clock's last chime faded: *I can give you one week. After that it must be archived and returned to its rightful owner.*

The clock's gears clicked as they reset. She slumped back into the chair. Even if she was trapped here for a month, it may not be long enough to solve the code.

She stared at the cup of tea on the desk beside her. *You are a jewel, Saunders.* She lifted the teacup and ventured a sip. Her chin crinkled. It was cold. The cup rattled on its saucer.

The sound of footsteps drew her eye back to the makeshift vanity mirrors. A visit from Sir Avery would be a welcome distraction to lighten her disposition. She straightened in her chair and pinched her cheeks.

The tap of footsteps passed by the door and faded down the corridor. Tillie huffed. Still not yet.

Her eyes lingered on their own reflection in the mirror. Her lids were heavy. Her hair was in need of attention. She wrinkled her nose. Aunt Prudence would have an apoplexy.

She leaned toward the mirror, turned her head to inspect her dilapidated coiffure and noticed the fractured reflection of her abandoned tea cup. She closed one eye. The reflected image disappeared from one of the mirrors. She smiled, opened her eye and closed the other eye. The image appeared to jump to the adjacent mirror. For a moment she was lost in the inane entertainment of image calisthenics. The distraction soon became tiresome; she searched the mirror for a more engaging amusement.

Her discarded transcriptions lay against the mirror, their reflection reversing the drawings. The pyramid, Delphi temple and depiction of Kali remained the same in reflection. The Mayan pictogram was reversed, making it an undecipherable, meaningless doodle. Tillie glanced over the reflection of the additional squiggles her father had added to the symbols. They too had reversed.

Her eyes widened.

"Of course!" Her voice broke the silence. "You *did* leave me a clue." She scooped the scattered notes together. "Da Vinci wrote his notes *backwards*. You need a mirror to read them."

She held a page of notes next to the largest mirror and compared the reversed symbols to those on the Cryptocron. They matched.

"You were clever, Father."

Tillie stacked the da Vinci notebook onto her father's journal and pushed them to the edge of the desk to make room to work. There were twenty symbols in all; not enough to represent the English alphabet. No, there were still four pictograms missing. Maybe Greek?

She reviewed her father's drawings. The picture of the sphinx had six symbols.

<<*Six*,>> said the Orb.

"Yes, I know." She stared for moment. *Six?* She raised an eyebrow. "Of course!" She scribbled the letters next to the corresponding pictograms: *S. P. H. I. N. X.*

Next, she examined the pyramid. Her grip relaxed on the nib. There were only five symbols. *Not pyramid... Egypt?* She smiled. Egypt had five letters: *E. G. Y. P. T.* She tallied up the newly encoded symbols. Ten.

She chuckled and extracted the remaining letters, teasing them from the inscriptions hidden within the illustrations her father had drawn, until twenty pictograms had been deciphered. There were still four symbols missing: *C, O, U* and *Z*.

Tillie rubbed her eyelids. She was tired and her stomach ached. She hadn't noticed the clock chimes while working and the lack of natural lighting made it impossible to tell the time of day.

"What time is it?" She glanced over her shoulder toward the wall clock.

A low grumbling broke the silence. She grabbed at her stomach and blushed.

"It *must* be time for breakfast. Where is Saunders, I wonder?"

She groaned and twisted in the narrow chair, trying to view the clock. Her hand reached out across the desk and knocked the stack of notebooks onto the floor with a thunk. As she retrieved her father's journal, a photograph slipped from its pages and fell onto her lap.

Tillie scooped it up. Her secret. It was the only photograph she had of her father. She kept it, breaking a promise to her aunt and uncle. Her father's pale eyes stared back at her, holding her gaze. She stared back, willing him to tell her the final part of the key.

She studied the photograph. Professor Nathaniel Kempthorne was a tall, straight-backed man with a rugged chin, his dark hair slightly tousled, yet with a precise moustache trimmed to perfection. He sat at his grand carved-oak desk, a plethora of notes and keepsakes strewn before him. In his hand was his familiar pen, the same pen Tillie now held in her own hand to decipher the same code it had written over a decade before.

Her mind wandered back to her father's study. She could smell the smooth sweetness of the toffees he would give her as she spent many long hours playing at the foot of that desk. Her favourite pastime had been playing with one of her father's treasures - a small statue of a sphinx, which resided on his desk and watched over his work as he pondered puzzles or concocted fanciful experiments. She could feel her father's presence even now, hear his voice. Words flooded her memory: "*It is one of a kind. It belongs only to us, given to me by your Uncle Meriwether.*"

It had been almost a decade since she had thought of the statue, a willing companion on many re-created and imagined adventures to far away, exotic lands.

It had a name. What was it? Yew? Eu...?

"Eustace!" she smiled. "I had forgotten all about you, dear Eustace."

Tillie ran her fingers over the photograph. There, on the desk was her dear friend, perched upon his dais of carved stone edged with decorative symbols. She squinted at the corner of the sepia-tone desk through the lorgnette. If her memory served her truthfully...

There, just visible, were the now-familiar markings. She scribbled them down beside the copies of her father's drawings. Seven in all, the first and last duplicated, as in her companion's name: *Eustace.*

She scribbled the letters next to the corresponding pictograms and placed her nib back onto its rest. She leaned back and folded her arms. Only two letters remained: *Z* and *O*. And how many words would require a *Z*?

She retrieved the Cryptocron and rolled it slowly in her hands. The decrypted symbols now shouted at her, demanding her to complete their task. She turned the rings on the cylinder. Shorter words formed and fragmented as she span each one slowly. The pictogram for the letter 'H' clicked into position on the first ring. She bit her lip. Now she just needed the key word.

"'H' for Henry," she said absentmindedly. "'H' for... Harrow? 'H' for...?"

<<*Homunculus,*>> replied the Orb.

"*Homonculus* has..." She counted on her fingers. "Ten letters."

Her arm slipped on the desk. Her elbow knocked the saucer. A drop of tea swirled over the edge of her cup as she sat bolt upright in her chair. Her hands trembled as she dialled each corresponding symbol on the rings of the Cryptocron.

She twisted the cylinder.

Nothing.

A chill rolled over her body. Her heart sank into her chest, burying itself into her lungs. She struggled to breathe against its weight. The cylinder slipped from her fingers and rolled across the desk.

What now? She threw her notes across the desk. Papers fluttered silently onto the carpeted floor. She buried her head in her hands. Moisture seeped onto her hand. She flicked the offending tear from her fingers. She would not cry. She took deep breaths, drinking in more air with each one.

"I will *not* cry."

<<*Homunculus,*>> interrupted the Orb.

"Quiet, or I will fetch the General's cane!"

<<*Homuncu--*>>

"We could be dug out at any moment," she hissed. "I do not have time to--"

Another wave washed over her; this time it spread calm and clarified her thoughts. The pressure lifted from her chest. She reached for the Cryptocron and felt its familiar weight in her hand. She smiled and dialled the sequence again: *H. O. M...*

Tillie held her breath and dialled: '*U'* The ring clicked into place.

She let the breath escape.

"I really should check my spelling next time."

She grinned and continued: *N. C. U. L. U. S.*

With each completed turn, there was a satisfying click. As the final letter snapped in place, a small puff of steam shot out of one end of the Cryptocron. A glass tube slid out of the cylinder.

<<*Finally,*>> The Orb warmed against her skin.

Her heart raced. She removed the tube's seal then tapped out the contents. A small roll of parchment tumbled into her hand. She unrolled the delicate missive. It was the cypher to her father's journal.

"Father always had a flair for the dramatic," she said.

Of Lies, Damned Lies, and Treachery

The monowheel sped across the bridge. Each revolution of its six foot metal wheel reverberated on the wooden planks. Its compact steam engine rattled, echoing the vibrations of the old bridge.

Wisps of grey engine smoke crept through the crisp night air towards Harrow's eyes; he adjusted his goggles, pushed his foot on the brake and decelerated to a more leisurely pace, one less conspicuous amongst the high class that flocked to Rotten Row to enjoy the newly popular pleasures of cycling.

He rode past the octagonal toll booth on the south bank, turned left towards the park and made his way along the tree-lined pathway. He smiled, leaned forward and pulled a small lever. The vehicle's wheel crunched on the pale gravel. The motor sputtered, then fell silent.

His gaze flicked from the path before him to the surrounding parklands for any stragglers. All was clear. He leaned to the left, rolling his vehicle between a thicket of trees, and emerged into a compact clearing with two small wooden sheds.

Harrow slid off his monowheel and wheeled it towards the smaller of the two structures. He surveyed the yard and, once satisfied he was alone, unlocked the door.

A faint glow greeted him as he entered the room. He leaned the monowheel against the opposite wall, lifted a small section of wood on the wall near the door, then slid a metal cover aside and pressed the recessed brass button inside.

Faint whirs echoed inside the walls. He removed his goggles and straightened his bowler. The ground beneath him lurched gently and descended slowly into the earth, taking Harrow with it.

The Ascension Chamber took less than a minute to reach its destination. A lanky man sat hunched over a wooden desk. He nodded as Harrow stepped from the platform. His skin was grey, as were the entirety of his eyes.

"I need to see the Professor immediately," said Harrow.

The man glared at Harrow. Harrow ignored him. He refused to use his employer's chosen title.

The man handed Harrow a linen surgical mask then returned to his work, scribbling something into a large journal.

Harrow made his way along the dim corridor until he found himself at a large metal door. Proudly emblazoned upon its surface was the cogged-ouroboros symbol of The Society. Any opportunity to remind them of *his* affiliations. Harrow rolled his eyes. Perhaps he thought it would keep his henchmen in line?

Harrow wrenched on the large door lever and entered. The antechamber was lit by two small carriage lamps. The light remained still, despite the breeze following him through the door.

Blue arcs crackled in the glass covers, revealing three unmarked doors in the wall before him. A small brass box was mounted near each door, each with a small speaker and a black button. He pushed the button next to the central door.

"Yes?" said a curt, disembodied voice.

"It's Harrow, sir. I have news about the escapees."

"Very well," replied the voice.

The door opened with a faint click. Harrow entered The Inventor's sanctum. Barely twenty feet in diameter, and octagonal in shape, every vertical surface was lined with luscious deep brown wood panelling. Carved archways reached up from each corner converging to form a circle around a disc of overlapping metal leaves.

Each wall was lined with bookshelves or glass cabinets crammed full of scientific equipment. Doors were fashioned into the shelving on four of the walls.

An ornate spiral staircase rose from the centre of the room and terminated mid-air, a few feet below the vaulted roof. In front of the staircase stood a large oak desk where Harrow's superior now squatted. The Professor scowled at Harrow, scrabbled on his desk for his leather mask and shoved it over the lower half of his face.

"Mask!" he hissed through his mask's air filters.

Harrow retrieved the mask he had been issued, donned it and apologised. He frowned under the camouflage. The Professor repeatedly pushed a button on his desk with his free hand. The other hand continued to hold his own leather mask firmly in place.

Another door swung open on the other side of the room. A short man in a white coat and surgical mask bustled into the room, scampered over to the desk and rolled up the Professor's sleeve. He pulled a long metal syringe from his bag and jabbed it into his superior's arm.

The Professor cursed. The pharmacist flinched. His hands trembled as he completed the ritual, removed the syringe and backed away from the desk.

The Professor slowly removed his mask and tentatively sniffed the air. He glared at Harrow.

"If you were not my son..." he growled.

Harrow swallowed. "I am sorry, sir. It won't happen again." He removed his bowler and bowed his head.

"In that you are correct." The Professor waved the pharmacist out of the room.

"It's safe now," he said.

"No, it is not." The Professor gritted his teeth as he rolled his sleeve back down. "You do not know what The Society has planned. I have seen some of their plans. London is not safe. England is not safe."

Harrow's eyes widened. "Pardon, sir?"

"Nothing." The Professor shoved his mask back in the top drawer then leaned forward. "Tell me your news, and it had better be good."

Harrow took a deep breath. Inheritance and prestige carried a high cost. Nonetheless, he was up to the task.

"I have tracked down a Department operative who escaped the explosion," he began. "A Mr Jackson. He was unaware of my involvement and has been dispatched."

"Was that wise?" asked the Professor.

"The Widow of Windsor is looking for a traitor, after the botched assassination attempt." He glared at his father. He should have trained his lackeys better. "Fortunately, Jackson was the mechanic who worked on the Bots. A dead man can not claim his innocence."

The Professor smiled. "Are there any others?"

"Only a few. I have someone constantly monitoring communications," he said. "If any of them try to contact the General, *I* will find them. We will be rid of the Department of Curiosities. It will just take a little time."

The Professor's eyes narrowed. His gaze wandered towards one of the bookshelves and frowned. "*They* are working on that too," he muttered. A bead of sweat formed on his brow as his fingers scrunched the corners of the papers lying on his desk.

Harrow followed his father's gaze towards the shelves. It was just a collection of stories. He raised an eyebrow. All that silver was sending the man barmy.

His gaze shifted to the far corner of the room. Amongst the specimen cases was a tall backed chair covered with a linen cloth. At its base, a golden glint of brass shone at the edges of the covering.

"How goes the work on the Automaton?" he asked. His father was passionate about his mechanical man and was always in a better mood when discussing it.

"Ah, yes." The Professor relaxed his grip on the papers. He rubbed his nose, took a deep breath and returned his attention to Harrow. A smile set slowly on his lips. "Have you found those files on Kempthorne yet?"

Harrow shook his head.

"I need that information to complete the experiments." The Inventor's hand slammed onto the desk. "It will not work without the final piece."

"I am trying, sir. There was nothing in the Upper Level files. There must be another vault with the older files."

The Professor swept the papers off his desk. "And I need my da Vinci notebook back. Kempthorne wrote his codes in it. If *they* crack the code, they will find me out. That cannot be allowed to happen, Harrow!"

"Allington and The General have been eliminated and, once the remnants have been dealt with, I will be the highest-ranking operative in London." Harrow took a step back from the desk. "I just have to wait until *She* summons me. Then I'll get the codes and be able to access the original files."

"Excellent, Harrow." The Professor pressed another button on his desk. The door on the far wall clicked open again. "You had better monitor communications personally until then."

Harrow nodded and exited the room through the unlocked door. He removed the surgical mask as he ventured down the dimly lit corridor on his way to the communications room.

Nine days was long enough. Tillie had grown tired of wasting time in rearranging the layers of endless skirts and had finally rid herself of the dessert-like confection of a dress. Mr Saunders had obligingly procured her some trousers from the Lower Level stores.

She rolled up the sleeve of her borrowed Chinese robe. The improvised outfit was unconventional, but proved excessively comfortable when sitting for hours at the desk. She fancied such an ensemble would also prove quite useful in future adventures.

Tillie snorted softly. What would Aunt Prudence say to that? She knew exactly what her aunt would say: *Decorum at all times!* Tillie flashed her gaze over the empty room and chuckled: but only when necessary, and only in public.

The Orb tugged and fidgeted on its chain. It often agreed with Aunt Prudence in matters of decorum. Tillie ran her fingers along the metal links, lifting the weight from her neck.

Though she revelled in the newly found freedom in private, she continued to wear the new stays Sir Avery had fashioned for her. She placed one hand on her chest and took a deep breath. Its reassuring support helped to relieve some of her rib pain. She felt invulnerable.

<<*Irrational.*>> The Orb's uninvited reproach rang through her thoughts. <<*Mission!*>> it demanded.

Her smile faded. Her hand returned to the journal and slowly turned the next page. Since she'd discovered the cypher key hidden inside the Cryptocron, it had been a laborious process to transcribe the various coded sections of her father's journal. A few answers had been found, but there were also more questions, hints and further references to a second journal hidden within the Department's Restricted Files.

She leaned her chin in her hand, swaying her elbow as she skimmed the notes until she found the next section of code to decipher. It was as if she could feel her father's presence, hear his voice as if telling her a bedtime story. The words were no longer simply scientific notations.

Her eyelids fluttered. His voice slowed. The words blurred.

<<Attention!>>

Tillie's head rang. Her hand slipped from her chin. She jerked up straight in her chair, stretched out her arms and glanced at the wall clock. Just after one. She sighed; it was too easy to lose track of time without natural lighting. She pulled herself to her feet, unbuttoned her trousers and draped them over the chair.

<<Continue.>> demanded the Orb.

"I'm tired." Tillie yawned.

<<Urgent!>> it hissed.

She moaned, gathered up the journal and note paper, then slumped onto the *chaise longue*. She slipped her legs under the covers, rested the book on her thighs and scribbled the transcribed words onto the note paper with one of Sir Avery's self-inking nib pens.

17th September, 1865

Inessa was upset this afternoon. She pleaded for me to be wary of Mr Cranshaw. She suspects my assistant of stealing my ideas and claiming authorship of my inventions. She is determined to keep him under surveillance.

I cannot believe it. I have trusted Cranshaw with my work for the Department for these past four years. He has never given me cause to doubt him.

18th September, 1865

I have made inquiries at the Royal Society. I could not find any evidence of patents or research filed under his name. I am reluctant to tell Inessa. Trust is important to her, understandable in her circumstances. This has placed me in an awkward position. Still, I do not regret my decision.

I will exercise caution and encode all future records regarding this matter, and of all research.

20th October, 1865
Inessa was inconsolable today. For the first time since I have known her, she will not confide in me. She locked herself in Matilda's bedroom and remained there the entire day.

22nd October, 1865
What a fool I am! Inessa has fled Adelaide. Several of my workbooks are missing. How could I have trusted her? Matilda is fretting. She misses Inessa terribly. I shall have to make inquiries for a nanny. I hope one day Myshka will understand.

Tillie's fingers traced one of the smudged circles that marred the dark ink of the journal entry. She had vague memories of a beautiful woman with pale green eyes and hair as black as ink. She remembered singing: a sweet, comforting voice with rich rolling 'r's. Tillie closed her eyes. Inessa. A smile flickered over her lips. She hummed softly:

> *I will weep on that night when you go.*
> *Sleep my angel, sweetly, softly.*

Then the woman was gone. She'd never known the woman's name until now. Her father never spoke of her. Tillie opened her eyes. Inessa had betrayed him? Tillie's smile melted away. No wonder her father wanted her memory forgotten.

<<*Sentimental.*>>

She huffed and turned the page to continue translating the entry:

23rd October, 1865

I have suspended my research indefinitely. I cannot report the theft. The Department was not aware of our connection. I have unwittingly endangered the security of the Empire, and have no way to prove my innocence. If there is any suspicion, even unfounded, that I allowed a foreigner access to my work, both Cranshaw and I could lose our positions. I should have heeded his warnings. How could I have doubted him?

The text returned to uncoded passages. Tillie put down her pen and frowned. She clenched her fist then stretched out the fingers of her right hand. She wiggled her fingers as she skimmed the pages until she found more coded entries, dated several years later.

21st August, 1874
I am to work on an important undertaking that could aid the Empire. If successful, this could be the beginning of a new age for the Empire. I have secured permission to retain Mr Cranshaw as my assistant, for the less sensitive areas of our research. The endeavour is of the highest secrecy. The Department is not to be informed of the particulars and Liberator has re-assigned me from the Department of Curiosities. All communications will be coded. For Liberator's eyes only.

Tillie gasped. "Father worked for the Department of Curiosities?" She stared at the words she'd just written: T*he Department is not to be informed of the particulars.* She frowned.

"What had he...?" Her eyes widened. "Of course, the Bots! Father must have created them while he was working for the Department. But that means..." She swallowed and shifted on the *chaise longue.* Her grip on the journal loosened; it fell back to rest on her thighs. "General Sabine knew Father?"

<<*Hush!*>> cautioned the Orb.

![125](gear icon with page number)

"Oh, you hush!" She placed the pen on the occasional table by the *chaise longue* with a clink.

How much did the General know? He *had* mentioned serving with Uncle Meriwether. Her heart raced. She gripped the edge of the *chaise* and sank her fingers into its plush velvet. Was there a chance he would recognise her? A chill ran up her spine and along her arms.

<<*No.*>> The Orb was cold on her skin.

"But the Department works for the Empire." She took a deep breath to slow her heart beat. An aching pain shot along her ribs. "...answerable only to the Queen. Surely Her Majesty must know the truth - know he's not a traitor?" Her voice cracked. Why hadn't She told the Department? Tillie's heart sank into her stomach and froze. She struggled to breathe.

"What if he was a--?" The word stuck in her throat. The journal slipped from her hand, dragging the notepaper with it. She caught the book and clasped it to her chest. The metal of her armoured stays pressed against her ribcage.

<<*Never!*>> The Orb twitched.

Heat pricked her skin.

"Damnation!" She jumped to her feet, yanked the Orb from her neck and flung it across the coverlet on the *chaise longue*. "No, never!" She shook her head. "Not father!" She slammed the journal on the desk and flicked though the pages to her last spot and translated the last entry on the page.

28th August, 1874

I have been working on a new prototype for the Horde. The work is all consuming. Mr Cranshaw was enquiring about my work, as has the General. I have tasked Cranshaw with another line of research while I am summoned back to London. I have insisted Matilda accompany us. I hope the trip will not be too tedious for my Myshka.

"That's why we came to London?" Tillie frowned and turned the page. An uneven stubble of paper remained where several pages had been hurriedly expunged. Smudges of ink tracked across the next page to a short notation. She flicked over the next few pages and scowled. Two years missing. Why? Who would've removed them? She turned back to the next coded entry.

December, 1876

I have been given final instructions as to the direction of my work. This research is key to the success of Liberator's vision. With India still in the grip of the Great Famine, this could prove vital. There is now pressure for absolute secrecy.

9th February, 1877

Some of my notations have been misplaced. My mind returns to Inessa's accusations that Cranshaw had been assuming authorship of my work. I could forgive the man of such vain actions. However I fear worse.

I have made inquiries. Nothing has been presented to the Department or Royal Society. It seems the information is lost to both Empire and Crown.

14th February, 1877

My blood runs cold. I may have wronged Inessa. Her suspicions may have been well founded after all. I have taken steps to ensure he will not access any information on the Horde.

I regret her parting and the part I played in it. Every day, I relive that moment. How could I have doubted her? I hope that she will be able to forgive me.

27th February, 1877

There have been rumours of an underground Society who wish to usurp the Crown. I have been watching Mr Cranshaw. I fear he may be selling our secrets to these unknown anarchists. I have sent him to Scotland on business while I organise everything.

28th February, 1877

I have informed Liberator of my suspicions. I have been instructed to ensure the protection of all the information with respect to the undertaking. The Files are now secure. They are now hidden in the Department's Restricted Files, as ordered. There is no safer place in London.

Tillie smiled. Every muscle in her body relaxed. Inessa *hadn't* betrayed her Father. He was *not* a traitor. But she still hadn't found enough proof to take her case to the Queen, to convince her to declare it publicly.

"I *need* to find those files."

Of Files, Piles, and Rarities

The knock on the door resounded through the room. Tillie slid her transcribed notes underneath her father's green journal and slammed it shut. She straightened her robe and pulled the neckline snugly.

Saunders peeked around the partly open door. "Lord Allington wishes me to advise you that the General will be accompanying you for dinner, Miss Meriwether."

"Thank you, Saunders," she replied. "Did I miss breakfast?"

"And luncheon, Miss," said Saunders as he stepped into the room. "I did knock, but you did not reply. I thought it best not to interrupt you."

"Yes. Thank you, Saunders. Will Lord Allington be at dinner tonight?" she asked.

"Yes. He's looking forward to it. We're having his favourite, sautéed mushrooms and venison pie."

She smiled. At least it wasn't kippers again.

"Is there anything else I can do for you, Miss Meriwether?"

Tillie glanced at the papers on her vanity-desk. She had to find her father's files. If anyone would know where to look, it would be Saunders.

"Did the Department's files survive the blast?"

"Unfortunately, all the Upper Level Files were lost in the explosion," he replied.

Damnation. Tillie's shoulders dropped.

"However, we have copies here on the Lower Levels." The man did not bat an eyelid as he freely proffered the information. "And none of the Restricted Files are stored above ground."

She fixed her gaze on Saunders and rested her hand on the journal. His eyes flicked to the desk and returned to meet hers.

"I believe you will find some of the information you require in the File Room, Miss Meriwether." He smiled.

She raised an eyebrow. Not much got past him, did it?

"You do have complete Lower Level access," he said. "I can show you the way."

"Thank you Saunders." She straightened her shoulders and rose from her chair.

He glanced at the trousers over the chair and cleared his throat. "Though you may want to dress for dinner, Miss." He bowed his head. "I shall wait for you in the corridor."

"Ah, yes." She tugged the trousers off the chair and nodded. Her cheeks warmed. At least her ribs were now sufficiently healed as to allow her to tighten her own stays.

Tillie followed Saunders along the maze of corridors and through a dimly lit section of brick tunnels. They continued down a narrow side passage, until they reached a solid iron door.

He pulled a thick metal disc from his trouser pocket and slipped it into a shallow recess on the door. It grated softly as he turned it anti-clockwise. A deep clunk echoed in the confined area.

"The Lower Level File Room," announced Saunders as he swung the door open and ushered her into the darkness beyond.

Cool air touched Tillie's cheeks. Something brushed along the wall next to her. A click broke the silence. Light blazed down on them. She winced and shaded her face as her eyes adjusted to the glare.

She peered into the dimness beyond the crackling tube light. They were in a metal-walled tomb filled with rows of storage shelves with rolling ladders. Each stack skimmed the ceiling.

"I will fetch you when dinner is ready," whispered Saunders as he slipped out of the room.

The door thunked shut behind her.

Tillie smiled and surveyed the shadows at least thirty feet away.

"This could take a while," she whispered. At least she wouldn't be disturbed. "Any ideas where to start?"

<<*Restricted.*>> The Orb's reply was quick.

She tucked the da Vinci notebook under her arm and ventured forward. Her boot heels clicked on the flagged stone floor, their echo rebounding from the darkness. She frowned.

"How far does this go?"

She slowed as she approached the unlit area. The floor gave way slightly under her boot. She froze. She stood on a brass plate, depressed below the level of the flagstones.

An illumination tube-flickered on at the end of the nearest row of shelves. The rows continued for another twenty feet before the shadows consumed them. A second brass tile lay in the floor at the edge of the unlit area.

Tillie approached the tile and stepped on it. Another light crackled to life to reveal a new section of files and a wall of drawers on the far side.

She peered down each aisle as she made her way to the end of the room. At the end was a plain door fashioned in wood to match the cabinets. An engraved, four-inch brass plate heralded the end of her search. This must be it. She had found the Restricted files.

"This is it!" She placed her hand on the door and spread her fingers across the dark, carved wood. She would finally get some answers.

A quick glance revealed no obvious handle. Her hand skimmed over the panelled surface, searching for a hidden latch, gently pressing each section.

Nothing.

She studied the door and traced the edges, then tugged gently at each carved motif.

Nothing.

<<*Plate,*>> suggested the Orb.

Tillie examined the brass nameplate, and nudged the cold metal with her fingertip. It swivelled downward to reveal a hidden panel with nine numbered buttons.

She gritted her teeth. The tendons in her neck tightened, creating sharp lines on her fair skin.

"I hate number codes." She rested her head against the door. A flutter circled her heart and washed over her entire chest. Sir Avery loved number logic. The edge of her mouth curled.

<<*Thirteen.*>> The Orb's voice flitted through her thoughts. She jerked her head away from the door.

"What did you say?"

<<*Thirteen.*>>

Her finger hovered over the first button.

The Orb grew heavy; a hot wave of annoyance rolled through her consciousness. This time the Orb was more insistent: <<*One. Three.*>>

She punched the corresponding buttons.

The door opened with a click.

"How could you possibly know that?" she gasped quietly.

There was no reply.

On the floor, just inside the doorway, was another brass tile. Tillie stepped onto it. A tube crackled near the door. Another lit up at the end of the narrow chamber. Old books and boxes were crammed into wooden shelves lining the walls. Dust tickled her nose as her skirts brushed against the neglected shelves.

She ran her fingers over the book bindings and box fronts, wiping off the layers of the years to reveal their faded labels. Some were scribed with titles or names. Others were branded only with dates, some marking secrets from almost a century ago. One box with significantly less layers of dust had been wedged between two of the ancient files. She peered at its label.

She froze. Her skirts, insisting on following Newton's Third Law, swished forward and slapped against the boxes. She coughed and batted away the plume of dust.

The box was labelled *'Eustace'*.

Tillie plopped down onto the floor and squashed down her billowing yellow silk skirts so she could access the box. She wrenched the box from its resting place and removed the lid.

Inside was a treasure trove of information. There were files on various foreign and British scientists, details on various inventions and their possible uses. She leaned into the box and rummaged through layers of papers. Nestled at the bottom of the box was a pocket-sized black notebook. She slipped off its rubber band and flipped through the contents. More symbols, this time with their key.

She grinned.

The Orb jiggled against her skin.

"I know, finally a code I won't have to break. Thank you, Father!" She slipped the da Vinci notebook from one of the bustle pockets under her skirt and compared the symbols. They were different. "It doesn't match anything in this, or Father's journal." She closed the notebook and slipped the rubber band back over its cover. "Now I just have to work out what it is the key for."

The Orb stopped moving; its metal globe warmed against her skin.

<<*Listen!*>> it hissed.

Footsteps echoed faintly on the stone floor in the main file room.

"Miss Meriwether?"

"Saunders?" She stuffed the black codebook into the pocket under her skirts, shoved the files back into the box and replaced it on the shelf.

She dashed out of the room, closed the door behind her, and slipped into the next aisle, then bent down and grabbed at one of the drawers to open it. It thudded on the floor.

"Damnation. Too far!" she cursed under her breath.

The da Vinci notebook slapped onto the flagstones beside her.

She gasped and sucked in a lung full of dust as she jerked her toe clear. A tight band clenched around her chest. She spluttered, and winced as a sharp pain ricocheted along her ribs. Her hands trembled as she wrestled to insert the drawer back into the hutch.

"Ah, Miss Meriwether. I have found you." Saunders stepped into view at the end of the aisle.

She nodded. A blonde ringlet fell over her face.

"Is it time for dinner already?" she asked.

"Dinner will be served in one hour." He eyed the open drawer. "Did you find what you were looking for?" he asked.

"Not quite." She coughed; the ringlet bobbed across her cheek.

"We can return tomorrow, if you wish."

"That would be splendid." She closed the drawer and picked up the notebook as she rose to her feet.

His gaze lowered to her yellow dress. "You may want to freshen up before dinner."

"Ah, yes." She glanced down at her skirt. Grey patches of dust clung to its folds. "I shall have to get a new launderer."

Saunders stared at the drawer, leaned forward and peered at the label.

He raised an eyebrow and shook his head.

Tillie's stomach grumbled.

"Did you say something, Miss Meriwether?"

"No, Saunders. It must be your imagination."

She spun on her heel and marched back along the file stacks.

Tillie's head was reeling. The Orb urged her on. She wrote quickly on the notepaper, trying to transcribe as much of her father's journal as she could before dinner.

1st March, 1877

I fear Mr Cranshaw was the real traitor all along. Inessa was innocent. I hope one day she will forgive me. I have concocted excuses to remove him from any crucial experiments related to the Horde and have encrypted the experimental logs, as ordered.

13th March, 1877

I have now been informed of the full scope of Liberator's vision, and have been given assurances that my concerns over the new revelations will be addressed. I must finish the final tests before Cranshaw returns from the north.

Her heart skipped. Almost there... She turned to the last page. It was torn, roughly in half. Smears of ink tracked across from the furrow to a partially smudged notation scratched in the margin:

My work notes must remain hidden.
Tell Matilda I didn't--
Tell Inessa I--

Tillie groaned and gripped the nib pen in her fingers until her fingers paled. Tell Inessa what? Tell me what? That he wasn't a traitor? He didn't lie to me all those years? Frustration growled in her throat. She flipped the page and peered at the remaining journal entry:

15th March, 1877

Today is the culmination of three year's work. The apparatus is set up. I have only a few more procedures to complete. I must confess it would be less demanding work with an assistant. If the final experiment is successful...

I have been assured that no good man - no innocent man - shall suffer. I have no reason to doubt the word of my superiors. I have hidden information in Inessa's treasured copy of da Vinci's notebook, lest I be judged wrongly for my actions.

May God forgive me. May he forgive me The...

<<Horde.>>

Tillie startled at the Orb's voice. Her hand jerked sideways and knocked the inkwell across the desk.

"Damnation!"

The ink bled over the edge and dripped onto her lap, staining her robe. She thrust herself away from the desk, sending the da Vinci notebook flying to the floor with a thud. The desk chair flew backwards and cracked against the wall. She snatched her father's journal and translated notes from the desk, careful to avoid any off-cast.

Ink dribbled slowly to the floor, pooled on the rug and seeped into the edge of the red leather binding of the book that lay there.

Of Photographs, Paranoia,
and Demises

T illie held the corner of the da Vinci notebook between her fingers and gently shook it. The ink had finally stopped seeping from the leather binding. Its sheen faded as it dried. She placed the notebook on the end of the desk and blotted up the remaining ink with remnants of the magenta gown that had been shredded during the destruction of the Ascension Chamber.

She settled on the edge of the fainting couch, trying not to avail it of its stated purpose.

"That was close," she whispered.

<<More careful,>> the Orb scolded and wiggled, as if nodding.

The wall clock chimed. Saunders would soon be arriving to escort her to dinner. She puffed the loose tendril from her face and inspected her ensemble. Large patches of black ink marred the skirt, their edges feathered as they had crept outwards.

"Oh dear." She sighed. Her already restricted range of attire had diminished even further and was now restricted to one green silk dress and the more masculine garments, not suitable for polite dinner company. Her shoulders slumped. "I hope we get out of here before all I have left is a man's dressing gown."

She changed into her remaining borrowed gown and inspected herself in the tallest of the vanity mirrors. She wrinkled her nose; she missed the neatness of a compact bustle. She held her breath and tentatively pulled her stay cords tighter. Her ribs didn't complain. She let the breath escape and smiled at her improved silhouette.

"That's better."

She studied the yellow, ink-stained gown, now draped over the back of the captain's chair. No doubt, Sir Avery would remark on her carelessness with regards to her apparel. Again.

"At least the notebook was saved," she whispered.

The open notebook lay on the desk. The ink had not seeped too far along the vellum pages. The cover had almost dried. The corner curled up on the damaged edge and the inside lining of the leather cover had separated from its base.

Tillie picked up the book and examined the end sheet. A triangular corner of thin paper poked out from under the vellum lining. She ran her finger over the surface. There was something under there. She traced the edges. Something rectangular.

She tugged at the corner of the vellum. It ripped. She winced. She'd been uncomfortable with her father's defacement of the Master's genius; she'd rather not contribute to the further destruction of such a valuable historical document.

Tillie retrieved a small knife from her pocket, slid it under the vellum and worked her way along the lifted edge. She slipped her fingers between the layers and coaxed out the contents: a postcard-sized piece of thin metal inside a tattered paper cover. One corner was torn, making the photographers stamp undecipherable. She opened the cover. Inside was a folded sheet of rice paper. This was definitely not part of the original notebook.

<<*Open it!*>> urged the Orb.

"Patience." Her hands trembled as she unfolded the parcel. The wrapping paper was covered in handwritten notes, in her father's hand, as was the metallic card. More coded scribblings. She flipped the card over. It was a tintype photograph of her father, standing in his office and flanked by a dark-haired woman and a light-haired man.

<<*Murderer!*>> hissed the Orb.

Her eyes widened. The Orb had never sounded so vehement, so furious. She scrutinised the photograph.

The woman had pale eyes and dark hair. Her dress shone under the daylight streaming through the window at the edge of the photograph; an outdated dress similar in style to that which Tillie now wore. The woman beamed at the camera with a warm smile. Surely she wasn't a murderer?

Tillie studied the fair-haired man's features, almost hidden in the shadow of his square-topped grey bowler hat. He was handsome, with a strong jaw and over-sized, frizzy mutton-chops. His eyes...

She studied them with her lorgnette; his eyes were turned away from the camera towards the others in the photograph. His gaze seemed to look past her father, settling on the woman. She couldn't place the woman, but the man was vaguely familiar.

There was a knock on the door. The tintype slipped from her hand onto the desk filled with mutilated historical works, ink-stained papers, a book of codes, a secret note and, now, an old photograph. How could she explain all this to Saunders and still keep her secret?

"Just a minute." She slapped the notebook shut, scooped up the notepaper and shoved it inside the pockets under her skirts. Next was the photograph, her fingers still wrapped around the precious memento.

"Come in," she said.

She noticed Sir Avery's green eyes first. Their corners wrinkled playfully. His moustache twitched as the corners of his mouth lifted in a smile. Then it dropped and the sparkle faded from his eyes.

"Are you unwell, Miss Meriwether?" His voice was soft.

She stared into his eyes and didn't reply. The words of the Orb echoed through her mind: *Murderer.*

"You're pale." His gaze flicked over her face. "You look like you have seen a ghost."

"You know very well, there is no such thing as ghosts, Sir Avery," she replied.

"Oh dear." He stepped towards her desk.

Tillie swallowed. Had she left something behind?

"What have you done to your dress?" he asked.

She let out a slow, quiet breath.

"I shan't tease you about the fate of yet another gown, Miss Meriwether." The smile crept back over his face. "It was at least twenty years old." He winked. "Though finding suitable attire for young ladies is *not* an easy task when buried under tonnes of rubble."

"Let me escort you to dinner, Miss Meriwether." He offered her his arm.

Her heart fluttered. She was glad to see him, but would never give him the satisfaction of knowing.

Fine china rattled gently as each of the three courses edged along the centre of the table, on a moving belt of articulated metal. A faint squeak accompanied the venison pie as it trundled toward them. Though the servings were meagre due to dwindling supplies, dinner was welcome, as was the company.

Tillie savoured each mouthful, thankful the kippers had run out a few days ago.

Her stomach still grumbled. She grimaced; though famished, she ate sparingly. Her ribs ached and her stays pressed against her stomach making her queasy.

Her eyes fluttered in the direction of her dinner companions, and settled on Sir Avery who was seated directly across from her. Neither man seemed to have heard her stomach's protestations. She took a shallow breath as she shifted uncomfortably in her chair. Perhaps she had cinched her stays a little tight? She wriggled her torso and ventured another slow breath.

"Are you well, Miss Meriwether?" Sir Avery lowered his voice. "How is your... err..." His cheeks reddened. "Does it fit?" he whispered.

"Yes, thank you, Sir Avery," she replied. "All is well."

The General dabbed his moustache with his linen serviette and chuckled softly.

"I am glad Cook did not succumb to the fulmination." He raised his wine glass to his lips and smiled.

"Most definitely," said Sir Avery.

"I miss asparagus," the General sighed. "When we surface, I shall ask Cook to buy fresh asparagus."

Saunders entered the room. "Communications are ready to be tested when you are ready, Lord Allington."

"Thank you Saunders," said Sir Avery.

Saunders passed a small note to the General, nodded in Tillie's direction and took his leave.

"Excuse me." The General read the note, meticulously folded it and slipped it into the inside breast pocket of his coat. "Our men have almost broken through the rubble. We need to find our traitor. Some of the Upper Level staff have survived, but I fear we can only guarantee the loyalty of the operatives here in the Lower Levels. Any suggestions?"

"I don't like Harrow," said Tillie. "He's always hovering."

"Hovering?" Sir Avery raised an eyebrow.

"Harrow?" The General shook his head. "No, no, no. That's his job. He's my right-hand man, head of Security. Been with us for years. There has never been any question of his loyalty." The General looked up at the ceiling and sighed. "Let us hope, for all our sakes, that he escaped the blast."

"But there's not much damage he can do in the Upper Levels, is there?" she asked.

The General didn't reply. All three silently regarded the ceiling.

Then, as if a toggle had been thrown, Sir Avery's attention snapped back to the dining table. He picked up his wine glass, took a sip and declared: "I think The Inventor is behind it."

The General followed suit, glass in hand, now seemingly oblivious to both her and the death that lay above them.

"Ah yes, but who is he working for?" he said.

Tillie regarded the two men. She peered over her glass, listening to their theories on potential traitors and who could be responsible for such anarchy, but always returning to the question of the Inventor's identity.

<<They've forgotten I'm here, haven't they?>> she asked the Orb.

The Orb twitched under her bodice.

"Tell me more about this *Inventor*," she said.

Both men paused mid-sentence and stared at her.

"Ah, Miss Meriwether." Sir Avery cleared his throat.

"There is no reason for you not to know. You *do* have Lower Level clearance." said the General. "He is a rival of the Department, and an enemy of the Empire. It's rumoured he worked on unsanctioned experiments with a scientist of our employ, a Professor Nathaniel Kempthorne."

She sucked in a sharp breath. *Father?*

"He was a traitor to the Department," said the General.

Sir Avery's knife clattered on his plate. "I've read the reports. There's not a lot of detail about the experiments."

Tillie slipped her hand under her skirts and into the hidden pocket. Her fingers clutched at the photograph. Surely, they knew her father was working for The Queen?

"He left about nine years ago. Before you arrived, Allington. Her Majesty ordered the information remain restricted." The General shook his head. "Diabolical experiments. He betrayed us..."

Tillie's scream caught in her throat. Her father would never betray the Queen, or the Department. It was Cranshaw. He was the traitor. She closed her eyes and let the air slowly escape her lungs.

"...and then was betrayed himself. His notes were never found; all the records were destroyed."

"And his assistant?" asked Sir Avery.

"Disappeared. There was a rumour he'd gone back to Australia." The General gulped down the last of his wine. "We don't know for sure. No one knows what he looks like."

"Then how do you know he is this Inventor?" asked Sir Avery.

"Ah, that's the curious thing. We received a communication from the Inventor. He claimed Kempthorne's work as his own, named specific details, warned us to take his demands seriously."

"Demands?"

"The blaggard wanted us to return Kempthorne's notes." The General poured himself another drink. "Even if we did have them, we'd never release them to a murderer."

Murderer? Tillie's heart twisted in her chest and froze. Each breath was more difficult than the last. Cranshaw had murdered her father? She wanted to scream, to shake them both until they listened: Cranshaw was the Inventor! *He* was the traitor, not her father. How could she make them understand?

She clutched the photograph, until the corners dug into her fingers. She fought the urge to thrust the photograph in their faces. But she'd have to explain how it came into her possession, how she knew the identity of those in it. They considered her father a traitor, and she would become the traitor's daughter.

The Orb squirmed. She felt its reluctance... No, there was something else. She felt a deathly chill against her skin. Fear. With the General's cane so close, it dare not reveal its presence. Its anxiety bled into her thoughts.

Her heart pounded. Her throat was dry. She clenched her teeth. She was *not* a traitor's daughter. She would *not* be defined by their misjudgement. She dug her fingernails into her palm.

But a photo didn't prove innocence.

Her other hand swooped up her wine glass. She swallowed some liquid calm and allowed her fingers to relax. She just needed more evidence.

All motion in the room seemed to slow. The men's voices slurred in her mind. The Orb's anxiety dulled until it was like a bee buzzing at the edges of consciousness.

She longed to confide in Sir Avery. She needed him to know the truth of it - of her family, of herself. She detested lying, especially to him.

"...presumptuous of an assistant," scoffed Sir Avery.

"Once a traitor, always a traitor," said the General. "Our information suggests he is currently working with a group of anarchists."

"I favour The Society," said Sir Avery. "It has their mark on it."

"That is still conjecture, Allington. We need facts." The General took a long sip of his wine. "But I agree. They excel at puffing themselves up above their station, and would pull down the rest of civilised society to do it."

Once a traitor. The words stung. She couldn't let Sir Avery know who she was. Not yet. She would *not* be branded a traitor's daughter.

A panel in the far wall slid open with a thunk. A hinged arm extruded itself from the cavity hidden behind. It slowly unfolded, deposited its load onto the table and snapped back into its hiding place. The hatch door slid shut. A silver platter slid onto the conveyancing belt and glided towards them.

Sir Avery inhaled deeply and grinned, now distracted him from conversation.

"Ah, dessert!" General Sabine leaned forward to snatch the platter from the mechanical runner. "What is your preference, Miss Meriwether?"

Tillie lowered her wine glass with deliberate languidness. The lusciously thick aroma of butter, sugared fruits and fresh pastry wafted upwards as the sweets passed. She retrieved a fruit-filled turnover with perfect flaky pastry. She nodded and smiled sweetly in the General's direction.

"Cook has excelled herself, yet again." Sir Avery ate his pastry and wiped a stray smudge of whipped cream from his moustache's extremities.

"I must take my leave now." The General's chair scraped as he rose from the table. "I have business to attend to. I'll meet you both in the Communications Room in, say..." He consulted his pocket watch. "Two hours?"

"Excellent," replied Sir Avery.

The door clicked shut behind the General.

An almighty roar reverberated through her head. She winced.

<<*Not traitor!*>> The Orb's screeched.

Tillie held her breath and waited for the onslaught to pass.

"You look as pale as one of those *Ghostmen*." Sir Avery placed his hand on hers. "Please, let me fetch the doctor."

She felt the warmth of his hand penetrate her skin. Her heart slowed. A wave of calm radiated over her chest and pushed the colour back into her cheeks. She shook her head.

"Then please tell me what is wrong, so I may be of some assistance."

She bowed her head to mask the tear that rolled down her face. She could not bear it if he thought ill of her.

"Migraine," she whispered.

Of Manipulations, Revelations, and Reunions

Harrow cradled his tea cup in both hands. There was no need to adhere to strict etiquette when closeted away for hours. Waiting.

He stared at the contraption before him: a small telegraph machine modified with alphabetical keys on one side. Several wires fed into a second machine equipped with a maze of levered buttons which hovered above a curved cylinder of paper.

Its design was based on the communication device developed by the Department of Curiosities. It had been easy to recreate the construction and, though not as sophisticated, it had served exceptionally well at intercepting the coded messages from the surviving operatives of the Department.

He scanned the list of names in a notebook on his desk. A couple had been crossed out. *Eliminated.* Top of the list was Mr Jackson, Bot mechanic, and he who would be blamed for the assassination attempt on the Queen, if questions were asked.

Harrow tapped the side of the teapot with the tips of his fingers. Still hot. He smiled, poured a fresh cup of black tea and sipped it. He swirled the liquid around his mouth and swallowed.

He waited. Still nothing; *hours* of nothing.

He ran his lip along the rim of the cup. It caught on the smooth fine china, dragged for a moment and snapped away.

Still nothing.

A single tap of a key broke the silence. Harrow's eyes flicked toward the cylinder. A single black mark blemished the surface of the paper-covered brass cylinder.

He put down his cup and waited for another key to fall. Nothing. He sighed and retrieved his cup. Another sip of tea. Still warm.

Tap, tap.

His attention returned to the device. A single lever quivered as it hovered mid-air before falling onto the cylinder.

Tap, tap, tap. The keys now rose and fell regularly, leaving their mark on the paper.

Harrow craned his head to read the message through the flurry of key strokes.

Attention all operatives.

Explosion survived. Assemble secondary site. Will confirm our arrival time within twenty four hours.

General Sabine.

Harrow's eyes widened. The corners of his mouth dropped.

"They survived?" They should have all perished. No one had followed him out of the smoke and flames as the Department's headquarters crumbled. He was certain. He'd waited for almost an hour, watching the building as it groaned and died. *How* had they survived?

He tore the sheet of paper from the machine's metal carcass. His hand shook as he folded the note unevenly and stuffed the message into his coat pocket. He gulped the remnants of his tea and wished it had been something stronger. He had to report the news. He had no choice.

He closed his eyes, took a deep breath and let it escape. Another deep breath; this time he held it until his lungs felt they would burst. He spluttered as he exhaled. He took another breath and frowned.

He snatched the list of names from the notebook and crushed it in his fist as he marched back along the dimly lit corridors towards his father's office.

"Sir, I don't understand how they could have survived the explosion." Harrow's voice was muffled. He fumbled with his protective mask and avoided his father's gaze.

"And yet they did, Harrow."

"You were there. You saw it. There must be tunnels," he suggested. "It's the only explanation."

"Perhaps the files I require are there as well?"

Harrow raised his eyes towards his superior, but avoided meeting his accusatory stare.

"You're not sending me back?" he whispered.

"Your assignment is incomplete."

"But, sir..."

"I need those files, Harrow," hissed the Professor, "and I require the return of the da Vinci notebook they stole from me."

"But they will track the Bot," said Harrow.

"You have their dead mechanic to provide a credible alternative, and shift any suspicion."

"Brown knows I delivered that Bot. They will check."

"Then you had better eliminate Mr Brown." The Professor glanced over the message again. "I doubt the Department will interview him before Sabine has regrouped his men. He'll want to assess his losses before organising his next offensive. Old habits die hard."

"The guards will be on alert." Harrow scowled. For once he was grateful for the concealment of the enforced linen mask. "After your men's failed assassination attempt."

"You are still a member of the Department of Curiosities. You have a valid reason to return to the scene to investigate." The Professor's teeth flashed as he smiled. "I am sure you can conjure up the appropriate papers to get close enough to signal your precious Bot." He leaned back into his chair. "I assume you built in a failsafe self-destruct programme."

"Yes, sir."

"Good. Then there's no need to tarry any longer. You will eliminate your loose ends and return to the Department to resume your position, retrieve the files *and* my notebook." The Professor interlocked his fingers and twiddled his thumbs. "That is all, Harrow."

A lank lock of hair fell over Harrow's forehead. Rain drops trickled down the lens of his spectacles and obscured his view of the path ahead. He wiped the glass with his handkerchief. Water dripped on the leaves around him, the constant beat almost masking the sounds of movement ahead. He remained hidden in the undergrowth.

Much to the amusement of Court, Mr Brown had taken to patrolling the Castle grounds nightly, only to return in the early morning hours, drenched from the rain. *Much to-do for a sprained ankle,* they whispered. *Paranoia,* said some.

True, Brown was overly suspicious, and exceedingly zealous when it came to the Queen's person. He was her loyal Scottish terrier, unwilling to drop his bone once his teeth had latched on.

Harrow knew Brown had wanted to sink his teeth into him from the day they met; he had recognised the animosity in the Scot's eye. Neither man trusted the other, having instinctively sniffed out opposing loyalties.

A faint snap of a twig broke the silence. Harrow twitched. He flicked his wrist. A hand crossbow slid out from under his sleeve. He locked the firearm in place and pushed a small button on its shaft. Four brass bolts revolved into position. The first bolt clicked home. His finger hovered over the trigger.

A gust of wind whipped the branches above him. A flurry of droplets swirled around his head and were deposited on his face. A large drizzle dumped down his neck and trickled under his collar. He mopped his spectacles and brushed the wayward tendril from his forehead, yet again.

Shadows danced over the ground in the fading light. They flitted across the path before him.

Another crack.

His finger flinched, sending a bolt flying into the bushes. He mouthed a silent curse and clicked the second bolt into place. He peered through the haze of the rain storm.

The bushes remained still.

Harrow wrapped his fingers around the small remote device in his vest pocket. The Bot's deactivation signal had a limited range. He could not afford to linger. He had to reach the inner wall of the castle before the next guard patrol was due.

He raised his crossbow to eye level, crept from his concealment and worked his way along the edge of the rough path, clinging to the shadows beneath the trees.

Leaves rustled behind him. His gaze skimmed a low line of bushes along the path. He fancied he saw a flash of light - something silver - and maybe a hint of grey amongst the lengthening shadows.

He slipped behind a tree trunk, retrieved a halfpenny from his trouser pocket and tossed it into the thicket. The leaves shivered.

He waited.

The crest of a grey bowler glided along the crest of the thicket and dipped from sight.

Harrow cursed under his breath. The Society had sent someone to make sure he got the job done. He tapped his finger on the crossbow. He'd wasted enough time. He stepped out onto the path and turned towards the hidden Man in Grey, tipped his hat and strode towards the castle.

The downpour had settled down to a constant drizzle. The outer stone wall of the Castle provided some shelter from the wind's fury. Intermittent squalls whistled though the woodland and stung his cheeks.

He checked his pocket watch. Ten minutes. His stomach lurched; the next guard patrol would pass by soon. He activated his Ascending Gear, scuttled up the wall on the metal telescopic legs and stepped effortlessly onto the top of the wall.

A couple of Bots trundled past seemingly oblivious to his presence. He ran his finger over the cog-shaped badge on his lapel and grinned - working for The Department did provide some benefits - then scurried off.

Once he'd reached the cover of the inner wall, he took out the Bot's Remote Activation Device and unfolded a ring of metal at the top of the box. On the device's face were two gauges. Harrow twiddled a dial on one end and waved the device to scan the area. A red needle flickered on the main gauge. He frowned and made a second sweep. The needle snapped to one side.

He flipped a switch on the side of the device. The needle on the second, smaller gauge flicked in the opposite direction. He chuckled, folded up the circular antenna and pocketed the device as he made his way back towards the outer wall.

A distant rumble echoed through the trees. Crashing sounds caught up on the wind gusts. He raised an eyebrow. The thought of the Man in Grey being chased through the woods was extremely gratifying. Perhaps The Society wasn't as infallible as their reputation suggested?

He ducked behind a bush at the edge of a clearing and scanned the

nearby area.

An unseasonal wind chilled the forest, obliterating the new spring leaves and renewing the autumnal drifts across the forest floor. Winter had returned to Windsor. Patches of the discarded jewels of Windsor's wild garden glowed ruby and gold on the forest floor as the last of the sun's light flickered through the canopy; a long shadow crept into the glade, consuming their glory.

The din grew louder. Brown blundered into the clearing, his shotgun at chest level. His ginger mutton-chop sideburns wiggled as he ground his teeth.

"I know you're out here," he announced in a thick Scots accent. "You should nae bothered blowing up your wee pet. I still have the papers." The barrel of his gun followed his gaze as he squinted into the undergrowth. "I will ensure your masters will know you for the traitor you are, Harrow."

Brown sniffed the air, ever his Mistress's little terrier. Harrow remained still. This wind was to his advantage, playing havoc with any tracking skill.

Brown sneered.

Harrow smiled. He slowly cocked the bolt on his crossbow.

A sudden calm in the gale provided a temporary hush. Brown spun in Harrow's direction and twisted to dodge the crossbow bolt as it sailed past his torso.

Damn!

"Sneaking up from behind?" Brown chuckled. "Never can trust a coward."

Harrow tucked and rolled into the clearing, as the shotgun fired into the bushes where he'd hidden. Debris lashed at his coat. His bowler dislodged and fell into a pile of wet leaves.

"I never did trust mechanicals." Brown flicked open his shotgun, rammed fresh ammunition home and snapped the gun shut. "I only trust my own eyes. And my eyes tell me that you are a coward as well as a traitor." He raised his gun and took aim.

Harrow's bolt loosed first, and lodged itself in Brown's forearm. Brown flinched, knocking his shotgun barrel off target. He lunged forward to grab Harrow's wrist, wrenched the crossbow loose and sent the final bolt flying harmlessly into a nearby tree.

Harrow scowled and slammed his forearm into the side of Brown's head. The crossbow's metal track sliced into Brown's skin as the weapon's strap broke. It fell to the ground with a wet thud.

Brown roared and swung back wildly; his fist whistled past Harrow's face.

Harrow chuckled and launched himself at his opponent. The butt of Brown's gun connected with his face. The crack echoed through Harrow's skull. His nose throbbed in pain. He swept his leg around and smashed it into the back of Brown's knee.

Brown bellowed as he fell to the ground. He slammed the metal shotgun barrel up into Harrow's chin, smashing his teeth together. Harrow toppled sidewards under the momentum. Brown grunted and thrust his boot into Harrow's groin. Harrow screamed in pain. His vision blurred. Brown rolled out of reach and dragged himself back onto his knees.

"You don't get to leave," hissed Harrow.

He scrabbled toward his opponent. He lunged at Brown's arm, grabbed the exposed end of his crossbow bolt and yanked the Scotsman to the ground, then flung out his arm and groped the ground for the shotgun. Instead, his fingers slammed into a jagged rock. He snorted, snatched up the opportune weapon and delivered a squelching blow to Brown's temple.

A half-smile flickered over his lips as he tossed the bloodied rock toward the trees at the edge of the clearing. It landed on the wet turf with a thud.

Brown's eyelids flickered. His breathing was shallow and ragged.

Harrow took a deep breath. He couldn't allow the man to live, couldn't risk him sharing his knowledge. He leaned forward. His fingers encircled the Scotsman's throat and squeezed.

Harrow rocked up onto his haunches. It was done.

He rose to his feet, as he scanned the path and the surrounding woodland. There was no sign of the alerted guard or his grey-bowlered stalker.

He examined his gloves. They were streaked with mud. Fresh blood had already seeped into the stitching. He clicked his tongue. A waste of a good pair of kid gloves.

A rivulet of warm blood trickled from his nose. He turned his hand to find a virgin spot of leather and dabbed one nostril with the back of his hand.

Leaves rustled behind him. He snatched up the shotgun and spun to face the intruder. The Man in Grey stepped out of the bushes, tipped his hat in Harrow's direction and surveyed the clearing.

"Good evening, Mr Harrow." The Man in Grey eyed Brown's body. His gaze lingered.

"Sir?" Harrow rose to his feet and brushed leaf litter from his trousers.

"I'm here to check on our investment. I sincerely hope you do not fail us, Harrow." His gaze darted back along the path. He flashed his white teeth and slipped back into the shrubbery.

Harrow scanned the undergrowth. The sun had finally set, cloaking the path in darkness. He tilted his head and listened. Nothing.

He dragged Brown's corpse toward the protection of the trees and kicked fallen leaves over the body.

Another breeze caught a tendril of hair, whipped at Harrow's forehead and caught his bowler, rolling it toward Brown's makeshift cairn.

Wind gusts rattled the canopy. Faint cries piggy-backed on each gust.

Harrow swallowed and glanced back toward the castle. An orange glow flickered across the low clouds. He needed time to escape.

He retrieved his hat, pushed back the strand of hair and secured it under the inner band.

The wind strengthened, lifted the fallen leaves from the burial mound and hurled them at his face. The surrounding trees shivered, adding more shrapnel to the bombardment. The flurry of leaves encircled him, tightening their grip as the wind whipped furiously.

He dashed back into the clearing and recovered his crossbow. It had snapped, shattering jagged splinters of wood around it. He ran his hand over the carpet of leaves. There was no sign of the string.

Flickering lights bobbed amongst the swaying trees, edging ever closer. He had run out of time.

Harrow grumbled under his breath and stalked off in the direction of Brown's quarters. There could be no loose ends. He fumbled in his coat pocket. His fingers wrapped around a small incendiary device. He must not fail.

The roof aperture of the subterranean room remained closed to the dark, silencing the unseasonal gales that raged above. Wayward branches scratched and tapped the dome.

Harrow sat near the doorway, waiting for the Professor to finish his business and allow him to report and receive an inevitable reprimand. He tapped his fingers on the smooth, polished wood of the chair and examined the tapestry upholstery. Jacobean, rumoured to have belonged to King James himself. His father liked expensive things. Even more so, if they carried provenance. They made him look important, feel important.

He eyed the canvas-shrouded chair in the far corner of the room. A bronze boot tip gleamed as it peeked out from under its folds. Harrow pursed his lips and seethed. His father also liked keeping secrets.

The Professor's raised voice filled the room. He sat at his desk, which in turn sat on a low dais, raising him above the rest of the room. The corner of his lip curled up in smug satisfaction as he looked down upon The Society's representative.

The grey-suited visitor stood at the base of the dais and leaned toward the desk, in order to converse without being overheard. His obligatory surgical mask bobbed up and down as he spoke quickly. Harrow cocked his head, straining to hear the conversation, his lip-reading skills having been rendered useless.

The Professor said little. The Man in Grey whispered in short bursts, with only the occasional word rising above the insistent murmuring: *Failure. Discovery. Notebook. Promises.*

The delegate's gaze flicked in Harrow's direction. His eyelids narrowed. Harrow heard his name. He returned the glare, direct and unblinking. He had done as instructed; he would not be blamed for the incompetence of others.

The Man in Grey took a step back, raised his chin and straightened his shoulders.

"You have one week to report on your progress with the prototype," he said.

The corner of the Professor's lip dropped slightly. His eyelid flickered.

"Is there a problem?" asked the Man in Grey.

"None," said the Professor. He flashed a bland smile.

"One week." The delegate's finger gently tapped his grey bowler as he turned on his boot heel, wrenched the linen mask from his face and strode out of the room. The mask fluttered to the floor at Harrow's feet.

"Harrow." His superior's voice was crisp and clipped.

Harrow twitched and sat bolt upright. His spine pressed against the tall back of the chair. He sucked in a quick breath. He traced his fingers along the smooth polished wood and exhaled a controlled breath.

The Professor pointed to the medical mask in Harrow's lap.

Harrow wrapped its cords around his ears, adjusted the linen mask and approached under the watchful eye of his superior. He stood in silence and braced himself for yet another verbal onslaught.

"The Society is not impressed with your handling of the Brown affair."

"They had a man in the grounds." Harrow snorted. "If they don't trust us, they should do their own dirty work."

"Burning down his lodge in the pouring rain was a miscalculation. She will know we're trying to hide something."

"*She* doesn't know who we are, sir," he replied. "Fire purifies everything. The Bot is destroyed. The paperwork is gone. There is nothing left to track to us... unless your men were identified, and that is not my fault."

"What if someone remembers you?" The Professor drummed his fingers on the lacquered wood desktop.

"I've only ever dealt with Brown," he replied. "He wouldn't admit he broke the strict rules against mechanicals in the castle, even if it was to protect *Her*."

"They will inquire within the Department," the Professor insisted. "What if they trace it back to me?"

"If we are diligent, we can lay this solely at The Society's door," he replied. "They are the known anarchists. You are merely..." Harrow paused for effect, "a rival scientist. There is no way they can connect you with The Society, is there?"

Harrow's gaze locked onto his father's eyes. There was doubt there. His heart fluttered. Good. All was going to plan. It wouldn't be long before he would gain control over his father's domain.

The Professor's shallow breaths quickened.

Harrow smiled under his mask. His father's paranoia was his weakness; it gave him an advantage, gave him control. Every time he resolved one of his father's anxieties, he gained leverage and became less dispensable.

"I've planned for that possibility, sir." He tossed a string-bound dossier onto the desk. "Here are additional files destined for the Department's records. They name the mechanic who built the Bots, Mr Jackson, as the one who delivered them to Windsor."

The Professor fiddled with the string on the package. His breathing slowed. "Excellent thinking." he said.

Harrow needed him to break if he was to assume his position. Just one more prod...

A hissing sound trickled down the metal tube that trailed the room's central spiral staircase. The message slipped out of the tube with a loud pop and fell onto the edge of the desk.

Harrow cursed under his breath. The moment was gone.

The Professor shook his head and blinked. He unrolled the scroll slowly. The gleam returned to his eye.

"Communications have intercepted a message from the General," he said. "Their men have finally broken through to the surface. Surviving operatives are to meet at Hyde Park, tomorrow at noon." He placed his elbows on the desk, interlocked his fingers and regarded his treasure: the covered chair in the corner with the bronze boot tip peeking out from under the canvas. A smile flashed over his lips.

Harrow's fingers twitched. One day he would lift that canvas and know his father's secret.

"The Society is not happy with the progress of your cypher machine. Its inability to crack the Kempthorne code has slowed progress on the prototype. We have less than a week to decode those experiment notes. I need the da Vinci notebook. It has to be part of the key!"

The Professor returned his gaze to Harrow.

"That meddling girl stole it from me. She *must* know something," he hissed. "Find out what she knows, and report back immediately."

Harrow clenched his fists.

"One week, Harrow. The Society has given us one week." The Professor's hands slumped to the desk with a thump. "You know what they do to traitors, don't you?"

Of Relocations, Meetings,
and Introductions

It was early evening by the time enough rubble had been cleared to allow the Department's surviving members to walk free of their entombment. Tillie emerged, wrapped in a blanket to hide her borrowed garb and unkempt appearance as much as to protect herself from the cold evening air.

Sir Avery studied her face in the moonlight.

"You look pale, Miss Meriwether. I think you've been out of the sun for too long."

"Not by choice," she replied.

He grinned. "Have you ever been to the seaside?" he asked.

Tillie nodded. She remembered playing in the sand as a child. Not in England, but Egypt, during one of the many adventures with her father. She adored Egypt.

"We could take the train to Southend," he said.

Her gaze dropped to the floor. Not Egypt?

<<*Not Egypt,*>> said the Orb.

"How thoughtless of me, Miss Meriwether." The corner of Sir

Avery's moustache drooped. "You must be exhausted after such an ordeal. I shall have to get you home to a comfortable bed." He offered her his arm.

"Should you?" she said, trying to hide a smirk.

"What I meant was..." Sir Avery dropped his arm. His face glowed red.

Tillie smiled. Egypt could wait for another day.

Tillie had longed for a hot bath; after almost two weeks trapped underground, she didn't mind where it was. She ran her washcloth along her bare leg. Warm water trickled down her calf.

Grace stepped up to the edge of the bath. Steam rose from the metal container she carried.

"Careful, Miss."

Tillie slipped her leg back under the surface. The hot water enveloped her. Her torso muscles relaxed, relieving the pressure on her ribs. They'd ached less with each passing day, allowing her to tighten her stays, but it was still difficult to lace them properly herself.

Grace laid out her underthings on the bed.

Tillie smiled; she'd missed the crispness of clean linens and was grateful to have Grace in attendance. She was also grateful not to be rattling around her aunt's empty house on her own. Most of all she was relieved to wear a gown, in any colour but cream or pale green.

By ten o'clock, she was ready to face the world, dressed in proper attire: a resplendent purple silk gown, her fully-equipped multi-functional bustle and Aunt Prudence's sturdy red parasol. She strode along the hallway towards the dining room, ignoring the Bots that skittered around the hallway and the Orb that complained around her neck. She was excited at the prospect of a hearty breakfast - at Sir Avery's expense.

He accompanied her to Hyde Park, where the surviving members of the Department of Curiosities had assembled as ordered by the General. They were searched, all credentials verified and alibis evidenced. Once processed, they were assigned carriage transport to their final destination.

It had been a long carriage ride across the Thames to a most unexpected destination.

Tillie studied the terrace houses on three sides of the orphanage grounds. Workmen scurried in and out of buildings as they unloaded crates off nearby carts as they ferried equipment to partially complete buildings on the unfinished side of the quadrangle.

She rested her gloved hand on Sir Avery's arm, as they strode along the path that edged the extensive courtyard. Gravel crunched underfoot. A tall, modestly-dressed woman glanced in their direction and entered one of the villas.

To Tillie's surprise, no one questioned their presence. The ongoing construction was quite advantageous. Even the orphans appeared to have grown bored watching the comings and goings and now busied themselves with wiping away the nose-smudges from the upper floor windows.

Tillie and Sir Avery continued their stroll toward the buildings on the far side of the green. A balding, sun-scarred man looked up from his gardening. He flashed a half-toothless smile and tipped his hat.

"Mornin'," he said.

"Good morning," said Sir Avery.

"You come to inspect the new work, then?" asked the gardener.

"Yes," replied Tillie.

"The rest of 'em went along to the new Master's house," said the gardener. "The one with the bicycle out front."

Tillie looked in the direction indicated by his grimy finger. A row of nearly-completed terrace houses stretched part-way across the final edge of the quadrangle. When complete, the ring of protective buildings would conceal the grounds from the outside world.

She scanned the length of construction in admiration. Very convenient.

<<*Very expensive,*>> said The Orb.

<<*But it provides a home to the orphans,*>> she replied.

<<*What cost?*>> asked the Orb.

<<*Don't be a snob. They deserve a chance to improve their station in life,*>> she replied, knowing that wasn't what the Orb had meant.

They paraded along the length of the buildings, feigning interest in the Gothic window arches, until they reached a partially built villa near the far end. Once inside the Master's house, safely hidden from prying eyes, a workman checked their papers and escorted them to an Ascension Chamber.

Tillie swallowed as she stepped inside. Her hand hovered above the lever. Her eyes skimmed over the walls and roof of the cramped room. Sir Avery placed his hand on hers and guided it onto the handle.

"It's safe," he whispered.

"You've said that before," she replied.

"It's been inspected. Trust me. It *is* safe." The edges of his groomed moustache lifted. His deep voice was reassuring.

She took a deep breath, nodded and pushed down on the lever.

The chamber descended slowly and rocked as it touched bottom.

Tillie stepped into a small antechamber with dark wooden panelling. A network of narrow tunnels snaked southward, away from the buildings' foundations. Workmen scurried along the tunnels transporting equipment, files and boxes to unseen parts of the new refuge.

"Welcome, Lord Allington," said a familiar voice.

"Good to see you, Saunders." Sir Avery grinned. "Has the General arrived?"

"He's waiting for you in the bunker," replied Saunders. "Please, follow me."

Saunders' footsteps echoed as they followed him along a vacant corridor, and through the maze of tunnels to an unadorned metal door.

General Sabine sat at his ornate desk. His calligraphed credentials already hung on the wall next to him. His cane leaned against his chair, never far from his sight.

He waved Tillie and Sir Avery into his new office and motioned them in the direction of a pair of deep-upholstered leather chairs near his desk.

She raised an eyebrow. The armchairs would have looked more at home in front of a roaring fireplace than in this concrete-lined subterranean bunker.

Large tapestry rugs covered the floor. A fully-stocked bookshelf occupied the wall behind her. An over-sized painting of Queen Victoria hung behind the General's desk; its eyes stared at her.

She flicked her gaze away from the portrait and studied the illumination tube installed above the General's desk. It cast a harsh glow over the room. She sighed. A warm fireplace would have been preferable.

The Orb's chain twitched around her neck. It grew cold against her skin, and stopped moving. She glanced at the walking cane, smiled and nestled into the cushioned leather as far as her bustle would allow.

The General looked up from his papers. Deep lines burrowed around his mouth; he seemed to have aged considerably overnight.

"There was an incident while we were trapped in the Lower Levels." His voice was gravelly and his eyelids heavy, as if he hadn't slept. "There's no doubt the explosion was orchestrated as a diversion and to keep us out of the way, if not to eliminate us entirely." He straightened his back and looked Sir Avery directly in the eye. "Someone has tried to assassinate the Queen."

Tillie gasped. Her hand clutched at her chest where she'd concealed the Queen's note in her stays. Sir Avery's moustache twitched. His fingers dug into the soft leather on the arm of his chair.

"Her Majesty's guards caught one of the men." The General glanced at Tillie. "Seems he's one of your Ghostmen, Miss Meriwether."

She remembered their paled flesh and haunting eyes. Her skin crawled. She frowned and shook her head. "They are not *my* Ghostmen," she whispered.

"He means the ones that attacked you," said Sir Avery.

"Is She... Is Her Majesty injured?" she asked.

"Injured, but alive," replied the General. "Court was informed She had an accident and fell down the stairs."

Tillie's fingers relaxed. It would not do to have her benefactor struck down before she could complete her assignment.

"The Society?" Sir Avery's grip on the chair's arm tightened until his knuckles paled.

"We don't know for sure, but it's suspected they are behind the plot."

"Let me question him," Sir Avery glared at the Queen's portrait. "He'll talk eventually."

"Unfortunately not," replied the General. "His tongue had been removed. *And* he is dead."

Tillie screwed up her nose. "How awful!"

"I am sorry, my dear. The Society isn't constrained by civilised behaviour. They are anarchists."

"And our traitor was most likely in their employ," said Sir Avery.

"And still is," said the General. "Saunders thinks someone has been intercepting our communications. If this is true, it means they have not finished with their plans."

Sir Avery eyed Tillie, then regarded the Royal portrait behind the General.

"Hence the alternative meeting place and the security." she nodded.

"Yes. It seems the traitor survived the explosion-- "

"Or we have two renegades in the Department," said Sir Avery.

Two? She frowned. The Orb had hinted as much.

The General nodded. "Either way, we must be vigilant. We cannot set up at our final command post until our traitor, or traitors, are caught."

Sir Avery dragged his eyes away from the painting. "If the Ghostmen do work for The Society, I wonder why they were trying to kill you, Miss Meriwether?"

The Orb fluttered near her breast. Her own heart fluttered in response. Had the Society discovered she was secretly working for the Queen? Had the General found out? Her heart raced. She'd been instructed to tell no one, not even the Department.

She avoided Sir Avery's gaze and swallowed.

<<*Calm down, he can't possibly know,*>> she replied. She waved her hand towards the doorway, and the labyrinth beyond, determined to change the subject. "I am impressed with the efficiency of the Department," she said. "To have all of this ready in such a short time."

Sir Avery eyed her and pinched his lower lip.

"The Bunker was one of our peripheral work stations. I don't think the engineers are happy we have taken over, albeit temporarily," said the General.

"Engineers?" She leaned forward.

"Yes," replied the General. "We have several larger projects being constructed. Little Nessie is one of them."

"Little Nessie?" asked Tillie.

The two men exchanged glances. The General nodded.

"Our dirigible," replied Sir Avery.

"Your..." She clasped her hands together and she edged further forward. "You have a dirigible! I've never seen a real one. But I thought--" She frowned. "The Embargo? Isn't it prohibited to fly over

London since the Dirigible War?"

"Technically." The corner of Sir Avery's eyes crinkled.

"We have Her Majesty's authority," said the General. "Information is restricted. Few in the Department know it exists."

"Then why tell me?"

"You have the required clearance, my dear." The General leaned forward. "But it is not to be mentioned outside this room. Is that understood? Lower Level Clearance only."

She nodded, and bit her lip to hide her grin.

"Can I see it?" she asked.

She never received an answer. A loud knock on the door diverted the General's attention.

"Mr Harrow has rejoined us," Saunders announced.

Harrow stepped into the room. A frown flashed across his forehead, seemingly unnoticed by either the General or Sir Avery. Harrow leered at Saunders. Tillie studied Harrow; there was no recognition in his eyes.

"Good to see you are safe, Harrow," said the General.

"Thank you, sir." Harrow bowed his head. His eyes narrowed as Saunders passed a folded note to their superior.

Saunders excused himself to return to his duties.

The General opened the missive. His mouth hardened.

"I don't think I have met Mr Saunders before," Harrow said.

"No." The General beckoned Harrow closer with a wave of his hand.

"I didn't know this bunker existed." Harrow stepped closer to the desk. "How many more have we?"

"It's not important," replied the General, his eyes remaining fixed on the note.

"Why was I not told?" asked Harrow.

"You did not need to know." The General folded up the note and placed it on the desk.

"But I am second in charge."

"You will report to Saunders, for now."

"Did he know?" asked Harrow.

"He organised it," replied the General.

Tillie noticed Harrow's jaw muscles tighten. He wasn't happy. She didn't have time for his games. She had too many other questions.

"You look puzzled, Miss Meriwether. I suppose you are wondering: *why an orphanage?*" The General smiled and switched conversations as if the topics hadn't altered.

She turned her attention to the General. "Yes, I was curious," she replied.

"Well, it was unexpected, was it not?" He chuckled. "This is only a temporary base of operations, however, it has afforded one unexpected bonus." He leaned back in his chair. "Some of the boys have proved to be exceptionally intelligent. We've decided to train a select few as Department operatives."

Harrow roused himself from his brooding and raised an eyebrow. "Very fortuitous."

"Yes." The General regarded Harrow. "How is the Queen?" he asked.

Harrow glanced towards the Queen's portrait, then shifted his attention to the General's desk. "I have heard reports she had an accident, sir. The doctor said she fell down some stairs. She is well otherwise."

The General nodded. "It was not an accident, Harrow." He picked up the message and tucked it into his coat pocket.

"Sir?" asked Harrow.

"Someone tried to assassinate the Queen," said the General.

"Do we know who, sir?"

"One of them was captured."

"Then we can find out who was behind the attempt."

"Killed, unfortunately," said Sir Avery.

Harrow bowed his head, for a just a moment. When he raised it, his demeanour had changed; he seemed more furtive, more apologetic, like a school boy who had been caught out. Neither the General nor Sir Avery seemed to notice. They seemed too intent on analysing the assassination attempt.

Tillie frowned.

"Sir, had I known, I could have been of assistance," said Harrow.

"How were you to know, Harrow?" asked the General.

"I should have realised the explosion could've been a diversion, sir." He pushed his spectacles firmly onto the bridge of his nose and backed away from the desk.

"There was no hint of a planned assassination attempt, and you had the survival of the Department as your priority," said the General. "Your current priority is to find the mastermind behind the plot. Who runs these Ghostmen?"

"Ghostmen?" Harrow's stance stiffened.

"Miss Meriwether has called them Ghostmen," replied the General.

"I want to know how they infiltrated the castle grounds?" said Sir Avery.

"Dirigible?" said Tillie with a gleam in her eye.

Sir Avery cleared his throat and rested his hand gently on her arm.

"The Empire won't be surprised via the skies again, Miss Meriwether," he said. "We learned our lesson after the Dirigible War. The Royal Guards watch the skies. They have the Harpoon guns to back them up."

"And, as you know, it is illegal for any airship to fly over London without Her Majesty's direct permission, my dear," said the General. "A dirigible would have been seen, and reported."

"Not *all* eyes are trained upwards against aerial attack," she said.

"All human eyes are," said Sir Avery. "The Bots patrol the grounds."

"Then, perhaps someone tampered with the Bots?" she asked.

She eyed Harrow. He was hovering again.

Sir Avery's moustache twitched angrily. "I don't see how--"

"We know the Russians have been trying to gain access to the Department for decades," said Harrow. "Perhaps they found a way to disable the Bots?"

"There was a scientist that got a little too close to the Russians in the sixties," replied Sir Avery. "Wasn't he was killed after he gave up secrets to one of their scientist operatives? What was her name?"

"Miss Baronova." Harrow straightened his shoulders.

The General raised an eyebrow.

"I read about it in the files," said Harrow.

"Didn't she disappear after the scientist died?" asked the General.

"I believe so, sir," replied Harrow.

"What was the scientist's name?" asked Sir Avery.

Harrow shrugged his shoulders.

The General leaned back in his chair. "Nathaniel Kempthorne," he said.

Tillie sucked in her breath silently. Her father had fraternised with rival scientists? Her heart sank.

The General glanced in her direction. She held her breath, dug her nails into her palm and feigned a smile. His eyes crinkled slightly at the corners.

"I knew him," he said. "He seemed an honourable man."

"Not honourable enough, it would seem," said Harrow. "He was a traitor."

"Was it ever proved?" asked Tillie. She tried to keep her voice even, despite the thumping of her heart.

"Not beyond doubt," replied the General. "But a dead man can't defend himself, can he?"

"Kempthorne created the original Bots, did he not?" said Harrow. "Perhaps he passed the designs to the Russian before he died?"

"That was almost a decade ago," scoffed the General. "Surely they would've used the information before now?"

"I think we need to look closer to home," said Sir Avery.

"Yes, I fear our traitor is someone within the Department," said the General.

Harrow crossed his arms. "It would be someone with access to the Bots, with the knowledge to modify them. Who's the mechanic in charge?"

"Mr Jackson is assigned to the Bot Project," replied Sir Avery. "He modified Kempthorne's original plans."

"Then we need to speak with Mr Jackson as soon as possible." Harrow smiled.

There was a knock on the door. Saunders wheeled in the tea trolley. The warm aromas of fresh fruit cake and cinnamon tea wafted under their noses as the trolley trundled across the room.

"I thought you may be in need of some tea, sir," said Saunders.

"Excellent timing, as usual." The General clapped his hands together. "Can you fetch Jackson? We need to talk with him."

"Ah." The tea trolley halted. China clinked. "That may be difficult, sir. Jackson has been missing since the explosion."

"Perhaps he was killed in the blast?" asked Tillie.

"That's unlikely, Miss," replied Saunders. "He had a meeting in London with the gear manufacturer that afternoon, to check on the rogue Bot you discovered in the Upper Levels."

"Sir, I tried to find all of our men after the explosion." Harrow slipped a piece of paper from his pocket and presented it to the General. "This is the list of the men who are missing. Jackson is on it."

The General skimmed over the note. "Mr Thompson is on assignment and Higgins is on the Continent."

He passed the note to Saunders who studied it.

"We have no information on Mr Jackson's whereabouts," said Saunders.

"Then he is our traitor," said Harrow.

"A missing man can't defend himself, either," said Tillie.

"It's obvious, Miss Meriwether," replied Harrow. "He had access and opportunity."

"It's likely, but not conclusive," she replied. "I'm sure you wouldn't like to be accused with only circumstantial evidence, Mr Harrow. There may still be a piece of the puzzle missing."

Harrow didn't reply. She did not like him. He reminded her of a boy she knew when she was young, always blaming others for his failings.

"*Another* puzzle for you to solve, Miss Meriwether?" Sir Avery smiled.

"Excellent idea, Allington," replied the General. "Saunders will keep you informed of the situation, my dear. In the meantime, he'll escort you to the Communication Room, adjacent to your private quarters."

"I could check Jackson's notes and the Bot blueprints, sir," said Harrow. "Perhaps I can find some pieces for Miss Meriwether's puzzle?"

"Excellent, Harrow. Saunders will show you to the File Room when he returns."

Tillie nodded her farewells and followed Saunders out of the room.

<<*Harrow lies,*>> hissed the Orb once out of the cane's reach. <<*Watch him.*>>

Of Correspondences, Confidences, and Lemon Tart

illie eyed the tapestry-lined walls of the Communication Room: garden scenes festooned with mythical creatures, medieval maidens in splendour and an eighteenth century pastoral scene of a young shepherdess in charge of her flock. There was even a matching tapestry fainting couch. She wrinkled her nose; she was not a big fan of sheep. They reminded her of some debutantes she'd met.

Saunders had apologised for the unfinished state, and the diminutive size, of the Communication Room; he hadn't expected it to have been pressed into service so soon.

Thankfully, the supposedly-calming decor had not spilled into her adjoining Sitting Room or bedroom. The gentle whoosh of an exhaust fan hummed above her, circulating the air and siphoning off the smell of fresh paint, which still clung to the teal-painted walls.

She closed the door to her quarters. A portrait of Queen Victoria rattled gently on the back of the door, keeping an ever-watchful eye over her subjects' work.

She examined the mass of brass, keys and wires of the telegraph messaging machine on the over-sized desk before her. It was smaller, but more elaborate than Harrow's coveted machine in the Upper Levels. Its complexity was more akin to the serpentine machine that she had worked with in the Lower Levels.

To her left, riveted to the wall with brass fixtures, were two long metal tubes. They emerged from the wall near the ceiling, ran down the wall and over the tapestries. A flexible metal hose ending in a brass trumpet-like cone was attached at the end of the narrower tube.

Saunders had explained the workings of both the telegraph system and the communication tube and supplied a brief list of instructions, with orders to destroy the paper before she left for the evening. She'd locked the metal door behind him as he left; only he, Lord Allington or the General were allowed access.

Tillie checked the clock; she dared not miss sending her report the Queen. She sat in the padded "Captain's" chair and checked Saunders' list; the telegraph machine was not dissimilar to the contraption in the Lower Levels. She reached behind the main key box and searched for the calibration cogs, then rotated the second one in the sequence. It clicked as she turned it downward two notches.

She typed quickly:

Liberator,
Relocation complete. Awaiting further instructions.
Homunculus.

She leaned back in the chair and waited. The reply came quickly:

Homunculus,
Search auxiliary files. Require any documents with regards to father's notes. Codename: Horde. Report immediately.
Liberator.

Horde. The Orb chilled against her skin, until it almost burned. Icy fingers clawed up her spine. Her heart froze. Her father had mentioned it, with dread, in his journal. He'd questioned the Liberator's - the Queen's - motives, despite having been given assurances that *no good man, no innocent man, shall suffer.*

The word echoed in her mind: *suffer.* Could the Queen be trusted?

"Suffer what?" she whispered.

The Orb remained silent.

She swallowed. <<*What shall I do?*>>

<<*Forgive me the Horde.*>> The Orb's voice was faint.

Her fingers trembled as she typed the final reply:

Message received. - H.

She flicked the cogs back to their original position and slumped back in the chair. Her heart pounded. She wanted to scream, to run, to escape this tapestry-lined prison. She scanned the room. The shepherdess brandished her crook and stared out at her and grinned, as if Tillie was a wilful sheep in need of reminding who was its keeper.

It had been hours since luncheon. Saunders had delivered afternoon tea and informed Tillie he would fetch her for supper. Until then she was to monitor the telegraph machine.

She took a deep breath and thrummed her lips in boredom.

<<*Wasting time,*>> said the Orb.

<<*Someone has to watch for incoming messages,*>> she replied. <<*It makes logical sense. Any messages will be in code, and I am the Communications Officer.*>>

<<*No time.*>>

<<No time for what?>> She reached past the machines to retrieve a small piece of cake from the tea tray Saunders had left for her: chocolate cake, her favourite.

<<Find traitor.>> The Orb's voice reverberated inside her skull.

She winced and shook her head. A piece of cake broke free, fell into the lap of her new purple gown. A few crumbs tumbled into the folds of the decorative pleating on her bodice.

"Bother." She brushed her fingertips over the gown and tried to recall Aunt Prudence's many lectures on the difficulties of removing various stains from silk.

<<Find Harrow,>> hissed the Orb. *<<Don't trust.>>*

"You don't trust anyone. I am surprised you trust me."

There was silence.

She pursed her lips. After five years of following the Orb's instructions, she still didn't know how it knew what she needed for her quest to exonerate her father, and where to find clues. She didn't understand how she alone could communicate with it. It never told her anything, just gave orders. Even Aunt Prudence had allowed her more freedom.

She clenched her hands. The Orb had been helpful, but she yearned for freedom to live her own life and not be controlled.

"I should ask the General to borrow his cane," she scoffed. "Then I could work in peace."

There was no reply.

"Do stop sulking." She smirked.

A succession of levers clicked as they rose and fell, leaving a flurry of black ink on the paper roll beneath them. After a few seconds, they sprang upward and were silent.

She glanced at her instruction sheet. Another click and the keys resumed their brief dance. She snatched her fingers away and waited a few seconds after the last key fell, before attempting another paper extraction.

A,
Men sent as requested. Jackson's body found.
Dead more than week.
Further instructions required.
S.

Tillie sniffed. It was a simple substitution code, easily decoded. 'S' needed to be taught a code which was harder to break.

She turned to the contraption on her left - a mass of alphabetised keys wedged into the bottom of an open mahogany box, inset with ornate marquetry veneer. A code book rested on a low stand above it. She flipped through its pages to find a more complex code. She wouldn't be responsible for intercepted information.

The message printed on a sheet of paper above the keys as she typed:

S,
Caught in Blast?
TM.

The machine remained motionless.

"Oh dear." She stared at the motionless keys and frowned. Perhaps 'S' couldn't decipher the new code?

<<*Is traitor?*>> replied the Orb.

Her heart jumped into her throat. What would she do if it was the traitor? Perhaps she could trick him into a trap for the General's men to capture him? Her heart froze. What if she made a mistake and he escaped? The General would know what to do.

She reached for the communication tube. An incoming telegraph whirred and clicked out the reply, this time in a satisfyingly complex code.

Felicitations Miss M,
Jackson murdered.
Please inform General.
Await instructions.
Yours
Smythe.

<<*Convenient,*>> said the Orb.

"Yes," she replied.

<<*Knew too much?*>>

"Perhaps he became a liability for The Society?"

<<*Accomplice?*>>

"Two traitors?" She flopped back into her chair. "But surely infiltration was less detectable with only one man in the Department? Dead men can't defend themselves, so we may never know for sure." She grabbed the speaking tube and blew into it. "Perhaps Mr Jackson is a distraction?"

"Message for you, General."

"Ready to receive, Miss Meriwether," replied the disembodied voice.

She rolled up both messages from Smythe, slid them into a metal cylinder and placed it the larger tube. She closed the hatch and wound the wheel beside it. The tube hissed. A sucking noise followed. The tube shuddered and, with a loud pop, the message was gone.

She poured herself a fresh cup of tea, sighed, and waited. Much of her new occupation required waiting. She reached forward for the last piece of chocolate cake. Her ribs twinged.

Tillie shifted in her seat and adjusted her bustle skirt so the contents of her pockets didn't push up into her ribs, grateful for the support her stays provided. Though the bones were healing, they were still tender and the return to her beloved bustle dresses had necessitated tighter lacing.

She pulled her father's diary from her pocket and laid it on the desk. She'd read every page, transcribed every symbol, deciphered every code. She thumbed through the diary, comparing various pictograms to those found in the da Vinci notebook. Again.

In the corner of one page was a doodle of a small, well-armed airship.

"A dirigible," she cooed as she tapped her fingers on the page. "Father used to tell stories about them, and the Airship Armada. I can't wait to see a real one." She grinned. The Department had a dirigible. Her heart fluttered. They could fly anywhere. Even Egypt.

"Oh, I would love to see Egypt again. Perhaps we could go digging for mummies?" She patted the Orb under her bodice. "You'd like that. Lots of sand and heat. You'd have lots to complain about. Unless the General came along as well."

The Orb fidgeted under her blouse. She laughed.

"That's not likely, is it? Perhaps Sir Avery could come with us?"

She paused for a moment. She imagined him dressed in a crisp linen suit, his sleeves rolled up and perspiration glistening on his arms. She tugged at her collar.

"Warm in here, isn't it?" She took a shallow breath. She longed for a walk in the open air, to feel the fresh breeze on her face. She tapped her feet on the floor. Slowly at first. Before long they were almost running.

She slammed the diary shut.

<<Don't stop,>> ordered the Orb.

"I've read it a thousand times."

<<Catch murderer.>>

"Why do you care so much?" she asked. "Cranshaw killed *my* father. Not yours."

There was long pause before the Orb replied.

<<Keep working!>> it roared.

The teacup rattled on its saucer. She grabbed her head and groaned. It throbbed from the force behind the Orb's demand.

"I need to return to the Restricted Files," she whispered, "and I can't do that until after supper."

She huffed and jumped to her feet. It took only a few steps to pace the length of the room. She clenched her fists and circled her tapestry cage.

"Do you realise, since I have joined the Department of Curiosities, I have been trapped underground the entire time, either by accident or necessity?" she hissed. "I think I prefer running over loose roof tiles to being closeted up in these tunnels. I need air!"

A sharp whistle whooshed down the communication tube.

"Pardon, Miss Meriwether?" It was the General's voice.

"Nothing, sir." Her voice faltered.

The Orb quivered.

<<*Not now,*>> she begged. She placed a hand over her chest and pressed until the Orb stilled.

"I have a reply for Smythe. Are you ready, my dear?"

She returned to the desk, flexed her fingers and readied them to type. "Proceed, sir."

She tapped out the code, as the General dictated:

Smythe,
Surveillance and follow only.
Suspect traitor may recover.
Inform of any interest in body, immediately.
Secrecy imperative.
Instructions known only Allington, Miss M, Saunders, myself.
Please confirm,
General.

The reply tapped out on the machine opposite:

Confirmed,
Smythe.

She spoke into the communication tube: "Confirmed, sir."

"Thank you, Miss Meriwether. I shall send Saunders to escort you to dinner." The tube crackled and went silent.

Tillie sighed. She had hoped Saunders would bring in a food tray. Her mind was reeling with questions. Where was Cranshaw, her father's murderer? Who was their traitor? Whom could she trust? She took a deep breath; socialising would take every ounce of concentration she could muster.

She returned to her adjoining private rooms, slumped on the edge of the bed and stared at her reflection in the cheval mirror. Strands of hair fell over her cheek from her braided coiffure. She pinned them back in place and searched her gown for any straggling crumbs. It would do for an informal dinner with work colleagues. She fastened the top buttons of her bodice and pinned the brooch her father gave her on the collar. She fingered the brooch.

"I won't stop looking, Father. I'll find Cranshaw and I *will* avenge you," she whispered.

With their liberation from the Lower Levels came the availability of fresh food.

Tillie savoured the last mouthful of salmon. She speared the remaining potato noisette and rolled it in the vestiges of the lemon sauce. Steam tickled her nose. She slowly breathed in the aroma. Cook had outdone herself, yet again. Supper had been divine: crab soup, poached salmon in lemon sauce with noisettes, roast pheasant and asparagus.

It'd been made even more enjoyable by the Orb's silence. Not a word throughout dinner. She wasn't sure if it was sulking, or just taciturn due to the proximity of the General's cane.

A faint snort echoed inside her ear. Her fingers tensed. She eyed her companions as they removed dessert plates of lemon tart and jellied fruit from the table's conveyancing belt, seemingly oblivious to the Orb's silent fuming.

"I believe lemon tart is a favourite of yours, Miss Meriwether." Sir Avery set a plate before her and smiled.

She licked her lips and nodded.

The General set down his silverware with a soft clink, and flipped open his pocket watch.

"It's getting late and I still have work to do," he said.

She swallowed a bite of lemon tart and patted the corners of her mouth with the now crinkled napkin.

"Setting up a new command post is damned inconvenient." The General turned to face her. "I do apologise, my dear. Allington here is much better company than an old goat like me."

"You're not an old goat, General," she said.

"Nevertheless, this old goat still has work to do and I must start early tomorrow." The corners of his eyes wrinkled slightly as he smiled at her.

"Good evening, General." Sir Avery nodded.

"Good night, Allington." The General stood, bowed and took his leave.

Tillie sipped the last of her sherry.

The chair leg scraped on the stone flagged floor as Sir Avery rose to his feet.

"I thought I might escort you to your rooms, Miss Meriwether," he said. "Navigating these wretched corridors can take a while to learn."

<<*Decline,*>> urged the Orb.

<<*We can trust him,*>> she replied. <<*He saved my life.*>>

"Thank you, Sir Avery." She slipped her arm around his.

<<*Trust no one.*>> The Orb's reply needled into her thoughts, this time accompanied by a sharp twinge. <<*Careful!*>>

She grimaced.

"Is there something wrong?" Sir Avery stepped closer, placed his hand on her elbow and frowned. "Are you unwell, Miss Meriwether?"

<<*No one,*>> whispered the Orb. <<*Must protect.*>>

"No, I am fine." She struggled to lift the corners of her mouth, to maintain a calm smile. "It's been a long day, and too much sherry gives me a headache." She patted his hand, tugged at his arm and strolled along the corridor, with him in tow and the Orb refusing to remain quiet.

Wall-mounted illumination tubes erupted into light as they strolled into the maze of corridors.

<<*Surely Sir Avery can be trusted?*>> she whispered to the Orb. <<*He made me armoured stays. We have the protection of the Department. We're safe here.*>>

<<*Protect me,*>> replied the Orb.

<<*I am sure he would protect you as well, if he knew you existed--*>>

<<*No!*>> roared the Orb. <<*Don't tell.*>>

Her head reeled under the assault. Her muscles tensed. A smile froze on her lips as she took a slow breath, careful not betray any emotion.

She glanced at Sir Avery. He was quiet, a tactic her father had often adopted. He relaxed his hold on her and strolled, chin raised to the world as his eyes methodically scanned the corridor. Gold buttons glinted on his turquoise jacquard waistcoat.

<<*He'll keep our secret,*>> she whispered.

<<*Harrow's friend,*>> hissed the Orb.

<<*He doesn't like Harrow.*>>

<<*Department loyalties,*>> said the Orb.

"I don't like Harrow, either," she said, out loud.

"Really?" Sir Avery paused mid-stride. His moustache twitched. "How candid you are, Miss Meriwether."

Tillie bit her lip. She hadn't meant to say that out loud. She cursed silently at the Orb; it was problematic conducting two conversations at once. Usually one ended up forgetting oneself. She longed to share her suspicions with him, but she needed to know where she stood on the matter of Harrow.

"His beak-like nose makes him look suspicious, don't you think?" She could feel the Orb's anger growing. *Breathe.* "And I don't like the way he hides behind his spectacles."

"I didn't think you were one to judge by appearances, Miss Meriwether." Sir Avery patted her arm gently. "True, he isn't the most sociable of fellows, but he excels at his job. He held the Department together while we were trapped, and discovered Mr Jackson's involvement in the assassination attempt. Surely that is in his favour?"

<<*Blames everyone,*>> said the Orb, drowning out Sir Avery's reply.

She opened her mouth to reply to the Orb but stopped herself, just in time. Yes, Harrow had been very quick in providing potential suspects. Perhaps too quick? But she had no real proof of his treachery. She'd have to remedy that as soon as she had an opportunity. She turned to Sir Avery, cleared her throat and forced a weak smile.

"Definitely too much sherry," she said.

"You do seem a little distracted this evening," he said.

<<*Blamed Inessa,*>> growled the Orb.

She closed her eyes, trying to ignore its accusations. Inessa? The name was familiar...

"Who was the Russian woman Harrow mentioned?" she asked Sir Avery.

"Before my time, I'm afraid. The General will know," replied Sir Avery. "The theory does warrant more investigation."

<<*Leave alone,*>> grumbled the Orb. <<*Innocent.*>>

<<*What makes you so sure?*>> she asked.

It didn't reply. There was another twinge of pain. She knew it would continue until she changed the subject.

"How long has Harrow worked for the Department?" she asked Sir Avery.

"Five years," he replied.

Five years? It was longer than expected. Surely he would have betrayed himself before now?

<<*Harrow lies,*>> hissed the Orb.

She remembered Harrow's discomfort in the General's office. <<*Quiet, I need to think!*>>

"Is he claustrophobic?" she asked.

Sir Avery blinked. "You ask the strangest questions, Miss Meriwether." He shook his head. "I don't know. Why do you ask?"

"I don't think he likes being confined underground," she replied.

<<*Guilty conscience,*>> said the Orb.

"Then it is fortunate he was not trapped with us in the Lower Levels," said Sir Avery.

"Yes, very fortunate," she said.

The last of the illumination tubes flared to life as they reached her sleeping chamber.

"It has been an intriguing evening, Miss Meriwether." Sir Avery bowed his head. His gaze lingered on Tillie's waist.

She took a shallow breath. She felt the heat rise from her breast, and flow into her face.

He leaned forward and gently brushed away the few remaining cake crumbs that clung to the silk of her bodice.

"Another gown blemished already?" he whispered.

She held her breath, trying not to respond to such a quiet intimacy.

His eyes met hers. His moustache dropped, taking his smile with it. He snapped his hand behind his back.

"I do apologise, Miss Meriwether. I did not mean to make you uncomfortable."

<<*Impertinent!*>> The Orb wriggled under her bodice.

His cheeks glowed pink under the harsh electric lighting. Sir Avery was usually logical and composed, keeping his emotions under control. She let out a slow breath and smiled.

<<*Stop flirting,*>> demanded the Orb.

<<*I am not flirting,*>> she replied. Aunt Prudence had said a woman's greatest power is the ability to beguile the weaker sex, to make men forget all logic and convince them what she wanted was what they wanted. Tillie was never comfortable with such manipulation, yet she found herself unconsciously fluttering her eyelashes.

Sir Avery's smile returned. She took a deep breath. His gaze flickered across her décolletage and darted away. He cleared his throat, his cheeks now tinged red.

Aunt Prudence would have been proud.

<<*Stop it!*>> The Orb burned against her skin.

She quickly released her breath. A small twinge ripped through her ribcage; the bones had not quite healed.

"Good night, Lord Allington."

"Good night, Miss Meriwether." His smile slipped slightly. With a nod, he bid her good night.

Tillie wrapped her hand around her door handle, peered back along the corridor and waited until Sir Avery turned down a side corridor. She released the door handle, spun on her heel and strode off towards the File Room.

<<*Finally,*>> grumbled the Orb.

Of Assignations, Suspicions, and Misappropriations

T illie's ribs ached. Something poked her in the back. She winced, rolled over and smacked her elbow onto a hard surface. A now familiar twinge gripped her torso.

"Damn these ribs," she hissed. She took a deep breath. Stale air and dust tickled her nostrils.

<<*Wake up!*>> screamed The Orb.

Blood whooshed through her ears as the world contorted under her. Her head spun. She flung out her hands to steady herself. Instead of soft silk sheets, her fingers encountered the resistance of chill stone tiles.

She cracked open one eye. The room was black as coal, with no street lighting for solace. She pulled herself up onto her elbows. The world jolted and spiralled in the opposite direction. She flailed at the air around her. Nothing was within reach. Her hand fell back to the floor; a tile subsided under the weight.

Harsh light flooded the room. She squeezed her eyes shut. A surge of pain seared along both optic nerves. It kick-started her consciousness and subdued the vertigo.

"Where am I?" She rubbed her eyes and tried to focus on the room.

<<*Restricted Files,*>> boomed the Orb's reply.

She cradled her head in her hands.

"Don't shout," she murmured.

Shapes separated and formed as her eyes adjusted to the illumination and observed the now familiar narrow room, with its shelf-lined walls. Beside her lay her father's journal, stuffed with her translated notes. Several boxes lay scattered over the floor. Squashed behind her was a bundle of purple silk and underskirts.

"I slept here all night?" She brushed off the under-trousers and straightened her half-unbuttoned bodice. "On the floor?"

<<*Like an urchin.*>>

She felt the Orb fidget against her bare skin; it glinted on her chest.

"Did you snicker?" she asked.

The Orb didn't answer.

She adjusted her collar and fastened the bodice buttons. "Being inaudible to the rest of the world has made you very impertinent. I shall have to teach you some manners."

The Orb sniffed - or it would have, if it had olfactory capabilities.

She gritted her teeth and pulled herself to her feet; not an easy task in full metal stays and nursing still-healing ribs, but she would not give the Orb the satisfaction of vocalising her pain, even if it was only psychogenic.

Fortunately, movement was easier without the encumbrance of the excess layers of skirting paraphernalia. She glanced at the masculine trousers she now wore under her customary skirts. They were practical, but tweed was not very glamorous.

<<*I must ask Saunders to order some more fashionable trousers,*>> she said.

<<*Not proper,*>> replied the Orb.

<<*A man can wear trousers. Why can't I?*>> She flicked her skirt

hems to the floor. <<*Aunt Prudence would have appreciated their practicality.*>>

She resealed the file boxes and replaced them on the wooden shelving. She retrieved her father's journal; it had fallen open to where her notes had been wedged into the spine. She flipped through to her last translated entry:

May God forgive me. May He forgive me the Horde.

Tillie slapped the journal shut and snapped the rubber band around it to secure the loose notepapers. She'd hoped to find more information in the entries. The night's efforts had been in vain.

She rummaged in the pockets of her multi-functional bustle and wrapped her fingers around an ink pen. It had been a gift from Sir Avery; a fantastic invention, holding the ink in a cartridge concealed in the pen's barrel. She noted the numbers of the boxes she'd just replaced, and jotted down a final annotation: *No further information found.*

She shoved the pen and journal into one of the concealed pockets in her bustle, shook the dust from her underskirts and slipped on the petticoat. It would *not* do for her to be seen cavorting through the corridors in trousers with an exposed bustle and underthings. She slipped the crumpled silk skirt over the petticoat and pushed and tugged at the overskirts, as she tried to smooth out some of the more prominent creases.

<<*Look at my clothes!*>> She threw her hands up in the air. <<*Sir Avery won't pass up an opportunity to comment if he sees this.*>>

The Orb didn't reply.

<<*Still sulking?*>> she asked.

<<*Listen,*>> it whispered. <<*Someone outside?*>>

She pressed her ear against the door. It seemed quiet in the main File Room. She held her breath, eased the door open and peeked along the closest row of shelves. It was unlit and appeared empty. She stepped out of the Restricted Files room, clicked the door shut behind her, and tiptoed along the aisle, careful not to let her heels hit the floor. She paused at the end and listened.

<<*I can't hear anyone.*>> She peered into the room. <<*We're alone.*>> She sighed with relief.

<<*Dark,*>> said the Orb. <<*Can't see!*>>

<<*I know.*>> She grinned as she loosened her laces and slipped off her boots. <<*But, if I can't see them, they can't see me.*>> She slipped back along the aisle, crept along the edge of the room toward the entry door.

Tillie easily found her way along the corridor warren to her rooms; Saunders had provided her with written directions. As expected, the illumination tubes flared into life as she stepped on the triggering floor tiles. As she turned left along the final corridor, the Orb twitched under her bodice. She paused mid-step.

Damnation!

She turned her head to listen. Faint footfalls approached behind her. She glanced down at her crumpled dress. She couldn't give Sir Avery the satisfaction of yet another opportunity to comment on the appearance of her clothes.

She glanced along the corridor ahead of her; there was nowhere to hide. Her heart raced as she side-stepped the trigger tile in front of her and padded in her stockings looking for refuge, her boots dangling by their laces from her fingers.

A click echoed along the corridor. She halted. Her heart pounded as she turned slowly to face Sir Avery's recriminations.

A silhouetted figure approached her, the glare of the illumination tube rendering his features unrecognisable. The figure lifted his head, hesitated, then continued forward slowly.

"Good evening, Miss Meriwether."

She recognised Harrow's voice.

Harrow activated the trigger-tile, stepped into the nearby pool of lighting and pushed his spectacles up the bridge of his arched nose. A scowl replaced his weak smile by the time he lowered his hand.

"Good evening, Mr Harrow," She moved her hand holding her boots behind her back. "I see the General has you working late tonight."

His neck muscles tightened.

"Just finishing up some loose ends," he replied.

<<*He lies,*>> hissed the Orb.

<<*Yes,*>> she replied.

<<*From File Room,*>> whispered the Orb.

She studied the corridor past Harrow's shoulder. <<*What was he doing there?*>>

Harrow's gaze met hers for the briefest of moments before disengaging. He sniffed and slipped his hand into his coat pocket. The Orb stirred at her breast.

"Have they found Jackson's body yet?" Harrow voice sliced through the awkward silence.

She shrugged and eyed Harrow as he wrangled a wayward lock of hair. Information about the mechanic's body had been restricted. Smythe had been told to inform the General, immediately, of any interest in the body. Harrow was certainly showing interest, albeit vague and tentative.

"The General doesn't keep me informed on everything," she replied.

"As Communications Officer, I'd expect you would be the first to hear any news."

<<*Secrecy imperative.*>> The Orb whispered, echoing the General's orders to Smythe.

"Nothing as yet, I'm afraid." She shook her head.

"I see," he said finally. "Then, I have a lot of work to do. We must find the traitor, then we can all get back to our real work." He cleared his throat. "Did you have any luck in the File Room?" he asked.

<<Don't trust,>> The Orb fidgeted.

"The thought of a traitor in The Department is quite unnerving." She placed her hand over her bodice to steady the Orb, and feigned a sigh, hoping Harrow didn't spy the Orb's movement under her bodice.

He peered over the edge of his spectacles, a faint curl licking the edge of his mouth. "Maybe there's something useful in Jackson's file?"

"You haven't checked?" she asked.

"I'm currently on orders elsewhere," he replied.

"Then I shall have to check for myself."

"I think that would be prudent. Good evening, Miss Meriwether." He grinned and marched off along the corridor, triggering a cascade of light as he moved further away from the File Room.

<<He knows,>> said the Orb.

<<You caught that, too?>> She took a deep breath. *<<How does he know Jackson is dead? And why is he so keen to have me check the files?>>* She bit her thumbnail and frowned.

<<Inform General.>>

"Of what?" Tillie whispered.

<<Traitor!>>

"Because of a slip of the tongue?" She shook her head. "No, I don't have enough proof yet," She peered after Harrow. What was he up to?

She crept along the corridor in his wake and slipped quietly along the now empty tunnel, avoiding each brass activation plate on the floor. She checked the side tunnel as she passed. It was dark. She continued onwards. The next tunnel was illuminated.

She crept into the tunnel. She checked each side corridor as she continued. The illuminated trail led back to the main entrance.

She glanced around the empty foyer. Where were the sentries?

A gentle thunk heralded the return of the Ascension Chamber. She checked the chamber's door. It was unlatched.

"He's absconded-- "

<<*Against orders,*>> finished the Orb.

<<*Where is he going? It's--* >> She glanced at the mantel clock on the sentry desk. <<*It's three in the morning!*>>

<<*Follow him,*>> urged the Orb.

"I have my orders." She yawned. "We are to stay in Department headquarters until the traitor is caught."

<<*Escaping.*>> The Orb jiggled. <<*Follow him!*>>

<<*Hush!*>> she demanded. She glanced down the surrounding corridors; they were all empty. She frowned. Where *had* the sentries gone?

Tillie slid the Chamber door open and scanned the walls. Her stomach knotted. Sir Avery had *promised* it was safe. She took a slow, measured breath, tugged at her bodice, straightened her skirts and swallowed as she stepped into the Chamber.

She had no choice; she would need proof if she was to accuse Harrow of any impropriety, let alone of treachery. She rammed the door shut and yanked on the lever.

"I shall blame you if this goes badly," she whispered to the Orb.

There was a faint clank. The walls hummed. A faint grinding sound vibrated through the walls as the chamber slowly made its way to the surface.

The Master's house was unlit. Tillie slipped behind the remaining packing boxes and made her way to the front door. It, too, was unlocked.

Gravel crunched outside the building.

She paused, and turned the knob slowly so as not to alert anyone lurking outside. There was a faint click. She winced and pressed her ear against the door and waited. There was no response.

She opened the door a crack. Droplets of rain tickled her nose and soaked into her kid gloves. A cool draft wafted through the opening, carrying a faint whiff of wood smoke. The children would be tucked up in dry beds, comforted by a warm fire.

A faint, rhythmic chugging echoed across the yard.

She pushed the door open a little wider and peeked across the orphanage green. Small puffs of steam rose into the air near the gatehouse. The faint shadow moved under its arch.

"Not fair!" she hissed. "He's got a monocycle."

Stones ground underfoot, as she stepped onto the path and scanned the yard. The Master's bicycle was propped against a nearby building. Wet grass squelched as she stepped off the noisy path and dashed over to the bicycle. The damp hem of her skirt caught on the chain as her foot landed on the opposite pedal. She tugged to free the material. A loud rip broke the silence.

She winced. "Blasted skirts."

<<*Hurry*>> screeched the Orb.

She wrestled the skirt free of the bicycle and fumbled at the clasp at her waist as she glanced over her shoulder toward the gatehouse. It was empty.

"Blast!"

She wriggled her hips to free herself of the skirts' bulk. The silk fell around her feet, followed by the petticoat. She hopped out of their embrace and kicked the extraneous garments away from the path. They plopped into the garden and sank, like a deflating balloon, into the fresh mud.

She whimpered. Still, there was no time to regret the decision; Harrow was escaping!

Tillie straightened her bodice and mounted the bicycle, this time unencumbered by swathes of ostentatious silk finery, and sped off in pursuit of the steam-assisted monocycle. She must have looked a sight in her intricately pleated purple silk bodice, still dusted with errant crumbs of chocolate cake, an exposed bustle and ill-matching men's trousers.

Wind rushed over her face and tugged at her bonnet, testing her skill at applying hat pins. She grinned and pedalled faster.

She shadowed the monocycle through the alleys and streets as Harrow made his way north towards the Thames. He turned onto the gravel paths of Battersea Park. She slipped off her bicycle, hid it behind a bush and followed the path in the shadow of the trees.

Harrow's monocycle skidded to a halt and ground into the loose stones. He scanned the path, then climbed off the still-idling contraption and wheeled it into a clump of nearby trees. Faint wisps of steam drifted up into the leaves.

She waited near the tree line and cocked her head to listen. A night bird flapped overhead. A fox barked. The monocycle's motor sputtered to a halt. A soft thud followed, then the sound of receding footsteps. Then nothing.

"Blast."

All was quiet. There was no movement in the trees; the path remained empty. She inched forward, following the edge of the path as it circled toward the river, as she searched for any evidence of Harrow's trail.

<<*Lost him*>> said the Orb.

"I did not lose him," she hissed.

She retraced her steps, widening the search to either side of the path. There was no sign of Harrow, or his monocycle. She made her way back to the hidden bicycle and scanned the parklands one last time.

"I can't believe we lost him," she whispered.

<<*Not me,*>> replied the Orb as it hung smugly around her neck.

Tillie returned to the orphanage, replaced the bicycle and collected up her discarded skirts. She strode directly to the file room, ignoring the damp tendrils of hair that clung to her cheek; she wouldn't sleep until she found out why Harrow was so keen to have her search Jackson's files. If she was quick, she could sort out the puzzle before the others rose for breakfast.

She'd never encountered Harrow in the File Room but, as Saunders' Upper Level equivalent, she'd assumed he had access. It was reassuring to know he hadn't had a chance to discover she had been searching the Restricted Files, but...

Her hand froze on the File Room door handle. Harrow had followed her along the corridor. He must have been coming from the File Room.

<<He lies,>> whispered the Orb.

<<I know.>> Her heart raced. What had he been up to?

She locked the door behind her. A single droplet of water dripped from her bonnet and splashed onto her nose. She sniffed. Her damp skirt bundle slipped. The trim haemorrhaged from the gash in the skirt and tumbled into a growing pool of water on the floor at her feet. She wedged the torn passementerie into the tears created by the bicycle's pedals, and grumbled as she ran her gaze over the sea of file drawers.

"What were you doing here, Harrow? What did you want me to find?"

She wandered along the nearest row and scanned the cabinets; each had a fine layer of dust. She glanced back down the aisle towards the Restricted Files. Her skirts had swept a trail though the dust during her previous visits.

<<I wonder if Saunders has noticed?>> she asked the Orb.

<<He notices all,>> it replied.

She grimaced. The man had a keen eye, but he was also discreet. Still, if he deemed her secretive jaunts as suspicious, he would report it. He was the General's man, after all. She twisted the brooch at her neck. She wasn't sure how much the General had been informed about her; he mustn't know about her visits to the Restricted Files. Not yet.

"We need a little diversion, I think," she whispered.

She unfolded her skirt bundle, wandered down the next aisle and dragged the material along the dusty shelves. She worked her way along a few aisles and crossed to the next section to repeat her ruse. She paused, mid-alphabet, and studied the drawers. The dust had already been disturbed here.

She snatched up the swathes of material that cascaded from her bundle, and edged along the aisle, scanning the floor and each drawer before she ventured onward.

The disturbance stopped abruptly about one-third of the way along the aisle. She ran her fingers along the labels: *I-v, I-x, I-z, J-a.*

"J-a?" she read out loud. "Jackson?"

She pulled the drawer out and thumbed through the cardboard satchels until she found one labelled *Jackson.*

The satchel contained diagrams on how to modify the Bots, notes on Jackson's service and background information; enough evidence to suggest he was the traitor, or at least in league with one.

The File Room clock chimed quietly.

Blast! Five o'clock already. In just over an hour Saunders would rouse her for breakfast. She examined her clothes: mud spattered boots, damp tweed trousers and torn skirts. Even Saunders would raise an eyebrow.

She snapped the band back over the satchel, tucked it under her arm and hurried back to her rooms to get changed.

Tillie's personal chambers consisted of two rooms: the Drawing Room was furnished with a fainting couch, desk and lockable cabinet. A wooden door led to her private bedroom.

She dropped the file satchel onto her desk and yawned. It had been a long night. She shuffled into her bedroom and scanned the painted walls and nodded in approval. Not a sheep in sight. A large, carved wooden bed dominated the bedroom. Soft, emerald bed clothes beckoned.

Her fingers sank into the soft down quilt and skimmed over the delicate embroidery of the silk cover. She longed to nestle under the covers, devoured by the soft feather mattress and clouds of Egyptian cotton, to dream of faraway places with warm sun and no drizzling rain.

She placed her skirt bundle on the vanity chair, kicked off her boots and let herself fall into comforting feathery bliss.

The grandmother clock chimed in the outer room. *Six o'clock.*
Blast!

She climbed out of the billowy depths of the bed clothes, stripped down to her underthings, and washed. She grabbed fresh linens and a turquoise ensemble, complete with military style jacket: no back lacing; perfect for unassisted dressing. The brooch her father gave her - a cameo carved from red sardonyx - finished off the outfit perfectly.

She sat at her vanity table and brushed her blonde curls; they had survived reasonably unscathed despite her nocturnal escapade. She braided her hair and tucked the last errant tendril in place. It fell limply along her neck. She clicked her tongue. This simply would not do. She would have to raise the subject of the lack of vital domestic help required for a lady. Perhaps Sir Avery could spare Grace in such dire circumstances.

Another chime signalled quarter to seven. Saunders would arrive at any minute.

She grabbed a hat box and pulled out a small purple bonnet with black feathers, twisted the lock of hair up and pinned the bonnet on top. She examined herself in the mirror.

<<*Acceptable,*>> said the Orb.

<<*Did I ask for your opinion?*>> she scoffed. Her stomach churned

and grumbled loudly. <<*At least I haven't missed breakfast, again.*>>

Tillie grabbed her father's journal and the black code book, and returned to the Drawing Room to lock them in the safe cabinet, away from prying eyes. She fetched the key and pushed it into the lock. The door moved under the pressure. It was unlocked.

Her heart dropped. She held her breath and tugged on the cabinet door. It was empty. The da Vinci journal was gone.

<<*Stolen.*>> The Orb burned against her skin.

She gritted her teeth and shoved the journal and codebook into a bustle pocket.

"Harrow!" she hissed.

Of Dead Men, No Tales, and Kippers

arrow pressed the black button on the announcement box beside the locked door of the Professor's office.

"Harrow reporting, sir."

The voice was crackly and curt: "Enter."

The door opened. The Pharmacist scuttled out and dodged Harrow as he stepped forward.

"He's not in a good mood today," he mumbled and shoved his medicine box under one arm.

"When *is* he in a good mood?" Harrow whispered.

The Pharmacist paused, widened his eyes and gulped. "Don't forget your mask." He shoved a linen mask into Harrow's hands and hurried along the corridor.

Harrow entered and waited at the foot of the dais. The Professor fussed over the papers on his desk, scribbling notes with his quill and grumbling with his customary dissatisfaction. A pale henchman stood at attention beside his desk and stared blankly across the room. His skin matched the colour of his eyes: a dull, sickly grey from years of enforced injections of silver to pacify the pathological fears of their employer.

Miss Meriwether had called them *Ghostmen*. Harrow eyed the Ghostman. The name was apt; he resembled a Dickensian ghost, sent to torture his father for his past, perhaps? Yes, Harrow liked that. He smiled under his mask.

"I trust you have good news for me?" the Professor asked Harrow. "The files?"

"Done, as instructed, this very evening," replied Harrow.

"Excellent. The Society won't tolerate any more excuses." The Professor looked up from his desk and glared at Harrow. "Nor will I."

Harrow swallowed. "The information will lead to The Society, as instructed."

"That will teach them to send their lackey to keep an eye on *me*."

"Sir, there is more news. The Department discovered Jackson's body." He waited, hoping the unexpected news would unravel a little more of the Professor's frayed ego.

"Jackson?"

"The Bot mechanic, sir," explained Harrow.

The Professor rammed his quill into its stand and leaned slowly back into his chair.

"You left the note, linking him to The Society?" he asked.

Harrow nodded. His mask moved slightly; a rhythmic fog swept over his spectacles, then faded. The tempo quickened with his breaths.

The Professor eyed Harrow. His lids narrowed.

"Is there a problem, Harrow?"

"No, sir." He could feel his pulse racing to match the quick pace of his nervous breath.

"Are you sure?"

Harrow licked his dry lips and adjusted his face mask, so his breath no longer clouded his spectacles. "I may have been followed," he said finally.

The Professor inhaled sharply. His face reddened.

Here it came: if there was anything that went wrong, he was usually blamed. Harrow bit his lip under the linen camouflage.

The Professor rose from his chair. It scraped along the tiles, teetered for just a moment, and slapped back onto the floor. He exhaled slowly and strode over to the far corner of the room to where his 'treasure' sat swathed in a linen cloth.

"The Society or The Department?" he asked.

"Sir?"

"Who followed you?"

"I'm not certain, sir. A man on a bicycle followed me from the orphanage. There wasn't enough moonlight to recognise him."

The Professor ran his fingers, ever so slowly, over the linen, catching it between his fingers. He tugged gently at the cloth. It slid to the ground revealing an automaton.

Harrow's eyes widened. It was a beauty: its skeleton was of brass and steel, its body encased partially in a skin of bronzed metal. The head was still incomplete, with empty sockets. Naked mechanical workings occupied the skull. A fitted leather glove covered one hand, the other was uncovered, revealing delicate wire tendons running down the arm and over the hinged fingers.

The Professor caressed its face.

"Bloody hell. This won't do, Harrow. Will I have to send someone to dispose of the body and clean up your failure... again? I've worked too many years on this prototype. I will *not* be thwarted now."

"But, sir? I have followed your orders-- " began Harrow.

The Professor shook his head. "The Department of Curiosities was not fully destroyed. Brown's death is suspicious. The Bot was not retrieved. Your cypher machine has not been successful, and that interfering girl stole my da Vinci notebook...." He slammed his fist onto the arm of the chair. The automaton shivered. The Ghostman didn't flinch. "That is not a very auspicious resume so far, Harrow."

Harrow straightened his back and smirked under his face mask.

"You wanted good news, sir?" He slipped a red, leather-bound notebook from his inside coat pocket. "The da Vinci notebook, as requested."

The Professor spun to face Harrow, a wide grin dominated his face.

"At last!" His fingers twitched.

Harrow crossed the room and handed the Professor the coveted notebook.

"There are some advantages to dining alone," he said. "I managed to retrieve the notebook while Miss Meriwether was flirting with Allington at supper."

The Professor chuckled softly, flipped through the notebook and skimmed the doodle-covered pages until he reached the ink-stained front endpaper. He tugged at the curled edge of the cover sheet, lifted it from the board and slipped his fingers under the vellum. He grinned, extracted a small piece of torn paper and examined it. His smile faded; he glared at Harrow.

"There was something in here." He thrust the torn scrap of paper into Harrow's hand. "Find out what was removed."

"Sir, I-- "

"No, you didn't. That's your problem. You're a disappointment, Harrow. It's best your mother's not alive to witness your failure. At least the influenza saved her that sorrow."

Harrow caught his breath. *And whose fault was that?* If his father had parted with just a little money for a doctor, his mother could have survived. He clenched his fists. He wanted to wring the git's neck. Barely a week after her death, he'd abandoned his only child to chase his ambition for scientific glory - all the way to the other side of the world.

Harrow would never forgive him. He would crush his father and assume control of his pathetic little gang. He had plans, big plans. Incriminating evidence would lead both the Department and The Society directly to the Professor. It wasn't long now...

He took a deep breath, relaxed his fists and swallowed. But not yet. First, he had to get away from London, out of England...

"Sir, I-- "

The Professor held up a hand to silence him.

"You will return to the Department and you will retrieve the cypher key," said the Professor.

"But sir, I was followed. What if I am caught?"

The Professor's gaze returned to the automaton. "Is there anything that can connect the Bots or Brown's elimination to me?"

"I don't think so, sir," he replied.

"Then you know what I must do if you are discovered," replied the Professor.

Harrow's fingers twitched. The Professor had an alternate refuge, with contingency plans to evacuate should his identity be jeopardised. Unfortunately, he wouldn't divulge its whereabouts, even to his own flesh and blood.

"Will you take me with you, father?" The words almost choked in his throat.

"If you are truly my son, you will do as I order."

Harrow remained silent. He clenched his jaw under the cover of the mask. If his tracker had been one of The Society's Men in Grey, they would eliminate him as a liability. If the tracker was from the Department, then it was possible they suspected him and would arrest him as a traitor. The Professor did not seem concerned about the prospect of losing his son, either to the Department or The Society.

Harrow swallowed. He needed more time. He had to make himself indispensable. Only then could he guarantee transport out of England and immunity from The Society's wrath.

"You'll need me to work the cypher machine after I retrieve the key." He eyed the Professor.

"Then you had better not get caught." The Professor waved Harrow from his presence, his attention not wavering from the automaton.

"Anything to be of service, sir." Harrow nodded and shuffled back toward the door.

"The Society representative returns in six days," said the Professor. "You have three days, Harrow."

Harrow pulled the door closed behind him, leaving it open just enough to peek through. The Professor cradled the head of his precious automaton in both hands, then turned to his Ghostman and spoke quietly. Harrow pulled a small ear horn from his pocket, wedged it up against the door crack and listened.

"Have my train ready. We're leaving London in two days. The Society won't have my prototype, key or no key. Harrow will remain here to distract The Society while I escape. I'll leave The Department and The Society to quibble over his fate."

Harrow whipped off his mask, spat on the floor and strode toward the Ascension Chamber. He had to be on that train.

The pungent stench of kippers pervaded the subterranean Dining Room. Tillie feigned a polite smile, shook her head and raised her hand in defence against the platter of salty flattened fish, proffered to her by Sir Avery.

He shrugged, shovelled a few onto his plate and returned the tray to the moving track along the centre of the table. She held her breath as the platter clattered past her. The General licked his lips and scooped up two pieces before the platter trundled back out of sight. The track whirred, paused and reversed direction. A faint, smoky smell broke through the kipper-stench.

She stifled a yawn and waited patiently for the rectangular tray of succulent, steaming ham to arrive. A plate piled with fried mushrooms followed. She took a long, deep breath, allowing the mouth-watering aroma to drown out the lingering smell of kipper.

The General smiled. "I thought you may prefer an alternative to kippers, my dear," he said.

Sir Avery swallowed the mouthful of kipper.

"Much appreciated, General," she replied.

"Excellent choice, General. Miss Meriwether isn't overly fond kippers."

"Neither is Harrow," said the General.

"Miss Meriwether is not overly fond of Harrow either," said Sir Avery. He took a long sip of tea, flicking his gaze from Tillie to the General.

Tillie sucked in a quick breath, almost choking on a mouthful of ham and glared at Sir Avery through slitted lids. She'd told him about Harrow in confidence. She swallowed the morsel and gritted her teeth. She needed to inform the General about Harrow's early morning excursion, and of his interest in Jackson's body. But, if she accused Harrow of stealing the da Vinci notebook now, it would seem to be in spite.

The Orb twitched, hampered in vicinity of the General's walking cane.

"Is that so?" The General raised a wiry eyebrow. "And how did he earn your antipathy?"

She noted the slight curl to the General's lip.

"I agree, he is not the most affable fellow, but he is a most useful chap." Sir Avery stifled a grin.

"Nor does he have the most pleasing countenance." He tapped his finger on his nose.

The General sipped his tea. His smile widened.

She clenched her fists. Her pulse raced. Muscles tensed in her neck, her jaw and her temples, threatening to capsize her carefully balanced bonnet. She opened her mouth, took a quick breath and pursed her lips.

Tillie felt a gentle hand on her arm.

"I am sorry, Miss Meriwether," whispered Sir Avery. "It was a jest, and in poor taste. I thought you were..." He removed his hand. "I didn't think you were serious about your suspicions about Harrow."

"I am always serious when it comes to treachery, Lord Allington."

The General's teacup clattered onto his saucer. "Explain yourself, Miss Meriwether."

"It may interest you to know Harrow was asking about the mechanic, Jackson." She patted her lips with a napkin. "And he left the orphanage last night, General; against your orders."

"Harrow?" The General raised an eyebrow and patted his moustache with his napkin. "The fellow doesn't have the gumption to disobey orders."

"I saw him leave, sir."

"And you left without permission, also, my dear?" said the General. She shifted in her chair.

"I followed him," she said, "but I lost him in Battersea Park."

"I am pleased to have such an observant recruit, Miss Meriwether." Crinkles formed around the edges of the General's eyes. He smiled and winked at her. "You needn't concern yourself about Harrow. He was following my orders; I asked him to investigate Jackson. No doubt that was the reason for last night. I didn't inform you, nor Allington. I assure you, he is a loyal operative." He smiled and poured a fresh cup of tea. "I congratulate you on your dedication, Miss Meriwether. I can see why Her Majesty was so taken with you. Keep up the good work, my dear."

Tillie finished her ham in silence and avoided Sir Avery's attempts to apologise. He'd made her look a fool. She couldn't accuse Harrow of stealing the da Vinci notebook now, especially not without absolute proof. Her heart raced; she felt like an outsider, a woman who had slipped into the Men's Club and accused one of their own of cheating.

She excused herself and made her way to the Communication Room.

Perhaps Smythe would have some news she could use?

Communications was not a very exciting occupation. The room was small. The cramped chair was not made to accommodate women's attire. The decorations, though well intended, were not to her taste. Woollen sheep stared out from tapestry fields, accusing her of negligence, having allowed Harrow to steal the da Vinci notebook.

She yawned and lifted her teacup. It was cold. She screwed up her nose and placed the cup back on its saucer. Five cups in two hours, each colder than the last. She sighed and glanced at the tintype propped up against the telegraph machine: Her father, Cranshaw and... Why couldn't she remember the woman? And why had her father hidden it in the notebook?

She sighed and reached into her pockets to retrieve the message that had been concealed with the photograph. Perhaps it held the answers. She unfolded the rice paper and held it to the light. Another code. Her shoulders slumped. Every time she solved one of her father's puzzles, another replaced it. Would it never end?

She flipped through her father's diary, searching for any clues or missed coded notations. There was nothing. She examined the transcription and read her father's words again. She needed to find his experimental journal. Perhaps it would provide the key?

<<*I wonder if Harrow filched it as well?*>>

<<*Most likely,*>> replied the Orb.

She slapped the paper onto the desk.

"I'm wasting my time!" she howled. "I should be following Harrow. He'll slip up eventually. I can't get proof if I'm shut up in here."

She shifted on her chair, repositioned her bustle and redistributed the valuables hidden in her pockets. Her stomach sloshed as she moved. A wave of nausea washed over her. She swallowed and rested her head on the desk. She had to remain, to do her duty; Smythe depended on her.

She remained motionless, waiting for the nausea to pass and for the telegraph machine to launch into life. Until then, she was a captive to the Orb's unrelenting barrage of demands and complaints - on the urgency of retrieving the stolen notebook, suggestions on various methods of capturing and punishing the treacherous Harrow. The words twisted through her thoughts, circling round and round, making the nausea worse.

She cradled her head on her hands.

"What if it wasn't Harrow?" she whispered.

<<No doubt,>> replied the Orb.

"The General seems certain it wasn't him."

<<Who else?>>

"Maybe we should review the facts?" she said.

<<Allington?>> suggested the Orb.

"Sir Avery?" She frowned and shook her head. "Impossible!"

<<Remember breakfast,>> it cooed. *<<Told secrets. Mocked you.>>*

Tillie scoffed and rose from her chair.

"He didn't mean it," she whispered.

<<You certain?>>

She covered her ears. A useless gesture; it wouldn't silence the Orb's prattling, but it made her point.

The Orb harrumphed.

She paced the carpeted confines of the room.

<<Not wanted. Men's Club.>>

"Do be quiet!"

The Orb fell silent.

Tillie sat down and took a deep breath. Finally, peaceful silence. She closed her eyes and imagined herself falling onto her bed, sinking into the warm mattress, her head cradled in the luxuriously plump feather pillow and the crisp, clean cotton sheets wafting over, caressing her body. Soft. Comforting.

She deserved a rest. It had been a long night.

Tap, tap, tap, tap. Tap.

She snapped to attention. The sheep still stared accusingly at her. The woven shepherdess leaned on her crook and leered at her from behind the telegraph apparatus on the desk.

Tillie's hands scrabbled for the arms of her chair so she could pull herself upright.

Tap. Tap. Silence.

<<*Message ends,*>> said the Orb, flatly.

She shook her head, extricated the paper from the cylinder and examined the message; Mr Smythe had learned his lesson and now used a more complex code. She smiled and scratched the message onto her notepad.

Dear Miss M,
Body retrieved and destroyed. Ghostmen under surveillance.
Inventor lair in vicinity of Battersea Park.
Inform G and A. Urgent.
Require instructions.
Yours,
S.

"How horrible. The poor man deserved a decent burial."

<<*Dead men...*>> said the Orb.

"Can't defend themselves," she continued.

She rolled up the missive and slid it into the message tube on the left wall. She cranked the wheel. The tube hissed and shook as the message whooshed its way to the General.

"I followed Harrow to Battersea Park, last night. I wonder..." She tapped her pen on the blank notepad page. "What if Jackson isn't the traitor? What if Harrow is working alone?" She didn't wait for the Orb's reply. "How else would he know about the body? It was restricted information."

She grabbed the communication tube and pressed it against her mouth.

<<*Intercepting communications?*>> suggested the Orb.

Perhaps he was listening now? She pulled the brass trumpet from her lips and stared at it. The General needed to know if communications had been compromised. She'd have to tell him in person.

She rose to her feet and froze half way. <<*But, the General trusts Harrow. What if he doesn't believe me?*>>

<<*Queen's Homunculus.*>> The Orb's words echoed ominously.

<<*I had forgotten about that.*>> She pushed her chair away from the desk. Her heart raced; though she didn't trust the Queen, she was still in Her employ and therefore outranked Harrow. The General would have to listen.

Of Reprieves, Messages,
and Little Nessie

Harrow sat hunched over an octagonal side table seconded from his room. His legs pressed against the narrow walls of the passage-like chamber sandwiched between the Communication Room and one of the store rooms. Few of the Department operatives were aware the auxiliary passage existed and, being a new installation, there would be little need for maintenance. This guaranteed Harrow uninterrupted eavesdropping. *A very fortuitous find.*

A reticulated tube snaked up the wall and pierced the pipe, which emerged from the Communication Room and clung to the roof on its way to the General's office. He held the ear trumpet at the other end of the tube against his ear.

Loose wires hung from the breached conduit and connected to a board with a mushroom-shaped light bulb, resembling a miniature version of the tube lighting in the General's office. He wiggled his shoulders and leaned against the left wall to avoid them and examined the scrap of paper found hidden inside the end papers of his father's precious da Vinci notebook.

His calf muscle cramped. He cursed, thumped his leg and slammed his chair against the wall behind him.

The bulb flickered ominously and dimmed for a few seconds. He wiggled the wires attached to the wooden base, sneered and turned over the paper. Faded lettering and scrollwork were barely visible in the faint glow. He pulled a jewellers' loupe from his coat pocket and examined the partial inscription: *...Street* and *...delaide.* He rubbed his chin. An address, perhaps?

He slipped his fingernail into the torn edge. There were two pieces of paper stuck together to form a pocket. He raised an eyebrow. A photograph. He leaned back into the chair and smiled. Now he knew what he was searching for.

A faint whistle trilled in Harrow's ear. He adjusted the trumpet, snatched up his pen and tapped the nib against the edge of the brass ink pot.

"Send a message, Miss Meriwether." The General's voice was faint, a whisper floating along the tube. "Be advised, Command security now increased. Continue Battersea surveillance. Exact headquarters location priority. Will await report. Confirm orders."

Harrow scribbled the message on his note paper and waited.

"Message received and confirmed by Smythe, sir," said Miss Meriwether.

"Thank you, my dear."

The tube fell silent.

"Thank you, General," whispered Harrow as he detached the ear trumpet from the tubing. He blew on the wet ink, folded the note and sealed it with a blob of grey wax. He rose, dodged the dangling wires as he eased his chair into one corner and flicked a toggle on the lighting device. In the darkness, he pushed against the blank wall. It gave way with a faint click. A fine line of light outlined the loose panel.

Harrow listened at the hatch and stepped into the back of a storage cupboard. There was no sound in the room beyond. He edged the cupboard door open an inch and peered through the crack. The room was empty.

He slipped along the wall behind boxes stacked along one side of the room and made his way to the surface.

Harrow flicked his gaze over the line of terraced houses and scanned the grounds.

"Mornin'." The gardener rose from his digging and tipped his hat as Harrow approached. "Lessons started hours ago. It's nice and quiet this time of day."

"Lovely roses," said Harrow.

"I almost lost them in this cold snap, sir." The gardener cut off a frost-bitten bloom and handed it to Harrow.

He slipped a note into the gardener's palm as he accepted the bloom.

"We won't be able to appreciate their beauty if it keeps up," he replied.

The gardener nodded as he pocketed the paper. "That would be disappointing," he replied. "I may need to fetch more supplies then, sir."

"That would be prudent," said Harrow.

"I'll take my leave then. Good mornin', sir."

The gardener scooped his equipment into his wheelbarrow and tramped towards the outbuildings.

Harrow excused himself from luncheon early, absconding with a bottle of wine to assist the passing of the afternoon's routine surveillance of Department communications. He'd been accustomed to sharing meals with Sir Avery and the General in the Upper Levels while the Department had resided at Prince's Gate, and wasn't impressed with the conversation afforded him by his re-assigned status. While he was accumulating an increased knowledge of magnetics and optics from his new work-colleagues, there was no opportunity to glean the tactical or operational information he had previously been privy to.

Harrow kneaded his forehead and groaned. He was wasting his time. He should be searching the Meriwether girl's belongings again.

He uncorked the wine bottle, poured a half a glass and sniffed it warily. The quality, like meal-time conversation, was also less than desirable. He checked his pocket watch; he'd been waiting five hours. It felt like ten.

He'd give it another hour; the Department's surveillance should advise him which train the Professor planned to board. He eyed the bottle, snapped the watch shut and filled the glass. It was going to be a long night.

His thoughts hearkened back to his father's words; he had two days to find the cypher key and missing photograph. He *had* to be on that train; he *had* to discover the location of the Professor's alternative headquarters if he was to usurp his empire. He'd managed to use the time, when the General thought he was checking the files looking for the traitor, to monitor communiques. He grinned; making use of the Department's surveillance to do so was a delicious irony.

Messages didn't start until mid-afternoon, as expected. All routine.

He poured another glass of wine and leaned back in his chair. Wires tapped his shoulder. He groaned, sat up straight and placed the glass to his lips, allowing the aroma to linger. He took a swig. It was sweet and strong, and slid down his throat in a not-unpleasing manner. A bitter aftertaste followed. He screwed up his nose; he preferred the General's personal wine.

Two glasses later, he was less annoyed with his situation. His eyelids grew heavy and fluttered in time with the flicker of the globe-lighting. His head lolled sideways, pressing into the hand holding the ear trumpet.

As the world dimmed, a faint whisper funnelled into his brain.

"He is most insistent, General." It was Miss Meriwether's voice.

"He's relocating? How much time do we have?"

Silence.

"Unknown, General," she replied.

"Has he confirmed which station?"

Harrow opened one eye.

"Not as yet," came her reply.

"Tell Smythe I need to know which train he will be on, Miss Meriwether. I won't have him escaping now, not when we finally have a chance to identify him."

"Yes, General."

"Send the following message to Her Majesty: Inventor preparing to leave London. Request urgent audience. Request Little Nessie for surveillance. Awaiting your reply, Yours General, etcetera, etcetera."

Harrow scrabbled to write down the message. The crystal glass fell to the floor, ringing momentarily before it smashed on the ground. The chair leg screeched through the shards as he sprang out of his seat.

The communication tube slapped his face. He dodged the lighting wires, bolted through the hatch and across the storage room, just in time to see the Meriwether girl emerge from the Communication Room.

He ducked back into the storage room and watched her from the doorway.

She frowned, shoved a collection of notepapers into the folds of her skirt and hurried down the corridor to the General's office.

The Communication Room door creaked as its spring pulled it to. Harrow slipped through the door before it clicked shut.

He found himself facing a large desk filled with a mass of devices, wires, brass tubes and keys. He raised an eyebrow. The General had made some upgrades.

Harrow sat down and ran his fingers slowly over the machines and reached his hand behind the key-filled mahogany box. His fingers searched rapidly, feeling their way over a series of cogs until he found what he was searching for. He grinned and rotated the cog two clicks downward, then gently rotated the next cog three notches upward. He leaned back into the chair and typed a coded message:

DOC sending operatives to prevent relocation. Increasing surveillance.
Request relief of assignment and rendezvous details.
H

His fingers trembled as he steepled them and touched his lips. He took a deep breath and stared at the device to his right.

There was no movement.

He glanced at the door and listened. How long did he have before she returned? His gaze darted across the room. On the floor, near the leg of the chair, was a tatty, green notebook tied with cord. He retrieved it and skimmed through the pages. It was a diary. Some sections were in code. He squinted and examined the text. Some of the pictograms seemed familiar. He turned the page. And another one.

The telegraph machine whirred. Tap. It echoed in the silence.

Harrow licked his lips. *Finally.*

Five more keys tapped slowly onto the paper.

Denied.

Harrow sucked in his breath and held it until it felt as though his lungs would burst. He breathed out shakily, and in broken gasps. He swallowed and turned to the mahogany box. He would not be left behind. He still had one more card to play, something his father would do anything to own.

His fingers caught the edge of the keys as he typed:

In possession of coded diary. Await instructions.

After a short silence, a message typed onto the cylindrical paper feed. Harrow snatched it from under the fallen type key. The key lever hovered then snapped back home.

Meet British Museum. 9.30 am.
Bring diary. Expect key in your possession.
-I

Harrow winced. He had searched the Meriwether girl's room and found nothing. The codebook had to be in her possession. Perhaps hidden under her skirts where he'd seen her concealing papers? He had to stay close and find an opportunity to check.

He reached behind the typing box and returned the cogs to their original positions. He struck a safety match; the sharp smell of sulphur irritated his nose as he watched the missive flare into flames and dissolve into ash.

Harrow dusted off his fingers. He grinned, slipped out of the Communication Room and strode toward the General's office in search of Miss Meriwether.

Hurried footsteps slapped on the stone floor of the adjoining tunnel. Light flooded the end of the empty corridor, illuminating the door to the General's office. Harrow pressed against the wall, retreated around the nearest corner to avoid the trigger tile on the floor, and flattened his body against the wall. He'd expected most of the Department to have retired by this late hour.

He extracted a small, circular-shaped box from an inside jacket pocket, and popped the catch. A dentist mirror flicked out and wobbled as a telescopic arm slowly extended. He eased the mirror just beyond the edge of the corner.

Saunders approached the General's office and rapped on the door. Sir Avery opened it. The lines on his forehead were deep. His moustache drooped.

"Come in, Saunders," he said. The door clicked shut behind him.

Harrow had no choice. He had to know what was happening. He had to find the Meriwether girl and shadow her until he found the key. He crept up and positioned an ear trumpet near the crack in the door and listened.

"Sit down, Saunders," said the General. "Miss Meriwether just decoded a message from Smythe. It seems the Inventor plans to depart from London on the Flying Scotsman, tomorrow morning. We have men on their way to the station to keep watch."

Tomorrow morning? Harrow's grip tightened on the ear trumpet. His father had demanded his man to have his train ready in *two* days, not one! That was earlier than expected. He'd lied. *Again.* He'd never had any intention of keeping their rendezvous. He cursed under his breath.

"You will be assisting Sir Avery with preparations, Saunders. I have an immediate audience with Her Majesty."

Chairs scraped on the stone floor.

"And, Saunders, no one is to leave the Bunker until we are ready to leave."

Harrow pocketed the listening device and slipped back into the adjoining tunnel.

How could Smythe have discovered the Professor's plans so quickly? Harrow had to catch that train. He had to know where his father hid his assets, all his secrets. He needed it all, if he was to take over. He clenched his teeth; he would not be left behind.

The office door clicked and swung open. The Meriwether girl stepped out. Allington followed.

Harrow waited.

"Do you really think we will be given permission to use *'You Know What'*?" she asked Allington. Her eyes glinted as she smiled.

"It was built for use in exceptional circumstances. These are exceptional circumstances." Allington's moustache twitched. "But, then again, one can never tell with the Queen."

"It's all so exciting," said Tillie. "Will we *all* be going?"

Allington shook his head. "Not for surveillance."

Her smile faded. "Pity." She sighed. "Then I had better return to work. Smythe may have more information by now."

"I just happen to be going that way. May I accompany you, Miss Meriwether?" asked Allington.

"If you wish. I left Saunders' map in the Communication Room."

Harrow cursed under his breath. The girl had more lives than a cat. He scuttled along the main corridor, ducked into an empty room nearby, and waited until all was clear.

With preparations to intercept the Flying Scotsman underway, there was increased traffic along the tunnels. Harrow had to leave now, before the General's orders spread and before the morning shift prevented him from leaving via the Ascension Chamber. The codebook could wait. The Meriwether girl wasn't going anywhere; it was more important to catch that train.

Harrow strode along the tunnels towards the exit. He held his breath as he turned down the final corridor leading to the Ascension Chamber. He would bluff his way out; he outranked most of the operatives. He was supposed to be here, as far as they were concerned.

The guard snapped to attention as Harrow strode into the antechamber.

"Good evening, sir."

"Yes." Harrow checked his pocket watch. It was almost two in the morning. A layer of sweat covered his palm. His fingers twitched. He thrust his hand into his pocket. He needed to escape in order to make his rendezvous at the British Museum and ensure he would be on the same train as the Professor.

The guard eyed the watch. "It will be a few minutes until the chamber returns, sir."

Harrow nodded.

"Ah, Harrow!" The unexpected voice echoed along the tunnel and fanned out into the antechamber.

Harrow's muscles tensed. He forced a smile as he turned to meet Saunders.

"Saunders." He nodded curtly.

"I'm glad I found you," replied Saunders. "I didn't realise you were assisting with the surveillance detail?"

"Something like." He slowed his breath and allowed his shoulders to relax.

"The General has an urgent task for you."

The Ascension Chamber clunked to the ground behind Harrow. His heart raced.

Too late.

He licked his dry lips. He had less than two hours before he was trapped in the Bunker. He had to get to the Museum in time for the rendezvous. His calf muscles twitched. He wanted to run. Before they discovered him. Before the Meriwether girl discovered he'd taken the da Vinci notebook, and the diary.

"It is time you were introduced to Little Nessie," said Saunders.

"Little Nessie?" Harrow raised an eyebrow.

"Our surveillance dirigible," replied Saunders.

Harrow's eyes widened. "We have a dirigible?"

Of Suspicions, Mechanicals,
and Machinations

Harrow followed Saunders along an unknown section of tunnels until they reached a small door. Saunders unlocked it and stepped into a room, no bigger than a cupboard. The floor shook as Harrow entered behind him.

Saunders pulled down on a brass lever. A series of whirs chattered overhead. The walls reverberated as cogs rumbled below them.

The auxiliary Ascension Chamber was more like a servant's entrance, little larger than a box; a coffin built for two. Harrow scanned the room. It could prove useful if he needed an alternative escape.

"Are there any more auxiliary Ascension Chambers in the facility?" he asked.

"You'd have to ask the General," replied Saunders.

Harrow clenched his teeth. There was a time he didn't have to ask. He smiled politely at Saunders.

"I'll do that," he said.

A faint smell of coal smoke seeped through the door crack as they descended. Then it was gone. The box shuddered to a stop. Saunders pulled another lever. The door jerked open.

Trickles of steam curtained the doorway and left droplets on the iron gate barring their way. Saunders pulled on the wall lever. The gate rattled and wheezed like a discordant accordion as it collapsed against the edge of the door.

Harrow winced.

"It's an old model," said Saunders. He flicked traces of rust from his palm. "The dirigible hangar was the first section built. The Bunker was built around it as a secondary base. Thankfully our engineers had time to improve on the design before it was needed."

Harrow stepped out of the Ascension Chamber. A carpet of water vapour swirled around his ankles. He glanced around the hangar. A massive pair of metal-bound wooden doors dominated the top-third of the far wall, reaching three stories high, large enough to launch a modest-sized dirigible. Other than the Ascension Chamber and the hangar doors, there were no other exits.

Robust curved steel girders rose to the ceiling, like a ribcage, to reinforce the entire structure. The external building windows, at the upper-most level of the walls, were bricked up. Large illumination tube assemblies stood at regular intervals along the centre of the hangar, clustered near groups of workers, machinery and contraptions, creating shadows in the far corners of the hangar.

He clenched his fist. What other secrets was the General keeping from him? How many more transport hangars were secreted away in the Department's tunnels? More importantly: how could he access them?

Saunders directed Harrow's attention toward the centre of the hangar. A large wooden vessel rested on the ground, surrounded by a box-like skeleton of wooden support beams. The vessel was almost forty-foot-long oblong with a vague boat-like appearance. Four large port-holes lined each side. A collection of large, paned windows covered the lower half of the hull at the stern, creating an observation compartment. Inside were two over-stuffed armchairs.

Thick hemp ropes trailed down both sides of the hull. Several men wrangled the ropes, yanking and coiling them into submission.

Harrow followed Saunders further into the hangar. There was a matching observation compartment on the bow of the dirigible. Spurts of steam gushed from the opposite side as a large mound of canvas peaked and rose slowly from the deck.

Men scurried around the hull, grabbed ropes and tied them to the netting covering the, now visible, balloon.

"Clear!"

The men scattered into the shadows.

"Harrow, meet Little Nessie," said Saunders.

"Why wasn't I told we have a dirigible?" asked Harrow.

"On a need to know basis, I'm afraid," replied Saunders. "Nothing personal."

Harrow's mind raced. If he could commandeer the vessel, he could follow his father's train and discover his bolt hole. He wouldn't have to continue tiptoeing around his father's fragile ego; he could implement his plan. He flexed his fingers. He glanced at the hangar doors. Too many witnesses; too risky.

"I thought dirigibles were banned in London?" he said.

"Her Majesty allowed the Department to have one, for use in extreme circumstances only. We cannot fly without Her permission." Saunders stared at the dirigible and rubbed his hands together. "The General has an audience with Her Majesty, to state our case."

A glimmer of hope. His heart pounded. If the dirigible surveillance mission was refused, he could extricate himself from the Bunker and still have time to rendezvous at the Museum in the morning.

"And if She doesn't give permission?" he asked.

"It's unlikely." Saunders shook his head. "Her Majesty wants the Inventor caught."

"Why such urgency?" Harrow frowned.

"I have no idea. The Queen rarely divulges Her intentions to us. We just follow orders."

Harrow nodded. "So what are our orders?"

"*You* are in charge of the surveillance."

Harrow smiled. *Excellent.*

"You'll fly Little Nessie over King's Cross Station," continued Saunders, "then widen your search back toward Battersea Gardens. You are to report immediately if there is any sign of the Inventor or his Ghostmen. We need to know which route he is taking, so we can follow the train and extract him outside London."

"How fast can it descend when we find him?"

"You don't," replied Saunders. "Under *no* circumstances are you to engage the enemy. We don't want anyone to know we have aerial surveillance."

"Quite so." Harrow smirked. The Widow couldn't afford to let her citizens know she was flouting her own laws; They'd start demanding access to her precious technology. After all, that is why the Department of Curiosities was established - to seize, control and hoard new technologies.

He checked his pocket watch. It was well past three o'clock: the hour of the wolf. His heart pounded. There was barely twenty minutes until the morning shift. It'd be impossible to escape after that. He tapped his pocket watch impatiently.

"Something wrong, Harrow?" Saunders raised an eyebrow.

"Just wondering when we leave?" He snapped the watch shut and dropped it back in his pocket.

"We have to wait for the General," replied Saunders.

Harrow slid his fingers into his pocket and ran them over the smooth metal of his watch. He flipped it over and over.

It had been a long night. The General had requested Tillie continue monitoring communications in the event Smythe should send new information. So far, there had been none.

Tillie buried her head into the feather cushion. Her cheek pressed against the lumps where studs secured the tapestry upholstery. She moaned. She much preferred the soft feather bed in her quarters. She rolled over, taking the cushion with her. A mistake: her hand fell over the edge of the couch, cracking her knuckle against the sharp edges of its carved wooden leg.

She howled in pain; her eyes opened in protest as she sat bolt upright. A twinge of pain shot through her still healing ribs.

<<*Wake up!*>> yelled the Orb.

She raised her head and glared, bleary-eyed at the clock. *Seven o'clock.* Barely three hours sleep? Even Aunt Prudence had never insisted she wake this early.

"Is there a message?" She cradled her throbbing fingers in her hand and shuffled toward the communications desk. The paper on the printing telegraph machine was blank.

The Orb did not reply.

She slumped back into the chair and cursed.

"Why did you wake me?" she moaned.

<<*Morning.*>>

"Probably." She leaned her head in her uninjured hand. "It's been two days. Just let me sleep."

<<*Catch Harrow.*>> The Orb's tone was gruff.

"You're not going to let me get any sleep, are you?"

The communication tube whistled beside her. She rolled her eyes and reached for the ear trumpet. Definitely no more sleep.

"Yes, sir?" she said, as cheerfully as she could manage.

"Saunders here, Miss Meriwether. I do apologise for the hour. I trust you slept well?"

She snuffled.

"The General has not yet returned. I had some tea and breakfast sent to you. I hope that is satisfactory. I'll be in the File Room looking for more information on Professor Kempthorne and his associates, if you require any assistance."

"Thank you, Saunders."

She retrieved the breakfast trolley from the corridor. She lifted the metal cloche from the plate and inhaled the warm aroma of fried ham. A smile caressed her lips. *Good man, Saunders.*

She crunched on a piece of toast and inspected the rest of the trolley. A large brown paper bundle had been wedged into the shelf below the food tray. She yanked it free. Her aching fingers fumbled to untie the string.

A fresh outfit was neatly folded inside the parcel: a midnight blue military-style bodice and skirt, trimmed in white, with a striped blue and white overskirt. Hidden amongst the folds of the skirt was her aunt's red parasol and a new pair of pale blue trousers, tailored in thick silk.

"Saunders, you are a gem," she cooed as she slipped on the trousers. They were a perfect fit.

<<Finished?>> asked the Orb.

She ignored the Orb and continued dressing, completing the jaunty ensemble with Aunt Prudence's red parasol clipped to her belt and the sardonyx brooch her father had given her at the collar. She fingered its gold setting and followed the features of the female portrait.

<<Beautiful,>> whispered the Orb, *<<Navsegda sozhalet.>>*

"Pardon?" she asked.

The Orb didn't reply.

She scoffed down breakfast - ham, eggs, toast, and jam. She dabbed her lips with a napkin, grateful no one had witnessed the spectacle.

"Now I am finished," she said.

Tillie yawned. Her arms grew heavy. Her eyelids fluttered. The illumination tube flickered. She twitched.

<<*Wasting time,*>> growled the Orb.

She moaned and adjusted her skirts in the chair. She'd been instructed to continue monitoring for messages in the Communication Room until the General summoned her on his return. Fortunately, Saunders had found the time, amongst his increased duties, to ensure she'd been supplied with adequate libations.

Tillie wrapped her hand around the teapot. It was starting to cool. She poured another cup of tea, dropped in four cubes of sugar and sipped it slowly. She wrinkled her nose; it was sweet, but not sweet enough.

She eyed the Queen's portrait over the rim of her teacup. *She* had commanded Tillie to ferret out any of her father's notes on *the Horde* and deliver them to Her. Tillie gulped down a mouthful of tepid tea.

Her father's diary had mentioned *the Horde*. He had voiced his concern about the project: *No good man shall suffer.* The words tormented her. Her father didn't trust the Liberator's intentions - Queen Victoria's intentions. Why should she?

<<*Don't trust,*>> whispered the Orb.

A shiver crept up her spine. What was *the Horde*, and what were the Queen's plans with it?

Her Majesty's oiled-blue eyes glared down at her from the door, reminding her of her duty. It was as if the Queen knew she intended not to relinquish her father's diary.

She shifted in her chair, was she to be always under the ever-watchful eye of her unwanted benefactor? She stirred her tea, hoping the as yet undissolved sugar would fortify her resolve.

<<*Find traitor,*>> grumbled the Orb.

She shook her head. <<*I need to find my father's notes on the Horde first.*>>

<<*Not here,*>> whispered the Orb. <<*Leave now.*>>

"You'll say anything to get what you want." She cupped her hand over her chest as if to muffle the Orb. "I can ask to accompany the General to see the Queen, if you want to go topside. I'm sure you two have a lot in common."

The Orb pressed against her chest.

"I thought not." A faint smile caught her lip as she sipped her tea.

<<Perhaps Harrow works for Queen?>> whispered the Orb.

Her heart leaped into her throat.

"I wonder what that blaggard is up to?" Her voice quivered as her hand fell away from her chest. She had no doubt he'd be skulking around the files or listening in on private conversations.

<<Stop him.>>

"But Sir Avery and the General don't believe me," she whispered.

The Orb grumbled. *<<Find proof.>>*

"I have no proof." She glanced up at Queen Victoria's portrait. "You called me your Homunculus. You made me your creature and trained me to become your clandestine investigator, to replace my father, didn't you? Well, I found these..."

Tillie reached into one of her bustle pockets for her notes and spread them out on the desk, along with the small black code book wrapped in a rubber band. She reached into the other pocket.

"And you can't have-- " Her fingers searched the cavity. Nothing. A cold wave of dread erupted from her chest and washed over her body.

The diary was missing.

She bent sideways, ignoring the nagging twinge in her torso, and delved deeper into the concealed pocket, groping into the corners. Her finger slipped through a ragged hole at the bottom of the pocket.

"Blast!"

<<No!>> screeched the Orb.

A sharp pain stabbed into the front of her skull, replacing the chill of dread with nausea. She winced.

"Don't yell," she pleaded. "It's not my fault."

<<*How?*>> it yelled.

How could the hole have gotten there? She searched her memories, retracing her movements over the past few days. She closed her eyelids; she was so tired. She gulped down a mouthful of tea to clear her mind. It felt like a stone in her throat, the muscles resisting the ball of liquid.

The bicycle...? She must have ripped the pocket when her skirts snagged on the bicycle. She remembered the uncomfortable seat that prodded and tugged at her trousers.

Her eyelids snapped open. The trousers! Her skirts would've protected the silk pocket; trousers would not. The pocket must have ripped on the bicycle after she removed her skirts.

The diary must have fallen out when she followed Harrow. She shook her head and swallowed again, trying to dislodge the lump in her throat.

<<*Careless girl,*>> hissed the Orb.

She covered her ears, trying to drown out the Orb. It was useless; there was no escaping its scolding.

<<*Message.*>>

The keys tapped rapidly onto the paper drum, behind her.

"It's not my fault. I had it yesterday morning."

<<*Message!*>> hissed the Orb.

She snatched the missive as the last key clicked home.

"Smythe has found the Inventor's hideout in Battersea Gardens. It's been abandoned." She snatched up her aunt's red parasol and attached it to her belt chatelaine. "We need to find the General immediately!"

Tillie strode along the tunnel until she reached the General's office. She knocked on the door and waited. The Orb jiggled against her chest. She knocked again.

"General?"

Saunders peeked out from the next doorway.

"He hasn't returned yet," he said.

"But it is after ten o'clock."

"The Queen keeps her own hours." Saunders shrugged.

Tillie nodded. True, one did not rush Her Majesty; one waited. She frowned and thrust Smythe's message in Saunders' direction.

"It's urgent."

"What is urgent, my dear?" The General's calm voice wafted down the corridor.

They both turned to face the General. He smiled.

"The Inventor has already left for the train," she replied, "and the Flying Scotsman leaves at ten!"

The General checked his pocket watch. "Hmm, quarter past ten," he whispered.

Saunders had already ducked back into his office, presumably to raise an alarm. The General ushered Tillie into his office. Saunders entered a few minutes later.

"I have advised Harrow to ready Little Nessie, sir."

"Harrow?" asked Tillie. The Orb fidgeted.

"Yes. He is in now in charge of the dirigible surveillance," replied Saunders. "She should be ready to sail."

"Good, Saunders. Advise Lord Allington he will be needed," said the General.

"Very well, sir." He looked expectantly at the General. "We only need confirmation of Her Majesty's permission."

"She has consented for us to use the dirigible but..." The General passed a sealed letter to Saunders. "But we are to avoid the City of London."

"But, sir-?" she began.

"-that will slow us down, General," finished Saunders.

"We can't defy our Queen, Saunders," said the General. He looked

Tillie in the eye. His smile faded, as did the glint in his eyes.

"No, sir." Saunders shook his head slowly.

"Then we had better get moving," said the General.

The Orb squirmed. Tillie knew what it wanted to say: *Follow Harrow.* She dug her fingernails into her palm. She *couldn't* leave Harrow alone, six hundred feet in the air, with both the General and Sir Avery. They were still in denial of his treacherous capabilities.

"General?" she asked.

"Yes, Miss Meriwether?"

"May I accompany you? I have good eyes. I know what the Ghostmen look like." She widened her eyes and fluttered her eyelashes. Aunt Prudence would have approved of the tactic. "And I have never flown in a dirigible before."

"And she is good with heights," added Saunders.

The General's gaze flicked in Saunders' direction, then returned to Tillie.

"I see. A conspiracy, is it?" he said. "Very well. Just as well you are dressed to travel, my dear. There is no time to pack." He clapped his hands together. "Follow me, Miss Meriwether. Saunders, inform Smythe to assemble the men here on our return."

Tillie grinned. "Thank you," she whispered to Saunders. She spun on the heel of her boot and marched out of the room behind the General.

Saunders, yet again, was a master of forward planning.

Tillie followed the General along the tunnels until they reached a small, unmarked door. He unlocked it. They stepped into a compact chamber. The floor shook as they shifted. He pulled down on a brass lever. A loud clank followed a series of whirs. The room rocked as it descended slowly. Her stomach twisted. She leaned against the wall and closed her eyes.

The chamber shuddered to a stop at the bottom. The General waved his cane over a metal box on the gate. It clunked.

She raised an eyebrow. The General wouldn't lock his men underground with no means of escape. "How many Ascension Chambers does the facility have?" she asked.

"As many as required, my dear." He winked. "But most are secret, on a need to know basis only."

He opened the door. An iron gate barred their way. Steam hissed across the floor. A wall of vapour obscured everything beyond the gate. The smell of burning coal belched into the chamber.

Clouds of vapour drifted over them and fell away to join the carpet of mist surrounding them. Fingers of mist clung to her face. Tillie stepped through the curtain of steam. The metal grill clattered shut behind them.

The steel-boned hangar was vast. She felt like she had been swallowed by a mechanical whale.

Workmen shouted and swarmed over a massive iron apparatus nearby. They ducked as it spat a burst of steam in their direction. A short, ruddy-faced worker cursed. He raised his head in their direction, nodded and trotted off, further into the hangar.

The stench of sweat and burning oil grew stronger as she followed the General further into the hangar.

Another cloud of steam from the machine rolled past them. The General led her toward the commotion at the heart of the hangar. The steam cleared. Tillie batted away the remaining vapour and halted. Her heart fluttered.

Little Nessie bobbed three feet above the floor. The ruddy-faced workman scurried up to its base and paused.

Harrow stood, hands on hips, by the stern, lecturing the workmen who struggled to retie the mooring rope. His hair was limp, his cravat loosely tied. He shook his head.

"No, no, no," he yelled, barely audible as another jet of steam gushed

roof-ward.

The dirigible jiggled and lurched a foot upward. The ruddy-faced workman edged up to Harrow, mouthed something and pointed in Tillie and the General's direction.

Harrow turned, pushed his spectacles back up his nose and strode toward them.

"Welcome, General. We'll be ready in ten minutes."

"Excellent work. Miss Meriwether will be accompanying us," said the General.

Harrow glared at Tillie. "It's bad luck to have a woman on board ship, sir."

"Little Nessie is a dirigible, not a ship, Harrow." The familiar voice of Sir Avery rang in her ears.

"Airship, sir," said Harrow.

"Superstition," replied Sir Avery. "I'll wager Miss Meriwether has a much better head for heights than you, Harrow."

Harrow stiffened.

Tillie smiled; she remembered Sir Avery's regard for her agility on roof tops, on the night they first met. It would be exhilarating to run along a moving deck, high above London.

"You took your time, Allington," said the General. "Everything set?"

Sir Avery nodded.

"We'll have a few extra passengers on this trip, Harrow." said the General.

As if on cue, the last of the armed men trickled out of the Ascension Chamber and trotted towards Little Nessie. Half a dozen in all.

Harrow eyed the troops, then turned his attention to the dirigible, now hovering several feet from the ground

"Are you sure, General?" he asked.

"Don't underestimate Little Nessie," replied Sir Avery. "She has hidden talents."

Harrow narrowed his eyes, and regarded the dirigible. "I assume you will inform me of these talents before I leave?"

"No need," said the General. "Both Sir Avery and myself will be aboard."

Harrow shoved his hands in his pockets; his gaze dropped to the floor. "Very well, sir."

He didn't seem happy with the revelation. Tillie's smile widened. *Excellent.*

The armed operatives swarmed up the chain ladder, over Little Nessie's deck and disappeared through various doors and hatches.

Harrow pursed his lips and motioned for her to follow. She studied him carefully. She did not trust him out of her sight.

"After you," she said.

He spun on his heel and scurried up the ladder. Sir Avery followed. Tillie climbed the ladder, manoeuvring her skirts around the railing, and stepped onto the deck of Little Nessie, happy to have an ally already on board.

She took a deep breath and surveyed the polished-wood deck. Her heart raced; she was on board her first dirigible! She would *not* let Harrow ruin the experience.

The vessel swayed as the General swung off the ladder and landed on the deck.

"What do you think, Miss Meriwether?" he asked.

"I think I may enjoy flying, very much," she said.

"Glad to be of service, my dear." The corners of his eyes crinkled as he chuckled. Tillie smiled; Grandfather-General had returned. He turned to Harrow. "Get those doors open," he said. "We have a train to catch."

Of Airships, Trains, and Flying Machines

The glass panel rattled gently as the train chugged along the track. The Inventor nestled back into the rich, velvet-upholstered seat and caressed the carved wooden armrest. He rested his head on the padded cushion and glanced out the window to his left.

Slivers of gold edged the orange cloud that ribboned across the morning sky. The glow of the polished brass fixtures glinted in the corner of his eye. A bright flare of light peeked over the horizon and spilled over the fields and houses, casting long shadows across the landscape. As the light extended across the horizon, the grey sky gleamed a brilliant blue, then faded as the sun rose.

The Pharmacist sat near the rear of the carriage. His eyelids drooped and his head lolled from side to side. A Ghostman entered through the rear door of the cabin. He staggered along the aisle as the carriage swayed over the tracks. He tapped the Pharmacist on the shoulder.

The Pharmacist twitched and rubbed his eyes. He checked his pocket watch, mumbled under his breath and nodded as the Ghostman ducked back out. He rummaged in his leather medical bag and took out a linen mask and a small, rectangular tin. He checked the tin's contents, fixed the mask over his nose and mouth, then rose from his chair.

His muffled footsteps plodded forward, along the carpeted aisle.

The carriage lurched. He stumbled, almost dropping the tin as he caught the back of a nearby chair.

"We shall be arriving soon, sir." He steadied himself and leaned closer to the Inventor. "I have your medicine ready."

"You're late," replied The Inventor, his attention still focused on the view outside. He rolled up his sleeve.

Tillie was alone on the deck. Aunt Prudence's red parasol tapped the handrail as she leaned over the railing. Thick canvas belts, attached to the railing at intervals, slapped rhythmically against the hull.

Harrow had accompanied the General below to the Observation Compartment. She'd contemplated following to keep an eye on him but, with a dozen of The Department's finest armed operatives aboard, he would have a difficult time undertaking any nefarious activities. The General would be safe for now, so she'd decided to take the opportunity to enjoy a new experience.

She sighed. Unfortunately, since both the General and his cane had gone below the Orb had not stopped barking orders. It insisted they catch the train, and she follow Harrow, search his cabin and possibly catch him in the act of treason. She ignored the incessant chatter and concentrated on the wind as it played with her skirts, slapped the canvas rail belts and buffeted her ears. A rogue lock of hair crept into her nostril. She laughed and removed the offending tendril.

"Careful!" yelled Sir Avery. He moved swiftly across the deck and halted several feet from the rail. "It's a long way to fall."

"I don't plan on falling." She flashed a mischievous grin in his direction, grabbed the rail with both hands and surveyed the world below them.

A patchwork of green fields and allotments flowed past beneath her. Animals and humans, as small as ants, were frozen in a tableau stretching to the horizon.

"Can we go any higher?" she asked.

His reply was snatched away by a strong gust of wind as Little Nessie turned to follow the course of the Northern Railway. She nodded and smiled as he mouthed a long, inaudible reply. "--are working on it, Miss Meriwether."

She giggled.

Sir Avery's moustache twitched as he smiled. She noted the effect her girlish laughter had on him - just as Aunt Prudence had predicted.

<<Stop flirting,>> demanded the Orb. *<<Must follow Harrow.>>*

<<Be quiet,>> she said. *<<And I am not flirting.>>*

She leaned over the railing and took a deep breath. Gone was the London smog and the stench of coal. They were far above the unpleasant smells of the country farms. She grinned.

<<I could get used to this,>> she said.

<<Not pleasure trip,>> snapped the Orb. *<<Work to do.>>*

<<Don't you ever think of anything else?>> Tillie turned her back on the landscape, perched her bustle on the rail and regarded Sir Avery. He had not approached her, but remained frozen at a safe distance from the edge of the deck. His eyes darted from her, to the rail, to the vast expanse of open air beyond the edge of the deck. Beads of perspiration glistened on his forehead.

"How long can we stay airborne?" she asked him, ignoring the Orb's reply.

Sir Avery grimaced and moved forward to hover near her elbow, while still remaining a respectful distance from the edge.

The Orb chuckled.

"Several hours, longer when the sails are deployed."

The dirigible turned again. A cross wind caught Tillie's skirts and whipped them against the rail. He reached out his arms, as if to grab her, and hesitated. He retreated a few steps.

"Please come away from the edge."

<<*Listen,*>> hissed the Orb.

"You're not afraid of heights are you, Sir Avery?" she asked, still ignoring the Orb.

"No," he replied, "but I am averse to falling."

Her memory flicked back to when they met, the impressive sight of Sir Avery dashing over slate tiles and shimmying down drainpipes.

"I seem to remember you being quite adept at negotiating rooftops," she said. "You didn't seem to worry about falling then."

His moustache drooped. "But I wasn't six hundred feet above the earth." His voice was shaky.

"Then go below, sir. Don't torture yourself."

"I can't leave you alone on deck," he replied. "General's orders: One must always be accompanied while on deck."

She rolled her eyes. "More safety regulations? The General lives for orders and regulations."

"He is a military man, first and foremost." The creases in Sir Avery's forehead softened.

She smiled.

"If you insist on staying," he said, "perhaps you should avail yourself of the safety strapping?"

One of the thick canvas belts had unwound itself and flapped in the air. Its free end slapped against the hull.

<<*Put on,*>> insisted the Orb.

"Please, Miss Meriwether," said Sir Avery. "It's too easy to lose your balance in an unexpected updraft."

She puffed her cheeks and grabbed the girdle's bifurcated end.

"Very well." She buckled the strap around her waist. "Now you."

Sir Avery raised an eyebrow in reply.

"Put on your safety strap, Lord Allington," she said, "or I shall inform the General of your flagrant disregard for following procedures." She rammed her hands onto her hips.

His eyes widened. He swallowed, stepped forward and groped blindly at the strap coiled to the railing, his gaze fixed on the deck.

<<*Concentrate!*>> The Orb squirmed under her bodice.

<<*I am not flirting,*>> she whispered.

<<*Must find train,*>> screeched the Orb.

Tillie closed her eyes and let the wind envelop her. A faint acrid scent wafted on the breeze. She opened one eye and searched the landscape below. White plumes of smoke trailed along the rail line into the distance.

"Over there!" She grinned, squinted in the direction of the Flying Scotsman and searched the track ahead. "There." She pointed further north. "There's a bridge over that valley." She unbuckled the safety strap. "I assume the General is also well versed in tactics, being a military man?"

Sir Avery nodded. He gripped the railing next to her. His knuckles whitened.

"You have good eyes," he said. "We should inform the General immediately."

He took a step away from the railing and fumbled with the strap's buckle.

"Hurry, Sir Avery." Tillie was already half way across the deck. "Our train is waiting."

The crew had assembled in Little Nessie's lower hold. Only the pilot and boilermen remained at their posts. The General had yet to arrive, and Harrow was conspicuous by his absence. Tillie frowned, and wondered what mischief he was orchestrating.

She stood behind the troop of operatives gathered before her. She stretched up on tiptoe to observe the proceedings.

Six strapping men, some of England's finest; each wore a harness wrapped around their torso. A life-line of thick silk rope attached them securely to the winch. They were armed with pistols, grappling hooks and devilish-looking knives. Strapped to their backs were over-sized blunderbusses: a silver ball jutted from one side surrounded by brass tubes, which coiled along the rifle's barrel to the muzzle. A mini-grappling hook perched on top of the barrel end; its cord funnelled along a tube back to a cartridge on the other side of the rifle body.

The troops eagerly jostled each other as they circled a large hatch in the floor of the hull. They checked their equipment, donned their goggles and readied to jump into oblivion below. The hatch intrigued her, as did the large brass winch secured to the floor near its rim. Sir Avery checked the gauges on the body of the winch assembly and swallowed. The colour drained from his face, until he resembled a wide-eyed Ghostman. His moustache twitched.

<<*It quivered,*>> said the Orb.

<<*Don't be horrible,*>> said Tillie. <<*If you can't say something nice, then don't speak at all. Or I'll ask the General to bring his cane.*>>

The Orb shuddered. The corner of her mouth curled in satisfaction. She'd finally discovered something to curb the Orb's increased bullying.

"Are we not joining them?" she asked Sir Avery.

He stared at the floor hatch and didn't reply.

<<*Reckless,*>> said the Orb.

<<*Not your choice,*>> she said.

The Orb fell silent.

The door behind them clanked. The men snapped to attention.

There was a faint chuckle beside her ear.

"Yes, you are going, my dear," said the General.

"We get to fly?" Tillie squealed with delight. "How?"

Sir Avery managed only a weak smile.

"You get these." Harrow stepped into view, carrying a large cylindrical contraption on each arm. "Personal Flying Machines."

"Confiscated from an Australian smuggler," said the General.

Sir Avery relieved Harrow of one of the flying machines and held it at arm's length.

"The cylinder contains a pressurised gas..."

His words faded as Tillie ogled the brass cylinders. So shiny. She could see her own reflection in their brilliance. She ran her hands along the pipes and grabbed the harness.

"How do I put it on?" She spun around, slipped her arms through the harness straps and pulled the contraption onto her back.

Sir Avery halted his lecture and blinked; his hands, still holding the harness straps, now encircled her waist. Her bustle nudged his arm as she snatched the ends of the straps from his hand and buckled up the harness.

He took a quick step backwards, transferring his hands to cradle the gas tanks until the straps were secure. The colour had returned to his cheeks.

Harrow handed Sir Avery the second Personal Flying Machine. Sir Avery donned the contraption and demonstrated how to adjust the pack to sit securely.

"You're not accompanying us, Harrow?" she asked.

"I have my orders," he replied. "I am to stay here with the General. The Personal Flying Machines are restricted to those with Lower Level clearance."

Harrow's face remained fixed, showing no emotion. He was up to something.

The Orb jittered. Tillie eyed Harrow out of the corner of her eye. She was not comfortable with leaving him alone with the General, in such close proximity of a gaping hole hundreds of feet above the countryside.

Harrow smiled at her. It was faint, but it was there.

<<He knows I suspect him. What should I do?>>

The Orb did not reply. She frowned; this time she wanted its opinion. She glanced at the General's cane and frowned. Blessings could also be curses.

Sir Avery jiggled the gas canisters and tapped on the pressure gauge. Tillie relaxed her muscles, trying to look as calm as possible, and returned her attention to the Personal Flying Machine.

"How do I start it?" she asked Sir Avery.

"First we..."

He swivelled two metal pipe-handles over her head. They clicked in place. She grasped them.

"Steering?" she asked.

"Yes," he replied. "Just apply pressure in the direction you wish to travel."

She pushed forward. The handles moved under her guidance.

"This," he indicated a switch at the bottom of the main body of the pack, "is the ignition switch. And this..." He indicated a large button on the right side of the pack, about elbow height. "This will get you back to the ground if you lose power."

Tillie grinned. It seemed simple enough.

The General stepped forward.

"Miss Meriwether and Gentlemen, I will remind you this is a retrieval mission. I have direct orders from Her Majesty. We need the Inventor alive." He turned to the troops. "And intact. Is that understood?"

The men nodded.

"Once he is retrieved, and you are clear of the train, Little Nessie will descend to facilitate your extraction." He turned to Harrow. "There is an extra flying machine prepared for you. Stop the train if there is any danger to the passengers."

Harrow narrowed his eyelids.

"Sir?" he said. "I thought-"

"Change of plan. We need to ensure the safety of the other passengers on board. That is your priority."

Harrow slipped on the flying machine and clicked the harness in place.

"Miss Meriwether, you are to accompany Sir Avery to First Class to apprehend the Inventor. The rest of the men will keep the Ghostmen from interfering."

There was a murmur of assent.

She carefully lifted her goggles over her head, hoping it would not disrupt her coiffure, and wrangled a ringlet back in place. The dirigible and the General would be safer with Harrow on the ground, though she'd have preferred to have someone accompany him, to keep an eye on him. At least he wouldn't have a chance to warn the Inventor.

The floor vibrated beneath her feet. A loud ratcheting echoed throughout the hold. A jet of air rushed through a crack at the rim of the hatch. The crack widened slowly, as the hatch slid open in front of them. Wind roared beneath them, whistling at the edge of the gaping maw.

Harrow stepped toward the hull hatch, flicked the ignition switch and stepped into the chasm. He hovered for a second, then plummeted out of sight.

She leaned forward and watched as he turned and sped northward toward the engine as it neared the bridge.

Little Nessie was now directly above the middle carriage, almost in position to drop the rest of her human cargo.

Sir Avery closed his eyes and ignited his flying machine. He winced as it rumbled into life, then took a deep breath and edged toward the hatch.

Tillie flicked the switch on her own contraption. A dull twinge gripped her rib cage as the initial vibration knocked on her spine. She took a, not too deep, breath and struggled to relax the muscles in her torso. The vibration settled into a gentle rhythm. The twinge eased until it was only a mild irritation.

Sir Avery leaned close to her. "Are your ribs still causing discomfort, Miss Meriwether?" he whispered. "You should inform the General."

"They are healing as expected," she replied. "There is no need to bother the General."

He nodded. "Very well. Then follow me, Miss Meriwether, into the heavens." He stepped into the air, screwed his eyelids shut and lowered himself out of sight.

Tillie stepped up to the edge. Her skirts fluttered in the churning air currents.

<<*Oh dear, I didn't think this through.*>> She grabbed the back of her overskirt with each hand and folded the edges forward, tugging them tight to tie a knot and tucked the ends into the harness strap, then stepped forward and descended into the void.

The air was cool. The swirling air currents abated as Tillie descended further from Little Nessie. She was alone in a vast sea of nothing. Free.

She slipped down through a cloud, barely feeling its chill touch, and surveyed the countryside below her. Sir Avery was a diminishing speck below her. She scanned the surrounding airspace and examined the train and track below. Harrow was nowhere to be seen.

Loose sections of skirt hem flapped against her body and crept toward her face as a zephyr played around her ankles, threatening to untie her skirts. She manoeuvred herself into the breeze to keep her skirts in place, thankful she'd remembered to wear trousers, then lowered herself toward the train.

Half way through her descent, the Personal Flying Machine's gas cylinders sputtered. They shuddered. Tillie plummeted five feet. The sudden jolt wedged her heart in her throat. A cracking pain shot through her torso. Her scream whipped away in the wind. The cylinder steadied; its reassuring, rhythmic vibration returned. The flying machine hissed innocently.

Sir Avery ceased his descent, hovered, and rushed up toward her.

The cylinders sputtered again. Her flying machine shuddered. Her heart froze.

"Not again."

<<*Sabotage!*>> screamed the Orb.

"Harrow!" she replied.

Gravity tugged at her heart, grabbed the wayward organ and slammed it into her stomach. Acidic chunks filled her throat. She grabbed at her bodice, trying to hold its contents in place.

"Matilda!" yelled Sir Avery as he swooped closer.

The wind tugged her skirts and yanked them from the harness. The material twisted and unfurled. It whipped at her face, wrapped around her arms and tangled her legs, digging her parasol into her side and pulling her off balance. She tumbled and spun downward towards the train.

A heavy object buffeted her mid-fall. It grabbed her arm and pulled her out of the spin and steadied her descent. She opened her eyes as Sir Avery wrapped his arms around her waist.

"Push the-- " His words were snatched by the howling wind before they reached her.

<<*Button,*>> screamed the Orb. <<*Push the button!*>>

Tillie twisted in the harness and slammed her elbow into the emergency button on the side of the pack. The cylinders coughed.

Sir Avery released her.

She dropped only a foot before the pack jerked her body upward for a second time. Her ribs burned. She wrapped her arms around her chest and moaned as she descended, gliding on the wind toward the carriages below.

Sir Avery followed.

She wobbled. She thrust her arms outwards to find her balance, then reached her hands backward. Soft canvas flapped against her fingers. She glanced behind her.

"I've got wings!"

Sir Avery grinned in reply. He shadowed her final descent and landed on the carriage roof next to her. They tiptoed along the roof toward the rear door.

"What happened?" he asked.

"The cylinders must have malfunctioned," she replied.

<<*Sabotage,*>> hissed the Orb.

"Both of them? At the same time?"

She tapped one of the gauges. "They're empty."

"That's impossible." He frowned. "I checked them myself."

He rapped the cylinder. There was a deep hollow clang. He frowned.

"I know you did," she whispered.

Little Nessie's shadow crept over them. They didn't have time to discuss Harrow's likely treachery now.

"We need to get in position." She patted Sir Avery on the shoulder.

They crept to the rear end of the carriage and climbed down to the door. The dirigible hovered above them, matching the speed of the train. It jiggled as the men descended out of the hatch and dripped down their ropes.

The engine's whistle screamed as the train chugged toward the bridge.

Sir Avery offered her a pistol.

"I've never liked guns," she said as she unhooked her parasol and hefted the heavy ivory handle in her hand. "Now would be a good time to see if your modifications were as good as you claim."

<<*Take the pistol,*>> urged the Orb.

She shook her head.

Sir Avery clicked his tongue. "As you wish." He loosed his grip on the pistol, letting the barrel drop to face the deck and replaced it inside his pocket.

Soft thuds above them heralded the arrival of the operatives.

"We had better keep moving." His moustache twitched. He winked at her, turned the handle and threw the carriage door open.

Of Pistols, Parasols, and Photographs

Tillie slipped her flying goggles down around her neck and scanned the dining car through the glass panel in the door. A well-dressed gentleman sat alone at the table near a side window to their right and shuffled through a stack of papers. Three pale Ghostmen stood throughout the carriage. One Ghostman guarded the far door, a second, taller, Ghostman stood near the gentleman occupant. The third was only a few feet in front of them.

The closest Ghostman spun to face them as Sir Avery opened the door and burst into the carriage. He batted Sir Avery's pistol from his grip. It skittered across the polished wood floor and wedged itself between a chair and table legs.

The gentleman jumped to his feet and retreated behind his bodyguard.

<<*The Inventor,*>> cried the Orb.

The Ghostman pulled a dagger from his boot.

Sir Avery lunged for his pistol and tumbled to avoid the Ghostman's follow-up attack. Tillie unclipped her parasol and stepped forward into the breach.

The door guard removed an elephant gun from under his heavy, woollen coat.

<<*Watch out,*>> screamed the Orb.

The gun exploded above their heads. Sir Avery threw himself to the floor. The slug punched a hole in the wall where he had stood.

Her ears rang from the blast. She stepped forward, thrust her parasol into the cloud of thick, white smoke before her and flicked open the canopy to protect Sir Avery. Her eyes stung as the taste of steam and sulphur filled her mouth.

"Not in an enclosed space!" yelled Sir Avery as he rolled towards the dining table.

<<*Leave him!*>> scolded the Orb. <<*Get traitor. Get murderer.*>>

The door guard aimed the elephant gun. Two shots? She'd gambled on it being a single shot rifle. Not even Sir Avery's science could stop a 0.577 Black Powder Express. She swore under her breath. The door guard fired his second shot.

Her shoulders tensed as she prepared for the slug to rip through the parasol, bringing inevitable pain. Instead, the canopy buckled, jarring her elbows. With a loud crack, the slug whizzed past and ricocheted back toward her attackers. The force threw her against the carriage wall, as the parasol's canopy sprang back into place.

The Inventor retreated towards the far door. The Ghostmen ducked for cover, their heads darting from side to side as they tried to track the bullet.

<<*Interesting*>> chuckled the Orb.

Her eyes widened. Sir Avery's improvements had saved her life. <<*Well, I did ask for a bullet shield.*>>

She glanced in Sir Avery's direction to thank him. He'd taken cover under the table. His hand reached out toward his pistol, just beyond his reach. Her gratitude would have to wait; she needed to create a distraction so he could retrieve it.

She yanked the parasol shut and slammed the ferrule into the jaw of the unsuspecting dagger-wielding Ghostman. His eyes bulged. His head snapped backwards as he gurgled in pain.

Sir Avery grinned and snatched up his pistol. The bodyguard surged forward to meet him.

The door slammed at the other end of the carriage. She glanced in its direction. The Inventor and the door guard had gone.

<<*Escaping,*>> hissed the Orb.

"I know," she yelled.

The injured Ghostman moaned, shook his head and scrambled to his feet. He lurched in her direction. She instinctively thrust her parasol forward at her oncoming assailant.

"Push the button," yelled Sir Avery, as he wrestled with the bodyguard.

Her thumb slid along the parasol's refurbished shaft, until it met an unfamiliar button. She pressed it. A shiny metal spike ejected from the tip of the parasol. She charged forward.

The Ghostman swung his fist into Tillie's stomach and roared in pain. Her metal corset rattled. The force of the blow swept her backwards and rammed her shoulder into the corner of a dining table. She slumped to the floor. The parasol clattered beside her. Her ribs screamed in agony. She struggled for air. The carriage swam and her vision blurred. Blood thumped through her ears, muffling the sounds of Sir Avery struggling with the bodyguard nearby.

<<*Move,*>> wailed the Orb. <<*Defend yourself.*>>

She struggled to lift her arms, to move her legs; her limbs refused to obey. She braced herself, but the expected blow never came.

The carriage shuddered violently.

She took a tentative breath and wrapped her fingers around her parasol handle. Where had the Ghostman gone? She squinted to search the dining car as her focus returned.

The Ghostman lay crumpled on the floor in front of her. His eyes stared back at her, wide and unblinking. He mouthed a retort and went silent. Blood gushed from a gaping hole in his chest and glistened in the light from the carriage window above her. The crimson liquid oozed from under his body and seeped into his woollen coat.

Beyond the fallen Ghostman, Sir Avery still grappled with his opponent for control of his pistol.

The tide of blood crept closer to Tillie's fingers. She blinked.

The front door of the carriage flung open. The Inventor and the door guard entered the carriage.

<<*He's trapped.*>> The Orb jiggled in delight. <<*Get him!*>>

Her limbs felt numb, too heavy to move.

<<*I think I broke another rib,*>> she whispered.

<<*Move!*>>

Pain racked her ribs with each gasp for air. She winced. Bile rose up her throat, threatening to fill her mouth.

<<*Move now!*>> screamed the Orb.

She took shallow breaths as she struggled to her knees and leaned on the window frame to steady herself.

The late morning sunlight streamed through the open window. She peered through it, along the track ahead. There were only a few more miles until they turned toward the bridge. A cloud of black smoke belched out from the engine's chimney and washed along the edge of the carriages. The taste of coal smoke dried her throat. Grit whipped her face and stung her eyes. She turned away from the window and scanned the carriage through streaming eyes.

The door guard moved forward, raised his pistol in Sir Avery's direction. She opened her mouth to warn him.

A thunderous explosion shuddered the carriage. It jolted forward. She struggled to keep her footing as the train groaned and increased speed. The door guard stumbled further into the carriage and waved his pistol wildly.

She shifted her weight to regain balance, raised her parasol and stepped between Sir Avery and the door guard.

The door guard steadied himself. This time he aimed at her. She flicked open the parasol and braced herself. The door guard squeezed the trigger. The hammer fell with a click as a deep rumble reverberated along the track beneath her feet.

The carriage shuddered a second time. The door guard's shot misfired and gouged into the floor. He lurched into the Inventor and slammed him against the side wall. Tillie was thrown across the floor in Sir Avery's direction. Pain seared through her body and down her arms. She shrieked.

Sir Avery tightened his grip on the bodyguard's neck, glanced at the splintered floorboards near him, then at Tillie. His moustache drooped.

"Matilda?" he whispered.

She gasped for air, not able to reply, her eyes streaming from coal grit and pain.

The bodyguard grinned, and rammed Sir Avery backwards into a nearby chair.

Sir Avery growled. He grabbed the bodyguard's wrist and wrenched it backwards with a sickening crunch. The bodyguard crumpled to the ground and writhed on the floor.

Sir Avery pressed his foot on the bodyguard's uninjured arm, snatched up his pistol and shot the door guard.

Sir Avery's moustache twitched. His eyes were cold. He raised the pistol in the direction of the Inventor and pulled trigger. It clicked.

Empty.

A shiver crawled under Tillie's skin.

She turned to face the Inventor. He remained motionless, staring at the door guard's pistol at his feet. His eyes widened.

Both men twitched.

Sir Avery threw himself forward, covering the distance before the

Inventor could grab the weapon. The two men landed on the floor next to each other. They blinked.

Sir Avery snatched up the pistol and crunched the butt into the side of the Inventor's face. The Inventor grunted. Blood trickled from his nose. He scowled and head-butted his attacker.

Sir Avery moaned and shook his head.

She crawled toward the Ghostman's abandoned dagger. The carriage lurched to one side as the train turned and sped towards the bridge. The weapon skittered across the floor.

"We're going too fast," she yelled over the clatter of the shaking carriage.

Loose papers fluttered to the floor.

The elephant gun lay only a few feet away. Her head reeled. The rifle blurred. She grabbed the edge of the table to steady herself, and stretched out her hand, ignoring the pain and curled her fingers around the rifle's butt.

The Orb pushed into her chest. It was warm. <<*Vengeance,*>> it hissed.

She dragged her body upright, rested on the edge of the table and glanced at the blank papers scattered across it.

<<*Something's not right,*>> she whispered.

The carriage swayed. The papers blurred. Her stomach churned. The men's skirmishing bodies twisted through the carriage refusing each other victory.

The Orb pushed harder, growing hotter. <<*Kill him,*>> it wailed.

She waited until her world stabilised. She raised the blunderbuss. Her finger tightened on the trigger.

She peered at the men.

"Something's not right." She lowered the gun and tracked the contorting body of the Inventor as he ducked another blow.

<<*Traitor. Murderer.*>> The Orb's searing heat seemed to burrow

into her chest. <<*Kill him, now!>>*

She swallowed.

"Don't make me shoot," she yelled.

Both men froze. The Inventor moaned.

<<*Now!>>* The Orb's demand reverberated through her mind.

Tillie looked back at the Ghostman lying in a pool of his own blood; a pool of her making. She didn't like guns.

<<*No,>>* she said.

"Shoot him." Sir Avery grinned.

"What if I miss?"

Sir Avery pushed his opponent to the ground and pinned him face-down on the floor.

Her hand trembled as she lowered the blunderbuss.

"I could have shot you," she said to Sir Avery.

"You wouldn't have." He winked at her. "It's empty. It only had two shots."

The Inventor kicked out in her direction. She eyed him.

"Something's not right," she said.

Sir Avery turned to her. His moustache wiggled. There was a hint of blood on one tip. She inspected his face.

"What's that on your forehead?" She studied a pale smudge on his brow.

He wiped his head. The smudge transferred to his hand.

She edged closer, took Sir Avery's hand, wiped the smudge with her finger and frowned.

"Cosmetics?"

She crouched down, biting her lip against the pain, and examined the Inventor's face. Two pale grey areas marked his face - one on his forehead, the other on his cheek - where the flesh coloured face paint had been rubbed off during the struggle.

She stared into his dull eyes - grey within grey. Her eyes widened.

The Orb twitched.

She gasped.

"It's not him," she whispered.

"Not who?" asked Sir Avery.

"This is not the Inventor," she said.

The Orb turned cold.

<<*Impostor?*>>

"I don't understand," said Sir Avery.

She leaned forward, dragged her thumb across the cheek of the struggling impostor and pursed her lips.

"He's an impostor." She thrust her thumb in front of Sir Avery's face. "He's a Ghostman in disguise."

"How?" Sir Avery raised an eyebrow. "Smythe is never wrong. If he says the Inventor is on the train, then he is."

"Never wrong?"

"Hardly ever," Sir Avery's moustache twitched.

"Then in this case, he has been misinformed. This is not the Inventor."

"A diversion?" he asked.

She nodded.

The Ghostman chuckled and squirmed in Sir Avery's grasp. He struggled to keep hold of his captive.

"Miss Meriwether, you'll find restraints in my pocket. If you'd be so kind as to do the honours."

She undid the buttons of his coat pocket and retrieved a set of chained manacles, closed them around the Ghostman's wrists. Gears whirred and clicked into place.

Sir Avery grabbed the manacle's chain and wrenched the impostor towards the forward door.

"Where's the Inventor?" he growled at the Ghostman.

The Ghostman did not reply.

<<*Tricked,*>> snarled the Orb.

"How can you be sure it's not him?" asked Sir Avery. "No one has seen the Inventor."

"I'm sure," she replied.

"How do you know?" he asked. "I need proof, Miss Meriwether."

She bit her lip. It was now or never. She had to trust someone. She slipped her hand inside her bustle pocket. "I have proof," she said.

<<*Don't,*>> scolded the Orb.

She fingered the edge of the photograph of her father and Cranshaw, whom she now knew to be the Inventor.

"Can I trust you, Avery?"

Sir Avery's eyebrow crumpled.

"You can trust me." His voice was calm, reassuring, rich and smooth like the toffee treats her father used to buy for her.

She pulled the photograph from its hiding place. She *had* to trust him; if they were to catch the real Inventor, he needed to know what he looked like.

<<*No!*>> roared the Orb.

"I have a photograph of him." She showed him the photograph.

Sir Avery squinted at the pitted tintype. Tillie watched his eyes track over the photograph. Her hands trembled. Had she made a mistake?

"He is the man on the left."

He glanced at her, taking particular interest in the brooch proudly displayed at her throat.

"I see," he said. "Are you sure?"

"Positive," she replied.

"And who are the man and woman with him?"

She snatched away the photograph. "Lost in history." She turned to the impostor.

"Where is your master?" she asked the Ghostman.

He did not answer.

Sir Avery grabbed his chin and forced his head upright. "It would be better if you tell us where he is."

The Ghostman avoided Sir Avery's glare and moaned.

"Check his tongue," said Tillie.

Sir Avery wrenched the Ghostman's jaw open and cursed under his breath.

"Removed, like the others?" she asked.

He nodded. "If this is an impostor- "

"Then *this* train must be a diversion," she continued.

The door burst open. A Department operative rushed into the carriage, followed by the crack of pistol-fire. He aimed his pistol at them. His scowl slipped into a smile. He lowered his weapon and stepped forward.

"There are no more Ghostmen on board, sir," he said. "You have the Inventor?"

"No, we don't," replied Tillie.

"Sir?" The operative raised an eyebrow and turned to Sir Avery.

"This impostor has led us on a merry dance, Robson." He threw the manacle chain to the operative. "This was a diversion, so the real Inventor could escape."

The train jolted, almost knocking them off their feet.

<<*Leave now.*>> The chill of the Orb numbed her skin.

Metal screamed beneath their feet. The train jerked forward, then backward. Glass shattered onto the wooden floor.

She toppled sideways and tumbled into Sir Avery. He grabbed her hand to halt her fall.

"Damn you, Harrow," she hissed.

"What the-- ?" grumbled Sir Avery.

"We need to get off this train," she replied. "We'll reach the bridge any minute."

"Splendid idea, Miss Meriwether," he replied. He nodded in Robson's direction.

Robson yelled the order into the adjoining carriage: "Disengage!"

The troops clambered out of the carriage windows, grabbed dangling ropes and climbed toward the dirigible. Tillie rushed to the rear door.

"Bring the prisoner, Robson. We may get some information out of him, yet." Sir Avery tucked his pistol inside his coat and followed Tillie.

Robson grabbed the Ghostman, dragged him to the side of the carriage and kicked open the external passenger door at the other end.

Tillie's boots clanged on the metal rungs as she mounted the ladder leading to the carriage roof. Her skirt pleating snagged on the rail as she climbed and yanked her backwards. She winced. Fortunately her armoured corset redistributed most of the force.

"Blasted skirts."

<<*Hurry,*>> urged the Orb.

She glanced at the smoking engine racing toward the bridge. Her heart raced even faster. She struggled to pull the treasured silk free.

"It's stuck!" She leaned forward and tugged harder.

Sir Avery grasped the skirt and wrenched it free. The momentum sent her careering forward and slammed her into the handrail and onto the roof of the carriage. A warm trickle ran down her forehead.

"Are you all right?" Sir Avery climbed onto the roof and offered his hand for assistance. The remnants of torn hem pleating dangled from his fist and danced in the wind.

She raised an eyebrow.

"I hope you won't blame me for ruining *this* outfit, Sir Avery?"

He chuckled, shoved the passementerie into his pocket and helped her to her feet.

Sir Avery's smile slipped.

"You're injured," he whispered.

She wiped her forehead. Steaks of blood stained her glove.

"Just a scratch." She steadied herself on the roof and searched the sky for Little Nessie. The sunshine glared in her eyes, obscuring the dirigible above them.

Another explosion shuddered the air. Bursts of hot, black smoke belched along the carriages and filled her lungs - foul tasting, acrid smoke. She spluttered, pulled on her goggles and peered through the choking smoke. Chunks of wood and metal showered over the engine. The front carriages curved awkwardly to one side as it raced onto the bridge, towards a smouldering gap of twisted metal, and to oblivion.

The roof below her feet shuddered.

<<*Run!*>> yelled the Orb.

All the carriages were now on the bridge. There was a sheer drop on either side. Her heart pounded.

"Run to where?"

Sir Avery ignited his flying machine and swung his arm around her waist. "Apologies, Miss Meriwether," he said.

Her cheeks burned. This was the fourth time he'd saved her. She couldn't let him make a habit of it. She took a deep breath and turned to face the engine, hoping he wouldn't notice her embarrassment and mistake it for swooning.

The engine slipped a few feet, dragging the carriages forward. The roof shuddered under their feet. She gripped Sir Avery's arm; her flying machine had been sabotaged and there was a one hundred foot drop below them. There were more appropriate occasions to assert her independence.

"Apology accepted," she whispered in his ear.

Sir Avery's flying machine sputtered.

"Not again," she moaned.

<<*No!*>> screamed the Orb.

Sir Avery growled and flicked a switch. There was a satisfactory hiss as the flying machine rumbled into life.

The carriage creaked and jerked forward. A deafening crack reverberated along the track. The engine whined and teetered on the edge of the track. Thick plumes of soot coughed into the air. Acrid smoke billowed from the engine and swallowed the fuel car as it slipped off the track. Glowing chunks of burning coal showered over the edge and dripped into the chasm below.

Sir Avery's Personal Flying Machine hovered for a moment. The dining carriage groaned, dropped away from their feet and plummeted after the rest of the train into the valley below.

The engine burst into flames. The explosion belched skyward and battered Tillie's eardrums. She screamed - or was it the Orb?

The Personal Flying Machine struggled to gain height.

The world became disarmingly quiet, muffling the second explosion, which thrust them upward. Little Nessie bobbed in the thermal updrafts as she descended to meet them.

"Don't let go," she whispered in Sir Avery's ear. She fought to keep her eyes open as the wall of heat buffeted them, and scanned the ground below.

Flames licked the bridge's wooden support beams below them, and crept along the edges of the carriages until they were engulfed. A few lucky survivors scrambled to free themselves from the wreckage, and scurried from the growing inferno. Others crawled, catching fire as they attempted to escape, stumbled and fell, sparking spot fires in the surrounding undergrowth.

The colour drained from his cheeks. His lips tightened. She buried her face into his chest and wept, grateful she could not hear the screams of the unfortunates.

The heat retreated as they crept higher.

"Almost there." His voice was muffled.

A scorching whirlwind buffeted them from above. A rush of heat rolled over her skin as they plummeted several feet.

Her heart leaped into her throat. She squeezed her eyelids shut and clung to Sir Avery.

"The dirigible!" His chest convulsed as he cried out, his voice barely audible over the roar of the explosion.

"General!" Her eyes snapped open. Her goggles fogged in the intense heat. Little Nessie spiralled past them, enveloped in flames.

A blood-curdling cry arose from the fiery depths of the gondola's fractured hull. The dirigible exploded. Blazing shards sliced through the air. Bodies tumbled toward the valley below.

Sir Avery launched the flying machine toward them and stuck out his free hand to grab Robson's arm. The machine wobbled. He grabbed the steering bar to control their descent. Robson's eyes bulged as his fingers slipped from Sir Avery's grasp. He dropped, grabbed Sir Avery's leg and held tight. The flying machine whined as the extra weight dragged them groundward.

Hot, black smoke rushed to meet them. The flying machine jerked and sputtered. A loud thunk echoed through her ears. Robson cursed. Sir Avery's grip relaxed. The flying machine quivered and went silent. She clutched at the harness and squeezed her eyes tight.

The wind whistled past them as they dropped.

The metal cut into Tillie's hand. The pain was dulled by the searing ache that grabbed at her chest. A warm trickle ran down her palm. Her eyelids refused to open.

Warm zephyrs washed wisps of hair over her face. A roar of flames followed, chasing the swarms buzzing in her head. Sharp pricks jabbed her leg. Leaves scratched her arms and rustled in the hot currents. She was alive!

<<*Where are we?*>>

The Orb didn't reply.

Her pulse raced. The pain in her chest magnified with each quickened breath.

"Concentrate," she whispered to remind herself she was alive.

"Slow breaths."

She sipped the air. Foul, pungent smoke filled her lungs. She coughed. More pain heralded a choked scream. Footsteps crunched nearby.

<<Stay calm.>>

Still no reply from the Orb.

Her eyelids fluttered open reluctantly. Colours drifted through a grey blur and resisted the urge to liberate themselves. A shadow crept into view and halted beside her. She blinked, unsuccessfully trying to clear her focus. Dark shoes nudged her shoulder.

<<Sir Avery?>> She opened her mouth but speech was still a memory.

She felt a tug at her hand, cutting the tintype deeper. Her fingers were slowly pried loose, and her father's photograph slipped from her grasp.

<<Thief.>> The Orb's voice was feeble and shaky.

The buzzing grew louder.

She tried to object, but managed only a pathetic moan. Objections, it appeared, were also but a memory.

Her brain signalled for her arm to move, to grab the bandit. It refused to obey. The shoe lifted, and turned. A twig snapped. The footsteps faded.

Another wave of heat buffeted her, bringing exhaustion in its wake.

Of Misunderstandings, Anguish,
and Walking Sticks

S moke trickled around the edges of the carriage window. The Inventor opened it and sniffed the air. Amongst the smell of coal dust and steam, there was a faint hint of salt. Gulls squawked in the distance. The Pharmacist waddled along the aisle toward him.

"I have your medicine ready, sir," he said. "We shall be arriving in Plymouth shortly."

The carriage shuddered. The Pharmacist's bag rattled. He winced, steadied himself and checked its contents.

"How long until luncheon?" asked the Inventor.

"Luncheon will be served on board ship, sir," replied the pharmacist.

"Excellent." The Inventor grinned, rolled up his sleeve, his attention still fixed on the view outside. "The sea air always gives me an appetite."

The buzzing faded. The smell of burning coal and singed leather clawed at Tillie's nostrils. Her chest ached.

<<*Where are we?*>>

The Orb didn't reply.

A chill gripped her chest. She held her breath as she sat upright and grabbed at her bodice for the familiar lump of her usually-vocal companion. The top few buttons were missing. Her torn collar hung limp against her exposed skin, weighed down by her father's brooch. Her fingers scrabbled under the lined silk and wrapped around the metal sphere. She took a deep breath.

"Why didn't you answer me?" she asked.

The Orb remained silent.

She huffed. <<*Stop sulking. There's work to be done.*>>

She scanned the littered valley. The train was a twisted confusion of burning wood and metal. Less than half a dozen civilians had emerged from the wreck. Robson had survived the dirigible explosion, thanks to quick reflexes and determination. He limped amongst the burning wreckage looking for survivors. Harrow skulked around the edges of the flames and carnage, like a mechanical carrion bird, still wearing an intact Personal Flying Machine.

Tillie pulled herself to her feet, determined to join the search for survivors. Brambles scratched at her skin and entangled her skirts. The deep, pleated petticoat hem ripped as she struggled forward.

She examined the shredded silk and linen, and her exposed tattered stockings. She tugged the material. It was no use. It was stuck fast. She eyed the blue and white-striped silk and sighed: such a waste.

She twisted her skirts over her bustle to reach the hooks on the waistband, and froze.

"My pockets!"

Her heart raced as she fumbled with the fasteners, and leaped out of the thorny jumble. She patted the hidden bustle pockets. The pockets were still intact and the back of her petticoat was barely damaged. She breathed sigh of relief; all the familiar bumps and lumps were there.

She removed the damaged hem and front petticoat panel, exposing her truncated men's trousers. She left the back panel intact to conceal the bustle and pockets from the photograph thief.

She examined her wounded hand. Smudges of dirt and dried blood stained her gloves. A ragged cut sliced through the material and into her skin.

Who had stolen the photograph and left her behind? She regarded the survivors. Any of them could have taken it: Sir Avery methodically searched the foliage and scattered pockets of dirigible debris, calling for the General. Harrow loitered close to Robson on the other side of the train wreckage. No one was searching this side of the valley.

She surveyed the surrounding area. Not far away lay a contorted leather armchair, its naked springs clothed in tufts of horsehair. Several clumps of wreckage surrounded it. She waded through the long grass and pushed aside bushes, searching for any signs of movement.

Her ears hummed.

<<*Have you stopped sulking?*>> she asked the Orb.

It didn't reply.

<<*Have it your way, then,*>> she said. <<*I need to find the General.*>>

The air buzzed behind her. She spun on her heel and searched in the direction of the noise.

The General lay motionless amongst dirigible wreckage, impaled by shards of observation glass and remnants of a flying machine peeled open by the blast. His face was pale. His limbs lay at awkward angles, not achievable at any age. His silver hair was streaked with blood and shone with an imperfect halo, illuminated by the flames licking the bridge supports. His breathing was shallow. Irregular. Laboured.

Tillie fell to her knees beside him.

A long gash tore over his right cheek and into his forehead. Shards of bone jutted from the empty eye socket. Blood trickled down his temple to where the eviscerated eyeball hung.

"General?" She could taste the salt as it rolled onto her lip. She wiped the tears from her chin.

"Not..." The corner of the General's lip twitched. His voice was faint and faltering: "...fast enough."

"Hush," she whispered. "Save your energy."

She dabbed the edge of his head wound. Deep furrows etched his face. He was old. Older than she had ever realised. She frowned and pressed her hand against his leg.

"Can you feel this?" she asked.

There was no answer.

Her heart sank. She cursed under her breath.

"General?" she whispered. "I need to get help."

A faint murmur was the only reply.

Her lip quivered. "Can you hear me, sir?"

"Yes." The General gasped for air. His lungs gurgled. "How?"

"How, what, sir?"

"Nessie." His remaining eye opened and stared, unfocused, past Tillie. His voice was feeble. The words were slurred. "Sabotage."

She glanced over the remnants of his Personal Flying Machine. It had peeled open from the inside, and not by the dirigible explosion.

"My flying machine was sabotaged as well," she said.

"Harrow..." he whispered. "Maintenance..."

"You believe me? About Harrow?" She held her breath.

"Forgive... me." The General's eyelids fluttered. "My dear."

She sniffed. Tears fell onto her hand. The General swallowed. The furrows around his mouth deepened. His hand grasped at the ground. A faint buzz flitted at the edge of her consciousness.

"Cane?" he whispered.

Tillie rose to her feet and searched the ground around them. A glint flickered amongst twisted debris wedged in some nearby brambles. She braced her side, reached across the bushes and leaned under a piece of warped wreckage, stretching her fingers out toward the General's cane.

Pain shot through her side. Her muscles spasmed. Her body convulsed. Branches scratched at her arms and face as she fell into the brambles. Her scream scraped her eardrums.

The Orb shuddered, but said nothing.

The buzzing grew louder. Her head spun, just before the nausea hit.

Footsteps thumped across the ground toward her. Twigs whipped her arm as the new arrival scrambled through the bushes.

"Miss Meriwether, are you injured?" Sir Avery's words rose above the ongoing roar of the flames. He clutched at his coat's side pocket. A hunk of torn striped, blue and white pleated silk overflowed from its top. "Are you in need of assistance?" His moustache twitched as he unbuckled his Personal Flying Machine and dumped its battered remains onto the ground beside his black boots.

She eyed his black boots and bulging coat pocket. Her heart pounded. What else did he have in there? Her father's photograph, perhaps? Every muscle in her body tensed.

"What are you doing here?" His moustache twitched as he scanned the surrounding undergrowth, the brambles and along the valley floor, anywhere but meeting her gaze.

Blood pounded in her ears. He knew! He had the photograph, and he knew.

"Miss Meriwether, are you injured?"

The fresh cuts stung her skin. Her hand throbbed. Her ribs complained. She ignored the pain and shook her head.

He narrowed his eyelids, inspected her face and torn bodice and frowned.

The brooch! She swallowed. She raised her hand to her throat, tucked the dangling collar – and the attached brooch – inside the torn neckline.

Sir Avery took her hand and helped her to her feet. She flinched.

"You're bleeding." He reached into his pocket, ripped off a piece of pleated trim and offered it to her.

"Thank you, Lord Allington." She wrapped the ragged cloth around her hand and wondered if now was an opportune time to flutter her eyelashes.

Sir Avery raised an eyebrow. "What are you doing so far from the search?" he asked finally.

The General! She cursed under her breath. She'd been too preoccupied with her father's photograph, with herself. She bit her lip. She'd never forgive herself if...

"I found the General's cane," she replied.

He retrieved the cane. "And the General?" he asked.

Tillie lowered her eyes and nodded.

His shoulders drooped. "Take me to him."

She led him back to where the General lay. There was a lot more blood now.

"Miss Meriweth..." The General stirred. "The cane?"

Sir Avery wiped it with his handkerchief and presented it to the General.

His fingers twitched. "Yours, my dear."

Sir Avery raised an eyebrow. Her jaw dropped. The Orb cooled against her skin.

She hesitated. This was no ordinary stick. This was a weapon, feared by the Orb.

"I..." She shook her head. "I can't, sir."

"Insist." The corner of his lip flickered. "Catch..."

Sir Avery offered her the cane. She took it, held it at arm's length and stared at it for some time.

"Queen's command." The General's eye closed. "Hom... un..." His voice faded.

"General?" Sir Avery's voice wavered. He cleared his throat. "Sir?"

She placed her hand on the General's chest. There was no movement. Sir Avery placed two fingers against the General's neck and leaned close to his face.

The spark faded from Sir Avery's eyes. His moustache dropped. The General had been his mentor for many years; she could only guess how he must feel.

She sat in silence, as he rose slowly to his feet and shuffled toward the wreckage. He faltered for the first few steps, paused, then straightened his back, tugged at his cuffs and strode toward Robson.

She sat in silence as Robson grinned and held Aunt Prudence's red parasol high into the air.

She sat in silence as Sir Avery issued orders, Robson nodded and hobbled towards her.

She sat in silence as Harrow stepped forward, smiled and greeted Sir Avery.

The Orb twisted under her stays.

<<No, he can't be,>> she whispered to herself.

The two men walked away, deep in conversation.

The Orb burned against her skin. Her head pounded. She wiped moisture from her forehead. Her hand was wet, the skin smeared red with blood. She stared at her torn glove and the exposed gash on her hand. The photograph was gone. Only Sir Avery had known about it.

"I trusted you," she whispered.

And she wept.

Of Lessons, Defences, and Parasols

T illie kicked the red parasol under the Parlour's *chaise longue*, adjusted the waistband of her trousers, and raised the General's cane above her head. The tip lolled forward. She frowned; it was heavier than expected.

<<Hurry,>> demanded the Orb. *<<Lift it.>>*

She twisted her gloved wrist and wrestled the weight of the ebony back into the air.

<<Attack!>> hissed the Orb. *<<Finish now.>>*

She grinned and lunged forward, extending her arm as far as she could reach. The sharpened tip sliced through Saunders' sleeve, narrowly missing his arm.

He lunged to the side, just in time to avoid the metal tip and slammed into the *chaise longue*. Its tassels shivered as it scraped on the carpeted floor. His fighting cane flew from his hand through the doorway, into the adjoining Communication Room and clattered onto the telegraph machine.

"Blast!" she hissed.

Saunders tumbled into the open doorway and rubbed his knee as he rose to his feet.

"Slow down Miss Meriwether. It's best not to practice the thrust technique at full speed until you gain more control."

"Why not?" She lowered the cane and frowned.

"The tip is sharpened, Miss. Training at reduced speed is for your safety." He examined his torn sleeve. "And mine. Perhaps you should practice 'the jab'? It's a little less energetic."

<<*Coward,*>> hissed the Orb.

<<*Hush!*>> She turned to Saunders.

"Where did you learn cane fighting?" she asked.

"The General," replied Saunders. "He picked it up from a chap he met in India."

Her lip quivered. She missed the General's grandfatherly comments. But there was no time to grieve now. She had to carry on and discover their traitor, avenge his death.

She took a deep breath and repositioned herself in front of the full-length cheval mirror Saunders had moved from the bedroom. She grinned at her reflection; with loose blouse, waistcoat and trousers, she looked more like a man. She squinted her eyes and imagined Lord Allington in place of her reflection. She rolled her shoulders and stabbed the sharpened cane tip in the direction of the mirror.

<<*Faster,*>> yelled the Orb.

She retracted her arm and repeated the jabbing motion. It was just as satisfying the second time round.

<<*Again!*>> demanded the Orb.

<<*I'm tired.*>>

"Well done, Miss Meriwether," said Saunders. "The movement should be short and sharp, so as not to allow your opponent a chance to rally a defence."

She jabbed at the reflection again.

"Excellent. The General would be proud. He thought you'd have the aptitude for cane fighting." He smiled and lowered his voice. "You're a quick study, faster than Lord Allington."

"Really?" Tillie grinned. She liked the idea of outdoing Lord Allington.

<<Flattery?>> said the Orb. *<<Feel better?>>*

Saunders nodded. "He's had too many years of tutelage by French fencing instructors. He's too polite, too predictable."

<<Is trick,>> whispered the Orb. *<<Is Allington's man.>>*

Her grin faded. The Orb had a point; a good overseer put his charges at ease, lulled them into complacency, making them easier to control.

<<Your overseer,>> whispered the Orb.

She eyed Saunders' reflection behind her in the mirror. He checked the telegraph machine as he retrieved his weapon.

<<Not trust Allington.>> The Orb's metal casing warmed against her skin. *<<Sent valet to watch.>>*

She'd seen Lord Allington speaking with Harrow, all smiles. Friendly. Perhaps the Orb was right? Perhaps Saunders had been sent to keep an eye on her?

She lifted the end of her cane, turned to face Saunders. Tapestry sheep stared at her from the Communication Room walls behind him. They watched Saunders examine the machine's receiving cylinder. They laughed at her as her 'overseer' returned to the Parlour and crouched into *first position*, ready for the next attack.

She raised the General's cane and gripped it until her knuckles paled. Had Saunders thrown his cane into the Communication Room on purpose, to check the telegraph machine? Had Lord Allington sent him to keep an eye on her, to make certain she wasn't withholding messages, or worse, divulging them?

A crack reverberated along her armoured corset stays, jolted the air from her lungs. She gasped and refocused. Saunders pulled back his weapon and snapped to attention.

"You must concentrate, Miss Meriwether. Don't leave yourself open to attack. Once you begin your strike, you must follow through."

<<*Cocky,*>> said the Orb.

She growled and jabbed her cane in Saunders' direction. He flinched out of the way and grinned.

"Excellent!" he said. "Use any opportunity, especially if your opponent is off guard."

<<*Finish it!*>> yelled the Orb. <<*Wasting time.*>>

<<*Quiet, I can't think.*>>

<<*Now!*>> ordered the Orb.

<<*Shut up!*>> "Leave me alone." Tillie swallowed. She hadn't meant to say that out loud.

Saunders lowered his weapon, stepped back and frowned. She lowered her cane and eased herself onto the *chaise longue.*

"My apologies, Mr Saunders." She batted her eyelashes for good measure, though recent experience had proved he was immune to such manipulations. "I am suddenly fatigued."

He nodded his head in a quick bow. "It is I who should apologise, Miss Meriwether."

<<*Make him leave.*>> demanded the Orb.

She didn't reply. She laid the walking cane on her lap and regarded its brass head. Her finger traced the lightning-pierced cog embossed into the metal.

"Mr Saunders, when the General discovered the listening Bot he did something with his cane. It seemed to disable the mechanical." She rested the cane's tip on the floor.

<<*No!*>> The Orb's yowl resounded in her mind.

<<*Too much noise.*>> She closed her eyes, trying not to visibly flinch, and ignored its protests.

"Yes, he called it his *Discombobulator.*"

"How does it work?" she asked.

"I believe it produces a magnetic field that disrupts mechanicals and some weapons." He smiled, stepped closer and held out his hand. "If I may?"

She nodded.

"The General was an expert in magnetic fields," continued Saunders. "He was always tinkering and engineering contraptions." He opened the top of the cane's spherical head to expose its workings: several small pins wrapped with copper wire wedged amongst a complicated mass of interconnected cogs of varying sizes.

Her hand hovered over the workings.

<<Don't!>> The Orb squirmed.

She smiled. The Orb was scared.

"And communications?" she asked Saunders.

"Possibly. I suspect that's one reason why he insisted on tube technology in the Bunker's Communication Room."

"How does it activate?"

Saunders closed the metal top and twisted his palm over the top of the cane's brass head.

<<Don--!>> The Orb's scream choked.

A shrill buzz rippled through her eardrums and whirled inside her head.

The Orb shuddered.

"Miss Meriwether?" Saunders was at her elbow, a frown on his face. "Perhaps you should turn it off? It does seem to have an exaggerated effect on particular individuals."

She shook her head. The nausea would pass and the Orb would remain silent.

"The General experienced increasing headaches," he said. "His physician was concerned about the effect of prolonged use."

"Thank you, Saunders. I'll take that under advisement."

Already the nausea had dulled to a light-headedness and the buzzing had dissipated. She clasped the cane closer, distancing it from Saunders.

Saunders cleared his throat. "Perhaps we should take a short break to check for messages?"

She clenched her jaw. The Orb was right; he was monitoring the telegraph machine. She tucked the walking cane under her arm.

"I'm sure I would have heard any incoming message," she replied.

"The machine has been quiet. I hope my little accident didn't break anything."

"That's not unusual. There's a lot of waiting involved in this assignment."

He laid his cane on the side table, strode into the Communication Room and checked the clock on the wall.

"It's getting late. Lord Allington is expecting a summons from Her Majesty, and she usually prefers to complete business before afternoon tea."

She followed, ignoring the judgemental glare of the woolly flock on the walls. Still, she hesitated.

"Won't the cane disrupt the machine?" she asked him.

"There's a small button on the side," he replied. "It allows the cane to filter out extraneous wavelengths and not affect our communications."

She ran her fingers around the collar at the top of the cane until she felt a recessed button. She pressed it. Her head pounded. The buzzing was of a higher pitch this time, and faded quickly

"Are you sure this will work?" she asked.

"I am sure," he replied.

"Does Lord Allington know about the cane's abilities?"

"Of course," replied Saunders. "The General trusted him in all things."

"I suppose he's busy now he's Director?" <<*And trying to avoid me.*>> She held her breath and prepared herself for a witty confirmation from the Orb. Her heart sank. It couldn't reply.

"Yes. The Queen has ordered a full inventory of the Curiosities."

She sat down, leaned the cane against the desk and checked the telegraph machine. The paper cylinder was untouched, the alphabetical keys still aligned, and the tube connections intact.

"You can tell Lord Allington everything is in order," she said finally.

The Orb twitched gingerly, as if to remind her of its presence and her overdue report. She glanced at the wall clock and swallowed. It was due hours ago, but it was impossible to send it while Lord Allington's bloodhound was sniffing around. She tapped her heel silently on the floor tiles.

"If Lord Allington is busy, he'll need your help." But would Saunders take the hint?

"He has everything in hand." Saunders leaned against the adjoining door frame. "He has Harrow organising the men."

"Harrow?" Her heart sank. It seemed confirmation of their collusion. "I thought you were second in charge."

Saunders raised an eyebrow. "I forgot, you don't like Harrow."

Was it that obvious?

Saunders grinned and leaned forward. "Neither do I," he whispered, with a twinkle in his eye.

She laughed.

"But the General trusted him, so--"

Saunders remained the loyal overseer, trying to catch her off-guard, but was he telling the truth? The Orb would have had an opinion to clear her doubts. She glanced at the cane and straightened her shoulders. She didn't need the Orb. She could think for herself. She cleared her throat.

Saunders' back stiffened. He pushed himself away from the door frame.

"We all feel the General's absence, Miss Meriwether," he said softly. "Lord Allington, most of all. He was loyal to the General. I think he really thought the General would outlive us all."

"But he knew the risks," continued Saunders.

"Who? Lord Allington?" She bit her lip. She'd have to guard her words now the Orb could no longer caution her emotions.

"No, the General," replied Saunders. "He survived India."

"India?" There was something in her father's journal about India... Perhaps Saunders could enlighten her? She turned to face him.

"What happened in India?" she asked.

"I don't know." Saunders rubbed his hands. His fingers twitched. "He wouldn't talk about it."

"Oh." Her shoulders dropped.

"You must console yourself with the knowledge he died doing what he loved, in the service of one he loved."

She turned back to face the telegraph machine and took a deep breath. Saunders had misread her meaning; she could use that to her advantage.

"Thank you, Saunders." She lifted her hand to her mouth as if to politely conceal a yawn.

"If you need to rest, Miss Meriwether, perhaps I could monitor the telegraph machine?"

She cursed silently. She needed him to leave. She was trapped. She had a report to send, a photograph to retrieve and her father's journal to find. The Orb was right; she didn't have time for Lord Allington's distractions. She eyed the telegraph machine; she *had* to send her report or endure the Queen's wrath.

"No, thank you, Saunders. I am perfectly capable of performing my duties." She tapped her fingers on her knee. What *could* she do to make him leave? Her fingers paused mid-air.

"Perhaps a cup of tea?" she said, "It's been a harrowing day and it's almost time for afternoon tea."

"I can ring for service," he said.

Blast!

"But everyone is so busy," she replied. "Be a good man and see if

Cook has any of those little apple pastries."

Saunders backed through the doorway into the Parlour. Tillie's heart leaped. She rose and shadowed him. The ruse was working.

"I'll see what I can do." He turned and scuffed his shoe against something under the *chaise longue.* He bent down and retrieved the discarded parasol. "It's best to practice with your usual weapon."

He rolled it over in his hand, as he returned to the Communication Room, and frowned.

A faint buzzing burrowed into Tillie's temples. Her head pounded.

She glanced at the weapon. Three of the spoke tips were bent. She ran her gaze along the soot-covered silk canopy to the spiked ferrule. Dark flecks of dry blood marred the metal; *Ghostman's blood.*

She flinched and stepped back, distancing herself from the weapon. Her bustle nudged the edge of the telegraph machine. She stared at the tip as Saunders rubbed his thumb slowly over the flecks. Her heart froze. She'd taken a life.

Tillie lowered herself into the chair.

"I'll have it cleaned immediately." Saunders finished dusting off the parasol. "Perhaps we could continue practice with your parasol?"

She looked away, searching for solace in the tapestries' calming pastoral scenes. Instead, the Shepherdess gathered her flock for protection and glared back, accusing her. The flock of sheep silently bleated. *Killer. Murderess.*

Her hand trembled. She hadn't known the extent of the parasol's modifications; Sir Allington had only said it would protect her. There was no warning he'd re-engineered it as a weapon.

Killer! Murderess!

There was no comforting reply from the Orb to absolve her, no witty retort to dissolve the pain.

<<*It wasn't my fault!*>> "I didn't know," she whispered to the Shepherdess.

"Miss Meriwether?" Saunders placed the parasol on the *chaise longue* and returned to the Communication Room.

She cleared her throat, looked him in the eye and spoke in a calm, authoritative voice: "There's no hurry, Saunders. I think I will lie down for a while."

Saunders didn't move. She frowned. Why wouldn't he leave? She feigned another yawn. Still he stood motionless, like a loyal watchdog. Her fingers tensed. It was her turn to put him off his guard. A servant he was, and she would treat him as such.

She took a deep breath and rose slowly to her feet. She turned to face Saunders and unbuttoned the top button of her blouse.

"I don't want to be disturbed. It's been a most tiring day."

"Lord Allington will be expecting you for supper," said Saunders.

Tillie glanced at the clock on the wall. Her hand twitched. Too many distractions. Too many interruptions. She needed to send her report to the Queen and find the stolen photograph. She couldn't do that while trapped in the Dining Room entertaining Lord Allington. An hour or two should suffice.

"Then he will be disappointed," she said. "I shall be taking supper in my rooms. I'll ring when I'm ready."

She swallowed and undid a second button. Her shoulders tensed. Would he call her bluff?

"But my orders were to--" His cheeks reddened. He retrieved the parasol, bowed his farewell and turned to leave.

The telegraph machine whirred. Its keys clattered onto the message paper.

Saunders spun on his heel to face the machine.

She eyed the message on the cylinder. It was a familiar code, used exclusively by Queen Victoria and addressed to her Homunculus.

<<Not yet!>> She snatched up the paper. *<<Damnation.>>* She'd written the Queen's code into her father's code book. Fortunately she'd

memorised most of it. She scanned the message and deciphered it in her head before Saunders closed the distance: The Queen offered the briefest of condolences on the demise of the Department's Director, then demanded an immediate audience with Tillie to explain the tardiness. Finally, she summoned Lord Allington to deliver his new orders.

She clenched her hand, wincing as a nail sliced into the wound on her palm. She couldn't let Saunders see the message. He was clever; if he had stolen her father's journal on Lord Allington's orders, he could eventually decode the message.

"You look pale, Miss Meriwether," said Saunders.

She folded the message in quarters, then eighths, and clasped her hand as she replied: "My hand is throbbing."

"I should check the stitches." He held out his hand. "May I?"

"It's nothing." She rubbed her hand and slipped the message into the glove of her uninjured hand.

"I do have some field medical training," he said.

She relented and peeled the glove off her injured hand. The wound was inflamed. A few of the stitches had come loose and there was bleeding where her fingernail had aggravated the wound.

"You'll live." He examined her hand. "but those stitches need fixing."

She tugged her hand free of his. It was obvious he was curious about the contents of the message. She had to say something.

"Thank you, Saunders, but I'm afraid I don't have time." She slipped the protective glove back over the wound, giving her time to think. "Her Majesty has requested Lord Allington's presence immediately, and I am to accompany him."

His lip twitched.

She glanced down at her attire: loose blouse with top button undone, truncated men's trousers, scuffed boots. Only her waistcoat was vaguely presentable for court. "*You* must inform his Lordship of the Queen's orders while I find something more appropriate for an audience with

Her Majesty."

He tucked the parasol under his arm, bowed his head and shut the door behind him.

She strode to her wardrobe and chose a purple outfit with green trim. A white blouse would complete the trilogy of the Queen's favourite colours, and perhaps lighten Her mood.

She slipped on the skirt and buttoned up the bodice, as she eyed the jewellery on the vanity table. She fingered the sardonyx brooch her father had given her, and traced the features of the profile. It seemed familiar. She peered closer at the figure. It had the same features as the brooch worn by the mysterious woman in her stolen tintype photograph.

She snapped her fingers away from the brooch. It was a link to the photograph - and to her father. *Damnation*. She wasn't ready for Lord Allington to discover the connection just yet.

Tillie examined her reflection in the mirror, primped her hair and sighed; it would have to do. She couldn't let the Queen wait any longer.

She plopped into the Communication Room's chair and retrieved the Queen's message from her glove. She read it again. *IMMEDIATELY* was typed in capital letters, as were the words: *CONFIRM MESSAGE RECEIVED*.

She bit her lip. She *had* to reply. There was no point proffering excuses now. Queen Victoria preferred her subjects to grovel in person. She reached behind the key box, located the calibration cogs and rotated the second one until it clicked into the required position. She leaned forward and typed her reply:

Message Confirmed.

Of Strawberries, Anarchists, and Queen Victoria's Secrets

F resh strawberries glistened in the polished silver bowl. A silver jug of thick cream and a plate of freshly baked petite pastries were laid out on the table beside them.

Tillie licked her lips. She could already taste their sharp sweetness.

"Do try one, Miss Meriwether," urged Queen Victoria, "before Sir Avery remembers himself and tears his attention away from his teacup. He is usually quite partial to strawberries."

<<*Spoils of the rich.*>> The Orb's voice was almost cheery, no doubt due the absence of the cane's constraint.

<<*Hush, not now,*>> entreated Tillie.

Her head no longer ached now she was beyond the cane's influence. Unfortunately, the Orb immediately avenged its incarceration by renewing its constant chatter and complaints. She clenched her jaw, having been relieved of her new walking cane before entering the Royal Presence; she longed for its return and renewed internal peace.

<<*She cannot hear,*>> said the Orb.

<<*And nor shall I.*>> Tillie ignored the Orb's reply and concentrated

on the tasty treats set out before her. She plucked a large strawberry from the bowl and took a bite. Sweet juice greeted her taste buds. Her muscles relaxed.

The Orb shifted under her bodice, its exuberance replaced by a sulky silence.

"Such sweet strawberries so early in the season?" she asked.

"We have an extensive hothouse, Miss Meriwether," said the Queen. "You must see it some time."

Queen Victoria took a sip of her tea. The painted gilt highlights on her fine china teacup glistened in the afternoon sun.

Lord Allington sat motionless, teacup in hand, and continued to stare at the carpet.

"Perhaps Lord Allington would like to attend as well?" asked the Queen.

"Pardon, Your Majesty?" His teacup rattled in the saucer.

"You seem out of sorts, Lord Allington."

He cleared his throat and set his cup and saucer onto the table. "I assure you, Your Majesty, all is in order. I am prepared and able to serve the Empire and bring this traitor to justice."

The Queen's ruby earrings sparkled and danced as she shook her head.

"All in order?" Her gaze slid down her nose and landed squarely on him. "General Sabine always spoke highly of you, but you've been careless, Lord Allington." Her stern voice bounced off the walls and reverberated in Tillie's eardrums. "*My* dirigible is destroyed and now I have to appoint a new Director to the Department of Curiosities." She tsked and flashed Her sharp, blue eyes in Tillie's direction. "At least Miss Meriwether had the sense to uncover the impostor."

Tillie lowered her head, avoiding the attention of both the Queen and Lord Allington; she glimpsed his reflection in the polished silver tea pot. A frown was etched deep into his forehead, his moustache wilted.

His gaze skittered over the tea table, avoiding Queen Victoria's scrutiny.

"As the Department's new Director, you will do everything in your power to apprehend this anarchist." Her eyelids narrowed. "Alive, mind you. He has something of mine I wish to have returned."

Tillie's eyes widened. Could it be *the Horde* mentioned in her father's journal? Would she finally discover the secret?

Lord Allington nodded.

Queen Victoria took another sip of tea. Her cup chinked as she set it back into its gilt-encrusted saucer.

"Take Miss Meriwether with you. She is sensible and seems to keep her head when the rest of you threaten to lose yours."

Tillie bit her lip, trying to keep it from curling, then nibbled a glazed pastry to make doubly sure.

A ruckus erupted outside the Parlour. Men shouted in the hallway. There was a snuffle and scratching at the door. The door rattled.

Queen Victoria rolled her eyes. "Enter."

The shouting ceased. Another rattle, and the door flew open.

A flurry of dark fur sped towards the Queen. Lord Allington leaped to his feet and assumed a defensive stance.

"Do sit down, Lord Allington."

He snapped to attention and slid back into his chair.

The dog ran around the room, tugged open the second set of curtains.

"Noble, do behave in front of our guests." The Queen smiled.

Noble jogged across the room and nosed around Her feet, catching her skirts as he did so. A brassy glint caught Tillie's eye. It shimmered over the curtains and skittered across the ceiling.

<<*Exposed!*>> The Orb squirmed. <<*Undone!*>>

She clasped her bodice collar. The buttons were secure. <<*Not you.*>>

She searched the floor for a source of reflection. Another glint of light erupted from under the hem of the Queen's skirt as Noble arranged himself at her feet. Tillie gasped inaudibly.

She examined Lord Allington's reflection in the teapot. Had he noticed it?

He raised his eyebrow. His gaze tracked the source of the reflection along the floor and halted. His eyes widened. He averted them immediately and caught her gaze reflected in the polished silver. His eyebrow fell. He'd seen it as well; it wasn't her imagination.

He shrugged and turned his attention to the plate of pastries on the tea table, his expression unreadable.

"Down, Noble." Queen Victoria scratched Noble behind one ear and patted him on the head.

The dog shook his head and plopped at her feet.

"Do you like dogs, Miss Meriwether?" The Queen straightened her skirts.

Tillie shrugged. "I haven't had the pleasure, Your Majesty."

The Queen tore a corner from her pastry and fed it to Noble. "I find them more loyal than most men." She leaned back and jerked a tasselled cord hanging behind her.

The Footman announced the new arrival: "The Private Secretary, Your Majesty."

<<Enforcer Ponsonby,>> whispered the Orb. The remark was slow, measured.

"Do come in, Lord Ponsonby," said the Queen. "This is Miss Matilda Meriwether, niece of Colonel Meriwether."

Ponsonby's eyes widened slightly. He smiled and nodded his head.

"I knew your..." There was a noticeable pause. "Uncle." His eyes lingered on her, a little longer than was comfortable. She squirmed under his gaze.

<<Did he mean he knew Uncle Meriwether, or father, do you suppose?>>

<<Yes,>> replied the Orb.

Ponsonby bowed. His neatly trimmed full beard seemed excessive compared to Lord Allington's elegantly waxed moustache.

"You know Lord Allington, of course," said the Queen. "He is our new Director of the Department of Curiosities. Make the paperwork happen, Lord Ponsonby."

The two men politely nodded in each other's direction.

"The Department will no longer be autonomous," said Queen Victoria. "You will report to Lord Ponsonby. He will conduct a full inventory of *all* Curiosities. He will approve each new acquisition and all non-essential items will be destroyed."

Lord Allington straightened his back.

"Lord Ponsonby will supply you with your new orders, Lord Allington." The Queen waved him in Ponsonby's direction. "Miss Meriwether will entertain Us until your return."

Lord Allington stood, bowed and followed Ponsonby from the Royal Parlour. The door closed behind them with a resounding click.

Noble twitched an ear, snored and continued to nap at the foot of his Mistress.

The two women eyed each other. Tillie knew they both had many secrets neither wanted to share. She sipped her tea under the scrutiny of her Queen.

Noble snuffled and rolled onto Tillie's boot. She nudged him away and continued to drink her Darjeeling.

"You know the identity of the Inventor," said Queen Victoria.

Hot liquid caught in Tillie's throat. She spluttered. The Queen was always one to get to the point.

"How did you know?" she asked.

"I have my ways, Homunculus. You know that." The Queen stroked Noble's dark fur. "What does he call himself now?"

<<*Don't tell,*>> hissed the Orb.

"I'm not sure, Your Majesty." She clutched her teacup. She should not refuse her benefactor, her Liberator, her Queen. But Lord Allington already knew and, if he was one of Her creatures, he would tell Her. If Tillie didn't tell the Queen now, her loyalty would be in question. "The only name I have is Cranshaw."

Queen Victoria frowned. "Cranshaw? Why does that name sound familiar?"

She plucked a strawberry from the platter and nibbled it. Her frown lifted. Her blue eyes studied Tillie through slitted lids, as if trying to pierce her soul to find the truth. "Do you know who Cranshaw is, Homunculus?"

<<*Say nothing,*>> demanded the Orb.

Tillie's teacup rattled onto its saucer. Was Lord Allington working for the Queen and had he already advised Her of the photograph's contents?

<<*Don't trust him.*>>

The Queen continued, not giving Tillie any chance of denial. "He worked with your father, on..." She paused. "On one of my projects."

Tillie relaxed. <<*Perhaps he didn't inform the Queen?*>> she said to the Orb.

<<*Not yet,*>> it replied.

Her father's journal entries flashed through her memory. There was a secret project commissioned by the Queen. He'd seemed disturbed with its ramifications. What was it called?

The Orb chilled against her skin. <<*The Horde,*>> it whispered.

The word echoed ominously. Her heart jumped into her throat. Less than a month ago, she'd discovered her father had been an agent of the Queen, her Homunculus. Now Tillie had inherited the title. She didn't relish inheriting *the Horde* as well - whatever it was.

<<*Don't trust Her,*>> said the Orb.

"Your father never mentioned him?" asked the Queen.

As a child, Tillie had been oblivious to her father's work and his associates. She had only recently discovered Cranshaw's existence.

She fought to calm her breathing. She fought to control the urge to scream, to run and hide. She concentrated on Noble's slow, steady breaths, watched his stomach rise and fall as he dreamed. She took a deep breath and met the Queen's calm blue eyes - and lied to her Queen:

"Father never spoke of his work." It was a half-truth; he'd never *spoken* to her about it. Written words didn't count. So, it wasn't a lie; it was an omission, but still potentially dangerous if the Queen should ever discover her deception. One did not mislead one's monarch, especially when one was Her personal agent.

Queen Victoria scrutinised Tillie and smiled.

"Find this thief, Cranshaw. He has something of mine." She leaned closer and whispered: "*I* want it back. At any cost."

Tillie bit her lip. <<*Any cost?*>>

<<*No.*>> The Orb shivered. <<*Don't.*>>

She ignored the Orb's order.

"If you would authorise access to some of the Curiosities, Your Majesty?" Her voice was calm. "There are several devices in the vaults that would assist me in your service."

"No." The reply was quick and without hesitation.

"But you authorised the use of the dirigible?"

"It is too dangerous, Miss Meriwether." The Queen's smile had melted. Her lips tightened as she glared directly into Tillie's eyes. "I will not risk public exposure of any more Curiosities. There have been too many accidents already."

"What I had in mind was much smaller than a flying machine-"

"No." Queen Victoria picked up a pastry from the platter and tossed it to Noble. The dog snatched it mid-air in his teeth. "It is not appropriate to flaunt such extravagances to those who cannot afford them. The *Mechanical Permit Restriction Act* not only ensures the Curiosities remain unseen by the public but also impedes corporate inquisitiveness. We cannot risk the uneducated masses gaining access to any of the technology. It is for their own good, Miss Meriwether."

<<For Her good,>> scoffed the Orb.

Tillie bit her tongue and fought the growing tightness in her head. One did not disagree with Her Majesty, Queen Victoria.

"You sound like Bertie. He's a bit too cosy with those lobbyists, the Gadgeteers." Queen Victoria narrowed her eyelids. "They want every citizen of the Empire to have access to mechanicals." She scoffed. "He calls it progress. I call it greed."

Tillie turned her cup on its saucer. She wanted to remind the Queen that her late husband, Prince Albert, had championed progress; he would most likely sympathise with these Gadgeteers as well. She picked up the cup and sipped the liquid. One did not contradict the Queen.

Queen Victoria picked up another strawberry and examined it.

"You're not sympathetic to the Gadgeteers are you, Homunculus?" Queen Victoria dusted sugar from her fingertips. "At best they are anarchists. Demanding Empire-wide access to mechanicals would only lead to civil unrest. What else would the lower classes do with all their leisure time?"

"I thought they just wanted permission to sell their goods here, Your Majesty."

"Lobbyists are just as dangerous as anarchists when they set out against their Queen." She shook her head. "They only wish to acquire the leverage to overturn my law so they can fill their coffers. We must control this so-called Industrial Revolution before it destroys our way of life."

<<Her way of life. Her control,>> said the Orb.

"But surely the Curiosities could be used to defend The Empire and still be controlled?" asked Tillie.

"History tells us what will happen." Queen Victoria glanced out the window and stared into the empty sky. It was widely known she wasn't overly fond of dirigibles. A faint metallic click emanated from beneath the Queen's skirts as she shifted in her chair. "Unleashing the Curiosities, even in the service of my Empire, will lead to war. Do you want to be responsible for starting a war on English soil, Miss Meriwether?"

Tillie lowered her eyes and shook her head.

<<*Always intimidation,*>> said the Orb.

"We created the *Mechanical Ownership and Operation Permits* to protect Our Empire and withhold perilous items from those who would seek to do the Empire harm. We require all our loyal subjects to abide by those laws. The Department of Curiosities was created to ensure such technologies are locked away. As an operative of the Department, it is *your* responsibility to prevent improper use of them. And as my Homunculus, it is your duty to obey me and ensure the safety of The Empire against such Anarchists."

<<*Ambushed,*>> hissed the Orb.

Tillie closed her eyes. Now she understood the deal she had made, the deal her father had made. She understood his last diary entry, his plea for forgiveness. Her chest tightened. Her ribs throbbed and echoed her quickening heartbeat. She had given her word too readily. She was trapped.

<<*Servitude,*>> said the Orb.

<<*To the Empire,*>> she continued.

<<*To the Queen,*>> corrected the Orb.

Lord Allington was now Department Director, but where did his allegiance lie? Was he a traitor in league with Harrow or was he the Queen's man determined to entrap both Harrow and herself as traitors? Her muscles tensed. She needed time to think, to reassess her situation. She took a long breath and opened her eyes.

"As ordered, Your Majesty."

Queen Victoria patted Noble's head.

<<*Good dog, Matilda,*>> sneered the Orb.

<<*Be quiet,*>> she said. <<*Or I'll fetch the General's cane.*>> She straightened her shoulders and re-directed her gaze forward, past the Queen. "My real concern is the presence of The Society."

"You need not worry. One of my operatives has infiltrated their ranks; your counterpart in The Society. They provide me with regular reports." The Queen grinned as she picked up the last cream-covered morsel. "And on time."

Tillie swallowed and gripped the edge of the chair to prepare herself for the Queen's wrath.

Queen Victoria laughed.

"*I* have many loyal spies."

<<*I'm a spy?*>> Tillie's heart shuddered. A hot wave of nausea flooded her body.

<<*For good of the Empire,*>> the Orb said flatly.

<<*For the Queen,*>> Her vision dimmed.

<<*Breathe,*>> ordered the Orb.

She strained to draw a breath. Her ribs tightened, constricting her lungs.

"Are you in pain, Miss Meriwether?" The Queen's voice was polite, but with no hint of empathy.

"My ribs," she replied.

"Such things happen in the line of duty. They will heal."

<<*Again,*>> said the Orb.

<<*Shut up!*>> Tillie fanned herself. "May I inquire if your Man in Grey has reported any hint of the Inventor's whereabouts?"

"Cranshaw has betrayed The Society. He broke contact the day of the Flying Scotsman incident and is believed to have fled the country. Ponsonby will have informed Lord Allington by now."

Queen Victoria rose to her feet and brushed crumbs from her spotless black silk skirts. Tillie jerked to her feet.

The Queen strolled toward the windows. A faint clicking accompanied her. There was no sign of a limp, no hint of the serious leg injury, resulting from the near-assassination only a month before.

<<I thought the doctor said she would be bedridden for months? Perhaps he over-estimated her injuries?>> she asked the Orb.

<<Listen,>> it whispered.

Noble snuffled.

Queen Victoria's feet fell rhythmically on the thick carpet, with a soft thud and a click. Her silk skirts rustled against each other. She halted before the large windows. The clicking ceased.

<<No limp,>> replied the Orb.

<<Mechanical limb?>> she asked. *<<It couldn't be; the Queen would never tolerate such a thing.>>* She regarded the woman who stood steadfast on two legs before her. Perhaps she would?

Queen Victoria turned to face her, silhouetted by the golden colours of the sunset.

"When the Inventor is found you will inform me first, before Lord Allington. Do you understand, Homunculus? That is why you were put in charge of Communications. You will inform me, then you may inform the Department. Understood?"

"Yes, Your Majesty."

"Bertie recommended Lord Allington for Director of the Department. What is your opinion, Homunculus?"

"Me, Your Majesty?"

"Yes. You've worked with him."

"He's..." She hesitated. If she declared him a thief, and in league with the traitor, Harrow, he could face the noose. And he *did* save her life. Until now, he'd always *seemed* loyal to the Empire. She swallowed. What if this was a ruse to test her loyalty as well? Could he be working for the Queen, with his own mission to find a traitor? Tillie took a deep breath.

"He's thorough, Your Majesty. And he's always seemed loyal to the Empire," she replied.

"There are rumours of an anarchist element in the Department of Curiosities, with possible sympathies for the Gadgeteers. Now General Sabine no longer runs the Department I must ensure its loyalty. You are to ferret out this anarchist element and report back to me. No one is above suspicion. I need to be certain of the Department's loyalty and I need time to reclaim my stolen property. It *must* not fall under the attention of the Department." Queen Victoria returned to Her chair, sat down and glared at Tillie. "Do I make myself clear?"

"Perfectly clear, Your Majesty."

"Excellent." The Queen tweaked her chin with her lace-gloved fingers.

"Your Majesty, what was stolen?"

"The plans for a prototype, called-- "

<<*The Horde.*>> The Orb's cry drowned out Queen Victoria's reply.

○

The familiar smell of cloves and smoky citrus still lingered, though it dwindled more each day. The General's polished wooden pipe sat untouched on the corner of his carved mahogany desk, as a monument to his memory. Queen Victoria's portrait still glared at the room from behind the desk.

Tillie sat in the overstuffed leather armchair she had adopted in the General's office. Lord Allington sat behind the grand desk. His jacket hung over the back of his chair. He'd rolled up his sleeves and he seemed determined to ignore her presence. His attention never wavered from the piles of papers strewn across the leather top. He scribbled notes, signed papers and mumbled.

She stared at the fireplace. The embers glowed half-heartedly, providing little warmth against the fresh air sucked into the room via the gently humming fans embedded in the air shaft above. Chunks of coal clinked and dislodged and fell through the grate. She flinched just enough for her ribs to remind her of their presence. She closed her eyes and took measured breaths, careful not to aggravate her ribs further.

According to the Department Physician, nothing was broken, just severely bruised, thanks to the support of the metal stays. He'd wanted to test a new gadget procured from Germany, to view her bones. She had declined. While she revelled in new technology, she did not wish to become the subject of overeager experimentation.

Her finger traced the edge of the lightning bolt symbol carved into the brass handle of the General's walking cane. It had been twelve days - twelve long days of waiting since returning to the headquarters. She'd been grateful for the silence the cane had afforded her. But as Saunders had predicted, her headaches were increasing in both severity and frequency.

The Orb, no doubt, would make up for lost time when the headaches became unbearable and she was forced to disengage the *Discombobulator.* For now, she was grateful for the silence, and the time to think.

She opened her eyes. Lord Allington still shuffled his papers and avoided conversation. She waited impatiently for him to enlighten her as to why he'd summoned her to his office, reluctant to let him out of her sight, until he led her to the stolen photograph.

She rested the walking cane against the arm of her chair. He'd assigned Saunders to continue schooling her in the art of cane fighting - a perfect ruse to allow him to monitor her duty hours in the Communication Room. At least Harrow hadn't been given the assignment.

When the Department had been informed of the Inventor's identity, Harrow had become agitated and more secretive than usual. Lord Allington, however, had remained calm. She shifted in her seat. He'd been consulting with Harrow more regularly. Nothing apparently untoward but, still, she needed to discover what they were planning.

She eyed Lord Allington. How long had he known of the Inventor's identity? He caught her gaze and stared back.

"Is there something wrong?" she asked.

"No," he replied. "I was just wondering what became of your lovely brooch."

"Oh!" Her hand moved to her throat. Had he recognised it from the photograph? She fidgeted with her collar. "I... I lost it in the explosion," she replied.

He frowned. "Unfortunate."

"Yes," she said.

"I shall have to buy you another." A faint half-smile flickered over his lips but his eyes remained sombre. He shuffled through his papers.

Her attention returned to the fireplace. He didn't take his eyes from her. She would've preferred to have been confined to the Communication Room rather than watched over like a child.

Did he suspect she was the Queen's spy? She struggled to keep her breaths even so as not to betray her thoughts. How long had he known? Was it the photograph or...

Her heart pounded. Her hands grew clammy. He'd attended her after the explosion of the Upper Levels of the Department's original headquarters. She placed her hand over her heart where she'd sewn the silk note the Queen had secretly given her at their first meeting. Had he seen it? The blaggard must have peeked. Her cheeks burned.

<<He lied!>>

The Orb squirmed under her bodice.

"You have been very quiet, Miss Meriwether."

She flinched at the break in the silence.

"Is there something you wish to discuss?"

She lowered her hand. She had many things she wanted to ask: Where is my photograph? Why do you trust Harrow? Why have you summoned me here? What she said was:

"We have so many Curiosities hidden away in the Department. Right here, under *our* control. We experiment. We improve. We catalogue. Why can't we use them?"

She'd had over a week to ruminate on the Queen's comments about the Gadgeteers and mechanicals. She took a deep breath. If Queen Victoria wanted her to play the part of a spy and ferret out Gadgeteer-sympathisers, then she would. But for her own reasons.

"We could have discovered the truth of the decoy if we had been allowed to fly directly over London. Lives could have been saved." She slammed the cane onto the floor, in a very General-like manner. "Surely there's a gadget that can find out who sabotaged my flying machine, something that could have saved...?" She licked salty liquid from her lip. <<...*the General.*>>

Lord Allington removed a handkerchief from his pocket. Her hand gripped the walking stick and pushed it away from the armchair. If he commented on her emotional state, she would make good use of her newly-acquired martial skills.

He raised an eyebrow. She gritted her teeth and clutched the cane tighter; the affectation was no longer endearing.

"As you know very well, no flying machine - airship, dirigible or balloon - is allowed over London skies. Not since the Dirigible War." He placed the handkerchief on the desk next to the General's pipe.

She nodded and echoed the Orb's words: "For the good of The Empire."

"And for the protection of Her Majesty and the Royal Family," said Lord Allington.

"But surely there is validation in using the Curiosities, in extenuating circumstances?"

He avoided her gaze, picked up his self-inking nib pen and scrawled notes on the paper before him.

"Under *no* circumstances," he said.

"Perhaps the Gadgeteers have a point in opposing *The Mechanical Permit Restriction Act* and fighting for the rights to own mechanicals for everyone, not just the rich and well-connected?

He narrowed his eyelids. "The Gadgeteers are profiteers and smugglers, in league with The Society."

She huffed. If he was the Queen's man, there should be no surprise in his reply. She was the patron and commander of the Department. If he was a traitor, surely he'd want continued access to its Curiosities? Still, his words stung; there are many Curiosities that could help those in need. Surely that is for the good of the Empire?

Lord Allington straightened the papers on his desk and leaned forward.

"What *did* the Queen say to you, Miss Meriwether?

"Nothing of consequence," she replied.

He clicked the cover back on his ink pen and placed it on the desk. She sighed with relief; she'd been spared the eyebrow affectation.

"I have rarely known Queen Victoria to have a conversation of little consequence." His moustache twitched; another mannerism that was no longer endearing.

She clenched her fist until the wound on her palm ached. She wanted to slap his face. Instead, she fluttered her eyelashes and replied:

"She said 'We are women in a world of men and we must stick together'."

His eyes twinkled, just for a moment. He blinked and the polite veneer returned.

"Did the General ever explain *exactly* what we do here in the Department of Curiosities?" he asked.

She remembered the General's words: "The Department of Curiosities deals in discoveries of things of a curious nature, that may have potential to benefit The Empire," she recited.

"And?"

"Research and storage of all things curious," she replied.

"In a manner. Her Majesty believes the discoveries are best kept secret and not accessible, and therefore not exploitable, to those not deemed safe." He sat back in his chair.

"Like the Gadgeteers?" She slumped back into her armchair.

"And The Society," he replied.

The Queen's portrait stared down at her, commanding her to obey. She dropped her eyes to the table. Lord Allington renewed his interest in his papers.

"Tell me, Lord Allington, have *any* of the Curiosities been used to aid the subjects of the Empire?" she asked.

He waited a moment before providing an answer. "None," he said.

Her eyelids widened; she was surprised by the tone in his voice.

"None?"

There was a pause.

"By Her Majesty's orders." He took a deep breath. "Do you trust me, Miss Meriwether?"

She straightened up in her armchair. How did she tell the Director of the Empire's most clandestine department that she suspected he may be in league with a treacherous swine who had killed not only a man she admired and respected, but also a train-load of unsuspecting innocents?

The fireplace crackled beside her. She narrowed her eyelids and stared into the flames.

"*Can* I trust you, Lord Allington?"

He opened his mouth, then seemed to reconsider his reply.

"The General advised me you are not what you seem," he said finally. "However, he did trust you with Lower Level clearance and mentioned something about family loyalty. He served with your uncle, I believe?" He eyed her and raised one eyebrow, slowly and deliberately. "Do I need to be informed of any outstanding orders? Is there anything you wish to tell me, Miss Meriwether?"

She didn't reply.

He cleared his throat. "Should I be wary of our conversations?"

"Don't you trust me, Lord Allington?" She executed a perfect flutter of eyelashes. Aunt Prudence would have been proud.

He steepled his fingers and placed them to his lips. "Who do you work for, Miss Meriwether?"

She examined the man before her. Either he was exceptionally adept at disguising his demeanour or he was genuinely concerned about her affiliations.

"My allegiance is with the Empire and I work for the Department." The words were true. "The General engaged my services at your recommendation." She straightened her skirts. "You were impressed with my agility on roof tops, if you remember."

Lord Allington blinked. Tillie smiled. She relished the moments when she caught him off guard.

"Why did you summon me to your office, Lord Allington?" She leaned forward in the armchair.

"Ah, yes." His moustache twitched. "I shall be away on an assignment for several weeks. Saunders will be in charge while I'm away. Harrow will continue with the inventory."

It was her turn to raise an eyebrow. There was something he wasn't telling her.

"I'll be investigating reports of smugglers. There are rumours The Society is involved," he said.

Tillie sprang to her feet. "May I come?" she asked.

He shook his head.

Her heart sank. He'd denied her request too quickly. She couldn't let him leave without knowing if he intended to use the photograph against her. She had to find a way to accompany him.

"I'm sure Her Majesty would approve my request to accompany you," she said.

Lord Allington's back stiffened.

"I don't know what to make of you, Miss Meriwether." His muscles relaxed slightly. "However, the General trusted you. He left written orders to give you complete access to the Department, its records and intelligence; I'm to give you complete co-operation." He shrugged. "And it seems you now outrank Harrow. He won't be pleased with the news." He smiled. "He needs someone to keep an eye on him, to make sure he doesn't get distracted." He handed her a folded communiqué. "You are now in charge of *all* communications. You must have friends in high places, Miss Meriwether."

Tillie bit her lip. Had the Queen informed the General of her commission? Her heart raced. How much did Lord Allington know? Was he in league with Harrow? Who had stolen her father's journal, and where was the photograph?

Her head ached. Her ears buzzed. There were too many questions writhing in her head and no one to confide in. A wave of nausea washed over her.

She swallowed. Lord Allington's admissions had given her hope; perhaps he wasn't conspiring with Harrow? Perhaps she could trust him? She needed to know the truth, even if she didn't like the answer. Most of all, she needed the photograph back.

"You said *complete co-operation*?" she said.

He nodded.

"Then I repeat my request to accompany you."

He grabbed the communication tube and spoke into it.

"Are we ready to proceed, Saunders?"

A muffled voice delivered its information and waited for the reply.

"Excellent. Tell Smythe to ready mobilisation procedures. I will require same for Miss Meriwether. You will be in charge of my personal affairs until we return."

She licked her lips and strained to hear the reply.

"Agreed," Lord Allington replied. "Inform Smythe it is required within the hour." He replaced the tube in its cradle. "I'll have someone relieve you in the Communication Room until our return. You have one hour, Miss Meriwether. Pack for hot weather."

Her eyes widened. *Egypt?* Her heart skipped. Finally, she would return to the place responsible for so many delightful childhood memories.

She reached for the General's cane and wrapped her hand around the head. It had warmed during the sojourn by the fire. She leaned onto its reassuring support. She stifled a smile. It was *her* cane now.

She nodded.

Lord Allington snapped to his feet. He dipped his head in a shallow bow.

The General's cane hummed under her grip. The Orb warmed against her skin.

"Please, may I have it back?" she asked.

"Have what back?" He frowned.

"The photograph I showed you on the train," she replied.

He shook his head. "What makes you think I have it, Miss Meriwether?"

She took a slow breath. She'd committed herself on this course; she could not go back now.

"You took it from me after the train exploded." Tears filled her eyes. "Please, I need it back."

He sat back in his chair and ran his fingers over his moustache. His frown deepened.

"Why would I take it?" He placed his elbows on the desk, rested his lip on his knuckle and regarded her. "The General was right. I shouldn't take you at face value, Miss Meriwether. I hope he is also correct in your loyalty to the Department. Can you tell me why the General trusted you?"

She stepped back to the armchair and eased into its comforting embrace. If he considered Harrow - an agent of the Queen - to be a spy, then he would consider her a spy as well. Her skin crawled at the very thought. She could not tell him the truth. A half-truth then?

Tillie smiled sweetly.

"Family connections," she said.

Of Trains, Dirigibles, and Steamships

Wooden hangers clacked as Tillie rummaged through the gowns in her wardrobe.

They would be away for several weeks. She bit her lip. She needed to send a report to the Queen before they left.

She listened at the door to the Communication Room. All was silent. She wrapped her fingers around the door knob and gently turned it, so as not to alert anyone on the other side. It was still locked. Lord Allington had already assigned someone to Communications, but why was she denied any access to the telegraph machine? Perhaps he didn't trust her after all?

She returned to the bedroom. How would she manage to pack in time? She studied the dishevelled pile of gowns: burgundy silk, purple silk with elaborately pleated bodice and a russet-coloured satin outfit with black trim.

After weeks of wearing ill-fitting dresses while trapped in the Lower Levels, she'd developed an aversion to green and yellow. Emerald green was acceptable, but only just. She would return to Egypt in style - and less detestable colours.

She retrieved her father's black code book from her bustle pocket, rolled off the rubber band and removed the photograph of Eustace, her childhood plaything, on her father's desk. Her father's eyes stared at her from the photograph. He smiled, as he always had when he reassured her all would be well, as he had just before their last holiday in Egypt.

Ah, Egypt. Many memories of her travels remained; she could almost taste the sweet coffee, smell the scorching Egyptian winds that rolled in from the desert, feel the sweltering heat of the days.

She screwed up her nose. Perhaps she should choose something cooler for day wear? She added two Egyptian cotton ensembles - one of teal with blue trim and white Belgian lace, and an exquisite dress of crisp white. She arranged the bustle skirt pleating so the wide midnight blue stripes fell pleasingly over the edge of the bed.

"That's better."

She ran her fingers through the remaining gowns hanging in the wardrobe, pausing at the blue and purple striped day dress given to her by Lord Allington. It was perfect for travelling. She sighed and tugged at the fastenings of her current practical, front-fastening bodice. The military-style bodice really was not her style. And it was emerald green. If only Mary were here to help.

Visions flashed through her thoughts: a white tablecloth, red blood, a naked ankle. She caught her breath. Her chin wrinkled. She closed her eyes and tried to erase the memory of Mary's crumpled body.

She missed the girl's fussing and Aunt Prudence's reprimands from atop the hallway stairs. The room blurred. She sniffed, wiped away the tears and glanced at her pocket watch. Less than thirty minutes to pack. There was no time for reveries.

She stacked the transcribed papers and notes on the vanity, along with the code book, the pocket watch and the photograph of Father and Eustace. She placed the walking cane on the tabletop next to her precious brooch. Her head throbbed in time with the cane's soft hum.

The Orb remained around her neck - and silent.

Tillie picked up the brooch. She couldn't wear it, not while the photograph with it was still missing, and could link her to the Inventor. But she couldn't bear to leave it behind. She kissed it, wrapped it in a handkerchief and tied it with one of the green ribbons Grace had given her.

She stood, hands on hips, and examined the collection on the vanity. Had she forgotten anything? She bit her lip. The da Vinci notebook, her father's journal and the photograph of her father, linking him to Cranshaw and the mysterious woman were notably lacking.

The Orb twitched next to her skin, still muted by the presence of the cane.

"I know," she replied. "I need to recover them, whatever the cost."

There was a knock on the door.

"Miss Meriwether?"

She spun towards the door. The woman's voice sounded familiar.

"Who is it?" she asked.

She scooped up the papers off the vanity and shoved them into her hidden bustle pocket. Her hands shook as she slipped the photograph back inside the code book and stuffed them in the other pocket.

"Miss Meriwether?" The doorknob rattled.

Tillie strode to the door.

"Grace?" She straightened her skirts and unlatched the door.

"Yes, Miss," replied Grace. "Lord Allington sent for me. I'm to be your companion during the voyage."

"He thinks of everything doesn't he?" she said.

"Yes, Miss." Grace scanned the dishevelled room. "Shall I pack?"

Grace was, as always, full of elegance. Her slender form glided through the room to the bed, with the languid ease of a dancer. Two large steamer trunks trundled along in her wake. She opened the trunks, unfolded their vertical compartments and marched to the wardrobe. As she returned for an armful of linens, her gaze swept over the vanity desk.

Tillie shuffled sideways, positioning herself in front of the vanity, hoping to block Grace's view of the mirror, and curled her fingers around the handkerchief-wrapped brooch.

"I must change into something less drab to travel. I do loathe green." She sighed loudly.

"We haven't much time, Miss. I'll pack, while you choose your travel attire." Grace turned to the crumpled array of clothing; purple and green hair ribbons danced behind her as she shook her head. She set to organising the jumble of gowns, isolating each outfit before it was straightened and arranged on the bed.

Tillie slipped the brooch into her pocket and joined Grace to inspect the dresses.

"I think this one is perfect for air travel." She pointed to the blue and purple striped day dress. "It would look splendid with my velvet carriage coat."

Grace nodded and hung the remaining bodices in the steamer trunk, and bundled the skirts into the larger drawers. She held up a pair of teal linen trousers. Her eyes widened. There were five pairs in all.

Tillie smiled. "For bicycle riding and chasing trains."

"Very practical, Miss." Grace smiled. "Are you expecting trouble while we're away?"

"My Aunt always said 'Be prepared for anything'," she replied. "Who am I to defy such wisdom?"

"Indeed, Miss, but you won't be needing them for now. Lord Allington would never allow trouble on his watch." Grace doubled them over, tucked in the legs and placed them all in a steamer trunk drawer, next to the Chinese dressing gown.

Tillie unbuttoned her bodice and dropped it onto the bed. The Orb shifted under her camisole and glinted near the neckline. She tucked it back out of sight and slipped out of her skirt before Grace returned with the striped outfit.

Grace eased the skirt over Tillie's head, tugged down the hem and primped the bustle folds into position. Tillie slipped her arms into the bodice. Grace pulled it tight. A sliver of pain radiated through her chest.

Tillie gasped and glared at her new companion. Grace winced, deftly buttoned up the front of the bodice and adjusted the lace cuffs.

"You are very efficient, Grace."

"Thank you, Miss. Someone has to be." Grace latched the trunks and clapped her hands together. "Now, hats?"

Tillie waved her hand in the direction of an assorted pile of hat boxes. Grace opened each box, checked the contents and stacked them beside the trunk.

"You will need something to protect you from the sun," said Grace. "Have you a Boater?"

Tillie pointed to a pale blue hat box on top of the wardrobe. Grace pulled down the box, extracted the hat and handed it to her.

Tillie leaned toward the vanity mirror and pinned the hat in place. Its dangling red ribbon flopped over her father's pocket watch on the vanity.

Grace reached forward and flipped it behind Tillie's shoulder, then snatched up the timepiece and flipped it open.

"We haven't much time." Grace eyed Tillie through slitted lids, clicked the watch closed and handed it to her. "I'll fetch someone for the trunks."

Grace whisked across the room and out the door.

Tillie opened the pocket watch. The engraving in the lid was faint:

To my darling
Love, I

Tillie sauntered along the corridors leading away from the main

315

corridor, dressed for an afternoon's promenade, complete with straw sun hat, walking cane and parasol. Grace followed with a stack of hat boxes in each arm and berated the three porters who struggled to keep pace. Saunders led the way, down an Ascension Chamber and along a set of deeper, bricked tunnels.

The cane's *Discombobulator* hummed gently in Tillie's palm. The Orb fidgeted against her skin, unable to complain, but she guessed its intent.

"We won't be late, will we?" she asked Saunders.

"We're almost there, Miss Meriwether," he replied. He activated another brass floor plate, illuminating the path.

A large circular door glinted at the end of the tunnel. It was recessed into the wall. Three thick metal rods pierced the surrounding frame. A short metal rod protruded from the wall, to the right.

He pulled a metal baton from his coat pocket and rapped twice on the metal door. A loud metallic thud replied. He slipped the baton into a hole in the rod, creating an over-sized lever, and wrenched the handle downward.

A loud clunk echoed through the tunnel. Saunders removed the baton and rapped on the door again.

Another thud.

A hissing sound crept along the tunnel, surrounding them. A rhythmic thumping followed, as each bar disengaged and slipped into the door frame.

A faint whir emanated from the other side of the wall. The door swung toward them. A young man with messy red hair, soot covered face and an infectious grin stepped forward. He towered above Saunders.

"Good afternoon, sir." The young man lifted his goggles. Two large white patches encircled his eye sockets, where the lenses had protected them.

Tillie sucked in her lip, trying not to laugh.

"I'll inform Lord Allington your party has arrived." He skittered off into the void beyond the door.

"This way." Saunders stepped through the portal.

Tillie, Grace, the trunks and their bearers followed.

The atmosphere changed as soon as they stepped through the portal. The earth-cooled tunnels widened into a cavern. A layer of humid air now warmed Tillie's skin. The air was thick with moisture, making it harder to breathe.

Her ears hissed. Hollow sounds echoed in the distance, their direction unfathomable in the unseen depths of the cavern. After so many weeks in the Department's warrens, confined to small rooms and narrow corridors, she felt exposed and vulnerable.

Tools clanked as workmen busied themselves around a massive steam machine. Leather hoses snaked out from the machine into the misty depths of the cavern. Intermittent bursts of steam disgorged in the party's direction, creating a veil that blurred the way ahead. One of the men cursed.

Saunders coughed loudly and cleared his throat. The workman jerked his head in their direction, jumped to his feet and nudged the man next to him.

"My apologies, Misses." He tugged on the brim of his grimy cap.

Grace pursed her lips and shook her head.

Tillie smiled; she had uttered worse when interred in the Lower Levels.

"Good evening, gentlemen." She dipped her head in greeting.

"Ex-orphanage boys," said Saunders.

"That explains their manners," whispered Grace.

"But excellent Steamers and mechanics," he replied. "We also have an engineer-in-training."

A chirrup emanated from Saunders' vicinity. His hand went to his waistcoat pocket. The chirrup continued.

"Excuse me, ladies." He fished out a small gadget, which vaguely resembled a rectangular pocket watch. With a turn of a knob at its crown, the cover popped open.

Tillie peered at the contraption. In place of a clock face was a mass of cogs. A small red light flashed in unison with the contraption's chirps.

Two shadows appeared just beyond the curtain of steam. A long leg pierced the vapour. The red-headed attendant had returned. He turned to Saunders and nodded. The other shadow hovered just beyond the veil.

Saunders snapped the case shut.

"I must leave you, Miss Meriwether," he said. "Cager will assist you from here." He excused himself and disappeared into the steamy depths of the cavern.

The lingering shadowy figure stepped out from the haze, raised his hand and pushed at the bridge of his nose.

Tillie gripped the handle of her parasol and wondered if any new enhancements had been added when Lord Allington had it repaired.

"Harrow, what are you doing here?" she asked.

"Saunders is otherwise engaged." One corner of this mouth curled upwards. "And Lord Allington was in need of an assistant on our journey."

A third figure strode through the steam toward them.

"After all, one does not travel without a valet." Harrow adjusted his spectacles. "Isn't that so, sir?"

Lord Allington glanced sideways at Harrow, then turned to Tillie.

"Pleasure to have you aboard, Miss Meriwether." He raised his elbow in her direction. "Harrow will show Grace to your quarters."

Tillie slipped her hand around Lord Allington's arm and was led through the mist.

Thick iron girders lined the walls of the cavern and framed the flat ceiling to create a web of interlocking joists. Workmen scuttled around at ground level, performing their duties.

Tillie scanned the cavern. Cager strode toward the hive of activity near an array of tube lighting in the centre of the cavern.

She froze mid-step.

A large dirigible bobbed several feet off the ground. It hung in the air like a gigantic bumblebee - an intriguingly impossible monstrosity that defied gravity.

She gasped in delight as she took in the spectacle.

It was almost three times the size of Little Nessie. The gondola resembled an over-sized submersible ship. Large metal bands encased the wooden hulk. Two rows of metal-rimmed portholes lined each side. Glass viewing bubbles were attached both atop and below the airship hull.

A small deck surrounded by an ornately carved balustrade crowned the main ship. Two large, long oval balloons floated above the gondola and tugged at a net of thick ropes, which held them in place. Sandbags hung from the periphery of each balloon; a mooring rope, as thick as a man's thigh, tethered the airship to a large metal mooring ring bolted to the ground.

"Miss Meriwether, meet Big Nessie," Lord Allington grinned.

She stifled a giggle.

"Surely the gondola is too large for the balloons?" she said. "It is so..." She searched for a polite word. "... cumbersome. It looks like an impossibly over-sized, blue-bottomed bumblebee."

"Yet bumblebees fly incredibly well, and prosper," said Lord Allington.

The engine convulsed.

"Higher," yelled the Head Steamer. "We need *more* steam!"

The air shuddered. Steamers crawled over the steam machine and yelled instructions over its irregular rumbles and ominous rattles. Tools clinked. Bursts of steam hissed out from the machine's innards.

The Head Steamer grimaced and wrestled with a lever resembling a railway switch throw bar.

"Watch it!" yelled Cager, as he rushed to join the Steamers.

The Head Steamer opened his mouth to reply and caught her gaze. A smile flickered over his lips and he nodded in her direction.

Cager grabbed the lever and pushed. Together they thrust it to the ground. One of the leather hoses quivered on the ground and flicked sideways. Steam hissed along it toward Tillie and her companions. A wall of heat rolled past them as it made its way along the pipeline toward a plated section of wall.

The plates rattled as the steam rumbled up inside the wall toward the ceiling.

Cager thrust his thumbs into the air and grinned. Lord Allington nodded and called to Harrow who was, as usual, hovering near the edges of the action.

Harrow emerged from behind the steamer trunks. Grace glided past him and issued instructions. The porters fell in line behind them.

A cloud of steam chugged along beside them and drifted closer to the dirigible. The tip of a ladder protruded from its core. The cloud slowed as it neared the dirigible's hull, and aligned itself with the upper observation deck. Tillie followed, mesmerised by the ladder machine.

The chugging sputtered. The steam dispersed. A sweaty Steamer sat on a mini steam engine. He manoeuvred the ambulatory ladder machine toward the dirigible. The top rung nudged the hull.

A hatch opened in the side of the hull. The Steamer nudged wheel chocks in place as he circled the machine. It shuddered into silence. The Steamer nodded in Harrow's direction.

An errant gush of steam hissed around Harrow's head as he climbed the rungs. He halted, growled at the Steamer and ostentatiously wiped his spectacles before entering the belly of the dirigible.

Tillie noted the smirk on Grace's lips as she followed, juggling the precious hat boxes in one arm.

Cager jogged back from the ladder machine. "Follow me please, Sir, and you too, Miss."

Another rumble shook the nearby plate wall as Cager led them to the ladder.

The dirigible crept higher, affording them a better view of the underside of the gondola. Large sky-blue canvases were slung across the bottom of each balloon. Tillie fancied she spied the occasional hand-painted fluffy cloud on the underside of the gondola's hull.

The steam machine chugged louder. The hoses shuddered. The dirigible rose even higher.

As it neared thirty feet from the ground, there was a loud crunch. The dirigible jolted upward, dragging the sandbags along the ground. Another sky-blue canvas erupted from under the viewing bubble.

The workmen cheered.

"Reel it back in," yelled The Head Steamer. He sprinted up to Lord Allington. "That was our last check, Sir."

"Excellent, Dodds. How are the new engines?"

"Everything is in working order, Sir." he replied. "We were just about to engage the new on-board engines."

It made sense. They'd need engines; the winds alone would not take them all the way to Egypt.

"Will there be enough fuel?" she asked.

"The water converters will provide enough fuel for the entire voyage, Sir." Steamer Dodds grinned and nodded. "The scoops will allow us to reload once we reach the Indian Ocean."

"Indian Ocean?" gasped Tillie. That was a strange route to Egypt. She frowned.

"We have the latest in German water-hydrogen conversion technology and Russian communication transmission systems," replied

Lord Allington.

"Communications?" She shook her head. "How? We can't drag cables behind us."

Lord Allington leaned close and whispered in her ear. "Cable-less technology."

"At least it isn't far to Egypt," She rubbed her hands together.

"Egypt?" said Cager.

He exchanged glances with Lord Allington. Lord Allington's moustache twitched.

"But," her smile faded, "you said pack for hot weather. I thought..."

Lord Allington shook his head. Her shoulders slumped.

But everyone goes to Egypt! She leaned her weight onto the walking cane.

"I think you are confused, Miss Meriwether," he said. "We're following The Inventor to Australia."

"Australia?" Her cane thudded on the ground. "How unfashionable!

The roof creaked and moaned above them.

"Watch, Miss Meriwether." Lord Allington gestured toward the steel-lined ceiling.

Nothing happened.

She nodded politely. *Behold the engineering prowess of the Department of Curiosities.*

"Patience," he whispered.

The metal joists jiggled. The roof lurched and grated. Cracks appeared where it met the walls. Clods of earth trickled from the edges and showered the cavern floor.

She examined the falling earth. It was covered in neatly groomed grass.

The grating sound reverberated through the cavern. The wall plates vibrated.

The ceiling inched downward, revealing an array of turning cogs built into the walls. The steam machine groaned and hissed behind them, as if to complain about the increased workload. The ceiling slowly descended several feet and hovered. A fissure appeared along the centre of the gigantic roof-disc. Each half teetered for a second before retreating toward the walls. More turf-laden lumps dribbled down.

Moonlight streamed through the gaping maw. Cool air descended and dispersed the clouds of steam.

The cogs ground to a halt. With a series of squeaks, the roof settled in place. The steam engine gasped and shuddered. There was silence.

A bearded face peeked over the edge of the precipice.

"All clear, Sir." His faint voice wafted down to the stunned gathering.

Lord Allington clapped his hands together and gestured toward the ambulatory ladder machine.

"Your dirigible awaits, Miss Meriwether." His moustache twitched.

She gathered her skirts and ascended the steps.

Of Gadgets, Tea, and Destinations

T illie sat by the porthole. Her hands pressed down on the top of her walking cane. Wisps of cloud kissed the glass. She leaned forward, rested her chin on her hands and stared out the aperture.

"Not Egypt?" she whispered.

<<*Not Egypt,*>> echoed the Orb.

Grace's shadow flitted across the glass, as she bustled around the cabin unpacking. She laid out Tillie's midnight blue velvet carriage coat and fluffed up its fur collar and cuffs. Crystals sparkled amongst the embroidered peacock feathers on the sleeves and collar.

"I've laid your travel coat, Miss," said Grace. "The temperature drops quite quickly as we go higher in the Aether."

<<*Too high!*>> screamed the Orb.

<<*I can't do anything about it,*>> said Tillie. <<*Stop complaining, or I'll activate the Discombobulator.*>>

The Orb sniffed.

She frowned and turned away from the porthole. "Have you travelled by dirigible before, Grace?"

Grace nodded. "Once. In the smaller one. We beat the train to Dover."

She smiled. "They fly faster, the higher they go."

Tillie looked at the porthole; flickering pinpoints of light pierced the night sky. The ground was a dark, featureless carpet below them. How much higher could they go?

"How long would it have taken to reach Cairo?" she asked.

"Two days. Perhaps less." Grace retrieved a matching pair of kid gloves and presented them to Tillie.

"Two days?" She blinked.

The Orb shifted.

"How long till we reach the Colonies?"

"About two weeks," replied Grace.

"Only two weeks?" Tillie's hands slipped off the head of the cane. She leaped out of her chair. "We could arrive before the steamship?"

"Indeed," replied Grace, "that was Sir Avery's intention." She pulled a hefty brass key from her pocket and slid it into the lock of the last unmarked steamer trunk.

Tillie moved closer. She'd wondered who it belonged to. The porters had strained to load it, though it was only half the size of her clothing trunk. She peeked over Grace's shoulder, curious to see what secrets it held.

"May I present your personal Cabinet of Curiosities," said Grace, "courtesy of Lord Allington. He doesn't trust everyone with the Department's creations."

<<*General's orders,*>> said the Orb.

"Perhaps it was the General's suggestion?" Tillie asked out loud.

"He doesn't do everything the General tells him." Grace shrugged. "I think he likes you." She turned the key.

Several clicks circled outwards from the lock and cascaded around the trunk. With a whir of a loosed spring, and a final clunk, the latch popped open.

Grace opened the lid slowly. A faint smell of sulphur wafted upward.

Tillie sniffed. "Gunpowder?"

"The trunk has an explosive trap, for those attempting unauthorised access."

Grace removed a layer of books and stacked them beside the trunk. A second wooden lid lay inside. A line of buttons ran along the two sides. Grace positioned a hand above the first button on each side and ran her fingers along the rows, counting the buttons. She pressed a button on each side simultaneously. The internal lid popped up.

"Remember, three and seven," said Grace.

"Three. Seven." Tillie nodded.

"Those numbers will prevent your hand from being blown off."

Tillie swallowed. She waited until Grace slid the lid from the trunk, before leaning forward to view the contents.

She gasped; never had she seen so many gadgets in one place. Brass, silver and polished steel glinted under the gas light. The smell of fresh leather caught in her nostrils. Carved wooden cylinders lay neatly packed amongst locked boxes, some with ornate metal attachments.

She opened one of the boxes. A decorated pistol lay on a pillow of green velvet. Metal tubes ran along one side, a glass valve attached to the other. A short telescope of etched brass was attached to the body of the weapon.

"Be careful with that," said Grace. "It is a *Disruptor* pistol. It can disable both magnetic and electronic fields."

The Orb went cold. It pulled around Tillie's neck and pushed into her chest as if shrinking away from the pistol.

"Electronic? Like the General's cane?" she asked.

"Almost," replied Grace.

Tillie eyed her out the corner of her eye. She knew a lot for a maid.

"It's used to disable mechanicals," Grace continued. "Not recommended for use during flight. It disrupts the engines." She snapped the box lid shut. "Much like your cane."

"That's good to know." Tillie placed the *Disruptor* back in the trunk.

Grace reached deep into the trunk and pulled out a leather face mask.

"You will need this if we have to venture too far into the upper Aether." Grace handed the mask to Tillie.

She glanced over the small brass cylinder and flexible tube attached to the face.

"How high is that?" she asked.

<<Too high.>> The Orb squirmed.

"No need to worry. An alarm will sound if we drift too high. You'll have a few minutes to put it on." Grace pointed to a brass knob under the tubing. "You twist this and breathe normally."

Tillie flipped over the mask and examined it. "Compressed air?" she asked.

Grace nodded and handed her a long leather belt and brass hook. She wrapped the belt around Tillie's waist, secured the mask to it, then stood back and smiled.

"Now you are ready."

"Ready?" asked Tillie.

"You have a meeting with Lord Allington before we reach the Channel."

<hr/>

Tube lighting reflected off the unadorned brass-lined walls of Lord Allington's office, illuminating everything with a warm, welcoming glow.

Taking pride of place in the centre of the cabin was a smaller version of the tracking sphere Tillie had seen in the Department of Curiosities' Upper Levels. It was by no means less impressive, and just as ornate. Three spherical shells slid over each other. Illuminated miniatures of sea-faring vessels, land transport and flying machines glided over the detailed world globe that lay at its core.

The innermost shell tracked Big Nessie's progress across the Channel. As she watched, the miniature dirigible froze and whirred. Its light faded as it twisted and rose to the middle shell.

Butterflies erupted in her stomach. Her head spun. Her vision blurred.

Miniature-Nessie twisted again and rose to the outermost sphere. Its light brightened.

One by one, the stomach butterflies landed. Her head stopped whirling.

Through the clearing haze she saw Lord Allington, sitting at his portable desk, apparently oblivious to the sudden shift in the Aether.

She leaned on the desk, careful not to knock the tea trolley next to it. The desk, immovable and steady, was a fine piece of craftsmanship and engineering: a travel trunk unfolded to convert into a fully-functioning travel desk, complete with drawers and lockable storage. Notes and plans lay strewn across its surface.

Lord Allington's eyes twinkled as he listed Big Nessie's features and pointed them out on the dirigible's floor plan.

"The Communication Room is-- " He glanced up from the plans. His grin faded. He returned the dirigible plans to his desk and placed a glass weight on one corner of the papers. "My apologies, Miss Meriwether. I forgot this was your first ascent into high altitudes."

He rose from his chair and gently ushered her to a nearby armchair.

"We must go higher now we've reached the Channel. The sudden drop in oxygen can make one light-headed. I should have warned you. Please forgive me. I'll instruct the pilot to warn you, next time we ascend."

He pulled the tea trolley closer and poured a cup of tea.

"This is a special blend, Miss Meriwether. Good for calming the nerves."

The cabin squirmed. The butterflies twitched.

The Orb groaned. She groaned. Her head fell into her hands. She held on tight.

<<Don't move,>> whispered the Orb.

"Mmmm, yes," she replied.

The sweet scent of vanilla tickled her nostrils. She closed her eyes, took a deep breath, allowing the vapour to fill her lungs.

"The nausea will pass, Miss Meriwether." He lifted a silver cloche off the tea trolley. "Cook has supplied us with a selection of cakes for the journey."

She nodded her head. There was always time for tea. She opened her eyes, gradually exhaled, and took the cup from Lord Allington.

The tea glistened. Steam danced around the rim. She took a sip. The butterflies settled.

The tracking sphere clicked loudly as Miniature-Nessie glided south over the globe, skirting the mainland.

"We're not flying over land?" she asked.

He shook his head. "The sea route is considerably safer. Several European watch stations are still active. It would *not* do to have an overzealous watchman report an unscheduled dirigible flight. Certain powers may jump to the wrong conclusion and think the Empire is finally retaliating." He sipped his tea. "There are too many factions in Europe with air flight capabilities. It's wise not to risk detection."

<<Vulnerable,>> complained the Orb.

<<They'll never see us at night,>> She eyed the strawberry cake on the tea trolley. He'd been right; she was feeling a little better.

<<No time for tea! Find Harrow.>>

She sighed and rose from her chair "I must-- "

The cabin twitched. The butterflies soared and rushed up her throat. She clutched her stomach and swallowed.

<<I'm not going anywhere.>>

The Orb grumbled.

Lord Allington frowned. He helped her back into the chair next to the desk.

"We won't cross land until we reach southern Africa where we'll catch the trade winds."

Higher? Her stomach dropped and started doing laps around her internal organs.

He offered her a piece of strawberry cake.

"No, thank you." She raised her hand. The thought of food joining the internal merry-go-round made her feel sick.

"Why do we need the winds? Don't we have engines?" she asked.

"Yes, but our power is supplied by converting water to hydrogen. When we cross Africa, we won't have easy access to water; we need a minimum fuel reserve for emergencies, so we'll avail ourselves of the wind currents when we can. However, Miss Meriwether, I'm afraid to do so means we *must* cross higher into the Aether." He indicated the mask on her belt. "For that, you will require the breathing apparatus."

A small mantelpiece clock on the portable desk chimed midnight. He checked his pocket watch.

"It's later than I thought. Harrow should have joined us by now." He snapped the watch shut.

She glanced over the plans under the glass weight on the desk beside her.

"Lord Allington, you mentioned cable-less communications. How is that possible?"

"Research, Miss Meriwether. We don't just lock away our acquired curiosities." He grinned. "A brilliant Italian scientist helped the General to extend the range of the device using an insulated aerial. His government ignored his talents, to our advantage." He lowered his voice to a whisper. "I'm considering inviting him to England. Best not mention it to Harrow when he arrives."

She still wasn't sure if she could trust Lord Allington. *Was* he was working with Harrow, and trying to trick her?

<<He doesn't seem to trust Harrow either,>> she said to the Orb. But could she trust him?

<<Caution,>> whispered the Orb. *<<Trap.>>*

"Why did you bring Harrow?" she asked.

Lord Allington poured himself a cup of tea, walked up to the Tracking Globe and examined the miniatures.

"He threatened to tell Ponsonby if I didn't allow him to come," he said finally.

She frowned. What did he mean exactly? Why would Harrow complain to Ponsonby if he couldn't join them on the mission?

<<Keep enemies close,>> said the Orb.

"And while we are aloft, he mustn't report back to his Controller." Lord Allington sipped his tea.

<<No permission?>> whispered the Orb.

She raised an eyebrow. Was Harrow going to report the use of a dirigible without permission? Which reminded her...

<<I need to send the Queen a report or she will insist I meet with her.>> She swallowed. *<<I can't tell Her I'm halfway to the Antipodes! What do I say?>>*

<<Lie,>> replied the Orb.

"When will I be able to familiarise myself with the new communication system?" she asked.

"Not until the engineer has it functioning."

She slouched into her chair. Her 'report' would have to wait. Queen Victoria would be *furious*, but at least it gave her time to construct a believable ruse.

The evening chill crept through the cabin. Tillie tugged the collar of her blue velvet coat tight to stop the cold creeping down her neck.

The cabin door swung open.

"Sorry I'm late." Harrow closed the door behind him. "I'm still finding my air-legs." His eyes scanned the room and lingered over the papers on the desk as he gravitated towards the tea trolley.

Lord Allington studied the recent movements of the tracking globe. A flash of the white of his eye suggested he was also interested in Harrow's movements.

Tillie lifted her teacup to her lips to conceal her smile. *<<He doesn't trust Harrow.>>*

<<Ruse?>> said the Orb.

Harrow fidgeted near the trolley. She watched the two men, watching each other.

"Tea, Lord Allington?" he asked.

Lord Allington raised his cup. "I'm fine."

Harrow nodded. "How do you take your tea, Miss Meriwether?"

"Lemon," replied Lord Allington.

He slipped a slice of cloved lemon into a teacup.

"I already have a cup of tea, thank you."

She sipped her tea; it took the edge off the increasing chill and the caffeine clarified her thoughts.

She scrutinised Harrow through the steam as it wafted up past the rim of her cup. He poured some tea, his hand hovered over the milk jug as his attention wandered back to the papers on the desk.

"Not taking milk today, Harrow?" Lord Allington circled the Tracking Globe, still sipping his tea.

Harrow's hand darted toward the lemon.

"No. I thought I'd try lemon for a change." He dropped another lemon slice into his cup and took a sip. His nose wrinkled, his lips pursed. He swallowed.

"You're not supposed to swallow the clove, Harrow." She lifted her teacup to hide her smirk.

The Orb jiggled.

"Pilot wants to know our heading." Harrow's teacup clattered onto his saucer. "As we all do, Sir."

"Ah, yes." Lord Allington returned to his desk, shuffled through the papers and pulled out a map with a course marked in red. He handed it to Harrow.

Harrow examined the map.

"We should make landfall in Adelaide in two weeks," said Lord Allington.

Harrow's lips thinned. "That fast?"

"With the new technology, Big Nessie is twice as fast as any steam ship currently in The Empire." Lord Allington grinned.

Harrow eyed him through narrowed eyelids. "Will Miss Meriwether be informing Her Majesty of our progress?"

Lord Allington's moustache twitched.

<<He knows.>> Her heart raced.

<<Impossible,>> hissed the Orb.

Her fingers twitched.

<<Don't fidget.>>

She clasped her hands in her lap.

"No, Miss Meriwether will not," replied Lord Allington. "The new communication machine is not ready yet."

Her fingers relaxed.

Harrow glanced over the desk and raised an eyebrow. She was unsure if his reaction was in response to Lord Allington's comment or to whatever had caught his eye on the desk. A crooked smile crept over his lips. He rolled up the map and excused himself.

She rose to her feet, placed her tea cup on the trolley and glanced over the desk. A detailed plan of the dirigible lay on top of a closed diary. The Communication Room on the upper level was clearly labelled. He would have been blind not to have noticed. She had no doubt he'd noted its position and would try to contact The Society.

<<Stop him,>> urged the Orb.

<<Quiet, I need to think.>> She placed her hand against her bodice. *<<There are too many questions I need answered.>>*

She waited until she could no longer hear Harrow's footsteps, then lowered her voice.

"The Queen is not aware of our journey?" she whispered.

Lord Allington shook his head.

Her eyes widened. The Queen didn't know! Her heart thumped. Perhaps he was working against the Queen? Her heart sank. Was he working for The Society?

<<He's worried Harrow will tell Her,>> she said.

<<Will you tell Her?>> asked the Orb.

Tillie didn't answer.

<<Don't trust him.>>

<<He can't be a Man in Grey?>> she replied. *<<Why would he be chasing Cranshaw half way around the world if he wasn't loyal to the Crown?>>*

The Orb cooled under her stays.

<<What if he discovers I belong to the Queen, like my father?>> She swallowed. *<<And She's ordered me to spy on the Department?>>*

"Miss Meriwether?"

The colour drained from her face. *<<He'd despise me,>>* she whispered.

"Miss Meriwether, are you unwell?" asked Lord Allington.

Her head jerked up in response.

"Is the altitude still bothering you?" he asked.

A quick reply was needed: "A little," she whispered.

He frowned and moved closer.

"You look pale." His hand cupped her elbow and ushered her back into her chair. "Perhaps you should avail yourself of the oxygen mask?" His voice was calm, relaxing.

<<Perhaps he would understand?>>

<<Tell no one,>> said the Orb. *<<Trust no one.>>*

<<I have to know,>> she whispered. "Why are you so concerned Harrow will inform Her Majesty?" she asked Lord Allington.

He sat beside her, ran his fingers over his moustache and stared out the porthole, avoiding her gaze.

"I thought The Department of Curiosities reported directly to the Queen," she said.

He opened his mouth and hesitated, as if choosing his words carefully: "We serve The Empire."

"Isn't it the same?" she asked.

He didn't reply.

<<Damning silence,>> said the Orb.

When he finally spoke, his voice seemed strained, tired. Uncertain.

"Have you seen those big harpoon guns that ring the Palace?" he asked.

She nodded.

"They were built to destroy airships like this. If the Queen knew we've built Big Nessie, she would double her firepower and never leave the Palace. And what good is a monarch who does not trust her own people?"

<<Treacherous,>> hissed the Orb.

"But The Department is loyal to the Crown," she said.

He bit his lip.

"Yet, if She thought otherwise, She would use every available archived Curiosity to protect herself. Even against us." He folded his arms. His shoulders rose and fell with his deep breaths. "I *know* the Queen championed you, Miss Meriwether; the General told me before he..." He pinched his bottom lip. "He trusted you. And you definitely don't like Harrow." He turned to face her. "Harrow threatened to inform Ponsonby of my plans to use Big Nessie to follow the Inventor unless he accompanied us; Sun Tsu said: *keep your enemies close.* I couldn't have him informing *anyone* of our plans." He stared into her eyes. "Can I trust you, Matilda?"

He held his breath.

She nodded slowly.

"I hope I've made the right decision," he whispered, barely audible. "The General was searching for something the Inventor stole. Something that could change the fate of the Empire. I mean to continue his search. I need your help."

<<He trusts me.>> Her heart fluttered.

<<Fool. He lies.>> growled the Orb.

<<Shut up!>> she said. *<<He needs my help.>>* She smiled sweetly.

"I'm searching for something called *the Horde*," he said.

Of Corridors, Cabins, and Trunks

S hafts of moonlight pierced the portholes and partly illuminated the passageway. Every muscle in Tillie's body seized. Numbness gripped her heart and crept over her chest; its tendrils crawled down her arms to her clenched fists. The Orb chilled her skin and remained silent.

She willed her leaden feet to move. How did Lord Allington know about *the Horde*? What did he know about *the Horde*? Her shoulders drooped.

She crept into the darkness, toward the Communication Room where she knew Harrow would be lurking.

The Communication Room was easy to find, having studied Big Nessie's plans. It lay directly under the main observation deck of the dirigible.

A sliver of flickering light marked the outline of the door ahead. She hugged the wall and tiptoed toward the lone door at the far end, avoiding the shafts of light splashed along the dim, claustrophobic passageway.

It was a plain door, purporting to be a broom cupboard. While not hidden, it would remain undetectable to those who did not know of its existence. Who would look in a broom cupboard but staff, all of whom she was certain would have higher clearance than that expected of the usual domestic staff? They probably outranked Harrow. Grace probably outranked him, possibly even Cook. Her lip curled. There was a perverse comfort in such a notion.

She bit her lip to stifle a laugh; she was too near the Communication Room to risk Harrow hearing her.

Tillie inched closer and cocked her head to listen for signs of activity. Clicking noises filtered through the crack. A repeated snapping sound followed. Someone growled.

<<*Harrow!*>> she gasped.

<<*Stop him,*>> ordered the Orb.

She froze. <<*I need to know what he's doing. If I barge in he may destroy any evidence.*>> She held her breath, remaining still and, most importantly, silent.

The clicking resumed after a few moments, this time at a much faster pace.

She pressed her cheek to the crack and squinted. <<*I can't see anything.*>>

A loud thud shook the door. She jumped away from the door and flattened her body against the wall.

There was a scrabbling noise, then silence. She backed further away and melded into a long shadow leading into a side passageway.

<<*Stop him now,*>> raged the Orb.

<<*Quiet. If you want to stop him, then go ahead. Personally, I would rather not meet him, alone, in a dark passageway, without a weapon. I should've brought the cane, or my parasol. I should not have listened to you.*>>

She poked her head around the corner. The sliver of light widened and illuminated the passageway.

Harrow stood in the doorway. He straightened his coat, pushed his spectacles back up his nose and ran his fingers through an errant lock of hair. He flicked the switch for the wall lighting and stalked down the walkway, muttering to himself as he passed the passageway where she hid.

Tillie waited until Harrow's footsteps receded, before she peeled herself away from the wall and entered the Communication Room.

The polished brass trim of the telegraph machine shone under the feeble electric light. The compact gadgetry was uncluttered; there was no familiar, intricate web of wires to dance around.

She examined the machine. A set of wires ran from the machine's heart to a second writing machine, resembling a Remington upstrike machine. Sheets of paper sat wedged under the keys.

She slid the top sheet from its cage. It was blank. She held the paper horizontally, the edge almost touching her eye, and squinted as she scanned the surface under the light. There were no indentations.

<<*No message?*>> asked the Orb.

<<*Surely he would've had time to send at least one message?*>> She tapped a few keys. The machine remained silent.

<<*Broken,*>> hissed the Orb.

<<*Perhaps Lord Allington was telling the truth; perhaps it isn't functional yet?*>>

Tillie slipped the paper back into position, flicked off the light and went in search of Harrow.

❂

Tillie climbed down the narrow ladder to the cabin deck, slipped along the passageway and paused at the end. The left corridor led back to her room. The corridor on the right led to the gentlemen's quarters. Both were empty. Perhaps Harrow had gone to the lower deck?

<<*Search the cabin.*>> The Orb jostled, pulling to the right.

<<*What if he returns?*>> she replied.

<<*Find journal,*>> it ordered.

She hesitated. There were no portholes along the curving internal corridors. She squinted, waited for her eyes to adjust, and strained to listen.

<<Hurry!>> hissed the Orb.

<<Quiet, I can't hear.>>

The Orb jerked at her neck, its chain dug sharply into the skin.

She flinched.

<<All right, I'm going.>>

She tiptoed along the corridor, careful to avoid her boot heel hitting the wooden floorboards.

Her boot heel clicked on the floor.

<Shh,> yelled the Orb.

A snuffle sounded behind the thin walls.

Tillie leaned her ear to the wall. There was another snuffle.

<<Allington snores.>> The Orb snorted.

She ignored the Orb's rudeness and continued to the next door. Harrow's quarters according to Nessie's floor plan.

<<Go in!>> said the Orb.

<<I need to check it's safe first.>> She reached into her pockets for a listening device and nestled its ear funnel against the door. The snoring from the adjoining room grew louder. She fiddled with its settings and listened again. She heard only the faint creak of the door against its frame as the dirigible rocked in the Aether currents. Beyond that, there was nothing.

She slipped a small lockpick from inside her boot and set to work, glad she hadn't forsaken all the accoutrements of her pre-Department adventures.

❖

Harrow's cabin was immaculate. Not an item out of place. It was almost too organised; the bed was perfectly made, with his steamer trunk placed squarely at its foot. A smaller trunk was stacked on the steamer, perfectly centred, as was the hat box atop it. Even the shadows cast by the faint moonlight seemed perfectly aligned.

Tillie searched the hatbox and the trunk. Each item of clothing was folded precisely. Shoes were wrapped neatly in paper to protect the starched shirts from any extraneous mud. Everything was in order with nothing to betray outside allegiances. No secret messages or instructions to prove his betrayal. No weapons - of mass destruction or of minor inconvenience. And no sign of her father's journal or the da Vinci notebook.

<<*That's odd.*>> She was sure Harrow had stolen them. Could she have been mistaken all along?

<<*Impossible!*>> The Orb warmed against her skin. <<*Harrow is traitor.*>>

She dropped the shoes back into the trunk. A hollow thunk resounded through the cabin.

<<*There!*>> hissed the Orb.

She knocked on the base of the trunk.

Thunk.

<<*A secret compartment!*>> Her heart raced. Her fingers traced along the inside edge of the trunk's base. The panel shifted slightly. She felt inside the walls for a latch.

Nothing.

She stepped back and examined the trunk. It was made of intricately carved wood. Small dragons climbed up the leather strapping; they reminded her of the Chinese puzzle box her father had given her on her eighth birthday.

"I wonder..."

She ran her hands over the outside of the trunk. The wood tickled her skin as she searched for any raised sections or concealed buttons. Her fingertip sensed a faint ridge in the centre of a panel. She examined it with her Lorgnette. A small, recessed square had been hidden in one of the dragons.

She placed the listening device against the trunk and pressed the square. A muffled twang reverberated through the wood.

The square popped outwards.

<<Which way shall I turn it?>> she asked.

<<Anticlockwise,>> replied the Orb.

<<Why?>>

<<Harrow left handed,>> replied the Orb. *<<Turn left.>>*

She hesitated. *<<What if someone else made the trunk?>>*

<<Turn left!>> The Orb was now uncomfortably hot on her skin.

She huffed, pursed her lips and turned the knob. Clockwise.

A faint tink funnelled down the listening device to her ear. Several clicks followed. Then, silence.

She winced. The Orb tapped on her chest as she listened for the consequences.

Seconds ticked by.

One.

Two.

Three.

Something snapped in the bowels of the trunk. Her heart lurched.

<<Told you,>> grumbled the Orb.

She took a deep breath. Her ribs twinged. She braced them with her hand, rose slowly and peeked into the trunk. The false base had flipped up at one side.

<<Is that so?>> She smiled. *<<I will entertain apologies at your earliest convenience.>>*

She lifted the base clear.

Several boxes lay in the bottom. Beneath one was a hint of green binding.

<<*There!*>> yelled the Orb.

Tillie wriggled the notebook free from its prison. Her hands shook as she flipped through the pages. It was her father's handwriting. She'd found his journal. Nothing had been removed. She closed her eyes, pressed the journal against her chest for a moment, then slipped it into her hidden bustle pockets.

<<*Safe.*>> The Orb seemed to sigh with relief and relax against her skin.

She reached back into the hidden compartment and pulled out an oblong wooden scroll box decorated in gold lacquer with a peony design and tied with a tasselled cord.

She untied the cord and tested the lid. It wouldn't budge.

<<*Locked,*>> said the Orb.

"It must be important," she whispered.

She carefully placed the box on the bedside table, pulled out her lockpicks and set to work. There was a satisfying click. She hesitated. Had Harrow protected his secrets with minor explosives as well? She scoffed; Grace had made her paranoid about traps. She bit her lip and ran the tip of the pick along the edge of the lid. There was no obvious trap.

She held her breath and eased the lid upwards. To her relief, the entire task was uneventful.

A wad of letters occupied the box. Some were tied with a red ribbon, others tied with a grey ribbon.

<<*Grey?*>> The Orb jiggled under her bodice. <<*Proof. Harrow is traitor.*>>

<<*They could be personal letters.*>>

<<*Incriminating letters,*>> said the Orb.

Her hand hovered over the letters; she wasn't comfortable reading someone's personal correspondence.

<<*Same as journal,*>> said the Orb.

"But that was father's journal," she whispered.

<<No difference,>> insisted the Orb.

She picked up the grey-bound letters. The Orb was correct; when seeking evidence of clandestine and treacherous acts, it was acceptable to delve into private communiques. There would be no harm if he had nothing to hide. And *he* would have no qualms if their positions were reversed. She clenched her jaw and slipped the ribbon off the bundle. Besides, he hadn't had *any* qualms when he stole both her father's journal *and* the da Vinci notebook.

She skimmed the top missive. The ink and lettering were consistent with messages received on the telegraph machine. It was addressed to Harrow and spoke of the Flying Scotsman, dates, times, numbers of operatives. One specific date stood out:

"Third of April," she whispered out loud. "The day after the General..." She gasped. The wound was still raw.

<<*Died,*>> concluded the Orb.

Her hand trembled as she read further:

Under no circumstances must the D.O.C. board train, or report back to the Widow. No loose ends, Harrow.

It was signed with a capital *'I'*.

<<*Inventor,*>> screamed the Orb.

The air rushed out of her lungs with the force of the Orb's outcry. She caught her breath, and struggled to slow her heart beat. Her head spun.

<<*Traitor!*>> screamed The Orb.

<<*Cranshaw,*>> she said. <<*He is 'Cranshaw'. He who has a name is not to be feared.*>>

Dull thuds echoed somewhere outside the room. A door banged shut.

<<*Quiet!*>> she demanded, careful not to articulate the words. <<*I heard something.*>>

Another thud emanated from the adjoining room.

The Orb twitched and warmed against her skin.

<<I've taken too long,>> she said.

<<Take message,>> demanded the Orb.

<<We have what we need.>>

<<da Vinci notebook?>>

Tillie shook her head. *<<We need to leave.>>* She relocked the lid of the scroll case, returned it to the trunk and replaced the false bottom.

She crept back to the door and listened. All seemed quiet. She wrapped her fingers around the doorknob and turned it slowly. The doorknob clicked.

Tillie peeked through the crack in the door. The passageway was empty. She crept out of Harrow's cabin and shut the door silently behind her, ignoring the Orb's continuing protests.

Footsteps tapped ahead in the darkness. She froze, and lowered her boot heel gently to the floor.

<<Not mine,>> she whispered.

<<Hide,>> urged the Orb.

Tillie pressed herself against the wall, slid into the deep shadows and felt along the wall for any means of escape.

The footsteps grew louder.

A convenient door handle offered a glimmer of hope. She held her breath and turned the knob. A faint click signalled the latch had disengaged.

<<Hurry, no time,>> said the Orb.

<<Quiet,>> she replied, *<<or next time I'll bring the cane. I may get some peace and be able to think.>>* If it was possible to glare internally, then she did so.

Light spilled into the corridor as she eased open the door.

The footsteps moved closer.

<<Hide,>> growled the Orb.

"Is that you, Smythe?" It was Lord Allington's voice.

There was a clatter of metal on porcelain.

She hesitated.

The Orb cursed.

"Close the door, man. It's creating a draught."

She swallowed and turned toward the room. A tall folding privacy screen concealed half the room from view. Lord Allington was nowhere to be seen.

The footsteps changed direction as they neared the junction at the end of the corridor.

She lowered her voice, mumbled something unintelligible and pulled the door shut behind her.

<<What are you doing?>> cried the Orb.

<<Trying not to get caught,>> she replied.

There was a splash. A glint on the wall caught her eye. She leaned sideways and spied a standing mirror near the far wall. In it was a clear reflection of Lord Allington leaning over a porcelain washbowl. His braces knocked against his thighs. The button of his trousers clacked against the bowl as he splashed water over his face. Droplets trickled down his bare forearms and dripped off his naked elbows.

He straightened up and reached out for a folded towel next to the bowl.

She gasped and stood bolt upright, the mirror no longer in line of sight.

<<Oh, dear.>> Heat burned her cheeks. She stepped back towards the door.

<<Footsteps outside,>> reminded the Orb.

She heard them, muffled by the walls. Her pulse raced, only serving to spread the heat beyond her cheeks. Faint beads of perspiration formed on her forehead.

She scanned the room, searching for an escape. The window was too far away, and they were airborne.

<<*Several thousand feet,*>> reminded the Orb.

<<*I know.*>> She turned her attention back to the room, looking for a way to avoid imminent discovery. She needed somewhere to hide. To her left was a bed, a crisp, white nightshirt folded neatly on the bedcover. A coat and shirt hung over a chair at the foot of the bed.

<<*Under bed?*>> suggested the Orb.

The heat in her cheeks intensified. <<*I can't stay there while he prepares to retire for bed.*>>

"Hand me my nightshirt," said Lord Allington, from behind the screen.

She stifled a curse.

<<*Do something!*>> hissed the Orb.

Her heart pounded. She took a step forward and checked the reflection in the mirror. Lord Allington's face was buried in the towel as he dried himself. She took a deep breath, snatched up the nightshirt and flipped it over the screen, not taking her eyes off the mirror.

"That will be all," he said, head still in towel. "Though," he lifted his head, "I could do with a nightcap."

Tillie edged back towards the door. The footsteps passed by Lord Allington's cabin. A door clicked shut further along the corridor. She listened for any further movement.

All was silent.

She reached for the doorknob.

Lord Allington shuffled behind the screen. The nightshirt slipped off the partition and was replaced by a pair of trousers.

In one swift move, she opened the door, slipped out, closed it behind her, then made a hasty retreat along the corridor to the safety of her own quarters.

Of Spies, Companions,
and Confrontations

T illie flung her camisole over her steamer trunk, slumped onto her
bed and sank into the soft mattress. A cushion of feather pillow
caressed her ears. A metal corset stay pressed into her back. She was
too tired to wrestle with her corset. She closed her eyes, rolled over and
buried her face in the pillow, drowning her troubles in the welcoming
comfort.

Sleep at last.

<<Don't sleep,>> grumbled the Orb. *<<Still work to do.>>*

She moaned as she reached out for her walking cane. Her fingers
flailed in the empty space beside the bed. She rolled closer to the edge
of the mattress. Her nails scraped against the wood of the bedside table.

<<That's odd.>>

She reluctantly lifted her head from the pillow and cracked open an
eyelid. The cane wasn't leaning against the bedside table where she'd
left it.

The Orb scoffed. *<<Will endanger airship.>>*

She sighed in frustration. It was right; Lord Allington had mentioned the *Discombobulator* could interfere with the dirigible's engines. She rolled over onto her back and removed its chain from around her neck.

"I'm sorry," she whispered. "I need to think tonight. Alone." She placed the Orb in the drawer of the bedside table.

It jittered as she closed the drawer, its reply muffled.

She frowned and scanned the room. Where was the cane? She reached down over the edge of the bed and searched the floor near the bedside table. Nothing.

She leaned over the edge as best she could in the metal corset, without aggravating her bruised ribs, and searched under the bed. A glint beckoned her.

"Not where I put you." She slipped off the bed, lay on the floor, stretched forward and grasped the brass handle.

"Miss Meriwether!" Grace rushed to her side. "Are you injured?"

She felt a petite hand clasp her upper arm. Another wrapped itself around her chest and lifted her easily from the floor, twisting her corset.

She winced, and transferred her weight onto the cane as she stood.

Grace grimaced, echoing Tillie's pain, and helped her to the nearest chair. Her eyes scanned Tillie's body. She clasped Tillie's face in both hands and stared into her eyes.

"Well, you don't have concussion," said Grace. She placed her hands on her hips. "What happened?"

Tillie eyed her new companion.

Grace was stronger than she looked. She wondered what other secrets Grace was hiding.

"I lost my balance," she replied.

"Perhaps it's the rarefied air?" said Grace. "Some people need longer to adapt to the reduced oxygen levels at this height. We need to get you out of that corset for a while, so you can breathe."

Grace relieved Tillie of the walking cane and rested it against the bedside table. She untied the cord and loosened the corset, one eyelet at a time, allowing for each rib to adjust to the change in support.

"There, that should allow you to breathe." The tugging stopped. "Your ribs would heal faster if you didn't have to wear this." Grace eyed the corset and screwed up her nose.

Tillie lowered her head and smiled. "My aunt would have told me to stop exerting myself so much when wearing stays," she said.

"She sounds like a sensible woman," replied Grace.

"She *was*." Tillie sighed. "But she championed stays."

"Lord Allington told me about your aunt. I'm sorry, Miss Meriwether."

"Thank you, Grace." She took a tentative breath. Her ribs didn't complain. "And, please, call me Tillie."

She picked hairpins from her bun; her blonde curls tumbled over one shoulder to her waist.

Grace rummaged through the folded linens packed in the steamer trunk and fussed over the clothing.

"Have you already unpacked your nightgown?" she asked.

"No, why?" replied Tillie.

Grace frowned. "I'm certain I didn't pack your drawers with your stockings."

Tillie glanced at the cane, now back where she'd left it before her meeting with Lord Allington. It seemed several items were out of place.

"Did you return to the room this evening, Grace?"

Grace shook her head. "Not until just now, Miss."

"Did you move my walking cane?"

"You saw me put it back."

"No, I mean earlier, when the trunks were delivered to the cabin."

"No." Grace crossed her arms. "I have no need to play with your gadgets. I have enough of my own to keep me occupied."

"No, you misunderstand me." Tillie held a hand up to calm her. "I wasn't accusing you of anything, Grace. Quite the opposite. The cane had been moved from where I'd left it." She glanced over the room and frowned. "Is there anything else out of place?"

Grace puffed her cheeks, let out a long breath and studied the room. As her gaze fell on the locked, unmarked steamer trunk, she paused.

"The hat box. It was on the trunk." She indicated the locked Cabinet of Curiosities.

Harrow had searched her room while she was searching his. The cheek! She placed her hands over her bustle pockets. At least the codebook and the rest of her treasures were safe.

Grace tugged at the lid. It remained secure. She examined the main lock.

"Scratches," she hissed. "Someone's attempted to pick the lock." She frowned. "We've got a spy on board."

Tillie flinched. She was growing to loathe that word.

"I will inform Lord Allington immediately," said Grace.

"No." The word spilled out of her mouth a little too quickly. She bit her lip. Grace was loyal to Lord Allington. Surely if her cabin had been searched on Lord Allington's orders, Grace would have done so and not left evidence behind, nor drawn attention to it. It was Harrow's work. It had to be. But she couldn't have him incarcerated just yet. She needed to find out if he knew of her indenture to Queen Victoria and make sure he didn't tell Lord Allington - or he'd never trust her again.

She took a deep breath, rose to her feet and smiled. She picked up her camisole, slipped it over her corset and buttoned it up.

"Fetch my bodice, please, Grace. I'm going to look for our spy."

"Miss, it could be dangerous," said Grace.

"Tosh. I promise I'll be careful," she said. "Besides, you approve of fresh air, if I remember. I shall inform Lord Allington myself."

"But, whoever did this--"

"My cabin has been violated by someone on board," she said. "I have the right to seek the blaggard out."

Grace cleared her throat. "You can't go dressed like that."

Tillie caught sight of her reflection in the standing mirror and froze mid-step. Her silk bustle skirt of blue and purple stripes was the only thing fit for public viewing. The matching bodice now lay half-folded on a nearby chair. Her half-unbuttoned camisole barely covered her stays. She pulled the strap back onto her shoulder.

Her hair fell in untidy ringlets on one side; the other was still meticulously pinned. Aunt Prudence would have had a fit if she were to venture willingly into public in such a state of undress. She lifted her skirts a little higher and smiled. And what would Aunt Prudence have thought about her trousers!

Grace shook her head and slipped the bodice over Tillie's arms and began buttoning it up.

"Aunt Prudence would have approved of you, Grace," said Tillie as she turned toward the cabin door.

"Miss, I haven't finished dressing you. The stays need to be tightened so I can finish fastening up your-- "

"Stop fussing, Grace."

"Miss, I really think I should tell Lord Allington."

"You stay here and guard the Curiosities." Tillie grabbed her travel coat of embroidered velvet and slipped it over her ill-fitting bodice. It would do. She wasn't being presented at court. She snatched up her red parasol, hefted the comforting weight in her hand, and strode to the cabin door.

It was extraordinarily late, even by Tillie's standards. The sky was dark. The full moon was setting, taking with it the light, and there was still no hint of sunrise.

She neared the end of a short passageway which should, if she remembered the dirigible plans correctly, lead to the upper observation deck.

She'd searched almost every inch of the dirigible and there was still no sign of Harrow. He couldn't vanish into thin air. The deck was the only place left to search.

On occasion she'd thought she'd seen a shadow following her but further investigation had proven her to be mistaken. The Orb would usually offer up its almost preternatural suggestions but, in the hurry to leave her cabin, she'd left it in the bedside table drawer. This was one time she'd wished she'd not craved silence.

The ladder resembled narrow, vertical steps, reaching up to a bolted hatch in the ceiling. She tugged a lever on the left wall.

The locking bolts slid into the wall. With a long hiss, the hatch dropped downwards. Her loose curls danced in the breeze - first a waltz, then a jig. Without warning they whipped wildly against her face. She grabbed the wayward locks, tamed them into a loose plait and climbed up onto the deck.

A chill wind blasted across the deck, as if coming directly from the Arctic. It clawed at her travel coat and whistled down the front of her half-buttoned bodice. She tugged the fur-lined collar tight.

The wind picked up. Intermittent gusts pulled at her skirts, swirled around her legs and exposed her boots and stockings. The silk billowed like a sail and threatened to launch her off the deck. She shivered and made her way toward the observation dome at the centre of the deck.

Shadows flickered behind her. She scanned the deck. The moon was low. Above her the painted canvases flapped against the enormous balloons, casting long, undulating shadows.

She strained to listen for any movement above the sound of the wind buffeting her ears. There was nothing; she was imagining things.

The wind died down. The faint putter of engine propellers chugged behind her. The securing ropes creaked. Otherwise there was silence. She was alone with the darkness. And the stars; bright, glittering stars, even more brilliant than she remembered from her trips to Egypt. There was no London fog to obscure the heavens. The dirigible flew above the dust, the grime, and the clouds.

She leaned against the rail and drank in the vast heavens around her.

"I could get used to this," she whispered.

"Good morning, Miss Meriwether."

Harrow!

She gasped and spun on her heel to face the unexpected company. His eyes were cold, betraying his manufactured smile. She gripped tightly on the parasol's carved ivory handle until her knuckles cramped.

"Fancy meeting you here." He nodded at her parasol. "Out for a walk with your parasol? That's a bit eccentric, even for you."

"I thought I'd watch the sunrise."

"The sun won't be up for an hour or two." Harrow pushed his spectacles up his nose and took a step closer.

"You must be careful up here, Miss Meriwether. It rained earlier in the evening and the deck is slippery. You don't want to have an unfortunate accident," he said. "Who would operate the telegraph machine?"

She glared at him.

An errant breeze flirted with the pleating at the hem of her skirt and plucked at her hair. Once introductions had been made, it returned and whipped the skirt against her ankles and yanked her coat making it almost impossible to manoeuvre her parasol. The sudden shift in weight threatened to pull her off balance. The wind circled and rushed from behind her. Strands of hair whipped her face.

She grabbed the offending locks, shoved them into her plait and turned to face the traitor; he stood between her and the hatch. She pulled wisps of hair from her lips and allowed them to float free. She pulled off her travel coat, exaggerating her agitation and hoping to distract him as she searched for an unobstructed way off the deck.

He stepped closer.

She glared at him through narrowed eyelids. Her grip tightened on the parasol and hefted the reassuring weight in her hands.

"There appears to be a rat on board." Harrow's eyes remained fixed on her.

"Better than a treacherous, murdering weasel."

"Did you search my cabin?" he asked through clenched teeth. He stepped closer and grabbed her arm.

So this was it: no more games. She opened her eyes wide and met his stare.

"Did you search mine?" she replied.

"What did you take?" He squeezed her arm.

"I retrieved my property." Her free hand searched for the railing behind her as she wrenched out of Harrow's grip.

Water droplets plonked onto her nose and splashed into her eyes. Another Aether tempest roared over the deck. Raindrops lashed her cheeks. A flurry of striped silk writhed around her calves. The chill blast seeped through her boots.

She cursed, shoved the parasol into the swathes of silk floating around her knees and thrust the garment deckwards. She stepped on the hem, ripped a split down the front of her skirt and exposed her trousers.

Harrow glanced downward, his attention lingering on her exposed ankles. The corners of his mouth curled. His lips parted slowly.

The hairs on the back of her neck stood on alert.

"You won't get the chance," she hissed.

He slowly raised his eyes and stared directly into hers. The hard line of his smile remained unaltered, as if frozen in the wind.

The wind died. Her plait slapped against her neck. Her skirts, which until now had tried the utmost to defy gravity, finally acknowledged the physics of the situation. She shifted her weight to compensate. Her wet skirts clung around her legs and dragged heavily as she moved.

Her loss of concentration allowed Harrow his opportunity. He lunged at her, grabbed the end of her plait and wrapped his fingers around her arm.

"Don't touch me," she spat.

She tugged her parasol free of her clothing, flicked it upwards and slammed the reinforced canopy into his arm, just above the elbow.

He yelped in pain and snapped his arm out of reach. The smile was gone.

Heavy raindrops spattered the deck and soaked into the silk of her bodice.

"You ignorant chav."

"Afraid to use my name, Harrow?" She chuckled nervously.

Harrow's eyebrow arched, rather unimpressively.

"I wouldn't be so confident if I were you," he snarled. "Mr Brown was overconfident as well, *my dear.*" His voice changed into a poor mimicry of the General.

She froze. It was as if she'd been kicked in the chest. She remembered the General's battered body, his tired eyes. If Harrow had meant to intimidate her, he'd chosen the wrong image. The General deserved justice for his death.

"Murderer and traitor." She growled and raised her parasol.

Harrow snatched a weapon from inside his coat and pounced forward in attack.

She dodged instinctively, but not fast enough. The blade sliced through her bodice and scraped along the metal stays. He grabbed for her bodice sleeve. Her heart pounded. She dived to the side. The buttons popped and scattered over the deck. The sleeve dragged off her shoulder. A sudden chill gripped her chest. She twisted to the side and slipped out of the bodice.

Harrow roared, threw it onto the deck and thundered after her.

She grabbed the railing to regain her balance.

"You, sir, are no gentleman."

"I never claimed to be, Miss Meriwether." He lunged awkwardly; his leather sole slid along the wet decking and he slammed into the railing. His knife clattered onto the deck, along with another object. Metal glinted dimly in the failing moonlight.

She squinted. Her father's face stared back at her.

"Thief," she screamed. "That's mine!"

"It's mine now," he hissed.

Sleet stung her skin. Water drizzled from her nose and chin. Wet hair clung to her face and neck. She wanted to scream out the truth. It was the only photo of her father's murderer.

"I need it." Her voice cracked.

He laughed and kicked the photograph. It skimmed across the wet deck and ricocheted off the glass observation dome.

Her muscles twitched.

The dirigible banked. The photo skittered further across the deck.

They both lunged for it. She kicked Harrow's knife toward the edge of the deck.

Tillie grinned.

Harrow cursed.

Big Nessie turned again; the knife slid away from the edge.

This time he grinned. He snatched up the knife.

Tillie lunged for the tintype. Her skirts clung to her legs, dragging as she moved. She kicked at the sodden material. A loose strip of ripped pleating dragged lifelessly across the deck and twisted around her ankle as she made for her escape. Her foot tugged the soaked ensemble and sent her sliding across the deck. She snatched up the photograph.

"Blasted skirts! They'll be the death of me!"

Harrow snarled and lurched toward Tillie.

Her fingers fumbled around the clasp of her skirt. She needed time.

"Why betray the Department?" she asked.

"I don't want to be second - or third - in charge," he said. "I deserve more, but first I need to control *the Horde*. And not my pathetic-- " He scowled. "The coward ran away and left me behind."

"The Inventor?"

Harrow scoffed. "I always thought that name was pretentious."

She tugged at her waistband. It wouldn't budge. She groaned and plunged the spiked tip of her parasol into the limp remnants of her skirt. She hacked through the material, grabbed one end and ripped the skirt from her torso. Her stockings and trousers were no insulation; the bitter cold seeped into her bones.

Another wind gust grabbed her skirts and lifted them away from the deck. The material flapped wildly in her hand. She remembered Saunders' training and his instructions on the unexpected attack. She smiled. Harrow would not win!

Harrow advanced, shepherding her toward the edge of the deck. He raised his weapon and grinned. She flung the improvised cloak in his face. It snared his weapon arm and obscured his view.

She ducked to the other side of the observation dome. Her wet fingers cramped in the cold. Her teeth chattered.

Harrow clawed at the heavy material, extracted himself from the entanglement and tossed it aside.

She edged toward the open hatch and watched for her chance to escape. When the time came, she'd need to move fast.

He started in her direction and stopped. Something fluttered at his feet. He bent down and picked up the object. A small black book.

"The code book!" She froze. She clutched at her exposed bustle pockets. In her haste to remove her cumbersome skirt, she'd nicked the corner of one of the pockets. "No!"

The pages fluttered in the wind. Harrow glanced at the book.

"The key!" He glared at her with a sickening smile. "Thank you, Miss Meriwether. You've saved me any further bother. My employer will be very happy." He tucked the codebook into his coat pocket.

"Give it back, Harrow." She gripped her parasol, determined to wipe the smile from his face, and dived forward.

He sneered and knocked her aside. She fell backwards onto the observation dome and cracked her head on the glass. The photograph fell to the ground and clattered on the deck. She shook her head and shivered. She was drenched. Her joints were stiff and refused to obey her command. She wiped the back of her head and examined the red smudges on her fingers as they faded and washed away in the rain.

"Let us end this little game." He advanced towards her. "Didn't anyone tell you not to bring a parasol to a knife fight?" He grinned, raised his knife and lunged forward to attack her.

Her reactions were dulled by the bitter cold. She dodged, too late. Harrow twisted at the last moment and wrapped one arm around her shoulders. His knife pressed against her throat. His other hand grasped her wrist, preventing her from wielding her parasol. He squeezed.

She clawed the arm at her throat. Her fingers slipped. He grinned and dug his nails into her tendons. The parasol fell from her hand.

"It is as it should be, Miss Meriwether. Did you really think you could win?" He kicked the parasol away. It glanced across the deck and ricocheted off the observation dome towards the railing.

She clenched her teeth. She couldn't let him win.

A warm trickle worked its way down her collar. Her head throbbed. Her ears rang. Aunt Prudence would have had useful advice. She always did. Fluttering eyelashes wouldn't work this time. But all men had their weaknesses...

She'd only get one chance. She took a deep breath, raised her foot and stomped on his instep. At the same time, she slammed her elbow into his groin.

Harrow gasped. His grip loosened. She dropped down, twisted away from his grip and swung her cramped fist into his jaw.

He screamed in pain and flailed his knife in her direction. She kicked him in the chest, catching him off guard, and retreated behind the observation dome.

Harrow stumbled backwards across the deck, slammed into the handrail and overbalanced.

Tillie plunged toward the rail, reaching out instinctively to catch him as he floundered for the leather safety strap. He missed. His eyes widened. He opened his mouth as he plunged over the edge of the deck, his scream snatched away by a gust of Aether.

An alarm clanged in the bowels of the dirigible. The wind roared above her, filled the canvas and slapped it against the balloons above. The deck pitched to one side as the dirigible rose higher.

"Not now!" She grabbed the safety strap and fumbled at her belt for the Aether mask. It wasn't there; in her haste to find Harrow, she'd left it in her cabin.

Damnation.

Her head ached. Her stomach churned. The dirigible banked again and rose even higher. She lost her footing, tumbled forward and slipped between the posts. A curtain of hair fell over her face, obscuring her vision. She gasped for air.

"I'm sorry, father," she whispered. Her arms ached. Her grip weakened. "I failed you."

The world closed in and smothered her.

Of Homecomings, Orders,
and the Good of the Empire

M atilda." The voice called to Tillie from the darkness. She grimaced and rolled over. She hated that name.

"Matilda?"

"Call me Tillie." She moaned and opened her eyes.

"Sir, she's awake!" Grace folded the wet cloth in her hands and retreated.

Lord Allington sat in a chair by Tillie's bed. A deep furrow scarred his forehead, highlighted in the failing light. His moustache quivered as a faint smile flickered over his lips.

"Glad to have you back with us, Miss Meriwether," he whispered.

Tillie raised herself onto her elbows. Her head spun. Her ears thrummed. The cabin twisted.

Lord Allington leaped from his chair and slipped his hand behind her back to ease her back onto the bed.

Her head throbbed. Blood pulsed through her ears, feeding the pain.

Grace frowned, moved closer and spoke to Lord Allington, their voices muffled.

Tillie closed her eyes and cradled her head. Her fingers brushed against loose threads, and felt along the rough edge of a bandage wrapped around her head. She remembered a loud crack, and stinging rain. She remembered her lungs bursting, and pain. A lot of pain. Someone had shouted: *Man overboard.*

She opened her eyes.

"Harrow?" She jerked upright and searched the room, fearing she'd see him skulking in the background, biding his time.

"What happened?" she whispered.

"There was an accident," he said.

"Harrow tried to kill you," said Grace.

Grace propped a clean pillow behind Tillie's back.

"You need to rest," said Lord Allington.

Tillie's gaze darted around the room, ignoring him.

"You're safe," he said. "He's gone." He eased her back against the pillow.

Her muscles relaxed. She scanned the cabin. Her walking cane rested against the bedside table. Her parasol wasn't visible. She remembered it skittering toward the edge of the deck. Her hand trembled.

"Aunt Prudence's parasol!" she gasped.

"No need to fret, Miss Meriwether." he smiled. "Grace rescued it."

Grace disappeared back into the shadows, returned with the red parasol and handed it to Tillie.

"Sir Avery had it repaired while you were indisposed," she said.

"Better than new." His moustache twitched. "Except for a small chip in the handle."

Tillie examined the carved ivory handle. She ran her fingertip along the hairline crack running part-way around the lip of the handle and over a small notch on the edge. Her heart pounded. This was the second time she'd almost lost the parasol. She clasped it tight. She'd lost too much on this journey: Aunt Prudence, the General, her father's code book and the photograph of him, his murderer and the mysterious dark-haired woman. At least she still had her father's journ--.

Her eyes widened. She grasped at her hip for her bustle and its hidden pockets. Her fingers scrabbled at the crisp linen sheets.

"Where are my--?" She glanced down at her body. Her corset was gone. She wore nothing but a nightgown. Patches of faded yellow bruising marred her arms and wrists. Heat crept up her neck and nestled in her cheeks. She pulled the sheets up over her nightgown.

"Who--?" She pressed her hand against her torso and swallowed. She'd sewn the silk communiqué from the *Liberator*, claiming Tillie as Her own, inside the corset. Her secret, kept close for so long, was now exposed.

Damnation.

But why had Lord Allington not mentioned the note? She glared at him. Was he tormenting her, prolonging her agony before he sprung his trap?

"Where are my clothes?" she whispered.

Lord Allington stepped back.

"Your clothes were covered in blood, Miss." Grace handed her a robe. "You were wet through and your corset needed repairs." She glanced in his direction.

"You were fortunate Grace followed you," he said. "If she hadn't realised you'd forgotten your Aether mask..." He eased himself back into the chair and shook his head.

Tillie glanced out the porthole. The sun was on the horizon; the darkening sky was tinged with orange and purple. She slipped the robe over her shoulders and tugged it tight.

"How long have I been in bed?" she asked.

"Three days," replied Lord Allington. He leaned his elbow on the arm of the chair. "It's been very enlightening."

"What has?" She eyed him through narrowed eyelids.

"You talk in your sleep." He crooked a finger over his lip in an unsuccessful attempt to hide his smile.

She clutched her bedclothes tighter.

"You had a fever." Grace glared at Lord Allington, dunked her cloth in a porcelain water bowl on the bedside table and wrung it out.

"And concussion," he added.

Grace placed the cloth on Tillie's forehead. It was cool, and soothed the pain. Her fingers loosened their grip on the bedclothes.

"Sir Avery insisted on watching over you," she whispered.

He cleared his throat.

Grace nodded, wiped her hands on her apron and retreated to the cabin door. "I think I'll fetch the tea." She turned on the tube light on the far wall and shut the door behind her.

Lord Allington's smile faded. "We have to talk, Miss Meriwether."

He dragged his chair closer to the bed, opened her hand and placed his own above hers. A square of folded silk fluttered onto her palm. Her ears burned.

She stared at the inked word facing her: *Homunculus*. She swallowed. He *knew*.

"We wear masks, both of us," he said. "I'm trying to work out which is your mask and which is the true you."

She clasped the silk missive and clutched it to her chest. She drew her knees up, dragging the bedclothes away from him.

"How *dare* you," she hissed. "I thought you a gentleman."

"No, Miss Meriwether, I didn't-- I mean--," He shook his head. "*Grace* found it."

She straightened her legs slowly, one at a time, and eyed him.

"The time for games is over, Miss Meriwether." He straightened in his chair and cleared his throat. "I need to know if I can trust you." His shoulders relaxed as he let out a long breath.

"Can I trust you?" she said.

"Me?" Lord Allington raised an eyebrow.

"I saw you," she said, "after the train crashed. I recognised your black boots." Her hand wrapped around the brass head of the walking stick. "Why did you take it and give it to Harrow?"

He tilted his head. "Give what to Harrow?" he asked.

"The photograph."

He threw open his hands. "Why on earth would I give it to Harrow?"

"I saw how he greeted you, after the crash. You are in league with him, aren't you?"

"In league?" He scoffed. "He works for the Department. As do you, Miss Meriwether. I do think you have allowed your feminine fantasies to--"

She slammed the end of the cane onto the floor, cutting him off. "Harrow worked for Cranshaw," she hissed. "He told me himself."

"My apologies, Miss Meriwether. It appears we are at an impasse." He straightened his waistcoat. "Very well, to show my sincerity I shall be the first to concede."

Concede? She crossed her arms. What other secrets had he learned while she was feverish?

"The reason I need to know if I can trust you..." He took a deep breath. "I believe Harrow was also working directly for Her Majesty and was spying on the Department."

She opened her mouth to reply. Her eyes widened. Harrow was a traitor, a murderer. He worked for Cranshaw; how could he be working for...

"The Queen?" Her voice was barely audible. "Is that why you refused to declare Harrow a traitor?" she asked.

He nodded.

"Why would She spy on her own Department?" Tillie had wondered why the Queen had asked her to do exactly that. As Lord Allington was *conceding*, perhaps he would enlighten her.

"The Department of Curiosities was created to protect the Empire." He hesitated. "Some of us believe the Queen is not making the best decisions for her people. There are rumours she's accumulating technology and keeping it from us."

"Isn't that the purpose of the Department?" she asked.

"Yes," he replied, "but some of it is too powerful for any *one* person to control, even the Queen."

"Like *the Horde*?"

He nodded. "The Department needs to discover what it is, verify the threat and neutralise it."

"Even against Her Majesty's orders?"

"Yes," he replied.

"For the good of the Empire?"

"The Department has vowed to protect the Empire," he said, "and I will uphold that vow."

"Even if the Queen declares you a traitor?"

"The Empire is more than the one who wears the Crown." He took a deep breath. "There, I am a man of my word, Miss Meriwether. I have told you my secrets." He pursed his lips. "Now it's your turn. *Quid pro quo.* I know you aren't working with Harrow; you would not accuse one of your own. Who is the *Liberator*? Who are you working for?"

He lifted his head and met her gaze. She relaxed her shoulders: he *was* an honourable man. He'd confessed his secrets, and kept his part of the bargain, though such words could be considered treason. She owed him same courtesy.

She took a deep breath. Would he hate her when she revealed she worked for the Queen?

She took his hand and smiled.

"We wear the same masks, Sir Avery. I pray you will forgive me mine."

She peeled back the bedclothes, wrapped the robe tight and made her way to the porthole. She stared at the vast night sky. The stars twinkled back, as if to reassure her.

"Professor Nathaniel Kempthorne was my father. He wasn't a traitor. He was following *Her* orders." Her heart raced as she waited for his reaction.

Sir Avery remained silent.

"He worked for the Queen until he queried Her motives. His assistant murdered him and fled, and Father was declared a traitor." She paused; she watched drops of water run down the glass, not game to turn and look Sir Avery in the eye.

Still, he remained silent.

Her head throbbed. There was one final admission she was reluctant to convey.

"The *Liberator* in the note is..." She cleared her throat and swallowed. "The Queen. She's ordered me to find Father's notes on *the Horde*."

"Yes."

Yes? Butterflies circled in her stomach. "And to spy on the Department." Her head reeled.

"As I expected."

Expected? She spun on her heel to face him. The cabin walls seemed to buckle.

He stood behind her and grinned.

"You knew?"

"You talk in your sleep."

"Then why make me say it?" she asked.

"I had to know you trusted me," he replied. "And I had to know I could trust you."

"And if I hadn't told you?" she asked.

"Then I would have had to neutralise the threat."

Her eyes widened.

"You wouldn't have--?"

"I'm glad we shan't need to find out."

She buried her head in her hands. Her world was spinning. The butterflies whirled faster.

"Then we are allies?" he asked.

She nodded slowly.

"And now you must send your report to the Queen," he said.

Tillie moaned, raised her head and tried to focus.

"I shall keep your secrets, Sir Avery. And in return I ask you to keep mine."

"So, we have an agreement."

The cups on the tea tray rattled as Grace entered the cabin. Sir Avery nodded in her direction. She poured a cup of tea, dropped in a slice of cloved lemon and handed it to Tillie.

"How much does Grace know?" she whispered in his ear.

"Everything," he replied.

She sipped her tea. It was tart but the bitterness of the cloves was refreshing. The warmth took the edge off the increasing chill as Big Nessie climbed into the Aether.

"Can we trust her?" she asked.

"I am your loyal companion, Miss Meriwether." Grace reached into her apron pocket and handed Tillie a photograph.

She examined the tintype. One of the edges was dented. Fine scratches scored the image. Fortunately, the faces were still recognisable.

"This was my father," she said.

Sir Avery peered at the photograph. "Is that Professor Waldran?"

Her eyes widened. "Cranshaw is Waldran?"

"And he was your father's assistant," he said.

"His name is Cranshaw," she replied. She was not afraid to say the name. "Cranshaw murdered my father."

Big Nessie's Communication Room was more like a broom cupboard than a workspace. It was less than half the size of its counterpart in the Bunker under the orphanage. Dark, wood-panelled walls made it appear even more cramped. Only one illumination tube flickered above the workspace.

The familiar flexible metal hose and brass speaking funnel was hooked onto one wall. A covered wire hung from the ceiling, looped over a ceramic cylinder and divided in two. One wire attached to the printing cylinder. A strip of paper wound over and through a series of rollers, past a set of punch-cogs and fed through a box beneath the cylinder and onto a narrow reel on the other side. A spherical array of keys was suspended above the paper on the cylinder.

There the similarity to the telegraph machines Tillie was familiar with, ended. The other wire attached to a platform of cogs built onto the solid wooden table wedged between the walls. Set into the front edge of the table top was a set of piano-like keys etched with letters of the alphabet. In place of calibration cogs was a numbered dial.

Tillie sat on the chair and adjusted her skirts. She turned the calibration dial to the Queen's personal setting. Her fingers hovered above the keys on the table. They twitched. Her Majesty had already forgiven her once for delaying her scheduled report by a couple of days. Tillie's heart pounded.

"It's been two weeks." She swivelled the chair to face Sir Avery. "Last time she demanded an audience. I can't attend if I'm on the opposite side of the world."

"It will become harder, the longer you delay." He placed a gentle hand on her shoulder. "It's best to contact Her on your terms."

She shifted in the chair, took a deep breath and keyed the message:

Liberator,
Report to follow.

Homunculus.

They stared at the machine. The cogs clicked and whirred, then turned. Tillie held her breath. The paper tape jiggled, spat forward and jerked through the rollers to emerge on the other side with a series of punched holes.

She peered at the punched holes. There was a pattern but... She frowned. Was this a new code?

The tape continued through the box under the paper cylinder. The keys above the cylinder burst into life and tapped out a message in Queen Victoria's specified code.

Homunculus,
Report overdue. Explain immediately.
Liberator.

Tillie reached for the keys and hesitated. She clenched her fingers.

"What shall I say?" she asked. "I can't lie to the Queen."

"Does she not lie to you?" he asked.

She bit her lip. Had the Queen lied to her? She recollected their short conversations and correspondence. Queen Victoria's words were always careful and precise.

"Have you never lied to Her?" he asked.

Tillie crossed her arms. Had she lied to the Queen? Her shoulders drooped. She had. *Once.* She'd misled the Queen about her knowledge of Cranshaw's assistance in her father's work. Her heart raced.

"It was more of an omission," she whispered.

"The best lies are based in truth." He patted her shoulder. "Tell her you were following orders."

She wiped her clammy fingers on her skirt and keyed her response:

Liberator,

Unavoidably detained. Harrow working for Inventor. Tried to escape. Followed. No time to report. First available opportunity to access telegraph machine.

-H

It wasn't a lie. She let out a long, slow breath. Her pulse slowed. The return message tapped onto the paper cylinder:

Homunculus,
Report location.
Liberator.

She caught her breath. "We weren't authorised to leave, let alone use a dirigible."

He leaned down and whispered in her ear: "Her Majesty did not *know* about Big Nessie."

"I can't tell her!" Tillie spun in the chair to face him. She could feel his breath on her face. "It will jeopardise the Department."

"Then don't," he said.

She shook her head. She didn't want to lose her only ally.

"We've planned for such a situation," he said. "It's imperative to make sure you retain the Queen's trust. We need to find out the nature of this *Horde*. If the Department will no longer be in a position to investigate unimpeded, you will be our best chance of discovering its secret."

Tillie swallowed. She keyed the message slowly:

Liberator.
Adelaide, South Australia.
-H

The return message came almost immediately:
H,
Defied orders.
-L

Her heart sank into her stomach.

"Tell her..." Sir Avery leaned against the wall and ran his hand over his moustache. "Tell her you didn't know your destination."

Again, the truth. She'd thought they were headed to Egypt, not the Antipodes.

"Tell her you had no option but to accompany me if you were to remain in the Department's confidence."

"But she'll declare you a traitor."

"Better a traitor to the Crown than to the people of the Empire." He shrugged.

"But the Department?" she asked.

"Not to worry, Miss Meriwether," he replied. "The Department has friends in high places." He chuckled. "We may have to go to ground, but we have protection."

Her eyes widened. She opened her mouth to reply. She wanted to say: *How high?* But there was something in his laugh that suggested if she didn't want to lie to Queen Victoria, she shouldn't ask.

"And grovel," said Sir Avery. "She likes grovelling."

She sent her reply.

This time there was no immediate response. She bit her thumbnail and thrummed the fingers of her other hand on the table.

"Why doesn't she answer?" she whispered.

The keys slapped their message onto the paper. She read it out:

Suspect D.O.C. acting against orders in South Australia. Suspected

of conspiring to smuggle mechanicals within Empire.

Find out how deep treachery goes. Remain until I am satisfied you have required information. You will report via Governor's Residence as per agreed schedule.

Confirm orders.

Liberator.

"Excellent!" Sir Avery pushed himself off the wall and leaned on the back of her chair. "That gives us time to find any information your father had on *the Horde*, what threat it poses and find out how to neutralise it."

He placed his hands on her shoulders. "And you can find your proof that your father was not a traitor."

She leaned back into her chair. She could feel his heart beating against her back. She closed her eyes and smiled. Six years ago she'd promised to clear her father's name. For six years she'd struggled to keep her promise. Now, finally, there was a glimmer of hope she would do so.

"Well done, Miss Meriwether. And you didn't have to lie to your Queen." He removed his hands from her shoulders. "I'll tell Grace to serve afternoon tea before we land."

The door clicked shut behind him.

She smiled and replied:

Liberator,

Orders confirmed.

Homunculus.

Tillie pinned the cameo on the collar of her blouse. She ran her fingers over the deep red stone and along the pale profile of the woman. There was no need now to conceal it; Sir Avery knew all about her father,

Harrow was gone and the dead couldn't reveal secrets.

She tugged at the lace cuffs of her teal sleeves. The bruises on her wrists, where Harrow had attacked her, were now barely visible. The bodice's long sleeves concealed the remaining vestiges of her other injuries. She pulled on her gloves and slipped her parasol into a triangular pocket on the hip of her skirt.

Grace entered the cabin and smiled.

"I'm glad you're feeling better, Miss Meri--"

Tillie wiggled her finger and tsked.

"You look much better, Miss Tillie," said Grace.

"Have we arrived yet?" asked Tillie. It had been too many years since she last saw Adelaide; she'd left as a small child, an orphan mourning the loss of her father. Now she returned a grown woman, determined to get justice for his death.

Grace nodded, picked up Tillie's boater and straightened its ribbons.

"Smythe has taken care of the trunks," she said.

Tillie dashed to the porthole and peered through the misted glass. She'd never seen the beach from the air.

Big Nessie flew toward a brick and sandstone tower constructed at the end of a railed jetty. A strip of white sand glared in the late afternoon sun. Red and blue dots fluttered in the sea breeze. She pressed her nose against the glass. She couldn't wait to go sea bathing!

"Won't they see us?" she asked.

"This is the main Aether port for Adelaide," replied Grace. "They won't notice another arrival." She thrust the straw hat in Tillie's direction. "You mustn't forget your hat, Miss."

She took the hat, set it on her head and turned back to stare out the porthole as she shoved the hat pins through the straw.

Thick chains rattled as they winched brightly painted bathing machines from the sea toward the wall at the edge of the foreshore. More bathing machines trundled along metal tracks on the sand, towards the water. Puffs of steam followed them. The machines eased into the water and continued several yards beyond the breakwater. More clouds of steam belched from them.

Each bathing machine had a cage-like contraption resting on its roof. One of the contraptions rose into the air. A metal arm swung forward and slowly deposited the cage into the water on the sea-side of the bathing machine.

The dirigible cabin door swung open. She saw Sir Avery's reflection in the glass.

"Time to go," he said.

She stepped away from the porthole.

Grace handed her the walking cane.

"What are the cages for?" asked Tillie.

"Sharks." Sir Avery smiled at her and tipped his hat.

"Sharks?" she echoed. Perhaps she could wait to go sea-bathing after all.

"Someone was taken two years ago. Since then there have been several attacks. It's bad for the bathing machine business, so they borrowed the invention from an operative in New South Wales."

She glanced back out the porthole. Sea bathers poured out of the bathing machines and splashed around in the confines of their shark enclosures.

Big Nessie's shadow moved across the water, shading the bathers as it turned to align itself with the Aether Tower.

Of Trains, Trolleys, and Retribution

The Ascension Chamber jiggled to a halt at the base of the Aether Tower. The door opened. The smell of salt and seaweed rushed through the iron gate to meet them. Tillie and Sir Avery stepped onto the jetty. Smythe and Grace followed.

Ropes creaked and slapped against the dirigible above them. A flat luggage trolley sat on a recessed metal track next to the tower. Steam hissed and cogs whirred as the Ascension Chamber rumbled upward to collect the rest of their trunks.

"Cager will bring the remaining trunks, Sir." Smythe ducked as seagulls squawked and dived over the jetty. One darted past Tillie's head and snatched food from the hand of a nearby child. His protestations faded behind them as they followed Smythe past the group of day-trippers and along the jetty.

Her footsteps clattered on the wooden boards. A warm breeze tickled her skin. She fanned her face; she'd forgotten how warm it was here in autumn.

Long shadows loomed before them as Smythe led Tillie and her companions down the left side of the jetty. The luggage trolley squeaked and rattled as it followed behind them towards the foreshore. Water lapped the jetty posts beneath them. Bathers splashed and laughed in the fading light. Chains rattled and clinked as another bathing machine trundled out to sea. Engines puttered on the foreshore.

Tillie could taste the salt and seaweed now. A gust of wind caught her boater and tugged at the hat pins. With it came the sounds of civilisation. The sound of engines grew louder as they reached the Promenade. Excited children squealed and dragged their parents towards the noise. More children ran from the beach, the chugging engine luring them like a Pied Piper. They swarmed around a brick and tin shed and under its striped awning, then broke away wearing grins as ice cream dripped down their fists.

A crowd had gathered around a Punch and Judy show set up on the other side of the jetty entrance. Working men mingled with well-dressed gentlemen. Ladies wrangled giggling children. Snippets of conversations wafted on the sea breeze - an eclectic mix of English dialects and foreign languages.

Punch squawked his *bye-byes*. The curtain fell as Tillie and her companions reached the square. The crowd clapped and dispersed. Others boarded a waiting steam tram or lined up at one of the various food stalls for an early supper.

"It's just like a day at Brighton," said Grace.

Tillie smiled.

"But the beach is less stony and the sea is warmer." She longed to feel the warm, soft sand between her toes, a reminder of less complicated times.

She breathed in the memories: the aromas of hot pies and perfume mixed with sweat, smoke and dust. She dusted off her skirt; she'd forgotten about the all-pervading dust. It lifted from the square as the crowd moved and permeated everything: the air, her clothes, her hair. She picked up a blonde curl and sniffed. Her heart fluttered. There was something else, a whiff of...

The Orb rolled against her skin. She slowly drew air in through her nose. It was a harsh, sour smell of burning nicotine. She halted and turned around to follow the scent. It reminded her of...

She sniffed again. It was almost gone. She turned into the direction of the breeze. It was definitely there; the familiar smell of tobacco. It reminded her of her father. She turned again. No, not Father. Perhaps the General? But there was no sweetness in the smell. She frowned. No, not the General either.

She stared into the crowd, searching for the source.

Myshka. The name floated on the wind, barely audible.

<<*Did you say something?*>> she asked the Orb.

The Orb shifted under her bodice.

"Miss Meriwether?" Sir Avery's voice drowned out any reply. He peered into the crowd, frowned and leaned closer. "Is something wrong?" he whispered.

She snapped out of the moment and smiled back.

"Errant memories," she replied.

"Smythe, find Miss Meriwether a cup of tea, and take Grace with you."

Saunders nodded and escorted Grace toward the Promenade.

"Do you remember much?" Sir Avery scanned the surrounding sandstone and brick buildings.

She shook her head. "Just phantoms."

"Of course." The creases at the edge of his eyes faded. "Your father worked in the Conceptualisation Co-operative before being recruited by the Queen."

"The Conceptualisation Co-operative?" she asked. "They create the mechanicals here?"

"Adelaide is host to many inventors and engineers from all over the world: Europe, Asia, Prussia." He whispered in her ear: "Even Great

Britain. The Co-operative is the name the locals give to the collective of laboratories set up throughout the city and surrounds to carry out research and development. A meeting of minds, as it were. It's a booming economy."

"And the Department has its own laboratory?"

He nodded. "Several. Paid for by Queen Victoria herself. Your father was assigned one, no doubt."

She held her breath. She'd thought her father had worked in secret.

"I didn't know there were other inventors here," she said.

"It's one of Adelaide's worst kept secrets," he replied. "The Queen denies knowledge, but the Department of Curiosities was created to regulate unauthorised mechanicals entering Her home shores."

A mechanical clanked behind her. Steam hissed. A steam-powered perambulator hummed and clicked past them. Tassels danced as it rolled along the promenade toward the beach. Proud parents strolled behind the contraption, deep in conversation.

Tillie leaned over the railing and scanned the beach. Many of the day-trippers had minor mechanicals and contraptions. She raised an eyebrow and lowered her voice.

"I thought all of the Colonies were bound by the Mechanicals Act?" she asked.

"Technically, yes." He leaned on the railing. "But we are far enough removed from London, and the Co-operative produces many contraptions of use to Her. As long as none are smuggled into Great Britain, even the Queen allows for indiscretions here."

"Smuggled?" she asked.

"Yes. The official function of the Department is to confiscate unlicensed mechanicals."

"Like Big Nessie?"

"Yes," he replied, "like Big Nessie." He cleared his throat. "Unofficially, some are useful for the protection of the Empire."

"Even if not sanctioned by the Queen?"

Sir Avery stared across the water, and didn't reply.

"At the behest of the influential *friend* you mentioned earlier?"

"Yes." A frown flitted across his brow. "You remembered that?"

"Yes." She leaned against the railing, next to him. It was obvious he wasn't ready to betray his friend's confidence.

The wind picked up. Waves crashed and foamed across the sand. The bathing machines' chains slapped the water.

A wind squall yanked at her skirt and threatened to steal her hat. The ribbons whipped her cheeks as she held it tight.

A woman cried out. A flora-endowed straw hat flew past and flopped into the water.

"Sir!' Cager's voice caught on the wind as he ran along the jetty towards them, waving. By the time Cager caught up with it, he was out of breath.

"What is it, Cager?" asked Sir Avery.

"We received a message, Sir," replied Cager. "He's here already."

"Cranshaw?" asked Tillie.

Cager nodded. "The passenger ship arrived a day early. He's boarding the Port train."

Sir Avery waved Smythe and Grace back from the Promenade.

"We have to get to the city train station before the Port Adelaide train." Tillie's heart raced. She hadn't come half way around the world to lose him now. "Once he leaves the station, he could go anywhere. Then, how will we find him?"

"If you leave now, you can catch up with him at the station," replied Cager.

"But the tram has already left," said Tillie.

"There's a train to the city, Sir," said Smythe as he and Grace rejoined them.

"Excellent," said Sir Avery. "You know where to send the luggage,

Cager."

Cager nodded and returned to the luggage trolley. Smythe ushered them across the square.

The train shuddered to a halt. Steam hissed across the platform and glowed under the light from the lampposts. Tillie patted the parasol snuggled at her hip. Her walking cane tapped on the platform as she stepped off the train.

Sir Avery led the way. They dodged bursts of steam from waiting luggage trolleys. Grace and Smythe followed.

"You, there!" Sir Avery hailed down a uniformed platform guard.

"Yes, Sir?" The guard's brass buttons glinted as he turned to face them.

"Has the Port train arrived?" asked Sir Avery.

The guard nodded. "Five minutes ago, sir."

"Stay here, Smythe." Sir Avery strode under the platform's scalloped roof towards the station house.

<<*Find Cranshaw,*>> whispered the Orb.

She pulled out the tintype photograph and pointed to the young Cranshaw.

"Have you seen this man?" she asked the guard.

He raised his lantern and peered at the image in its crackling light.

"He has red hair," she said, "And he's older now."

The guard nodded slowly. "He had an entourage and demanded a wagon for his crates."

Her shoulders slumped. "We've missed him."

<<*Keep searching,*>> urged the Orb.

"Oh, no, Miss. There was a delay in unloading his trunks," said the guard. "And he insisted his own men do it." He pointed to the other station platform. "They're just starting to unload now."

<<*Hurry,*>> growled the Orb.

She led Grace and Smythe to the end of the second platform. The train's engine sighed and clicked as it belched smoke from its lungs and settled on the tracks. Sash windows rattled as attendants made their way along the train.

She searched the crowd. Passengers chattered. Their shoe heels clacked on the platform as they strolled toward the enclosed part of the station. Luggage rolled and thumped onto trolleys. Workmen cursed. Steam hissed. The occasional seagull bemoaned its empty stomach.

A short man in a grey suit loitered by the station exit. Black mutton-chop whiskers emerged from under his grey bowler. He tipped his hat in the direction of two grey-skinned trolley attendants. A wooden crate, as large as a coffin, creaked against strapped trunks and cases as the trolley rolled toward the street exit.

A red headed gentleman, the lower half of his face concealed by a leather filter mask, nodded back in reply.

<<*There!*>> hissed the Orb. <<*Near the trolley.*>>

Her heart raced.

"Over there!" She thrust an accusatory finger in the direction of the red-headed man. His head jerked in her direction.

<<*Cranshaw!*>> Tillie and the Orb snarled in unison.

He stared at her for a moment, then dragged a case from the trolley, dislodging the end of the crate.

One of the Ghostmen grabbed the end of the crate. The other frantically pushed levers, hurrying the trolley toward the exit.

The Man in Grey pulled the brim of his hat over his eyes and slipped out of the exit towards the street.

The trolley blocked the red-headed man's exit. He hesitated, then turned on his heel and dashed toward an open passageway on the other side of the station.

"No!" She stomped her walking cane on the ground.

<<*Stop him,*>> whispered the Orb.

She grabbed Smythe's arm. "He's getting away. Fetch Sir Avery."

Smythe scanned the station and marched into the crowd.

<<*Don't let him escape,*>> demanded the Orb.

Her fingers twitched as the red-headed man disappeared along the passageway. She was not going to allow her father's murderer to escape.

<<*Catch him.*>>

"Wait for Sir Avery." She pushed her portmanteau into Grace's hands and dashed after her quarry.

A whistle pierced the surrounding hubbub as she dashed through the open passageway. The crowd hushed.

"Miss, you can't. You're not permitted--" The guard's voice was drowned out by a second whistle.

Tillie ignored him and continued her pursuit. She followed the sound of retreating footsteps along the passage. A door slammed up ahead. She glanced over her shoulder. No one followed her. She was alone.

She slowed her pace as she approached the door at the end of the passageway.

<<*Can you hear anything?*>> she asked the Orb.

<<*Hurry. Don't waste time,*>> it hissed. <<*Open the door!*>>

She took a deep breath and eased open the door. She gripped her cane and scanned the darkness as she pulled the door shut behind her.

The moon had not risen yet. A warm wind kicked up the dust from the nearby shunting tracks. In the distance, Tillie could barely make out the shadowy outline of a humped figure picking its way across the tracks toward a brick wall on the far side of the train yard. He paused, ascended the wall and disappeared over the top.

<<*Get him!*>> the Orb demanded.

She groaned. Her boots crunched on the gravel as she gave chase.

There was a roar on the other side of the wall. The low rumble grew louder as she approached. A figure rose slowly above the wall. His hands

388

gripped handles on either side of his body. Two large cylinders peeked out from behind his shoulders. The bottom of his harnessed contraption glowed like a giant firefly hovering above the wall. Red hair floated in an updraft of heat. He stared at her, his eyes hidden behind thick-lensed goggles, his laugh muffled by the leather mask.

She stared at him. Flecks of grey tinged the flaming locks; he looked older than she'd imagined.

He stared back.

"Cranshaw?"

<<*Murderer!*>> The Orb's scream sliced through her head.

She winced.

"How could you possibly know?" He peered at her through narrowed eyelids.

Murderer. The word echoed in her ears.

<<*Kill him.*>>

Tillie ground her walking stick into the gravel. She was *not* going to let him go free. Her father deserved justice. She smiled. The corner of her mouth twitched. She twisted the head of the cane. It hummed under her palm. She pointed it at Cranshaw as if she were cursing him.

Cranshaw wobbled in the air. The flying machine sputtered. He dropped a few feet. Its rumble waned. The firefly glow faded. He cursed and fell into the darkness beyond the wall.

She ran to the wall, wrangling her skirts as she struggled to get a foothold in between the bricks.

Damnation.

The silenced Orb thumped on her chest.

"I know, I know," she hissed. "He's getting away."

Her boots thudded on the gravel. She unhooked her skirt and let it fall to the ground.

"I know who you are," she yelled, as she climbed unencumbered.

She dragged herself onto the top of the wall, swung a leg over the other side and hesitated. She peered over. To her right, near the street, was a pale stone building with arched windows and edged with dark brick quoins. Walls lined three sides of the area, blocking any errant nearby street light.

The yard was pitch black, as dark as the Aether but this time there was no railing or twinkling stars to comfort her. There was no telling how far Cranshaw had fallen - or how far she could fall.

<<*How far down is it?*>> she asked the Orb.

The cane buzzed. Her head thumped. The Orb didn't reply.

<<*All right, you win.*>>

She disengaged the *Discombobulator*. Scrambled orders bombarded her, stabbed and ricocheted about her head. She screamed and buried her head in her hands.

The words coalesced: <<*Catch him. Kill him!*>>

Then there was silence.

Gravel crunched in the distance.

<<*Now!*>> ordered the Orb.

"How far down is the drop?" Her voice was barely audible.

<<*Not far,*>> replied the Orb. <<*Hurry, they come. Must follow.*>>

She lifted her other leg over the wall and lowered herself down. Her feet dangled in the air.

<<*How much further?*>> she whispered.

<<*Trust me,*>> replied the Orb.

Until now the Orb had proved trustworthy. It had protected her. She took a deep breath. It was correct. She couldn't let Cranshaw escape justice again; she *had* to follow, like Alice, she was about to fall down the hole after the White Rabbit.

She swallowed, lifted her fingers off the brick and let go.

Of Secrets, Automatons, and Endgames

T illie dropped to the ground with a gentle thud. She leaned against the wall, ran her fingers over the comforting rough brick and took a deep breath. It had only been a few feet; she was now back on *Terra Firma*. She straightened her bodice.

There was a scuffling noise. A faint breeze. A whiff of sour smoke tickled her nostrils.

Tillie sniffed. There was nothing. She was imagining things.

She raised her walking cane and cocked her head to listen. Hooves clopped on the far side of the building. A guard whistle trilled in the train yard, demanding attention. There was a far-off click, followed by a squeak of an un-oiled hinge, from the building.

A vertical sliver of dim light marred the blackness, and was gone.

<<*Go,*>> yelled the Orb.

She hesitated. The yard was pitch black. She would be advancing blindly.

<<*But I can't see.*>> she said.

<<*Follow,*>> urged the Orb.

<<*Is it safe?*>> she asked the Orb.

<<Get him!>> it hissed.

She made her way slowly toward the building; first she swung her cane in smooth arcs before her, searching for obstacles, then eased her foot gently on the unseen ground; one silent step after the other. The building's arched windows loomed above her like massive black eyes watching her every move. She listened at the door. All was quiet.

<<Hurry,>> growled the Orb.

The door opened easily. She gritted her teeth waiting for its squeak. It was faint. She held her breath. There was no movement inside. She let out a slow breath and nudged the door again. There was a thunk of hollow metal. She leaned down and searched behind the edge of the door with her fingers.

<<Don't!>> barked the Orb.

Tillie snapped back her fingers. She knew enough not to question the Orb's warnings.

She eased the door further open and stepped inside. Her boot sploshed in a pool of liquid. Warm water seeped into the leather. A stench of bleach mixed with a faint metallic odour assaulted her nostrils. She wrinkled her nose.

Cranshaw's discarded flying machine lay behind the door. One of the cylinders was dented and cracked. Liquid seeped across the floor.

She stepped out of the liquid, shook her boots and scanned the room. Shadows flickered in the meagre light of the single illumination tube on the far north wall. Next to it, a not-so-dusty wine rack was wedged under a set of servants' stairs leading up to a closed door. The rest of the store room was an assemblage of wooden shelves filled with boxes and tins of various sizes. Crates were crammed in almost every cranny, and cupboards lined the visible walls. An unlit coal burner squatted against the outside wall, its chimney piercing the floor above. A shovel leaned against a drum of coal.

Scratching noises issued from in the far corner under the stairs. Tillie paused mid-step, and waited. The sounds continued: scratch, thunk. Scratch, scrape. Curse. Thunk.

She flattened against the shelves and searched for a vantage point as she made her way along the cover of storage crates and shelving. Draped over one of the crates was Cranshaw's abandoned coat. Pale blotches spattered up one sleeve. A mechanical device peeked out from under the scorched cuff. She retrieved the mechanical: a small metal box, button on one side and several key-like projections from the top. She put it on the shelf, to investigate later.

"It has to be here." Cranshaw's voice was close.

She shifted a stack of candles and peered through a gap above the cardboard boxes of matches on the shelf in front of her. Cranshaw still wore the leather mask. His goggles were pushed up onto his forehead, forcing his red hair to escape out at odd angles. He pulled at a makeshift bandage on his arm. The sleeve was ripped. His hand was scorched, red and bleeding. A pistol lay on an empty shelf beside him.

He grunted, dragged a box from the cupboard and dumped it on the ground. He positioned his arms around the cupboard and pulled. The blood vessels in his temples swelled. One side of the cupboard jerked forward a few inches, then halted. He cursed and dived back into the cupboard to remove more boxes and tossed them aside. One ricocheted off the edge of the shelf concealing Tillie and knocked a slew of candles over her.

She jumped back and gasped. Cranshaw snatched up his pistol and stepped forward.

"Show yourself," he growled.

She clutched her cane and stepped out from behind the shelves.

He manoeuvred his head to look past her.

"You are alone?" He raised his revolver.

<<*Kill him,*>> whispered the Orb.

She didn't answer.

"Where is Allington?" he asked, "And his valet? Harrow, isn't it?"

<<*Murderer,*>> hissed the Orb.

"Harrow is dead," she replied.

Cranshaw's eyes darted back to meet hers.

"Dead?" He lowered the pistol slightly.

"He fell from a dirigible, somewhere over the South Atlantic Ocean."

"You killed my..." he whispered. A frown flickered over his brow and was gone. "...son." His mouth snapped shut.

His son? Her grip loosened on the walking cane. It felt as if someone had punched her in the guts.

"I didn't mean..." she said. "He tried to kill me."

<<*Is a trick,*>> yelled the Orb. <<*Murderer. Must pay.*>>

"He failed again?" Any sign of a grieving father had passed. "He was supposed to stop your airship, at *any* cost." The veins bulged on his temples again. "He failed to destroy the Department. He failed to assassinate the Queen. The Society will blame me. They are not forgiving."

<<*Kill him,*>> growled the Orb.

Cranshaw's pistol wavered wildly in the air.

"He told you where to find me, didn't he?" he spat. "I should have cut his tongue out!" He lunged forward and grabbed for her arm. "The world will be mine, and I intend to walk all over it. You will *not* stop me."

Tillie flinched and twisted away from his grip. She slammed into a shelf. Boxes and tins rained off the shelves, plummeted over their heads, bounced off limbs, and poured across the floor. She ducked, whirled her cane and flipped the pistol from his hand.

A shot fired wildly as it spun across the floor. The crate behind her shattered.

They both dived away, to opposite sides of the store room. She rolled and wrapped her fingers around the pistol.

Her heart raced. She pointed the pistol directly at Cranshaw's head, aiming its barrel directly between his eyes. At this close range, she was unlikely to miss.

Cranshaw obediently lifted his arms. He looked much older than the youthful scientist in the photograph. They *all* looked much happier then. She remembered her father's young face. He'd never been allowed to grow old enough to allow the lines of age to settle on his face.

<<Make him pay.>> The Orb dragged on the end of its chain.

Her hand trembled. She remembered her father's one-sided smile, the way he tugged at his shirt cuffs to rescue them from inside his jacket sleeve. She remembered his calming voice, as he read her favourite stories. Other memories had faded. Long ago. She rested her walking cane in the debris of the crate and raised her free hand to steady the pistol. Had she really known her father at all?

Her gaze shifted from the pistol to the dishevelled man before her, and looked him directly in the eyes. The greyness of his sclera was the colour of his Ghostmen; the flecked blue of his irises was that of her father's favourite suit.

She wondered if Alice would pull the pistol's trigger and risk falling down the rabbit hole forever.

"What was he like?" she asked.

"Who?"

"My father."

"I don't know your..." His voice trailed off as he peered more intently and traced every line of her face. His gaze froze on the brooch at her throat. He opened his mouth as if to speak. Instead, he stood mute, his attention transfixed on the piece of jewellery.

"Little Matilda?" he finally asked. "You must be Kempthorne's little brat."

"You may call me Miss Meriwether."

"*Meriwether*, is it now?" He scoffed. "Is that where She hid you?"

She nodded silently.

"Do you remember when I gave you toffees for your birthday?" he asked.

"My father gave me toffees," she replied.

Slowly the corner of his mouth crept up in barely-concealed amusement. The smirk grated on her every nerve. Her grip tightened on the pistol's trigger, revenge still only a thought away.

<<Shoot!>>

"Your father was not the heroic humanitarian you think," he said. "Ask your precious Queen about it." He dragged himself to his feet. "Kempthorne was careless with everything, and everyone, in his life."

<<Liar!>> The Orb was now dead still. *<<Shoot him.>>*

She clutched the butt of the pistol. Her knuckles paled.

"You lie," she hissed through clenched teeth.

"You were too young to remember," he snickered.

Her heart raced faster. Heat crept up her neck. Pain radiated from her clenched jaw, its fingers clawing over her skull. She fought to hear his words over the screaming Orb.

"Why did you kill him?" she demanded.

"Is that what you were told?" he replied. The smile remained as he lowered his hands slightly.

<<Murderer.>> The Orb twitched. *<<Don't listen. Punish him now.>>*

She groaned in frustration. Her finger twitched as it fought the urge to squeeze.

"You stole from him!"

"That I did. But murder?" He returned her direct gaze. "No. He was dead before I had a chance."

<<Destroy him!>> The Orb's voice boomed through her entire body. Her innards squirmed. She remembered the dying Ghostman on the train carriage floor - his eyes staring at her. She remembered the

look in Harrow's eyes as he slipped away from her on the dirigible. Her trigger finger relaxed slightly.

<<No!>> screamed the Orb.

<<Shut up! SHUT UP!>> Her reply drowned it out. Her finger moved away from the trigger.

"Why did you do it?" she asked Cranshaw quietly.

"Because he had what I wanted, what I could not get."

"And that was worth killing for?" She wouldn't give in until he confessed. She had to be sure. She would not condemn a man for something he did not do.

"Someone has been rewriting history again?" His arms slipped lower. "She has a habit of doing that."

"Who?" she asked, thankful the Orb had quietened down.

"Our dear Queen: Victoria, Empress of India and of all which she surveys." He bowed slightly as he spoke, lowering his head and placing his arm behind his back.

"A Gentleman does not malign his Queen." She raised the pistol and aimed between the eyes of the traitor. "Who are you working for?" she demanded.

"Ah, never stand in the way of a woman's revenge."

"I..." *Revenge?* Her finger cramped. "I want... I want justice for my father's murder," she stammered.

The Orb burrowed into her skin. *<<Shoot,>>* it whispered.

"Is that what you really want?" He eyed her as he stepped back toward the coal burner, not taking his attention off her. "Professor Nathaniel Kempthorne and I go way back, Miss... Meriwether. I think you should read the Department's files more closely. Though you may be disappointed in what the history lesson has in store for you."

Her nails dug into her palm. She stepped closer.

"Why?" she said. "Was it the money? When he resigned, you were out of a job." She shook her head. "Or did you want to claim his work as your own?"

She searched his eyes. Cranshaw's eyelids flinched.

"That was it?" She slipped her finger onto the trigger. "You thieving traitor."

"Not traitor." He wiggled his finger. "You'll find the Queen wants the research as badly as I."

Tillie swallowed. She knew he was speaking the truth.

"But not for the good of the Empire," she said.

His eyes widened. "Now who's the traitor?" His lip curled.

A whistle pierced the air. She glanced towards the doorway.

<<Weapon!>>

Cranshaw lunged at her, slapped away her pistol with a coal shovel and dived forward.

He swung the shovel at her face.

The Orb's warning gave her time to react. She pulled the trigger as she dodged the attack. The bullet sped through the space he had just vacated, and ricocheted off the brick wall behind him.

His weapon caught the side of her firearm and wrenched it from her hand. Her wrist cracked. She roared in pain. The pistol clattered across the stone floor, out of reach.

She spun to confront her attacker.

Cranshaw swung again. She replied with a resounding punch, and swept her leg in the direction of his feet.

He jumped back. "Too slow, *Matilda*."

She scrambled to retrieve her walking cane as he regained his footing, took careful aim and whirled the cane over her shoulder, bringing it down in a perfect arc onto Cranshaw's shoulder. The cane circled above her head, as she prepared for another attack.

A loud crack broke her concentration. Tillie spun towards the sound. Something whistled past her ear.

"Avery?" she whispered.

She turned back to defend herself from Cranshaw's next attack. He lay crumpled on the floor. Blood already pooled around his body. There was evidence of scorching on his linen bandage, ripped from his sleeve. She examined the skin on his hand, burned and blistered, with white bleach burns.

She leaned closer and removed his mask. Faint wrinkles framed his eyes. A permanent furrow lined his cheeks where the mask had sat. He stared at the brooch hanging from her ripped collar.

"That was her brooch..." His words were faint as his breathing slowed.

His gaze dropped. His eyes widened.

"It worked?" He gasped.

"What worked?"

He licked his lips.

"Tell me, do you hear voices, Matilda?" he whispered.

<<*Murderer. Traitor. Thief.*>> snarled the Orb.

She shook her head.

"Do people think you're mad...?" His breath was ragged, his voice faded to a whisper.

The Orb jiggled furiously. She placed her hand over her chest and held it still. She needed to concentrate. She needed to find out about *the Horde* while he still conscious.

"What is *the Horde*?" she whispered.

"You *don't* know, do you?" His snicker was feeble, his grin lop-sided. "End of freedom in the Empire," he whispered.

Even now he spoke in riddles.

Blood trickled from his wound. She reached for his coat and pressed it hard against the wound. Blood seeped through and drenched the material.

"I can't..." Red liquid oozed between her fingers. "I can't stop the blood," she said. "Please, tell me," she begged, "you're dying."

"*The Horde...*" He closed his eyes.

She leaned closer.

"Army..." His breaths slowed. "Automatons..."

Footsteps thumped outside in the darkness.

"Sir Avery?" Tillie lowered Cranshaw's body onto the ground and rose slowly. She reached for the walking cane, twisted its brass head and hefted it in her left hand. It buzzed. Her head hummed as she crept back to the doorway.

Whistles sounded beyond all three walls. A crackling lantern bobbed towards her, accompanied by running footsteps.

"Miss Meriwether?" The voice was hushed.

"Avery!" She stepped out into the darkness and waited.

There it was again: a hint of a smoky, sour aroma.

Sir Avery examined her as he as he strode towards her. His hair flopped over his eyes. His trousers were ripped at one knee. He leaned against the door frame and winced in pain. He spoke in short bursts as he fought to fill his lungs.

"Do you smell that?" she asked.

He drew a short breath. "All I smell is bleach and coal smoke."

She scanned the darkness. She was positive she hadn't imagined it this time.

"The shooter? Did he harm you?" he asked.

"Didn't you shoot him?" she asked.

He shook his head. "He got away."

His lantern hovered above her arm. He cradled her injured wrist in his hand.

"Nothing serious," she said.

"I'll fetch the surgeon as soon as we catch Cranshaw," he said.

"He's in there." She jerked her head in the direction of the storeroom.

Sir Avery raised his pistol, similar to the *Disruptor* Grace had shown her in the Cabinet of Curiosities, and strode into the storeroom. She followed him. Cranshaw was gone. There was a large pool of blood where he had lain.

"But, he was dead," she whispered.

"The dead don't walk, Tillie," said Sir Avery.

Sun streamed along the platform. The mechanical luggage trolleys kicked up dust as they trundled back and forth to the rear carriage. Particles of dust hung in the air, reflecting pinpoints of light, then settled to the ground.

Air pumps clicked and thumped. The train's engine hissed. Men dodged bursts of steam and passengers clambered into the carriages and reached through the windows to wave farewell to their loved ones. Near a rope draped across the passageway where Tillie had chased Cranshaw the night before, a station guard hovered.

Tillie slipped her arm around Sir Avery's and manoeuvred herself so the guard would not see her. Warm gravel crunched underfoot as they strolled out from the shadow of the station roof towards the First Class carriage. Smythe waited by the steps, a portmanteau in hand.

Her walking cane hummed. Her palm vibrated. Her head buzzed. The Orb remained silent. She rubbed her temple. A headache was an acceptable cost for a private farewell, especially after the Orb's recent abominable behaviour.

An itch crawled along her wrist. She extracted her arm and scratched the tight linen bandage.

"The physician said you must leave it alone." Sir Avery took her hand and wrapped it around his arm. "You're fortunate it's not broken."

She groaned.

A nearby carriage window rattled; glass screeched and slammed into its frame. Scraping metal fingertips and a grinning skull flashed through her memory. The automaton.

She froze mid-step, and clutched Sir Avery's arm.

"Cranshaw had a working automaton in his laboratory," she whispered. "We're too late!"

"Then why was he still looking for your father's experiment notes?" Sir Avery shook his head and frowned. "I think that automaton was in that long crate, and I think he brought it here to find out how to make it work." He cradled her hand in his. "That's why you need to keep looking for your father's notes. They should enlighten us on how to neutralise it."

"But it's been too many years," she said. "I don't know anyone in South Australia. Where do I start?"

"Grace will help," he said.

The engine whined. Steam hissed. Straggling passengers strolled toward the carriages. A plume of white smoke gushed from the funnel and collected under the platform roof.

Hot currents burst along the platform, kicked up Tillie's skirts and blasted her ankles. She recoiled from the train, towards Sir Avery. He caught her and smiled. She felt the warmth of his body against hers, and his breath on her neck. She blushed.

She glanced up at him. Aunt Prudence would've encouraged her to make the most of the situation. It was to be expected; they were a good match.

"I shall miss working with you, Tillie." He took her hands in his.

She smiled and waited. Aunt Prudence would have approved.

The train whistle echoed through the station. The smell of coal smoke filled the air. A convenient cloud of steam rolled across the platform.

She closed her eyes. Social conformity be damned; she'd always thought it vexing a woman should have to wait for any man. She stretched up on her toes and kissed him.

It was pleasant enough, but not as expected. There was no tingle, no flutter. It was like kissing a brother. If she were to seriously consider the match, surely she should expect something more?

The smoke cleared.

"Avery, I--" She bit her lip. How did one refuse a Lord? "Perhaps we should--?"

She stepped away and proffered her hand in farewell. "I shall miss you, Avery." Her voice was barely audible as it struggled to escape her dry throat.

Avery rocked back on his heels and smiled. "That's what I admire about you, Tillie Meriwether; you know your own mind. I'm honoured to call you a friend and colleague."

She took a deep breath. The burning faded from her cheeks.

He took her hand and shook it gently. "It will be boring back home without you, Tillie," he whispered.

Her eyes widened. "What will happen to the Department of Curiosities?" she asked. "The Queen is not happy. She considers you, and the Department, disloyal. Are you sure your influential friend will be able to protect you?"

He nodded. "I am sure."

"But how will I find you when I return to England?" she asked Avery.

"There's a quiet spot in Scotland," he replied. "Contact Smythe there when you return."

"Scotland is a big place. How do I find this *quiet spot*?"

He leaned closer and whispered: "Grace will show you."

"All aboard!" The guard's whistle shrieked.

"Sir, we must leave." Smythe smiled and tipped his hat in Tillie's direction.

"*Au revoir*, Miss Meriwether." Avery bowed his head and bounded toward the carriage to meet Smythe.

The platform guard folded up the carriage steps and blew his whistle a second time.

Pistons clacked and hissed.

Tillie waited until the train left the platform. She took a deep breath, turned on her heel and strolled under the station's corrugated iron roof to join Grace.

A new adventure awaited.

THE END

Acknowledgements

Thank you David and Sharon for their endless support,
to my beta readers Sue, Sonia, Lynne and Katie.
Thank you to Susan and Ivan Rehorek for Russian translations.
Thank you to Blake Canham-Bennett (Blakesby Hats) and Kaye
Inverarity (The Galley of Costume) for their advice on the history of
hats. Thank you to Terry Brown (Dragonsblood Creations)
for the outfits used on the cover.
Cover models: Blake Canham-Bennett and Felicity Mary.
Lastly, a big thank you to Narelle Harris for heeding the call to find a
surname for Professor Nathaniel Kempthorne

About the Author

Karen J Carlisle lives in Adelaide with her family and the ghost of her ancient Devon Rex cat. She loves fantasy fiction, gardening, historical re-creation, and steampunk and can often be found plotting fantastical, piratic or airship adventures.

Karen has always loved chocolate and rarely refuses a cup of tea. She is not keen on South Australian summers.

www.karenjcarlisle.com
https://twitter.com/kjcarlisle
www.instagram.com/karenjcarlisle
www.goodreads.com/kjcarlisle

Other Works

The Aunt Enid Mysteries
Aunt Enid: Protector Extraordinaire

The Adventures of Viola Stewart series

Available in paperback:
Doctor Jack & Other Tales
Eye of the Beholder & Other Tales
The Illusioneer & Other Tales

Also available separately as eBooks:
Three Short Stories
Doctor Jack
Three More Short Stories
Eye of the Beholder
From the Depths
Tomorrow, When I Die
The Illusioneer

Aunt Enid: Protector Extraordinaire

With a Twist of the Nib: For When Time is Short
(A short story collection)